LOST CHILD

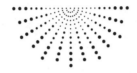

D S BUTLER

D1566710

Deadly Obsession
Deadly Motive
Deadly Revenge
Deadly Justice
Deadly Ritual
Deadly Payback
Deadly Game

http://www.dsbutlerbooks.com

For my readers - thank you for your support!

CHAPTER ONE

I think about the day I lost Jenna all the time. It's always with me.

People say the pain lessens over time, but I'm not sure that's true. Every time I remember, my stomach twists as I'm reminded of how I let everyone down, my sister most of all. I only took my eyes off Jenna for a second. But a second was all it took to lose her.

The day it happened, the twenty-fifth of May, was a bank holiday. The weather was sunny and warm in the small market town of Woodstock, in Oxfordshire, a hint that summer was finally on its way after a cold and rainy spring. I had grown up in Woodstock. The town seemed so ordinary and safe. Perhaps, that was why I'd let my guard down. Nothing bad happened in Woodstock. It was a quintessentially English town, a safe haven.

My father had died suddenly five years ago, shortly before

my sister, Kate, had fallen pregnant with Jenna. As Mum wasn't keen on rattling around the big house on her own, and Kate and her partner, Daniel Creswell, were living in a one-bedroom flat, it seemed logical for them to move in with Mum for a while.

Kate and Daniel married the year after Jenna was born, and Daniel progressed well in his career as a graphic designer. I was sure they could have afforded to buy their own place after the first year, but there was no need. The arrangement worked well for everyone. The house was large enough for Mum to have her own sitting room, and she was tolerant, easy to live with and adored Jenna.

Kate liked to joke she had a live-in babysitter. When I look back at that time now, I wish I had appreciated it more. We had so many happy memories.

Although I'd moved away from Woodstock, I hadn't gone far. I had a one-bedroom flat in Oxford, near the train station. I enjoyed living in the hustle and bustle of the city, but I came back to Woodstock every weekend. Sunday lunch at my mother's house was a ritual I didn't want to miss.

It was a good job Mum was easy-going because I'm sure living with Daniel Creswell would have driven most people to distraction. It wasn't that he was a nasty man, and he didn't treat my sister or Jenna badly, but he could be condescending and always wanted to be the subject of the conversation.

If you told him you had a pet elephant, Daniel would have a bigger one and the box to put it in. The constant one-upmanship irritated me, but Mum and Kate didn't seem to notice. The simple truth was they were nicer than me.

On the day it happened, my patience was already wearing thin with Daniel. He'd dominated the conversation yesterday over Sunday lunch, droning on about how successful he was and describing his recent business trip to Barcelona. When I asked whether he'd gone to see any sights, he informed me he wasn't there as a tourist and was far too busy to explore the city. I hadn't done anything more than roll my eyes, but that was enough for Mum to send a chastising look in my direction. I was very familiar with that look.

One day a week in Daniel's presence, I could tolerate, but because today was a bank holiday and it was the Wood-stock spring fête, I was in his company for the second day in a row, and he was starting to grate on my nerves.

The fête was held in Woodstock primary school's playing field. There weren't a huge number of attractions, but I'd been doing a pretty good job of avoiding him, slowly walking around the make-shift stalls that sold homemade jam, fragrant candles, tea and small cakes.

The smell of freshly-cut grass carried on the breeze, and the sun was warm on my skin. Children's excited laughter came from the stocks where they were pelting one of the female teachers with sopping wet sponges. Her once wavy hair hung in lank, dripping strands.

She caught me watching and grimaced. "Do you want a turn?"

I shook my head, grinning. "No, thanks!"

They were raising money for a good cause, maintaining the communal gardens. I stopped to watch for a while, laughing when one small boy grew sick of his poor aim and rushed up to squeeze water from his sponge onto the teacher instead.

When a few sharp words rose above the general chatter around me, I turned to see Daniel had his hand on my sister's arm. The rigid way my sister stood next to her husband made me think they were arguing. Her body was tense, and she held Jenna's hand tightly.

My niece, Jenna, like most three-year-olds, didn't like to stand still. She was tugging Kate's hand and bouncing on the balls of her feet, eager to participate in the fun.

There were children running everywhere, laughing with delight. The fête was set up for young children. Face painting, a bouncy castle, balloons, an ice-cream van, and for the older children, there was tinny music blaring out from one of the stalls with a minor local celebrity, Robin Vaughan, holding court.

Robin Vaughan wore a garishly-bright Hawaiian shirt and dark skinny jeans. Not a good look for a man in his fifties. I didn't understand the attraction, but the kids seemed to love him.

I dragged my gaze away from Robin and his cringe-worthy attempts to impress the youngsters gathered around him and turned back to my sister. I didn't want to listen in on their private conversation, so I waited until Daniel turned and stalked off before walking towards her.

"Is everything all right?" I put my hand on her shoulder.

Kate blinked and smiled brightly. "Of course, everything is fine. Isn't the weather amazing? I can't believe the sun is shining on a bank holiday. Wonders will never cease."

She was babbling and talking about the weather, so I knew something was wrong, but whatever it was, she didn't want to confide in me. At the time, I thought it was only a minor tiff between husband and wife.

I smiled down at Jenna who had progressed to whining and yanking on her mother's arm. "I want the bouncy castle."

I ruffled her soft blonde hair and looked at where she pointed to the inflatable, red bouncy castle and frowned. It looked very big, and I worried it might be a bit too rough for a child Jenna's size.

"I think that's for bigger boys and girls, Jenna," I said and watched her small face crumple. I should have used the distraction technique.

"We'll see what Mummy thinks," I said, turning back to Kate, but she wasn't paying attention. She was looking over my shoulder, watching her husband, Daniel, talking to one of our friends, Pippa Clarkson. Pippa was in charge of a stall selling handmade candles. She'd been in Kate's year at school and was a couple of years older than me. She'd made quite a success of her candle business, even managing to employ Kate part-time to help fulfil orders. Pippa's husband, Mark, was nowhere to be seen.

Next to Pippa stood Phil Bowman. He was supposed to be helping but he looked blankly down at the table, his arms hanging by his sides.

"God, he looks awful," I muttered.

"Hmm?" Kate sounded distracted and kept her gaze on Pippa and Daniel.

"Phil Bowman," I said and felt my chest tighten. "How long has it been now?"

Kate sighed. "Eight months."

"Poor bloke."

Phil had lost his wife and daughter in a car accident on the A44. He'd been driving but survived without a scratch. His wife and daughter hadn't been so lucky. Today, he looked grey, worn out and out of place. The people surrounding him were smiling, joking and laughing, but Phil looked like he was using up all his energy just to stay upright.

He was only a few years older than us. I'd dated his younger brother, Luke, for a while. It was years ago, but I could remember how I'd been so impressed by Phil. He went to music gigs, wore a leather jacket and seemed so mature and exciting. When I was sixteen, he'd bought Luke a bottle of Strawberry 20/20, and we'd sipped it while sitting on the bench behind the cemetery. I'd been slightly easier to impress when I was sixteen. These days, I preferred wine to fruit-flavoured alcohol.

Phil had been one of life's successes. He'd had it all. After studying Chemistry at Oxford, he had settled into domestic bliss with his wife and daughter. That all ended eight months ago.

He kept his gaze lowered, avoiding all the curious glances from locals. It was hard to keep things private in a small town where everyone knew each other's business. It was to be expected, I supposed, but I found it claustrophobic and stifling at times. I looked around, wondering where Luke was. He'd been his brother's almost constant companion since the accident, but today he was nowhere to be seen.

Kate's face tightened and she reached down to stroke Jenna's hair, as though reassuring herself her daughter was still safe. "I can't imagine how you can get past something like that," Kate murmured.

Frustrated at her mother and aunt, Jenna stamped her foot. "Mummy," she said, drawing out the word to pronounce every syllable.

"Just a minute, Jenna. Mummy is talking," Kate replied. Her voice was calm as it always was when she spoke to her daughter.

Jenna could be headstrong and was prone to tantrums, but it all washed over Kate. She patiently dealt with every one of Jenna's outbursts, calmly explaining to Jenna why she couldn't do all the things she wanted to.

I'd tried the logical conversations Kate was so fond of with Jenna but found they didn't suit me. I preferred the distraction technique when it came to dealing with my three-year-old niece.

But today, it was Kate who seemed distracted and impatient. It was very unlike her. I reached out for Jenna's hand. "Why don't I take Jenna to the bouncy castle?"

Kate smiled gratefully at me. "Thanks. You're an angel."

Jenna bounced along beside me, her tiny hand warm in

mine. She had so much energy she found it impossible to walk in a straight line. She swung our arms, giggling and skipping beside me.

I've replayed that moment in my mind a thousand times since then, wondering if someone was watching us, waiting for the perfect time to strike.

CHAPTER TWO

I can remember every detail of what Jenna wore that day. The long pinafore dress in her favourite pink swirled around her small legs as she walked. She'd decorated the dress with butterfly stickers, which were her current obsession. Over the top, she wore a cream cardigan, hand-knitted by Granny, and interwoven with pearlescent pink ribbons. Her shoes were practical rather than pretty. Velcro sandals, built for comfort over style. Even they had to be pink, though.

As she looked up at me, excited and already bouncing, her round cheeks dimpled in a smile, and her big blue eyes were bright as she looked up. She was so trusting. She feared nothing.

We were almost at the bouncy castle when another child stepped in front of us. I guessed she must have been about five years old. Her curly hair was scooped back in a ponytail. Her face was vividly painted with pink and white in the shape of a butterfly, and I knew before Jenna even opened her mouth she would demand a butterfly of her own.

Jenna stopped dead, staring at the bigger girl in front of us.

The child looked vaguely familiar, and I smiled at her and her parents, who were following close behind.

"You look very pretty," I said, which earned me a shy smile.

Jenna tugged at my hand. "I want a butterfly."

"Please," I corrected automatically. "I want a butterfly, please."

"Please, Auntie Beth?" She looked up at me, thrilled at the thought of getting her very own butterfly, and I turned back to the stall. A crowd of children had gathered around the face painting station.

But then I saw the woman in charge and shivered.

It was Dawn Parsons. I felt a prickle over my skin and held Jenna's hand a little tighter. It was hard to explain my aversion to Dawn. It started when I was a child. Dawn had always been a big, lumbering girl. She wasn't fat, but everything about her was thick and solid. She wasn't ugly, either, just lifeless. Her face lacked all animation, and I don't think I'd ever seen her smile.

Her clumsy, slow movements made her a prime target for bullies, and at one time, when I was in year seven or eight, I'd felt sorry for her. That only lasted until the age-old adage became true. Individuals who are bullied often become bullies themselves.

I had been walking home after school when a group of older boys from our school decided to torment Dawn. They called her names, pulled on her schoolbag and poked her with their fingers, running away before she could react. They never crossed the line to violence, but it was cruel, and it made me feel sick.

With an older sister and her friends to stick up for me, I'd never had to worry about bullies. But that day, Kate was off school with tonsillitis, and I didn't know what to do. I wanted the boys to stop, but I wasn't brave enough to speak up.

Trying to ignore the bullying, I'd crossed to the other side of the road, which in retrospect, wasn't a good idea because that side of the road didn't have a pavement and the grass verge was perilously close to the small brook that snaked along the same path as the road.

When the boys were tired of their game, they shouted one last volley of abuse at Dawn and ran.

I saw Dawn's shoulders shaking. I thought she was crying and paused to ask if she was okay. But when she saw me looking at her, the words dried in my throat.

Her normally dull eyes flashed angrily at me, and she stomped her way across the road towards me.

I took half a step back, too afraid to run. Dawn had always been much larger than me.

"What are you looking at?" she demanded, spittle flying from the edges of her lips.

I was too scared to reply and shook my head.

Dawn loomed over me and then a look of spite distorted her features as she lifted both hands and shoved me firmly on the chest.

It wouldn't have been so bad if the brook hadn't been behind me, but I lost my footing and fell heavily on my side, hitting the water with a splash, soaking myself and getting covered with mud in the process.

Dawn stood there, silently chuckling to herself.

I finally managed to scramble out and ran all the way home. The brook was only a couple of inches deep, and other than a few bruises, I was unhurt. I never told anyone what had happened. Mum scolded me when I got home dripping wet and splattered with mud, assuming I'd been messing about in the brook, and I didn't correct her.

After that day, I no longer felt sorry for Dawn Parsons.

Jenna reached up to tap me on the hip, demanding my attention.

"We'll do the face-painting after the bouncy castle," I said, hoping that Jenna would have forgotten about it by then.

I didn't like the thought of Dawn's thick, stubby fingers applying greasy makeup to Jenna's face.

Dawn hadn't changed as she'd grown up. If anything, she became more insular and less sociable. She still lived at home in the old thatched cottage with her mother, and as far as I knew, she hadn't held down a full-time job for more than a couple of months.

Jenna looked at me and then at the face-painting stall, and I could tell she was deciding whether to make a fuss. Time to use the trusted distraction method again.

"Come on, I'll race you," I said.

I kept hold of her hand and pretended to let her drag me along, protesting she was going too fast. Jenna laughed in delight. She had a competitive spirit and liked to win at everything.

Kate would tell me off when I let Jenna win the games we played. She insisted Jenna had to learn she wouldn't always win at everything. But I figured that was my prerogative as her aunt. I didn't have to make sure Jenna was a good loser. I was just there to help her have fun.

Her cheeks were glowing when we made it to the bouncy castle. I slid a couple of pound coins out of my pocket to pay the grey-haired man, who stood beside the discarded shoes at the front of the inflatable castle.

A group of Chinese tourists gathered on the edge of the street. Most of them snapped photos on their phones. I supposed an English fête was quaint and charming to them. One man, a little taller than the others, snapped away using a fancy camera with a long lens.

Jenna was in such a rush to get on I had to physically grab her and remind her she needed to remove her shoes first. Luckily her pink suede sandals were fastened with Velcro straps. I set them to one side before lifting her onto the bouncy castle.

She lost her footing almost straightaway, falling and

landing on her backside, and she giggled with glee as the bouncing from the other children jostled her.

"Go on," I said, encouraging her. "Try to bounce,"

It had taken a little while for Jenna to regain her footing, and each time she fell it made her giggle even harder.

A woman was standing on the opposite side of the bouncy castle. I guessed she was a mother watching one of the other children, except she wasn't really watching. She was tapping out something on her smartphone.

I turned my attention back to Jenna. She'd found her footing and actually managed a couple of jumps before she fell down again.

Her cheeks were flushed, and I started to worry that I should have taken off her cardigan. It was unusually warm today.

"Are you too hot?" I called out. "Come over here and let me take your cardigan off."

She shook her head, and I knew she suspected me of trying to lure her off the bouncy castle before she was ready. Jenna was wise to the ploys of adults.

I exchanged a look with the woman beside me.

"She knows her own mind, that one," the woman commented dryly.

"She certainly does."

It didn't really matter, though. I could take her cardigan off as soon as she was finished.

I saw a larger boy jumping exuberantly, bouncing closer to Jenna, but before I could call out a warning, the boy stumbled and fell against Jenna. I bit my lip, barely holding myself back from climbing onto the castle myself and picking her up.

The tumble had shocked her, and she landed with a bump. The happy expression left her face in an instant. She sat there for a moment, eyes wide, as the older boy picked himself up, said sorry and then carried on bouncing.

Jenna's lip wobbled, and if I didn't intervene, it wouldn't be long before she started to cry.

I opened up my arms, and she scrambled forward on her hands and knees towards me. I gathered her up, kissed her on the forehead and told her what a brave girl she was.

"Was that fun? Did you bounce very high?"

Jenna nodded, torn between wanting to cry and listen to me praise her jumping skills.

"How high did you jump?" I asked.

She pointed up to the sky, and I grinned. "That's amazing."

When I was sure tears had been averted, I put her back down, slipped her shoes on and then tugged at her cardigan. "Let's take this off, shall we? It's a bit hot today."

I took her hand again, and we set off back towards Kate and the rest of the family. Halfway back across the field, I groaned. I was an amateur. I should have brought Jenna back the other way so she didn't see the face painting again.

The mishap on the bouncy castle was now completely

forgotten, as Jenna grinned gleefully and pointed at the face-painting station.

"Can I have a butterfly now?"

I glanced over. Dawn was still there. She looked up and made eye contact, staring blankly at me. I shuddered.

"No, we'll do it later," I said.

Jenna pouted. "I want a butterfly," she said, her voice trembling as though her heart were breaking. It was incredible how young children could go from feeling on top of the world to shedding tears within a few seconds.

I had no idea how Kate dealt with the rollercoaster of Jenna's emotions every day. It was exhausting. Out of the corner of my eye, I saw something silver catch the sunlight. I turned. Helium balloons were on sale at another stall just a few feet away.

The perfect distraction.

I knelt down beside Jenna and said, "Look over there, poppet. They've got balloons. Would you like one?"

Jenna hesitated. I knew she wanted a balloon, but she also wanted a butterfly painted on her face. She was getting wise to my distraction technique.

I decided to play my ace card. "That one over there has got a butterfly on it. Do you want that one?"

That did the trick. A broad smile spread across her face, and her cheeks dimpled. She nodded.

"Come on, then."

Holding Jenna by the hand, I walked over to the balloon stall.

A middle-aged woman, wearing deep plum lipstick, smiled at me. I didn't know her name but recognised her. She worked at the local coop. There was a young man with scruffy brown hair standing beside her making balloon animals. Jenna was transfixed as he twisted the balloon and made it squeak.

"What's it supposed to be?" I asked, nodding at the blue balloon in his hand.

"A giraffe," he said, frowning. He didn't look at me. His face was screwed up in concentration.

The woman beside him chuckled. "It looks more like an overweight sausage dog. What can I get you, love?"

"Can I get one of the helium balloons, please? The one with the butterfly."

I didn't have enough loose change in my pocket, so I let go of Jenna's hand to pull my purse out of the back pocket of my jeans. I handed the woman a five-pound note and then took my change.

I put my purse back in my pocket and said thank you as I turned around to give the balloon to Jenna, but she was gone.

I didn't panic at first. I held up the balloon and called out to her. "Jenna, I've got your butterfly balloon."

When Jenna didn't come racing back to claim her balloon

immediately, I looked over in the direction of the face-painting station and sighed.

I bet she'd run over there.

My chest was tight, and anxiety prickled my skin, but I fought back the panic. She would be fine, I told myself. She can't have gone far.

I marched forward, scanning the area for Jenna. It wasn't easy. There were so many other children at the fête. They seemed to have multiplied.

Directly in front of me, a young child sat on a chair, patiently waiting for his face to be covered with tiger stripes.

A young child about Jenna's height stood beside the chair. She had the same pale blonde hair. A wave of relief rushed over me when I saw her, but as I got closer, a stab of panic punctured the relief. Her hair was too short. It wasn't Jenna.

I think it was at that point the first coils of panic started to spread through my stomach.

"Has anyone seen Jenna?" I demanded as I reached the face-painting station.

Dawn Parsons wasn't there anymore.

Instead, a younger woman who'd been carefully painting streaks of bright orange on the face of the little boy in front of her turned to me. "What's wrong?"

The little boy with the tiger paint pulled a face, baring his teeth to roar. The other children laughed.

"Have you seen a little girl, three-years-old, blonde hair, pink dress?" I asked urgently.

The woman's gaze drifted down to the little girl I'd mistaken for Jenna only seconds ago.

"No, that's not her."

I turned around in a slow circle, scanning everywhere for Jenna.

Maybe she went back to the bouncy castle?

But before I looked there, I had to tell Kate. I felt sick.

I jogged over the field, heading for my family, and with each step, I tried to convince myself that Jenna was probably already there. Of course, she must have gone straight back to her mother to tell her she wanted to have her face painted.

I was a few feet away when Kate turned to look at me.

Jenna wasn't by her side. Kate stood next to my mother, and Daniel was still talking to Pippa.

"Have you seen Jenna?" I asked.

The look of horror on Kate's face was like a knife to my stomach.

Jenna was gone, and it was my fault.

CHAPTER THREE

Mum held onto Kate's arm. "Where did you last see her, Beth?"

"The balloon stall. I was buying her a balloon." I gestured pointlessly to the silver, helium balloon I gripped in my left hand.

Kate's gaze dropped to my other hand. I was still holding Jenna's cardigan.

We spent the next few minutes desperately searching for Jenna. Every adult we knew at the fête and some of those we didn't began to search for her, looking under tables, behind trees and anywhere else a three-year-old child could possibly hide.

I rushed back to the bouncy castle, muttering a prayer under my breath. Did Jenna decide to go back there? But if she had, why didn't she answer us when we called?

I stumbled on a tuft of grass, and the balloon slipped from my fingers. I desperately tried to capture the ribbon before it drifted too far. My hand closed around thin air as the balloon travelled upwards, taunting me. I couldn't be trusted to hold on to anything.

She wasn't there. No children were playing on it now. The grey-haired man was slowly deflating the castle.

Kate was white as a sheet, and I couldn't think where to look for Jenna next. I liked to be in control and organised, but the logical side of my brain had deserted me. I walked around in a circle calling Jenna's name.

I heard a shout, and everyone in the vicinity turned.

It was Mrs Gallagher, the headmistress of Woodstock primary school. "Has anyone checked the playground?"

The playground. Of course. It was just around the side of the school and had a brightly coloured climbing frame that fascinated Jenna. We could see it when we walked along Burgess St.

"I'll look now," I called back, already running toward the playground. I needed to do something.

I ran flat-out, my converse shoes thudding against the grass.

It didn't take me long to circle around to the back of the school, but the fenced-off playground was empty. There was no one around apart from two little boys chasing each other with sticks.

I bit down on my bottom lip. They weren't much older than

Jenna, and yet here they were, safe, and playing without any adult supervision. I'd only turned my back on Jenna for a few seconds. It wasn't fair.

I turned away, walking quickly back across the school playing field, still looking everywhere for Jenna as I made my way back to my family.

I met Kate's eye and shook my head. "Sorry, she's not there. I think we should phone the police."

"I've already done it." Daniel's voice was cold, and he couldn't even bring himself to look at me.

Mum reached out and touched my shoulder. "Have a look around the car park, Beth."

"The car park? Why would she be there?"

Mum shot me a meaningful look I couldn't interpret. Rather than waste time asking further questions, I jogged over to the small car park. There were only twelve cars parked on the crumbly tarmac. Most people at the fête were locals and would have walked to the event. I walked around each car, but there was no sign of Jenna. Then it hit me. I knew why Mum wanted me to go to the car park.

If someone had taken Jenna, they would find it hard to carry an upset three-year-old very far on foot without drawing attention to themselves, which meant they'd use a car.

I strode across the tarmac to the exit. There was only one way in and out. I'd stop every car before it left if that's what it took.

But no one was leaving. Everyone was taking part in the search, calling out Jenna's name. Besides, if someone abducted Jenna, would they leave their car here in plain sight?

I scrunched up my eyes and rubbed them with my fists. How could a three-year-old child go missing in a place like this? Woodstock was safe. The fête was meant to be fun.

I wrapped my arms around myself, to try and stop myself shaking. It didn't work.

I saw the woman from the balloon stall walking towards me.

"I'm sure we'll find her," she said when she was a few feet away from me.

The brown-haired young man, who'd been making the balloon animals, stood beside her, shuffling from foot to foot awkwardly. He didn't talk.

He looked shifty. I narrowed my eyes. Did he have something to do with it? But he couldn't have. I'd been watching him the whole time. Watching him when I should have been watching Jenna. He wouldn't have had the opportunity to take her.

I shook my head. "I don't know how it happened. I only took my eyes off her for a second, just to pay you for the balloon."

The woman gave me a nervous smile and patted my arm. "I know. You mustn't blame yourself."

But of course, that was exactly what I did.

The police were quick to arrive. At first, there were only two uniformed PCs on the scene, asking questions, and then more of them came as the minutes ticked past, and they expanded the search.

It took me ages to accept that Jenna was really missing and not just hiding or playing a game. I held on to that hope as long as I could. It was a slow, sinking realisation, a feeling of dread that invaded every cell in my body. For Kate, the realisation came faster and harder.

It hit her when she was talking to the first police officers on the scene. They'd found one of Jenna's pink shoes in a nearby street. I wasn't close enough to hear what they said to her, but I couldn't miss Kate's anguished cry in response.

The lady from the balloon stall raised a tissue to her eyes, and I stepped around her. I needed to do something. Even if Jenna had been taken, there was a chance we could get her back if we acted quickly.

I pulled my mobile phone from my pocket and tapped on the video app. I wanted a record of these cars and their number plates.

"Beth Farrow? Can I have a word?" I turned to see a uniformed PC behind me. He was short for a man, roughly my height, and slightly built.

He had a frown on his face, obviously wondering what I was doing. I lowered my phone.

"I thought I'd take photos of the number plates, you know, just in case it was important later."

He gestured to the corner of the small car park and pointed to a camera mounted on a pole I hadn't noticed before. "There's CCTV. We'll look at that asap. Now, if I could just ask you a few questions? I understand you were the last person to see Jenna?"

He didn't actually say it was my fault, but I saw the judgement in his eyes.

I nodded slowly. "Yes, I bought her a balloon. I only took my eyes off her for a moment... and when I turned back, she'd gone."

I was still trembling and thrust my hands into my pockets to stop my hands shaking.

The uniformed PC nodded. "I'd like to talk to you with the rest of the family if you don't mind." He pointed to the corner of the school playing field where Kate, Daniel and Mum stood talking to another officer.

"I need to stay here," I said. "I want to make sure no one drives off. If someone abducted Jenna, they'd use a car, wouldn't they?"

The PC frowned as though he thought my response was inappropriate in the circumstances. "As I said, we will take a look at the CCTV. Did you see Jenna near the car park?"

I blinked back tears and shook my head. "No, but she isn't anywhere else." I gestured hopelessly at the cars.

He put a hand on my elbow and led me towards my family.

"Right, can you tell me exactly where you were and what you were doing when Jenna disappeared?"

I told him every single detail I could remember.

That was the first time I had to tell the police about Jenna's last known whereabouts, but it wasn't the last. Before the day was out, I'd described and lived through those minutes again and again and again.

When I made it back over to Kate, I wanted to reach out and hug her, but I hung back, standing on the outskirts of the family group.

A plainclothes policeman was talking to Kate, and when he finished asking her questions, he turned to me and saw the cardigan I was still holding.

"Is that Jenna's?"

I nodded.

"Did you find it?" His tone was urgent.

I didn't understand what he was getting at. "I took it off her. She was too hot after the bouncy castle."

He nodded at a colleague. "We'll take that if you don't mind."

He turned to Kate with a kinder expression and said, "We will get it back to you as soon as possible."

I kept telling myself the police did this sort of thing all the time. They would find her within minutes.

But they didn't.

The rest of the afternoon passed in a blur until slowly people began to give up on the search. The school field slowly emptied as people returned home.

The drone of a lawnmower sounded in the distance, and across the street, someone was washing their car. How could their lives be carrying on as normal when Jenna was missing?

The police told us we should go home and wait. We'd been assigned a female family liaison officer, who escorted us back to the property, as though she feared we'd get lost on our own.

As we walked back to the house, I felt a glimmer of hope. Had Jenna made her way back home? Maybe she'd darted off, chasing a butterfly and then couldn't find her way back to the fête and decided to walk home. I knew that was wishful thinking, but I couldn't resist holding onto that last vestige of hope.

Kate was deathly silent, and Daniel babbled on about his confidence in the police force. I think it was more for his benefit than Kate's.

I stopped listening. On the opposite side of the road, I saw a Chinese couple, walking arm in arm. He had a fancy camera around his neck, and I recognised him as the man who had been taking photographs earlier. What if he'd managed to catch Jenna on that camera?

I flew across the street, away from my family and the police officer escorting us.

"Stop!" I called out. "I need to see your camera. It's urgent."

A frown puckered the man's forehead, and his wife clutched his arm. I don't think they understood what I was saying.

When I reached them, I pointed at the camera around his neck. "I want to look." I jabbed my finger at the camera. "At the pictures."

He didn't move fast enough, so I tried to remove the camera myself. He clung firmly to the straps and looked horrified as though he thought I wanted to mug him.

"Please, I just need to look at your photographs."

I felt a hand on my shoulder, and then the family liaison officer stepped in between the man with the camera and me. "I don't think we need to look at those right now, Beth. Let's get home."

"But I saw them. They were taking photographs opposite the school at the fête. There might be something important on his camera, a photo of Jenna."

The family liaison officer's calm expression wavered for a moment, but she maintained her position in front of the Chinese tourists.

Every year we had coachloads of tourists in Woodstock. They loved to come and see the old English town and visit Blenheim Palace. What if this couple got back on their coach and never realised they had a vital photograph of Jenna?

I took a deep breath. The Family Liaison Officer wanted me to stop making such a fuss and get back to my family, but I couldn't. It was a long shot, but he might have something on that camera.

"Leave it to me," she said, making me stand a short distance away so I couldn't overhear their conversation.

She launched into a long-winded explanation. They finally seemed to understand what I wanted, and smiles broke out over their faces as they nodded. She handed them a card, and then they went on their way.

I put a hand to my forehead and fought the urge to run after the tourists. What was to stop them going back to China without showing us any of the photographs? We had no contact details for them.

"What are you doing? You didn't even look at the camera."

She pursed her lips together and put a hand on my shoulder, guiding me back to my family. "He's given me the memory card, and I told him he could collect it from the station tomorrow. We have the photographs. Leave the investigation to us, Beth."

Shamefaced, I met the stony gaze of Daniel Creswell. He wanted me to leave. I had no doubt about that, but I couldn't leave my mother and Kate, not now.

I shot an apologetic look at Mum and then turned to Kate. She was holding herself as though she were made of glass and one wrong move would cause her to splinter into a million pieces.

Not long after Jenna went missing, Kate stopped holding herself together, and the result shattered all our lives.

CHAPTER FOUR

Two years later.

I blinked in the bright sunlight and raised a hand against the sun's glare. The beginnings of a headache throbbed behind my eyes. I wasn't sure whether it was the sun or the alcohol. Probably a combination of both.

Friday brunch in Dubai was a tradition that I never missed. There was a large group of us here today at the Address Hotel. The food was good, and the free-flowing alcohol was even better. We'd finished eating and had come to sit outside by the pool bar. May in Dubai could be intensely hot, and today was no exception. Ram, a Nepalese waiter, handed me a cold towel, and I thanked him. I'd spoken to him before. I knew he thought we were odd to sit outside when it was so hot.

"Mad Dogs and Englishmen," I said as he took our order for another round of drinks.

He frowned at me.

"Noel Coward."

The confused frown remained, and I told him it didn't matter. I didn't feel like explaining further.

I leant forward, picked up my gin and tonic and then settled back in the comfortable cushioned seat beside the pool, watching Mark and Adrian lark about. They'd had too much to drink as usual. When I had too much to drink, I became melancholy, isolating myself from everyone. When Mark and Adrian had too much to drink, they played the fool, hamming it up for laughs.

The waiters at the pool bar walked around them, shooting them occasional disapproving looks.

The sky was a perfect blue, unblemished by clouds. The hotel overlooked the sprawling Dubai mall, and all around us, modern skyscrapers glinted in the sunlight. The biggest of them all, the Burg Khalifa, towered over us. Music started up in the distance, indicating a fountain show was imminent.

"Are you okay, hun?" Sylvia sat down on the chair next to me. She held her cocktail glass at an angle, suggesting she was a little worse for wear. Her make-up was perfect, though, as was her carefully tinted and blow-dried hair despite the heat.

I worked with Sylvia, which was why I was friends with this group of people. Friends was probably a generous description. They put up with me tagging along because I knew Sylvia, and I liked going out with this loud, gregarious crowd because it stopped me thinking about the past. They didn't know much about me. I kept to myself.

After Jenna had gone missing, the media was intense. They'd camped outside the house, of course, but that wasn't the worst of it. That much I had anticipated. I hadn't expected journalists to sidle up to me and start conversations as I waited in line at a coffee shop. I hadn't expected journalists to call me at work, and I certainly hadn't expected a journalist to lie their way into Kate's hospital room.

I was far more careful now. I didn't trust people easily. But I liked Sylvia and envied her decadent, carefree lifestyle.

I smiled up at Sylvia and raised my glass. "I'm fine. You?"

Sylvia flopped back into the chair, spilling a little of the bright red cocktail on her white sundress. "Oh, bugger. This is Jil Sander. Why is it I always spill things on my expensive clothes?"

"Sod's law, I guess." I took a sip of my drink.

She ran her hands nervously over her dress, smoothing the creased fabric and bit her lower lip. I knew her well enough to sense she wanted to say something else. So, I waited for her to continue.

She put her cocktail on the small table between us and took a deep breath. "Are you going to apply for the promotion, Beth?"

We both worked for the same Arabic media company. The staff were treated well, and the pay was excellent, especially as the salary was tax-free. My role had nothing to do with the media. My duties involved chasing after my fifty-year-old boss and doing practically everything for him because he was incompetent. He was a nice guy just not very tech-savvy. He broke out in a sweat every time I tried to explain how Outlook worked. I could probably find a more challenging job or even another more demanding job with the same company, but my daily tasks were easy and uncomplicated, and right now, that suited me just fine.

Sylvia had started working at the company two years before me, and I guessed she was keen to land this promotion.

"I don't think so. I'm happy with things as they are," I said. I had no driving ambition to climb the corporate ladder, not here. Dubai was only ever meant to be a break, somewhere I could escape to, and get my head straight before I screwed things up even more.

Dubai had been my brother-in-law's idea. Daniel thought I needed to get away and start afresh. I didn't agree. At least, not at first. It was a year after Jenna disappeared when he first mentioned the idea. I was sitting at the kitchen table with him and Mum when he brought the subject up.

I dismissed the idea immediately, staring at him as though he'd lost his mind.

Daniel had taken a deep breath and exchanged a look with my mother, which infuriated me. I hated the way he did that. As though it was him and my mother united against me, trying to make me see sense.

"Hear me out, Beth," he'd said. "I think the break would do you good. A friend of mine has a job available, great pay with a generous holiday allowance. It would be perfect for you."

I shook my head. "I couldn't."

"Why what's keeping you here?" he asked, unable to hide his exasperation as he gestured around my mother's kitchen.

He couldn't be serious. I didn't want him here, sitting at the same old, scrubbed pine table where our family had shared so many happy memories. Daniel was a reminder of how that happiness had evaporated.

I kept my eyes fixed on the rose-printed tea set displayed in the huge dresser set back against the kitchen wall. I focused on the old, familiar objects in the kitchen rather than Daniel's face and spoke slowly, hoping my words would penetrate his thick, insensitive skull. "I couldn't leave Mum now. Not after everything that's happened."

I glanced at Mum, and she reached out to hold my hand. "I think it's a good idea, Beth."

"You do?" I frowned at Mum. She looked tired, beaten down by life, and I knew that was, at least partially, my fault. "But I couldn't leave you now."

She gave a pained smile and tightened her grip on my hand. "You're not to worry about me. Besides, I have Daniel looking out for me, and it wouldn't be for long. Just until you get your head straight. I can visit, too. I've already looked at flights. I could come and see you at Christmas."

I was silent. They had planned this.

The only sound in the kitchen was the ticking of the antique clock Kate had bought Mum for her birthday a few years ago. I wondered how long they'd been discussing how to solve my problems behind my back.

Looking back now, I could understand why they were so worried. My behaviour had been reckless. I'd lost my job, fallen behind on my rent and visited the police station at least once a week with fresh names I demanded they investigate.

At first, the police had humoured me and promised they would look into whomever I'd chosen as my suspect of the week. They'd soon grown tired of me, though, and Daniel told me outright my behaviour was embarrassing.

I'd lost my job two months after Jenna's disappearance. In the immediate aftermath, people had been kind. My boss told me to take as much time as I needed, but that was just something people said. They didn't really mean it. He certainly didn't, and I'd needed more time than he was prepared to give.

My life was a mess, and I didn't know how to fix it, so I took the only option open to me. I left the UK and headed to Dubai.

I closed my eyes, remembering.

"Hey, are you listening to me?" Sylvia's voice penetrated my thoughts, and I forced myself to smile.

"Sorry, I just drifted off for a moment. What were you saying?" I took a sip of my gin and tonic. The outside of the glass was wet, and the ice cubes had already melted. That was the downside of living in Dubai, but May was pleasant compared to August when you could open a window and the rush of heat felt as though you'd opened an oven door.

"I'm going to go for it," Sylvia said. "The promotion, I mean. Will you put in a good word for me with Dave if he asks about me?"

"Of course."

My mobile beeped with the sound of an incoming text message, and I leant forward to fumble beneath my chair for my handbag. I'd put it under there in the shade. It was so hot in the sun it could melt your lipstick. I knew that from experience.

My mobile felt hot to the touch, and I tapped on the screen to view the text message. There was no name, just a number, which meant the number wasn't stored in my phone's memory. I clicked on the message to open it.

A picture appeared on the screen, and my stomach clenched. I sat up quickly, to get a better look. The glare on the screen made it difficult to see. I used my bag to shade the screen and then I started to shake.

A bubbling sensation formed in my chest, like a silent scream erupting under my ribs.

"What's wrong? Beth, you look like you've seen a ghost. It's not bad news, is it?"

I shook my head slowly. I hadn't seen a ghost. I'd seen Jenna.

I shoved my phone back in my bag and stood up, dumping

my drink on the table. "I have to go. I'll see you on Sunday."

I didn't say goodbye to anyone else in the group and didn't wait for Sylvia to answer. I strode away, skirting around the pool and heading for the hotel. My heart was thundering in my chest as I pushed open the glass doors. Inside, the air was cool, and the change in temperature made me shiver. My sandals slapped against the pale, cool marble floor.

I didn't get far before Ram stopped me. He was smiling and holding out his phone to me. I shook my head not understanding what he wanted.

"Sorry, I have to go, Ram. I'll see you next time."

"It's Noel Coward. Mad Dogs," he said grinning, pointing at the video he'd found on the internet.

"Oh, yes. Very good."

His face fell at my lacklustre response. I felt bad but couldn't even attempt a conversation about Noel Coward right now. All I could think about was Jenna's photograph, and questions were whirling around in my mind. I couldn't focus on anything else.

I walked past the reception desk and headed to the chairs in the lobby. I'd intended to get home and look at the photograph again in private, but I couldn't wait. My hand was shaking as I reached inside my bag for the phone. Holding my breath, I opened the message again. Had I imagined it? Was I going mad?

I stared at the screen. It was Jenna. She was older and had lost some of her babylike plumpness, but her eyes were the same. I zoomed in on the image. She had two small moles on her left cheek, close to her mouth.

I stifled a sob and blinked away the tears that made it hard to focus. There was no doubt in my mind. It was a photograph of Jenna.

CHAPTER FIVE

I tried to call the phone number that sent the message multiple times but got a recorded message, which told me the number was not in use. It made no sense. The photograph had only been sent from that number a couple of minutes ago.

I took one of the taxis waiting outside the Address Hotel and gave the driver instructions to my apartment. I lived in an apartment block next to the Ibn Battuta Gate Hotel, just off the Sheikh Zayed Highway. The location suited me perfectly. It was close to the metro station, and there was a shopping mall across the road. Life was easy in Dubai.

I paid the taxi driver after he drove up the ramp and stopped outside the hotel's main entrance.

I nodded at the doorman, who was one of the regulars, but felt too tense to smile. Inside the hotel, I turned left to the residential apartments, ignoring the tourists gathered in the main hotel lobby.

I jabbed my finger on the green button, calling the lift impatiently. When the doors opened, a couple who lived along my corridor emerged, and I gritted my teeth and tried to force a smile.

Before they could initiate a conversation, I quickly cut them off. "Nice to see you. Must rush, sorry."

I stepped into the lift and pressed the button so the doors would close and cut me off from prying eyes and people who might want to chat.

Alone in the mirrored lift, I clutched my bag to my chest and looked at my reflection. My cheeks were flushed, and my dark hair was a mess. I raked a hand through the tangles, making it look even worse.

Had I imagined it? I wanted to look at the picture again, but I was paranoid I would do something stupid like press the wrong button and delete the photograph.

The lift dinged as it reached the sixth floor, and I exited before the doors were fully open. My sandals slapped along the marble corridor as I walked to my apartment. One of my neighbours was carrying a bag of rubbish to the chute, but I lowered my head and avoided eye contact to head off any conversation.

I pulled my proximity card out of my purse and held it to the pad on the door. When it clicked, I pushed down the handle and staggered inside, shutting the door behind me and leaning back against the cool wood.

I hadn't been running or even walking that fast, but I was out of breath. My hands were shaking as I lifted my bag in front of me and set it on top of the island in the centre of my small kitchen.

The main living area of the apartment was open plan. Only the bedrooms and bathrooms were behind closed doors. The windows were tinted to keep the heat out, and the furnishings were dark as were the floor tiles, which meant despite the dazzling light outside, the apartment was dimly lit. I switched on the light and then reached for my phone.

Even though I'd looked at it twice now, the image of Jenna still stole my breath away.

I took my time, focusing on every inch of her face, making sure I hadn't made a mistake.

I was still avidly gazing at the photograph when there was a knock at the door, which made me jump.

I left the phone on the counter and walked to the door, using the peephole to look and see who was outside.

It was Jose, the property manager. In front of him was a large container of water for my water cooler. I'd forgotten I'd asked him to bring me some more water when I'd left for brunch.

The tap water in Dubai was desalinated, and although it was fine for washing and cooking, many people wanted bottled, or what was commonly referred to as sweet water to drink. Most apartments came with a water cooler, and the water was cheap to buy.

I considered ignoring him, but Jose would have known I'd

only just got home. The last thing I wanted was for him to let himself in to check everything was okay.

I tried to relax and pulled open the door.

"Thanks, Jose," I said as he came in, lugging the heavy water container.

"Shall I put it on for you?" he asked cheerfully.

I wanted to be on my own as soon as possible, and there was still water left in the old container on the cooler.

I shook my head. "No, it's fine."

When I first moved here, I'd struggled. The water containers contained five gallons and were heavy. It was essential to position them perfectly over the water machine, so the lid punctured in the right place. Otherwise, you'd end up with water everywhere. But I'd learned how to do it now.

Usually, I would ask after Jose's wife and daughter, who were still living in India, but today, I had no time for that.

"Thanks very much, Jose. I'll see you later." I practically pushed the poor man out of my apartment.

Alone again, I turned back to my phone.

I took a screenshot, preserving the evidence. Then I saved a copy of the photograph and emailed it to myself. I wasn't sure why, but I was paranoid that this picture would disappear and nobody would believe me. Then I looked again at the phone number. It was a +44 number, which meant the number was registered in the UK. I tapped out a text message.

Who are you? Where is Jenna?

My heart was racing, but I needed to think clearly. My emotions were all over the place. One minute, I was thrilled, and then the next, I was wondering whether I was mistaken. What if it wasn't Jenna?

Pacing the small kitchen, I clutched my phone, but there was no response to my text message. I couldn't wait any longer. My mother and Daniel needed to know about the photograph.

Taking a deep breath, I rushed to get my laptop from the bedroom. I used video calls to keep in contact with Mum. It was nice to see her face, and it seemed more personal than a normal telephone call. Today, I had another reason for using a video call. I wanted her to see the photograph.

I pressed the call connect button and waited for her to answer. The call rang and rang, and no one picked up. I chewed the edge of my thumbnail and tapped my foot impatiently on the floor.

Was she out? I glanced at my watch. It was lunchtime in the UK. I could call her mobile, but this wasn't the sort of news I wanted to deliver if she was out shopping or having lunch with friends. I wanted her to be at home when I told her. Maybe I would have to call Daniel first? The idea made my chest tighten, but Jenna was *his* daughter.

I lifted the hair off the nape of my neck and felt the sticky sweat drying on my skin. Crossing over to the side of the room, I adjusted the air-conditioning and turned up the fan speed. The cool air against my skin gave me goosebumps.

Ignoring the low hum of the air conditioning in the background, I tried to connect the call again. This time Mum answered.

Her familiar face came into view, and she pushed her glasses up on her nose and peered intently at the screen.

"Hello, Mum."

"Hello, love. I was just thinking about you. British Airways have got a sale on, so I was thinking of booking my flight early. You can get some good deals if you shop around and —"

"Mum, I have to tell you something."

Mum frowned, picking up on my tense and urgent tone. "What is it?"

My mouth suddenly felt dry. I wanted to tell her, but I was afraid she wouldn't believe me. I'd run her ragged with my theories and possibilities on what could have happened to Jenna two years ago.

But I couldn't hold back. "Someone sent me a message." My voice sounded foreign and brittle. "Mum, they sent me a picture of Jenna. She looks older, but it's definitely her."

Mum didn't reply. She didn't even move. She was so still that for a moment I thought we'd lost the connection and her image had frozen on the computer screen.

"Mum? Are you still there?"

"Beth, it can't be Jenna." She sighed heavily. "I thought we were past all this. You've been getting on so well."

I shook my head and held up my mobile, showing her the photograph. "I know, but it is her. I'm sure of it."

Mum scrunched up her eyes as she squinted at the screen, trying to get a better look at the photograph.

"It looks like her, but it can't be, Beth. Be reasonable. Jenna is gone."

I frowned, turned the phone back to face me and stared at the screen. She was wrong. It was Jenna. I knew it.

"It's just because you can't see it properly," I insisted. "Wait a minute. I'll email it to you."

I used my mobile phone to access my emails and attached the image of Jenna to a message. I typed Mum's email address at the top and pressed send.

I waited for what felt like ages until I heard the tinny beep of Mum's computer as it received the incoming email.

Mum shuffled about in front of the screen, and I tried not to be impatient as I waited for her to access her emails.

When I couldn't bear it any longer, I asked, "Mum? Did you get it?"

The sound of her crying told me she had. She removed her glasses and bowed her head.

Tears prickled at the corner of my eyes. "It's good news, Mum. I know it's a shock, but don't worry. We'll find her. It means she is still alive. I'm coming home. I'll get the late flight tonight if there's room. I'm going to send you another email. This time, I'll send you the telephone number that sent me the photograph. I'll bring the phone back with me, but I need you to tell the police and Daniel, of course. Can you do that?"

She pinched the bridge of her nose and looked up. Wiping the tears from her eyes, she nodded. "Yes, I'll do it."

A warm, hopeful feeling eased the tightness in my chest, spreading through me and pushing back the terror I had been experiencing for the past half an hour. Now that someone else had seen the photograph, and agreed it was Jenna, I didn't think I was going mad.

I glanced down at my phone again. The photograph was definitely of Jenna, and now we had a chance to get her back.

CHAPTER SIX

I managed to get on the night flight back to Heathrow for an extortionate amount of money. Entering the airport made me feel nervous. Since arriving in Dubai, I hadn't been back to the UK. Mum had visited me three times, but I hadn't felt the need to return.

Truthfully, I didn't want the whispers to start up again. After walking into a shop or a pub in Woodstock, I'd been greeted by sideways glances and whispers. What a tragedy. What a waste.

I edged forward towards the check-in counter, already exhausted even though I hadn't started my long journey yet. The bright artificial lights in the departure zone hurt my eyes. The flight would take seven hours, and I already knew I wouldn't be able to sleep. I was emotionally exhausted and wrung out, but far too busy thinking about finding Jenna to get any rest.

An Indian family in front of me shuffled forward towards the check-in counter. I eyed their luggage in disbelief. It looked like they'd brought all their worldly goods with them. I only had a small carry-on with me. I'd been in such a rush to pack, but now, I wondered whether I should have packed all my belongings. Would I be coming back to Dubai? If we found Jenna, I wouldn't want to leave the UK again, and I had no idea how long the search would take us.

I shoved a hand through my tangled hair and then searched through my handbag to pull out my passport. I'm sure Sylvia would help me out if I needed her. She could pack up my stuff and put it in storage or even ship it over to the UK for me.

I hadn't called her yet, and I hadn't even let my boss know I was leaving the country. It was too late to disturb him now, so I would have to call him tomorrow morning after I'd landed.

There were murmurs of disapproval in the queue behind me as the woman behind the check-in counter tried to explain to the Indian family that they would need to pay for excess baggage.

When it was finally my turn to check-in, the woman behind the counter smiled and quickly and efficiently checked my ID and wished me a pleasant flight.

I passed through security and strode through to the departure lounge, pulling my case behind me.

Despite the late hour, a woman, wearing heavy make-up, stood at the front of the shopping area, holding a bottle of perfume to spray on passers-by. I dodged out of her way. The last thing I wanted was to smell of cloying, heavy perfume all the way back to London.

I rubbed a hand over my forehead, feeling my headache surface again.

Standing close to the wall to avoid the foot-traffic, I rummaged around in my bag, looking for paracetamol. I knew I had some in there somewhere. When my fingers located the foil packet, I walked towards Starbucks.

Caffeine and paracetamol would hopefully get rid of this headache before it got any worse.

It was strange seeing the airport so busy at this time of night. So many tourists crammed into coffee shops and browsed the electronics shop opposite me. A jumble of people milled about, some looking happy, some stressed and anxious.

I ordered an Americano and carried it over to a small table, wheeling my little, black case underneath the table, out of the way. Then I swallowed my tablets with a mouthful of scalding hot coffee.

I pulled out my phone and messaged Mum, letting her know I'd managed to purchase a seat on the night flight and what time I would be arriving at Heathrow.

She replied straight away to tell me she'd spoken to Daniel and the police. She asked if I needed a lift from the airport, and almost as an afterthought, added ominously that the police wanted to talk to me tomorrow morning.

I don't know why that made my stomach churn. Of course, the police would want to speak to me. This was a new lead and could be a critical development in Jenna's case.

I didn't intend to pay for a hire car. They were ridiculously expensive. The transport between Oxford and Heathrow was pretty good. Perhaps not quite as convenient as having my own car, but it would do. I certainly didn't want Mum driving at that time in the morning with this news hanging over her head. It was good news, but all the same, it would be a distraction.

I quickly tapped out another message telling her I'd get the coach to Oxford and then the bus from Oxford to Woodstock. I glanced at the screen above me, praying that my flight wouldn't be delayed. So far, so good. Everything seemed to be running on time.

I removed the lid from my coffee and stared down into the dark liquid. I was afraid to go back. Afraid that this lead would turn into nothing. I fought against the urge to look at the photograph of Jenna again.

I bit down hard on the soft inner flesh of my cheek and tried to fight the tears. I didn't want to cry. Not now. Not here.

Oh, Kate. Why couldn't you have held on a little longer?

The flight was busy. When I'd flown out to Dubai, the plane had been relatively quiet, and I'd had a spare seat next to me, but today we were crammed in like sardines.

If I'd had the money, I would have opted for business class.

I was in the middle of three seats. To the left of me was a large American man who sat by the window. He introduced himself as Steve, from Texas, then folded his arms and looked out of the window. To my right was a British woman, who got out her knitting as soon as she sat down and began click-clacking her needles together. It was such an old-fashioned thing to do that I couldn't help staring at her in surprise.

She didn't look that old. I pegged her at mid-fifties, but she had a kindly, motherly air about her.

Our take-off was smooth, and once we were in the air, the stewardess came along the aisle with drinks. I ordered a gin and tonic. I needed it.

The lady next to me ordered a glass of red wine, and the Texan gentleman ordered nothing but promptly closed his eyes and fell asleep. I wished I could do that.

I sipped my drink, trying to ignore the memories that were bombarding my brain. But it was no good. I had nothing to do on the plane except think.

Six months after Jenna disappeared, Kate had tried to take her own life. The police found her parked in a secluded country lane, slumped over the steering wheel. She had taken packets and packets of paracetamol. My sister didn't die immediately, which was unbearably cruel. In the hospital, when she'd recovered consciousness, I'd sat beside her for hours, holding her hand and talking to her, making her promise me she wouldn't give up hope.

I hadn't managed to get through to her. The dull resentment in her eyes told me that. But I thought we'd have more time. I intended to stick to her like glue. Between us, Daniel, Mum and I would make sure she wasn't left alone. Never again, I told myself, would we give her another chance to do this.

The trouble was, she didn't need another chance. Once was enough.

A day later, her liver began to fail. One of the nurses heard me crying in the corridor and tried to explain that this often happened in paracetamol overdose cases. It may have been kindly meant, but her medical explanation didn't help.

Her death had devastated us all. Jenna's disappearance was horrifying, but Kate's death sent me over the edge.

I squeezed my eyes shut, but even so, a solitary tear escaped and ran down my cheek. I wiped it away quickly, but not quickly enough. The motherly-looking lady in the seat next to me turned around.

"Are you all right? You're not afraid of flying, are you?"

I opened my mouth to say I wasn't, and then decided it was probably easier to go along with her assumption. That way, she wouldn't ask any more questions.

"A little," I said.

She let her knitting needles fall on her lap and reached over to touch my hand. "There's nothing to worry about. I've done this journey loads of times now. I've just been to visit my son. He's been living in Dubai for five years and has done ever so well for himself."

As she chattered on in a soothing voice, I relaxed back into my seat and allowed her words to wash over me.

CHAPTER SEVEN

The coach journey from Heathrow to Oxford took longer than I'd expected due to the heavy morning traffic. During the flight, I had been buzzing with nervous energy, impatient to start looking for Jenna. Since I'd seen the photograph, dozens of questions had been floating through my mind. I needed to be back in the UK to fit the pieces of this puzzle together.

But now I was getting closer to home, the doubt was setting in. The unknown taunted me. Was the photograph genuine? Who had sent it?

Someone out there knew Jenna was alive. Someone had sent that photograph, and I had no idea who it was. Friend or foe? Were they trying to help or were they playing games?

In Dubai, I'd lived a fairly anonymous life and had found

safety in that anonymity, but now I was back in the UK and heading to Woodstock, I felt vulnerable.

The grey clouds hung low in the sky and resulted in a steady drizzle. As the coach travelled along the motorway, the spray from the surface water made visibility difficult, slowing us down.

The coach was busier than I'd expected, and I'd had to put my carry-on case in the luggage compartment at the bottom of the coach.

As we got closer and closer to Oxford, my nerves increased. My foot tapped on the floor, and I wiped my sweaty palms on the legs of my jeans and hoped I wasn't annoying the woman next to me with my constant fidgeting.

I couldn't sit still.

I tried to calm down and think the situation through logically. What did I know so far? I knew that Jenna was alive. That was the most important thing.

In the photo, Jenna looked older than when she'd disappeared. My niece had been kept from her family for two years. She hadn't looked malnourished, and there was no visible bruising apparent in the photograph. I wanted to believe that meant she hadn't been mistreated, but I knew some injuries couldn't be seen from a photograph.

I shivered.

The combined breath of all the passengers on the coach had made the windows steam up, making me feel claustrophobic.

If the police could find out who sent the photograph, then surely, they'd be able to locate Jenna quickly and bring her home. But deep down, I couldn't help worrying it wasn't going to be that easy.

When we finally arrived in Oxford, I was one of the first to disembark, eager to get out into the fresh air.

That proved to be a mistake.

The steady drizzle continued as we waited for the driver to open the luggage compartment at the base of the coach, and the persistent rain soaked through my lightweight coat. I had hoped it would be warmer and stupidly hadn't packed anything more substantial than my lightweight, cream linen jacket.

How could I have forgotten about the English weather? I waited patiently for my luggage, and as soon as the over-weight driver heaved it from the base of the coach, I scrambled towards him, thanking him. I raised the handle and then quickly strode off, wheeling my small case over the uneven pavement. I wasn't sure whether they'd changed the times of the bus, which travelled between Oxford and Chipping Norton, stopping at Woodstock on its way, but if the times were the same, I might just be able to catch the next bus with seconds to spare.

I walked briskly along the paved frontage of the bus station and saw that the bus, a double-decker, was already parked in its bay.

I even recognised the driver, which made me smile for the first time that day. I climbed on the bus and apologetically paid with a five-pound note. Bus drivers these days seemed very keen on passengers having the exact fare, but I didn't have any change on me.

The bus driver pretended to make a fuss, rolling his eyes and tutting, but he grinned at me to show me he was only joking. "Since it's you," he said with a wink. "I'll make an exception just this once."

He handed me my change, and I ripped off the paper bus ticket, thanking him and then dumping my case in the designated area at the front of the bus before going to sit at the back.

There were only a few other passengers on the bus, and I had the whole back seat to myself. The rain hadn't let up and was now streaming down the windows.

I licked my dry lips and tried to swallow the lump in my throat as the bus drove out of Oxford, passing all the familiar sites, Debenhams, the sandy coloured university buildings, The Randolph Hotel, The Ashmolean Museum and The Eagle and Child pub.

As I gazed out of the rain-splattered window at the buildings and shops, I tried to convince myself that Oxford was perfectly safe. Coming back to Woodstock was a good thing. I would find Jenna and bring her home. Things would never go back to the way they were before, not now that Kate was gone, but I owed it to my sister to make sure Jenna didn't slip away from us again.

The thought of my sister made me catch my breath. It wasn't always like that. Now that some time had passed, I could remember her with a smile instead of tears most of the time, as long as I was prepared.

But sometimes when I'd let my guard down and memories zipped through my mind without warning, it caught me unprepared.

That's when I realised the pain would never go away. It would always be there, lurking just beneath the surface.

The journey to Woodstock took twenty-five minutes, and as the bus passed the entrance to Blenheim Palace, I reached for my bag and then leant over to press the bell, signalling to the driver I wanted the next stop.

The bus pulled up opposite the Marlborough Arms, and I struggled with my case, yanking it over the metal bars, then thanked the driver and stepped down onto the pavement.

The rain was coming down harder now, and I should have run for shelter, but I could only stare blankly at the bus as it accelerated away. The familiar old buildings made of Cotswold stone, which had once looked so welcoming and homely, now seemed to crowd around me menacingly. The small, multi-pane windows glinted darkly, and it was easy to imagine faces behind the dark glass looking out and watching me.

I shivered and then yanked my case behind me as I moved closer to the sandy buildings, trying to get some shelter from the rain. I walked past the town hall, crossed the road and stopped beneath the navy blue awning of Betty's Teahouse.

Bedraggled and slightly breathless, I decided to wait until the rain lessened a little before walking to Mum's house. As the rain hit the awning, it sounded like tiny bullets ricocheting off the canvas.

Raindrops splashed in puddles at my feet, splattering my legs and forming dark blue splotches on my jeans. I pushed back my hair, and my fingers caught in tangles.

The bell above the teahouse door sounded as a middle-aged woman emerged carrying her groceries. I stepped to one side, apologising as she passed me.

As she'd opened the door, a rush of warm air had left the teashop. It smelled of freshly-baked bread and coffee, and my stomach rumbled.

For a moment, I considered going inside. I told myself it was the sensible thing to do. I wasn't avoiding going home. It just made sense to stay inside until the rain stopped.

Mum's house was only a short walk from the teashop, but with the rain hammering down, I would end up looking like a drowned rat if I attempted to make the journey now.

The sweetly-fragrant hanging basket beside me, heavy with drooping fuchsias and orange begonias, dripped on my shoulder.

I stepped a little closer to the building and pulled out my phone to text Mum and tell her I'd be home in twenty minutes. She replied almost immediately, telling me the police would be there in an hour's time.

I was lost in thought and didn't pay attention to the low voice beside me. It wasn't until I felt a hand touch my shoulder that I whirled around, eyes widened in alarm.

CHAPTER EIGHT

"Sorry, Beth, I didn't mean to startle you."

It was Luke Bowman. His fair hair fell over his bright blue eyes, and he pushed it back as he grinned at me. He'd hardly changed. He still had the same boyish grin, and his eyes still crinkled at the corners when he smiled.

"I didn't realise you were back," Luke said, his smile fading slightly when I didn't greet him enthusiastically.

I forced myself to smile and raised my arms to hug him. "I only got back today. I landed this morning."

"You've been in the Middle East, right?"

I nodded. "Yes, Dubai."

His grin widened again. "Well, it's really good to see you. I don't suppose an international jet-setter like you has time for a coffee?"

I hesitated, and he looked out at the terrible weather. "It doesn't look like the rain is going to stop anytime soon. We may as well wait it out in comfort."

He stepped away from me and held open the door to the teahouse. I shrugged. I was planning on sheltering inside the teahouse anyway, and a little company wouldn't be so bad.

"All right," I said. "A cup of coffee sounds good."

Inside the tea shop, it was darker still, but it felt cosy rather than oppressive. The lady behind the counter, who was carefully putting cakes onto a tray, smiled warmly at us as we entered. We made our way to a table beside the rain splattered window, and Luke pulled out my chair before sitting down himself.

"So, what is new with you?"

It was a normal enough question, but I tensed before replying. I reached out to pull the small paper menu towards me, even though I didn't need to look at it. The menu hadn't changed since I had last been here over two years ago.

"Not much," I said and tried to smile, keeping my eyes fixed on the menu.

I could feel the weight of Luke's gaze but refused to look up. He knew me too well, and I didn't want to tell anyone about the photograph before I'd had a chance to talk to Mum. It wasn't because I didn't trust Luke. It was tempting to confide in him. He'd been a good friend, and it was only my escape to Dubai that had cut down on our contact.

"What have you been up to?"

He smiled, noticing my none too subtle deflection.

"Coping with a frantically busy clinic for the most part. I shouldn't complain. It's earning me a good living, and I enjoy going to work every day."

"I'm glad it's going well."

Luke had made sacrifices to get the career he'd dreamed of since he'd been a teenager, but it had been worth it. He looked content and relaxed. He'd studied veterinary medicine at Nottingham University after transferring from Warwick and had bought into a veterinary practice four years ago.

"You don't look overworked," I said. "In fact, you look happy."

Luke's expression grew serious. "You, on the other hand, look anything but happy. Do you want to talk about it? Did something go wrong in Dubai?"

I shook my head.

"No, something didn't go wrong in Dubai, or no you don't want to talk about it?"

I smiled. "It's not something I can talk about right now." I fiddled with the paper menu. "There are other people I need to speak to first."

"Fair enough. If you change your mind, you know where to find me. I'm a good listener."

"I remember. Are you still living on Union Street?"

Luke nodded. "Yes, I should buy my own place instead of

wasting money on renting, but I've grown attached to the place. Actually, that's not true. I'm lazy, and moving sounds too much like hard work to me."

We both turned as a female member of staff dressed in black, wearing a white apron, approached our table.

"What can I get you?" she asked.

"I'll have a white coffee, please."

Luke raised an eyebrow. "No toasted teacake?"

I shook my head. "Not today."

I used to love coming in here on Saturday mornings with Kate for a pot of tea and a toasted teacake oozing with butter. I bit down on my lower lip and tried to force the memories away.

Luke placed his order: a teacake and black coffee with cream on the side, and the woman walked back toward the kitchen.

"How is your brother?"

Luke eased backwards into his chair, and his features tightened.

"He's getting by," he said after a momentary pause.

I was a hypocrite. This was a hard subject for him. I didn't want to talk to him about Jenna, so why did I feel it was okay to make him talk about his brother, Phil, and remember that difficult period in their lives.

Before I could apologise and change the subject, Luke said, "He is still living in London. He has a professorship at

Imperial College now, but he does occasionally come back to Oxford."

"Do you get to see him when he comes back?"

Luke gave me a half smile. "Only if I arrange it." He shrugged. "I miss how things used to be. But Phil can't help it. This is his way of coping. He focuses on work."

"I don't suppose you ever really get over something like that," I said.

Luke frowned and turned to look out of the window. The rain was still hammering down and showed no signs of letting up.

"I'm sorry," I said. "I shouldn't have brought up the subject. Why don't you tell me how your new veterinary practice is going?"

"It's going really well. We've been incredibly busy, and it's been a lot of hard work to get established, but things are slowly starting to come together. I was lucky to get in on an up-and-coming practice. I dread to think how much hard work would be involved in starting one from scratch."

We paused in our conversation as an older lady came to serve drinks and Luke's toasted teacake.

She beamed broadly as she put down my coffee cup and turned to Luke. "It's lovely to see you. Thanks to you, Mittens has had a new lease of life after the medicine you prescribed for him."

She smiled in a motherly way at Luke, and I almost expected her to reach out and ruffle his hair, or maybe pinch his cheeks, but she didn't. Instead, she put a white paper bag on the table.

"I know you didn't order it, but I know how much you like them."

She smiled at me, patted Luke on the shoulder and then walked off.

Intrigued, I leant forward and nodded at the white paper bag. "What is it?"

"I imagine it's a millionaire's shortbread," Luke said. "I'm sure you remember they're my weakness."

I grinned, remembering countless occasions when Luke and I had bought cakes from this very shop and then walked to the bus stop munching on them.

He peered inside the white bag and nodded. "Yep, I was right."

"It's nice to see some things haven't changed," I said, and I meant it.

I sipped my hot coffee as Luke entertained me with tales of his life at the veterinary clinic.

"We mainly deal with small pets, dogs and cats. We don't handle many larger animals."

"No horses?"

Luke shook his head. He'd always loved horses, and I'd always thought he would specialise in equine care. When we were in our early teens, we had taken to walking around the local stables on Saturdays, and even though his parents couldn't pay for expensive horse riding lessons, we would watch the younger children riding their ponies around the small circuit. Once some of the staff had got to know us, they were happy to let us do some mucking out for them, in exchange for a few lessons. I'd loved the soft-tempered ponies the best, but Luke had adored all of them, from the temperamental grey mare down to the miniature Shetland pony.

"Smaller animals are a better career choice," Luke said.

"I suppose there are always people wanting treatment for their dogs and cats."

Luke nodded. "Exactly."

My coffee cup was still half full when I noticed that the rain had started to ease. Despite the shock of the photograph of Jenna and the upcoming interview with the police laying heavily on my mind, I had enjoyed seeing Luke again. But I couldn't afford to waste any more time. I wanted to speak to Mum before the police arrived at her house. Reaching for my jacket I'd hung on the back of my chair, I muttered a quick apology to Luke. He hadn't even finished eating his toasted teacake yet.

"The rain is easing up," I said. "I'm going to make a dash for it. Sorry to rush off like this."

Luke shook his head and wiped his buttery fingers on a napkin. "It was nice seeing you again, Beth. Maybe we could meet up before you go back to Dubai?"

"Sure," I said shoving my arms into the slightly damp linen jacket. "I'd like that."

"What's your number?"

I opened my mouth about to reel off my mobile number and then remembered that I probably wouldn't have my phone for long. No doubt I would have to hand it over to the police as evidence, and they would keep it for as long as they needed.

"I'm about to get a new phone," I said, not wanting to give Luke a full explanation right now. "But I'll be staying at my Mum's, and you know the landline number there, right?"

Luke smiled. "I do."

I pulled my purse from my bag and rummaged through it to find some money to pay the bill, but Luke held up a hand. "Don't worry about it. My treat."

"Thanks."

I said goodbye, leant down to kiss him on the cheek and then headed out of the tearoom.

Outside, the rain had lessened to a light drizzle. The hanging baskets were drenched and dripping steadily. I walked quickly along the High Street, wheeling my case behind me. Luke, hadn't changed at all. I felt bad for not letting him know the real reason I'd come home, but how could I tell him about the photograph before I'd spoken to Mum, Daniel and the police? It wouldn't be fair, and I didn't want to do anything that could have a detrimental effect on the police investigation.

I was lost in thought as I reached the end of the High Street and prepared to turn left into Rectory Lane. Because I'd walked this way so many times in the past, I was functioning on autopilot, but I came to a sudden stop as a figure appeared directly in front of me.

It was Pippa Clarkson, and she had stopped dead in the middle of the pavement to stare at me.

Woodstock was a very small town, so I really wasn't surprised to run into another person I knew. Pippa's reaction did surprise me, though.

Her face appeared frozen.

I smiled at her. "Hi, Pippa, how are you?"

Pippa continued to stare at me, and I shifted awkwardly under her gaze. I began to think she wasn't going to answer me, but finally, her expression cleared, and she put a hand against her forehead.

"Beth! I'm so sorry. I wasn't expecting to see you. It was such a surprise."

She shook her head and took a couple of steps forward to clear the distance between us before pulling me in for a hug. "Nobody told me you were coming back."

I took a step back and shrugged. Pippa had been a good friend of Kate's and seeing her again made me feel Kate's absence keenly.

"It was a spur of the moment thing," I said. "In fact, I have to hurry because I'm supposed to be meeting Mum now. She's waiting for me."

Pippa stepped to the side of the pavement to let me pass. "Of course, sorry." As I walked past her, she turned and added, "Why don't we meet up and go for a drink or a meal while you're back in the UK? You are just visiting, aren't you? Or are you coming home for good?"

I had no idea. It all depended on how the search for Jenna went, but I couldn't say that to Pippa. Instead, I carried on walking, and said, "Meeting up would be lovely."

I didn't really mean it, though. Spending the evening with Pippa would be difficult because it would be so hard to see her without Kate. Not wanting to hurt her feelings, I said goodbye and then rushed on towards Mum's house before she could make any definite plans.

CHAPTER NINE

Our old family home held many memories. The main section of the house was made from Cotswold stone and double-fronted with small windows, but over the years, newer sections had been added, and the overall effect was a jumble of odd and quirky shaped rooms. We'd loved playing hide and seek when we were growing up because there were so many nooks and crannies.

The house was originally the Old Rectory and was partially hidden behind a tall wall made of Cotswold stone. I trailed my fingers along the crumbly, sandy stone and then stopped at the gate. The gate was a relatively new addition. Mum had installed the intercom system and large electric gate after my father died. She said it made her feel more secure, but today, the gate was open, probably because she was expecting me to arrive.

I slipped inside and closed the metal gate behind me. It shut with a metallic clang.

I walked up the familiar garden path, breathing in the fresh green scent of the herb garden mingled with the smell of damp earth.

The old apple tree was still there, it's gnarly branches reaching up to the sky, and the last of the pinkish white blossoms still clung on in patches.

Mum must have been watching out for me because I didn't even have a chance to knock on the front door before it opened.

"Beth!"

I let go of my case and enveloped Mum in a hug. I could smell her Oscar de la Renta perfume, and tears stung my eyes as I hugged her tight.

"It's good to see you, Mum," I muttered against the shoulder of her grey cashmere cardigan.

She took a deep breath and moved back, keeping her hands on my shoulders as she studied my face.

Her eyes were unnaturally bright and shiny with unshed tears.

"It's really her, isn't it, Beth?"

"I think so."

I turned away and shut the front door behind me, wheeling my case out of the way and back against the wall. I linked my arm through Mum's as we walked to the kitchen.

She had so many questions, but I didn't have any answers.

I put my handbag on the scrubbed pine table in the centre

of the kitchen and pulled out my mobile phone. With a couple of taps on the screen, I accessed the message and the photograph of Jenna and showed it to Mum.

She held her breath as her trembling hand reached out for the phone, and her fingers touched the image of Jenna's face.

"I don't recognise the number," I said. "So, I have no idea who sent it. It could be the person who took her...or somebody who's seen Jenna and recognised her from the news reports."

Mum looked at me, dazed. "I think that's the first thing the police will want to look into. They'll probably take your phone and try and trace that number."

I nodded. "I hope they've already made a start on tracing the phone number. They should be here soon, shouldn't they?"

We both glanced at the large, antique kitchen clock on the wall.

"Yes, they should be here within the next ten minutes or so."

A tentative smile played at the corner of Mum's mouth, and I knew she was reacting to this situation just like me. One moment I felt a rush of euphoria to think that Jenna was still alive and that we might get her back, and in the next moment, I was flooded with doubts. Was this some kind of horrible trick?

She reached out and grabbed my hand, squeezing it gently. "I can't believe this is really happening, Beth."

Before I could reply, the front door opened, and I turned in surprise.

My surprise was replaced by irritation when I saw that Daniel had let himself in. Of course, he had every right to be here, but he didn't live here anymore, so why did he still have a key?

I took a deep breath. Now wasn't the time to mention it. Why couldn't I be more understanding? After all, Jenna was his daughter, and how could I blame him if he didn't much like me? I'd been the one to let go of Jenna's hand. She had disappeared under my watch.

"Daniel," Mum said brightly. Her gaze quickly darted between Daniel and me as she sensed the change in my mood. "I'm so glad you could get here in time. Beth's only just arrived. The police will be here soon."

Daniel was wearing a dark grey suit. He didn't look his usual polished self, though. His tie was loosened and at an odd angle, and his hair was messy as though he'd been continually raking his fingers through it.

He nodded at me. "Beth."

There was no smile. No polite small talk. But then I was sure, in his opinion, I didn't deserve it.

"Why don't I make us a nice cup of tea?" Mum smoothed her grey cashmere cardigan over her grey woollen skirt.

"I'll give you a hand," I said.

But she shook her head. "No need. You talk to Daniel."

I shrugged off my linen jacket and placed it over the back of one of the chairs before sitting down at the kitchen table.

Daniel took the chair opposite me.

"Can I see the message?" His tone was brittle as he asked the question.

I pushed my phone across the table top towards him, and he picked it up to look at the screen. I knew it wasn't the first time he'd seen the image. Mum had shown him the photograph only minutes after I'd sent it to her, and they had been able to enlarge the image and study it on a computer screen.

Daniel's expression changed, and he looked pained as he looked at the screen.

"It's her. It's definitely her, Daniel." I rested my forearms on the table and leant closer to him. We'd had our differences in the past even before Jenna went missing, and I knew that was largely my fault. But I wanted us to work together now. If we wanted the best chance of getting Jenna back, we needed to.

Daniel shook his head. "I don't know. She looks different."

I frowned. "Of course, that's because she's older. It's been two years."

"I'm quite aware of how long it has been, Beth," Daniel said through gritted teeth.

I closed my eyes and took a breath. "I know. I'm sorry. But you can't really doubt that it's her, can you?"

Daniel looked up from the photograph and narrowed his

eyes as he stared at me. I shifted uncomfortably under his scrutiny.

"How have you been, Beth?"

To anyone else, his question may have seemed courteous, a pleasant exchange of small talk with his sister-in-law before the police arrived, but I knew Daniel better than that. He was referring to my episodes.

After Kate had died, I'd felt I owed it to her to find out what had happened to Jenna. I was desperate for some kind of resolution, and I followed every trail I could. I'd latched onto the silliest of coincidences and declared it evidence. I'd wasted police time and made Mum sick with worry on top of everything else she'd been through. Instead of getting resolution, the only thing I had achieved was to make life more difficult for Daniel and my mother.

I clasped my hands together and rested them on the table in front of me, trying to look like a woman in control of her emotions. "I'm fine. Dubai has been good for me."

Daniel said nothing. He just nodded and then looked back down at the screen.

The moment Mum set the teapot down on the table, there was a knock at the front door.

I got to my feet, but Mum put a hand on my shoulder. "Sit down, Beth. I'll get it."

I didn't turn around but could hear the murmurs of conversation after Mum opened the door and felt my stomach knot as I heard footsteps approach.

Why was I so nervous? I wanted to speak to the police. There was no reason for me to worry. Because I'd caused them trouble in the past with my insistence they follow-up every ridiculous lead I'd brought to them, I was worried that they wouldn't take me seriously. But this was different. This was a genuine lead, a real development.

I didn't recognise either one of the officers which surprised me. I thought it would be the same detective inspector in charge of the case. Jenna's disappearance had only been two years ago, and the detective inspector hadn't been anywhere near retirement age.

Mum's face looked pale and tense as she introduced us to the police officers. The grey-haired man was called Detective Inspector Rob Sharp, and his name suited him. His facial features were sharp and pointed. His nose was long and narrow, and his eyes were close set like a predator's.

The woman beside him, dressed in a smart black trouser suit and pink blouse, was Detective Sergeant Leanne Parker. Her face was round, plump and healthy. Shallow dimples dented her cheeks as she smiled at us.

They held out their hands to shake ours, and then we all sat down around the kitchen table. Mum poured the tea, and the china rattled a little as she passed the detective inspector his cup.

"I think it's best if you tell us in your own words what happened yesterday when you got the message," Detective Inspector Sharp said. His voice didn't sound like I'd expected. It was low, melodious and calming.

I nodded and twisted my hands in my lap. "Of course. I got

the text message yesterday. It was mid-afternoon in Dubai, so late morning here, in the UK. I'd been out for lunch with friends at a hotel, and we were sitting outside after lunch having a drink when I heard the message tone on my phone. I didn't recognise the number, but I saw the picture and... Well, it was a bit of a shock. The sun was shining on the screen. I couldn't see properly, so I went straight inside and looked again, and I saw immediately that it was Jenna, my niece. I was sure of it."

"Did you show any of your friends the photograph while you were there?"

I shook my head, not understanding the significance of the question. "No, it was such a shock, and I just wanted to be on my own. I took a taxi and went home and then when I looked at the photograph again, I knew that I had to tell my mother and Daniel because I was sure it was Jenna. I called my mother and showed her the photograph."

Mum nodded confirming my story. "That's right. Beth showed me the photograph over a video call, and I wasn't sure at first because I couldn't see it very well on her phone, but then she emailed me the photograph, and well, you can't deny there's a very striking resemblance to Jenna."

Detective Sergeant Leanne Parker jotted something down in a small notebook. I was surprised. I thought everybody did everything on electronic devices these days.

Detective Inspector Sharp turned back to me. "And after you spoke to your mother, what did you do then, Beth?"

I wasn't sure why my movements were so important.

Surely that had nothing to do with whoever had sent the photograph.

"I sent my mother another email with the phone number so that she could give it to you, and then I booked the next flight to the UK. I arrived at Heathrow this morning."

Detective Inspector Sharp nodded. "I see."

He followed up by asking me more questions about the friends I had been with over brunch, and then he turned to Daniel. "What did you think when you saw the photograph, Mr Creswell?"

Daniel's expression darkened, and he frowned. "What did I think? I was shocked. I couldn't believe it was Jenna."

"Do you believe it is a genuine photograph of your daughter?"

Daniel sighed and rubbed his hands over his face. "I don't know. It looks like her. I want to believe it's her, but…"

I watched Daniel carefully. Why wouldn't he believe it? He had the evidence right in front of him.

Detective Sergeant Parker turned to me. Her gaze briefly flickered down, taking note of my clenched fists, and she smiled. "You did the right thing, Beth."

"Have you been able to trace the number yet?" I asked.

The sergeant exchanged a glance with her boss and then shook her head. "It's early days. We are working on it."

I couldn't help feeling disappointed. They'd had the

number all night. Surely, they should have made some progress by now.

"I called the number, but I got a recorded message saying the number was not recognised. Was that the wrong thing to do?"

Leanne shook her head. "I think it was a natural response. But I'd ask you not to try to communicate with them again without letting us know first. In fact, we would like to keep your phone and do some analysis."

I'd been expecting that, so I nodded. "Of course."

Daniel pushed the phone across the table to the detectives, and Leanne placed it in a plastic evidence bag.

After everyone had finished their tea, and another round of questions had been asked, Detective Inspector Sharp got to his feet. "Thank you for your time. We will be in touch very soon. DS Parker will leave her contact details with you, so if you have any questions, you can get hold of her directly."

"Is that it?" I asked.

I couldn't believe there wasn't more going on. I hoped it was different behind-the-scenes. For all I knew, they could have a whole team working on tracing and tracking down Jenna back at the station.

"For now. I take it you're staying in the UK for a little while?"

I nodded.

As the detectives prepared to leave the kitchen, Daniel spoke up. "I've got a question," he said.

Everyone turned to look at him.

"Yes?" Inspector Sharp prompted, waiting patiently for Daniel's question.

"Will you be able to tell if this is really a photograph of Jenna?"

He shot a glance at me, but couldn't maintain eye contact for long.

"We have a technical team looking at the image. We should have more answers for you soon."

CHAPTER TEN

After the police and Daniel had left, Mum went to phone her sister, Aunt Mary, who lived in Aberdeen. She was worried the story about Jenna's photograph would break before she had the chance to let our close family know and prepare them for the onslaught of press attention.

She took the phone to the sunroom at the back of the house to make the call, and while she was occupied, I wheeled my case towards my childhood bedroom.

Three of the bedrooms were downstairs, and a further three were upstairs. The attic had been converted, so the upstairs bedrooms had sloping ceilings. My parents' bedroom was the largest room upstairs and had an en suite bathroom. Even though my father passed away some years ago, I still thought of it as my parents' room rather than just Mum's. The other two bedrooms upstairs were smaller and used as guest rooms.

The main living area of the house was open plan. The kitchen was the heart of the house and was where we held most of our family gatherings. There was a living room through an archway off the kitchen. A large room, it had space for three mismatched sofas as well as a couple of armchairs close to the wood burner.

At the far end of the living room was a small corridor that led to the three downstairs bedrooms. My bedroom was the first on the left, opposite the bathroom.

I paused with my hand on the doorknob and looked further along the hallway at the other two doors. Right at the end, was the smallest room, which had been Jenna's. The room next to mine was Kate's room, and it was the room she had shared with Daniel while they'd lived here with Mum. Despite that, I would always think of it as Kate's room.

I turned away and pushed open my bedroom door.

Mum had made up the bed with fresh white sheets. The room itself hadn't changed much. It was decorated with the same pale lilac walls and bright white woodwork as it had been when I was a teenager.

A rickety, white painted dressing table, topped with a large mirror, was set back against the wall close to my bed. My cream jewellery box was on top of the dressing table just as I had left it. Kate had a matching one, but hers had been red.

Above the heavy oak chest of drawers was a large picture frame, stuffed full of photographs of Kate and me when we were growing up. I needed to unpack and get back to Mum, but I couldn't resist looking at the photographs.

I smiled as I looked at the familiar images. Kate using her hand to shade her eyes from the summer sun, holding a melting ice cream and grinning. Kate and I dressed in matching Christmas jumpers, pulling goofy faces for the camera. Kate, Pippa and I dressed as witches on Halloween. Kate and I the year we decided it was a good idea to have our hair permed.

I couldn't help grinning at that photograph. We'd thought we looked the business.

I took a deep breath, pushed away from the chest of drawers and knelt down to unzip my case. I hadn't brought much with me, but I'd already made the decision that I would be staying in the UK for as long as it took to find Jenna. It was then I remembered I hadn't even called into work and explained my absence.

I muttered a curse and reached for my mobile phone before remembering the phone was with the police.

Damn. I hadn't thought to store the phone numbers anywhere else. I would have to email Sylvia and ask her to pass on a message. Or maybe I could use Mum's computer to look up the company telephone number and asked to be put through to my boss.

I really should have planned this better. I was pretty sure I wouldn't be going back to Dubai. We had to look for Jenna and to do that I needed to be in England. However long it took, I wouldn't give up. Even though I wouldn't be going back to that job, I didn't like letting people down.

I quickly unpacked, putting most of the items in the chest of drawers and hanging up my linen jacket on the outside of the wardrobe to let it dry off.

Then I selected a navy-blue jumper and shrugged it on.

I grabbed a brush and ran it through my hair, not daring to peer into the mirror on my dressing table. I already knew I looked terrible. I didn't want confirmation.

First thing tomorrow, I decided, I would get a new phone. My phone was my lifeline. I relied on it for so many things: emails, text messages, looking things up on the Internet. I had no idea how long the police would need to keep mine for, and I didn't think I could survive very long without one.

I left my bedroom and made my way back to the kitchen. There was no sign of Mum, so I decided to make us both a cup of coffee. I noticed she had a fancy new coffee machine, but I didn't feel confident using it without instructions, so I spooned some instant granules into two mugs and switched the kettle on to boil. It was strange being back. Nothing had changed. But it was nice. I had a sudden vision of us bringing Jenna back here, welcoming her back into the family. She'd find it strange, of course, at first. But we'd spend all our time making sure she felt loved again. I brought myself up short. What was I thinking? Even if we found Jenna, she wouldn't be living here. She'd be with Daniel, her father.

When the kettle finished boiling, I poured hot water into the mugs and then added some milk. Mum and I both liked our coffee strong, with only a splash of milk.

Kate had been completely different. She liked her coffee

milky, with two spoonfuls of sugar. She'd taken after our father in that respect.

I missed them both so much. It was hard not to think that if my father had still been alive, none of this would have happened. He died far too young from complications after minor surgery. At the time, I didn't know there was no such thing as minor surgery. Anything that involved a general anaesthetic was a risk.

I carried the mugs of coffee out to the sun room, a long, narrow room at the back of the house. The large windows looked out onto the garden, and it could get uncomfortably hot in the summer, but on a rainy day like today, with occasional bursts of sunshine, it was a pleasant place to sit.

As I got closer to the sunroom, I could hear Mum talking on the phone. I overheard something that made me pause and listen guiltily.

"I think Beth is okay," Mum said. "Daniel is worried, but I know Beth. She wouldn't do anything like that."

My hand tightened on the mug. What wouldn't I do?

I hesitated, but then forced myself to stop eavesdropping. It wasn't a good idea. No one heard good things about themselves while listening in on private conversations.

I stepped onto the tiled floor of the sun room and smiled brightly at Mum as I held out the mug of coffee.

She mouthed the word thank you and reached up to take it from me.

"I'm just talking to your Auntie Mary," she said. She held up the phone. "Say hello."

"Hello, Auntie Mary," I said loudly.

Mum put the phone back to her ear and said, "I better go now, Mary. I'll talk to you soon. Of course, I will. I'll let you know when there are any developments. Bye for now."

She pressed the red end call button on the telephone and then leant back against the floral cushion on her rattan chair.

"Well, that's one job out of the way. I didn't want Mary finding out from anybody else."

"Is there anyone else you need to tell?"

Mum shook her head. "No, I don't want anyone inadvertently releasing the news before the police are ready. We'll just deal with everybody else's questions as they come." She took a sip of her coffee. "I just can't believe it's real, Beth. That Jenna is still out there somewhere. I can't help thinking that if only Kate had waited…"

Mum's voice trailed away, and I reached out to squeeze her hand. "I know. But the best thing we can do for Kate now is get Jenna back."

"I would have thought the police would have some leads by now. Do you think they know who sent it and don't want to tell us?"

I shook my head. "I don't know. I can't see why they wouldn't tell us if they'd managed to trace the number."

Mum stared out at the rain-soaked garden. It was less than

twenty-four hours since we had seen the photograph of Jenna. She smoothed a hand over her grey wool skirt, a gesture that was so familiar to me and betrayed her anxiety. Our world had been turned upside down with the discovery that Jenna could have been alive all this time. Feeling anxious was only natural, but I knew her well enough to sense that she was holding something back. I wasn't going to push her on the subject, though. If she wanted to confide in me or question me, I would let her do it in her own time.

We sat in silence for a moment, enjoying the sun, which had broken through the grey clouds and streamed through the large windows.

After a brief hesitation, Mum turned to me and said, "You shouldn't pay any attention to Daniel's reaction today, Beth."

That surprised me. Mum and Daniel had always got along well, and I couldn't help wondering whether something had happened recently to cause Mum to change her opinion of him.

"Why do you say that?"

"He's finding it difficult. I think he had come to terms with the fact Jenna was gone for good, and now he can't bring himself to hope he could get her back."

That made sense. "He is probably afraid that it will all come to nothing. I can understand that."

"He was in a wretched state after it happened. We all were."

I nodded at Mum's mug. "Don't let your coffee get cold."

After she picked up her mug and took a sip, she turned back to me and asked, "Why do you think they sent the photograph to you, Beth?"

That question had been worrying me for a while, and I hadn't yet thought of a logical answer. It would have been far easier to send the photograph to Daniel. My phone number and phone were both from Dubai, and it wouldn't have been easy to track down my number. If someone was trying to help us find Jenna, then why hadn't they sent the message to Daniel? He would have been the logical choice. After all, he was Jenna's father.

I shrugged and shook my head. "I have no idea. It doesn't make any sense to me. Do you think Daniel was a little off with me earlier?"

Mum hesitated before replying, and I could have kicked myself. What a stupid question! It had been my fault. If I had kept an eye on Jenna as I was supposed to, she wouldn't have gone missing. He had every right to dislike being in the same room and breathing the same air as me.

"It's not anything personal, Beth," Mum said carefully. "This has brought up a lot of memories for Daniel. It's only been eighteen months since Kate... I think he is struggling with the possibility that Jenna has been alive all this time."

"But it's good news. Surely he's pleased we have a chance to get Jenna back."

"It's not that simple. I don't think he can allow himself to believe or even hope he could get Jenna back. It's hard to remember how it was for everyone else at the time. We were all hurting so badly, but Daniel has managed to put some semblance of a life back together, and I think he's afraid of his carefully constructed new life tumbling down...It's not that he doesn't want Jenna back," she added hurriedly when she saw the look of disbelief on my face.

I nodded. "I can understand he's scared this might all come to nothing. What I can't understand is why the police haven't traced the number yet. It can't be that hard. They've had the number and the photograph since last night."

Mum nodded thoughtfully. Her face was tense, and I sensed there was something else she didn't want to tell me.

"What is it?"

She blinked, smoothed down her skirt and shook her head. "Nothing, I was just thinking things over."

"You know why the police are dragging their feet, don't you? Tell me. If they're not taking us seriously, I'll kick up a stink. Go to the local newspaper."

Mum sighed and put a hand on my arm. "Press attention is the last thing we want, Beth. I might be wrong, but I spoke to Daniel last night, and he said..."

I frowned. "Said what?"

"Don't get upset," Mum said, and I immediately felt my blood pressure rise.

"Just tell me."

"He wanted to know if I thought you could have made changes to the photograph."

I shook my head. "Changes to the photograph? What's that supposed to mean?"

Mum watched me closely for a moment, waiting for the penny to drop. The sun disappeared behind the clouds, and I shivered.

"He thinks I've made this all up somehow? He thinks I made changes to the photograph to make Jenna look older?"

"He didn't say he believed that, but he wanted to know if it was possible. I'm pretty sure he has spoken to the police about the possibility. He told me he was going to."

I put down my mug because my hands were shaking so much I was about to spill the contents everywhere. "How could he? He could have ruined the whole investigation. We need to trace whoever sent that photograph. If the police think I've made it up, they may not bother. Whoever sent the message, could have already dumped their phone. We could be too late. We could lose our only chance of getting Jenna back and…"

I broke off mid-sentence as a new sinking feeling overcame me. "You don't believe I've made this up, do you?"

Mum shook her head rapidly and reached out to squeeze my hand. "Of course, I don't. I know you could never do something like that. But I have a feeling that's why the police haven't been quick to let us know they have traced the call."

I ran a hand through my hair. "I don't believe this. They're not even going to bother to look for her because they think I've made it up?"

"I didn't say that, Beth. Calm down."

"It's hard to keep calm when people are accusing me of something like that."

"It's not an accusation. Daniel is finding it hard to process everything. He's wrong. I know that, and I told him so."

I sat back in the rattan armchair, my hands clasped together to try to stop them trembling. I was furious. But I really had no one to blame but myself. If I hadn't caused so many problems for the police two years ago, I wouldn't be viewed with suspicion now.

I turned to Mum and noticed for the first time how this had aged her. The lines in her forehead were deeper, and her lips were clamped together in a thin line. She looked as though she was bracing herself for the next life blow.

Her voice wavered a little as she said, "I can't help worrying Daniel's suggestion the photograph is not genuine will mean the police will focus on the wrong angle."

A wave of guilt flooded through me. If my behaviour two years ago prevented the police from taking this new lead seriously, then I could be responsible for letting Jenna slip away from us for the second time.

"So, since I sent you that photograph last night and you told the police and Daniel, nothing has been done to look for Jenna?" I asked, ignoring the bitter taste in my mouth.

Mum shook her head. "The police have to take any fresh news in Jenna's disappearance very seriously. I'm sure they traced that call as soon as they got the number."

"Then why haven't they told us that?" I asked, exasperated.

"Because I think they are waiting to see how we react. I imagine they've already traced the number, but for some reason, they're not convinced the photograph didn't come from you."

"But if they've traced the phone number, they must know who sent the message."

"I think they're probably holding information back."

"But that's not fair."

"I know."

I leant back against the plush cushions and clutched the material of the seat cover. "The photograph has given us more questions than answers. Where has Jenna been all this time, and who has been keeping her from us?" I tried to swallow, but my mouth was dry. I leant over and took a sip of my coffee. "She looked healthy in the photograph. I mean, she wasn't smiling, but perhaps the person who took her has been kind to her."

"Maybe." Mum's eyes filled with tears. "I suppose we won't know until we get her back."

"Where did we put the Detective Sergeant's card?" I asked, getting to my feet. "They said we should contact them if we had any questions."

"We haven't given them very long, Beth. They only left an hour ago."

"I know. But I'm going to try and persuade her that this was a genuine message. They've had the phone number and the photograph since last night. I'm sure they want to do all sorts of clever stuff with my phone to try and work out if I sent it, but while they're occupied with that, they're not looking for whoever really took Jenna."

Mum thought that over for a moment and then nodded. She handed me the cordless telephone. "The card is in the kitchen, next to the fruit bowl."

CHAPTER ELEVEN

As Mum had said, the card was in the kitchen next to the fruit bowl. Picking it up, I gazed down at the cream-coloured card and felt a fluttering of nerves in my stomach. I had to convince the police this wasn't some wild goose chase. Somehow, I needed them to believe I was trustworthy. Mum was right. They wouldn't simply ignore the photograph, but if they thought I'd manipulated the image, some of their focus would be wasted on me.

The number on the card was a direct line, and the Detective Sergeant answered on the third ring. "DS Leanne Parker."

"Hello, this is Beth Farrow. I spoke to you this morning about my niece's disappearance."

There was a slight hesitation on the line before she replied. I heard the rustling of paper. "Yes, what can I do for you, Beth?"

I took a deep breath and held the telephone closer to my

ear. "This is a difficult situation." I'd worked out what I was going to say before I picked up the phone, but now with the phone clamped to my ear, I forgot the clear, rational words I'd planned to use, and instead, I blurted out, "I've just been talking to my mother, and she suggested that Jenna's father, Daniel, might be worried that this isn't a genuine photograph. He suspects I've made it up."

What must she think of me? The police must deal with all sorts of family issues and troubles in the course of their investigations, but had this Detective Sergeant ever come across anything as messed up as this? The idea that anybody would create false evidence when a child's life could be in danger made me feel sick. Did she think I was capable of that?

When I'd first seen DS Leanne Parker this morning, I'd thought she seemed approachable. She had an open, friendly face and looked like the kind of woman you could go out with for a drink and chat. As far as first impressions went, I judged she was down to earth and sensible. I hoped I was right.

She took a long time to answer, before she finally said, "I see."

Was that it? Wasn't she going to reassure me that they were treating this photograph seriously and tell me they had a team of detectives tracing the number right now?

"I need to know that you don't believe I manipulated the image. I need to know that you're going to look for Jenna." My voice was strained and showed my desperation.

"We are, Beth. We are going to be looking into every possible scenario. I can promise you that."

I let out a shaky breath and leant heavily against the kitchen counter. "I'm glad to hear it," I said. "Have you managed to trace the number yet?"

"It's our top priority, and we are looking into it now. We will update you and the rest of the family when we have new information to share."

She was using generic words and platitudes. She was blanking me, and it was infuriating.

"This is really not good enough, Leanne. For one thing, I'm sure it doesn't take the police long in this day and age to trace a telephone call. I can't help feeling you are deliberately hiding things from us. And that's not on."

At that moment, Mum walked into the kitchen carrying the coffee mugs and gave me a disapproving look. I'd flown off the handle when that was the last thing I should be doing if I wanted them to believe I wasn't the crackpot Daniel thought I was. I needed Detective Sergeant Parker and Detective Inspector Sharp to be on my side.

"I'm sorry," I said. "It's just unbearable not knowing what's going on."

"Look, I know waiting for answers is hard. But we are progressing with the investigation. There are certain things I can't share with you at this stage because the investigation is ongoing, but as soon as we can give you an update, we will."

That didn't exactly fill me with confidence. Why couldn't

she just tell me now? "Surely, you can at least tell me if you've managed to trace the number."

"It's not quite as simple as that."

"What's that supposed to mean?" I tried and failed to keep the tone of my voice free from anger.

"It's not a mobile phone number." She sighed. "I can't say any more at this stage. Please, Beth, I know it's really hard but try to be patient, and I'll get back to you tomorrow."

"Okay." That was all I could manage. The phone call hadn't gone the way I intended, but keeping her on the line wouldn't help. I wouldn't get any more answers, and losing my temper would set the investigation back even further.

I didn't understand why she said the message hadn't come from a mobile phone number. It made no sense because I had seen the number on my phone. Bewildered, I said goodbye and hung up and then relayed the conversation to Mum, who seemed just as confused as me over the fact the message hadn't come from a mobile phone.

We made ham and tomato sandwiches and sat at the kitchen table together, picking at them. Neither of us had much appetite, but making lunch was something to keep us occupied and pass the time. We puzzled over what the Detective Sergeant had meant, and in the end, I started to believe I'd misunderstood.

After lunch, I decided to go for a walk, but Mum wanted to stay home just in case the police rang with news.

"You might want to avoid Blenheim Palace, today," she

said. "They've got an event going on, so it will be incredibly busy."

I nodded as I shrugged on my linen jacket. "I was just planning to have a quick stroll around the town," I said. "I won't go far."

I didn't head straight for the High Street, figuring it would be too busy. Instead, I walked around the back of Rectory Lane past a group of thatched cottages. One of those cottages belonged to Dawn Parsons's mother.

I couldn't help looking in as I walked by. Like most traditional thatched cottages, the windows were very small, and inside, the cottages were dark. The outside looked picture perfect, like something on a postcard or a chocolate box. The walls of the house were painted white, and a yellow rambling rose grew around the doorway. It was hard to believe someone like Dawn Parsons grew up in such a pretty environment.

I looked at the house carefully, wondering if Dawn or her mother were home, but Dawn's mother's car wasn't in the driveway. Of course, she could have sold the house by now for all I knew, but their family had lived there so long I couldn't imagine Mrs Parsons wanting to live anywhere else.

I wondered if Dawn was still living with her mother. I guessed she probably was. I couldn't see her doing anything else with her life now.

What had Dawn seen that day? She'd been questioned by the police like everyone else. She told them she'd been at the face painting station, and after Jenna had disappeared, she had joined in the search. But I knew better. She hadn't been at the face-painting stall when Jenna went missing because I'd noticed she wasn't there. Of course, she'd made up some excuse about getting a fresh supply of those waxy face paints out of somebody's car.

I thought she was lying, and I insisted the police look into her. That was probably when it started, my desperate clutching at straws. I only managed to annoy everybody. Daniel said I was wasting police time. In his opinion, I was getting the police to chase after people like Dawn for no reason at all apart from my personal vendetta.

I was outraged and expected Mum and Kate to tell Daniel he was wrong. They didn't.

Now that two years had passed, I was ashamed of how I'd acted. Daniel had been going through the worst experience imaginable, and I should have backed down, been more understanding. I was trying so hard to put everything right, but it wasn't possible. Nothing I did would change what had happened. Selfishly and cruelly, I'd lashed out at Daniel, and we had a huge row in Mum's living room.

As we shouted at each other, Kate had said nothing at all. She sat in an armchair with a cup of cold tea in front of her, her arms wrapped around her body, shivering. I should have picked up on the signs earlier, but I thought Kate's reaction was normal for a mother who had lost a child.

She could hardly bring herself to be in the same room as me in the weeks after it happened. She blamed me, and I know she didn't want to feel like that, but she just couldn't help it.

I had lost the most precious thing in the world to her. She trusted me, and I let her down.

I took a deep breath and shoved my hands in my pockets, walking away and leaving Dawn Parson's house behind.

I wound my way around the back of the Co-op and then walked passed the old garage, heading away from the town. As I approached the front gate of Blenheim Palace, I walked with purpose, with long strides and a fast pace, even though I had nowhere to go. I was trying to walk fast enough to leave my memories behind.

A large coach was pulling out of the Blenheim Palace drive-way, and I stood back and waited for it to pull out onto the main road.

More tourists. There were tourists there the day Jenna went missing. It could have been any of them, and they could have taken her anywhere. Maybe a tourist had taken her, and now they were having second thoughts. Maybe the guilt was too much for them, and that was why they had reached out with the photograph. I preferred to think Jenna had been taken by someone like that. Maybe a poor, child-less couple who'd wanted a daughter so much they decided to steal one. It was one of the nicer options that ran through my mind on a daily basis. There were other possibilities I didn't even want to consider.

I walked until I reached the roundabout leading to Bladon and decided I'd gone far enough. I turned to walk back the way I'd come, keeping my pace up. Rather than go straight back home along Rectory Road, I decided to take a detour and walk up by the older houses in old Woodstock.

There was a house there that was said to have belonged to Geoffrey Chaucer's son. Several stone steps led up to the other end of the High Street. An archway of green shrubs enclosed the steps and gave it an otherworldly feel.

I walked up the steps past the higgledy-piggledy houses full of charm and character and then paused beside the odd one out. Robin Vaughan's house. It was now hidden behind an imposing Cotswold stone wall. There had been an outcry in the community when he'd arrived because he had wanted to do all sorts of modifications to the old building, and many in the area thought the building should be listed.

At least, the wall he built around the house was made of Cotswold stone, and in a few decades, it would blend in and look like all the other stone built structures in the vicinity.

I think that one of the reasons Jenna's case had so much press attention was because Robin Vaughan had been there when it happened. I thought of him as a B-list celebrity, but it seemed even B-list celebrities sold papers. At first, we had held out hope that the press attention would help us find Jenna faster, but we were soon disillusioned. All they cared about were sales and digging up dirt. Neighbours and friends we'd trusted sold stories to the press, and we ended up losing much-needed support and not knowing who we could trust.

I was almost at the top of the steps when I noticed someone in front of me. The green branches overhead blocked out most of the sunlight. The stone steps were narrow, so I stepped to the side to let the woman coming towards me pass. When she was two steps away, I recognised her. It was the lady with the deep plum lipstick who'd been manning the balloon stall the day Jenna had gone missing. The sight of her stole the breath from my lungs. It shouldn't have. She lived in Woodstock. It shouldn't have been a surprise to see her again, but I gave an involuntary shudder as a prickle spread over my skin.

She seemed equally dumbstruck when she recognised me.

A hesitant smile played on her lips, and she raised a hand and then lowered it again as though she didn't quite know how to react.

"Hello, how are you?" She managed to smile.

It was a normal, polite question, very British and reserved.

I nodded. "Fine, thank you. Nice to see you."

We passed a few seconds with the usual small talk: *I haven't seen you around lately. I've been away. Typical weather for spring.* Neither of us mentioned Jenna or Kate.

After our conversation had lapsed into an uncomfortable silence, I said I had better be going and said goodbye. I wanted to get home.

I walked briskly along Rectory Lane, and I was just passing the old thatched cottages again when I could have sworn a curtain moved in one of the upstairs windows in Dawn Parson's house.

I stopped dead, staring up at the window. There was no discernible movement. No sign there was anyone there, at all.

I realised I was holding my breath. I was so sure I'd seen

the curtain move. Was I seeing things? Or was Dawn up there watching me?

I shivered.

I could go and hammer on the front door, demand she let me in and explain why she was spying on me. But that was overreacting. It was the sort of thing I would have done two years ago. Now, I was supposed to be in control and acting logically. I had no proof anyone was even in the house. Perhaps a window was open in another room and a breeze had shifted the curtain.

I looked away and carried on walking, only to turn back when I was a few feet away just to make sure. The window was dark and empty.

Even though my own eyes told me there was no one there, I felt a tingle along the back of my neck as though I were being watched as I headed back to Mum's house.

CHAPTER TWELVE

When I got back to Mum's house and stepped through the front door, I realised how ridiculously I was behaving. It was just a house. The police had investigated Dawn Parsons at the time and ruled her out as a suspect. I couldn't let my old fears take hold of me now. What I needed was a clear head. At least, I hadn't been stupid enough to go up to the front door and confront her.

When I'd first seen my counsellor, which I'd only agreed to under protest to keep my prescription for sleeping tablets from my GP, she'd told me to use the tried and trusted technique of counting to ten before I acted. It was trite, but sensible advice. Unfortunately, I was never able to follow it.

I walked quickly towards the kitchen, ready to ask Mum if there'd been any news while I was out, but before I could say anything, she looked up and shook her head. She was sitting at the kitchen table, and I wondered whether she'd been sat there since I'd left.

"Nice walk?" she asked, trying to smile and show some interest for my sake.

"It was good to get some fresh air. But it didn't take my mind off things. Everything keeps going around and around in my mind, but I can't make sense of it. I don't understand why the message came to me. Daniel doesn't trust me, and neither do the police, it seems. It would have been better if whoever sent the message had sent it to Daniel instead."

I shrugged off my jacket and sank into the chair opposite Mum. "It's going to be tough on all of us over the next few days as we wait for answers. But I don't want you to worry about me, Mum."

Mum's eyes crinkled around the edges as she smiled. "You're right, it is going to be difficult, but if we get Jenna back, this agonising wait will be worth it."

Putting my palms flat against the scrubbed pine table, I pushed myself up and asked, "Shall I make us a cup of tea?"

Before Mum could answer, there was a knock at the door.

As she went to answer it, I filled the kettle at the sink. I flicked the switch on the kettle and grabbed a couple of mugs. Hearing voices, I walked towards the edge of the kitchen so I could see through the archway and across the living area. I'd recognised the visitor's voice but couldn't place it.

Gasping when I saw who it was, the mug I was holding slipped through my fingers and smashed on the floor.

Mum and her visitor both turned at the noise.

"Crap. I'm sorry."

"It doesn't matter. I've got plenty more," Mum said, forcing a cheerful tone into her voice.

The visitor followed her towards the kitchen. I took a step back. Marjorie Parsons. It had been two years since I'd last seen Dawn's mother, but she hadn't changed a bit.

She was wearing a beige raincoat that ended mid-thigh and didn't suit her dumpy figure. Her hair was curled close to her head in an old-fashioned style.

She smiled at me. "I heard you were back, Beth. It's lovely to see you. How long are you staying?"

"Um, I'm not sure yet."

I shot a glance at Mum. I was waiting for her direction on how much we should say. We didn't want to let the cat out of the bag too early. If we weren't careful, the news about Jenna's photograph would be all around the town. Mum had a smile fixed on her face, and she didn't act as if this was anything but a normal social call.

"I was just about to make a cup of tea. Would you like one?" I forced myself to make eye contact. I'd put Dawn's mother through hell with my accusations against her daughter. More than once I'd seen her in tears over the things I'd said, and I felt horrendously guilty. She must have been a good friend to Mum while I'd been in Dubai.

"I don't want to intrude," she said. "I heard you were back and wanted to say hello."

"You wouldn't be intruding, Marjorie," Mum said firmly. "Stay for a cup of tea."

Although I would have preferred to be alone to brood, I didn't want to appear rude. I carefully knelt down to pick up the shards of porcelain that had scattered over the floor.

As Mum made a start on making the tea, Marjorie smiled down at me.

"So, tell me how you've been getting on in Dubai? Your mother says you're doing ever so well. She is very proud of you."

I wished Marjorie wouldn't be so nice to me. If she were more like her daughter, it would be easy to despise her. But there was nothing in this motherly, kindly woman that I could hate. That didn't mean I was comfortable in her presence, though. Her being here reminded me of my bad behaviour two years ago and made me feel like I was drowning in guilt.

"It's been a lot of fun," I said, plastering on a smile. "You can't beat the sunshine."

Marjorie gave a chuckle. "I think the heat would be too much for me! I prefer a nice English summer."

I smiled again politely and looked around for the dustpan and brush to dispose of the remaining tiny fragments of the shattered cup. "It's not so bad," I said. "Everywhere is air-conditioned nowadays."

"It does sound exciting. Your mother showed me some photographs of her last trip and said you had a very important job, so I'm glad they could spare you for a trip home."

I glanced at Mum, who had her back to me and was pouring hot water into the teapot. She had always liked to brag about Kate and me. Even after I'd fallen off the rails, despite everything, she was still proud of me. I swallowed the lump in my throat.

After I brushed up the last of the remains of the mug and deposited them in the bin, Mum set the teapot on the table. I sat down and joined them for tea.

The atmosphere was awkward, and it was obvious an apology was needed to clear the air. I didn't relish that idea, but I couldn't bury my head in the sand and pretend I'd never made the allegations against Dawn. It was my bad behaviour that had caused so much upset, and I needed to take responsibility for it.

"I owe you an apology, Mrs Parsons. I made some accusations, unfounded accusations, and I know they were very hurtful. I wasn't thinking straight at the time. I hope you can forgive me."

"Of course, Beth. It's all water under the bridge now. It was a horrible time, and I do understand. Actually..."

She smiled as Mum passed her a cup of tea and then bit down on her lower lip before continuing, "I wondered if you might have time to have a word with Dawn at some point."

My physical response must have been answer enough. I gritted my teeth and my body tensed. Seeing Dawn Parsons again was the last thing I wanted to do. The police may have cleared her, but she still gave me the creeps.

"Sorry," Marjorie said, her cheeks colouring with embarrassment. "Forget I mentioned it. You're probably far too busy. I imagine you've got a lot to fit in before you go back to Dubai."

Mum said nothing. She didn't need to. She expected me to extend the olive branch by agreeing to talk to Dawn.

"It's just that Dawn is terribly shy. You know what she was like at school, and she hasn't got any better. In fact, for the last two years, she's cut herself off from anyone her own age. She doesn't even try to apply for jobs anymore." It was like the floodgates had opened as Marjorie Parsons told us all about her worries over her daughter.

I sympathised. It couldn't be easy living with someone like Dawn, but I didn't see what it had to do with me. I couldn't spare any energy worrying about someone like Dawn. I was too busy worrying about Jenna.

"I don't think I'm the best person to talk to Dawn," I said, intending to let Marjorie down gently. "We were never really very close."

The look of disappointment on Mrs Parsons's face made me feel like a heartless cow. But why should I feel bad? Dawn had always been horrible to me. She'd had a disappointing life, and I felt sorry for her, but it wasn't my problem. It wasn't down to me to solve her problems.

Even though Mum did nothing but politely pass a plate of biscuits to Mrs Parsons, I could feel her judgement.

"Maybe I'll try and find some time," I muttered.

"That really would be very kind of you," Mrs Parsons said. "Dawn's always looked up to you."

I almost choked on my tea. That was a ridiculous statement for two reasons. One, Dawn was nearly a foot taller than me, and two, she had made her disdain for me very clear by shoving me into the brook. But I didn't say any of that to Mrs Parsons. Instead, I smiled and nodded and then took a large bite out of a ginger nut biscuit.

I sat quietly drinking my tea as Mum and Mrs Parsons discussed church business. I prayed for the telephone to ring with news on Jenna, but we didn't hear anything from the police for the rest of the afternoon.

CHAPTER THIRTEEN

After Mrs Parsons had left us, Mum picked up her Kindle and went to sit in the sunroom to read. I asked to use her computer and went online.

Mum had embraced technology in the last two years. She had a desktop Mac computer in the wide entrance hall as well as a laptop. I opted to use the Mac and sat in the small swivel chair in front of it.

I wanted to buy a new phone. I didn't want to get tied into a contract, so I ordered a pay-as-you-go sim card, opting for next day delivery.

I took a quick look at a couple of websites advertising the latest phones, but in the end, decided to go to Oxford tomorrow and buy one, unless we got news from the police before then. It would get me out of the house and keep me busy, and that was exactly what I needed.

After scrolling through my email inbox, I quickly typed a

message to Sylvia, explaining I'd be staying in the UK longer than expected. In a few days, I'd probably have to call her and ask a big favour. She was the only person I'd feel comfortable asking to help ship my stuff back home.

I replied to a curt email from my boss, apologising for my absence and explaining some of the simpler tasks that he would be expected to do without my help. He was probably already rushing around the office panicking.

Once I'd finished with my emails, I started to shut down the computer but stopped as a thought occurred to me. Mum had saved the photograph of Jenna to the computer's desktop. I opened it up. Seeing it there, on the big screen, took my breath away.

I studied the image carefully, trying to see whether it had been doctored. Could somebody be that cruel? Why would they try to trick us after all this time? But nothing about the picture indicated it had been altered. It looked like a genuine photo to me, but then I was no expert.

I looked at Jenna's immediate surroundings, hoping to pick up a clue about the location. I didn't recognise anything in the background. That was disappointing, but at least it suggested this was a new photograph.

If it were an old photograph of Jenna, which had been altered to make her look older, I probably would have recognised where the photograph had been taken.

Jenna was standing on a lawn beside a tall, dark green hedge and she wasn't looking directly at the camera. Her legs were slightly apart as though she was walking and the camera had caught her in motion. Whoever had taken the picture was looking down on Jenna. Had the photograph been taken from higher ground? Was she in a park, a playground?

I couldn't tell much about the time of year from the photograph either. The grass looked reasonably healthy, and the sky was blue. Jenna was wearing a pink cardigan, but no coat. Did that mean it had been taken recently? A month ago, it would have even been too cold for a little girl to be out in the garden without a coat.

I pushed away the thought that Jenna might be living with someone who didn't care enough to ensure she stayed warm. I zoomed into the picture until the edges went fuzzy. The sides of Jenna's trainer were damp from the wet grass. Blinking away tears, I remembered trying to fasten her shoes after she'd been on the bouncy castle on the day she went missing. I'd messed that up, too. I closed my eyes, trying to drive away the memory of the police officer handing Kate one of Jenna's shoes they'd found in a nearby street.

I refocused, turning my attention to the hedge. The amount I knew about plants could fit on the back of a postage stamp. No one could ever accuse me of being green-fingered.

The leaves were green, so that suggested the photograph was taken in spring or summer, but what if it was an ever-green hedge? Mum would probably know. She and my father had always been avid gardeners. Mum love to spend time pottering in her garden. I didn't want to ask her, though. She might start to worry I was veering headlong into one of my wild goose chases. Instead, I searched the web until I found a forum where expert gardeners offered to identify plants. I stared at the screen and then shrugged. It was worth a try.

Deciding that posting the image of Jenna was a bad idea, I took a screenshot of one section of the hedge and zoomed into the leaves. The edges were a little blurry, but it would have to do.

I signed up to the forum, entering an email address and typing in a password, and then waited for the confirmation email, drumming my fingers on the desk. The wait gave me time to doubt myself. What did I really expect to achieve from this? Was I going too far again? The email appeared on the screen, and I clicked the link to confirm my address. Two minutes later, I had signed into my account and posted on the forum, asking for help to identify the dark green hedge. I sat there and refreshed the screen hoping for a reply. Of course, that was a ridiculous expectation. Nobody would respond that quickly.

Taking a deep breath and ordering myself not to pin my hopes on something so unlikely to help, I switched off the computer, stood up and stretched.

It was a long shot, but it felt good to be doing something positive. It was unlikely that the hedge would be a kind of rare plant only found in one area of the UK and would miraculously be able to tell us where Jenna had been when this photograph had been taken, but it felt better to do something proactive instead of sitting around, twiddling my thumbs, and waiting for the police to come back to us.

CHAPTER FOURTEEN

After fixing a simple pasta dish for dinner, I opened a bottle of red wine for us to drink with the meal and ease our frayed nerves. After the day we'd had, we needed it. Mum's gaze kept flickering over to the telephone, but the phone remained stubbornly silent. There had been no fresh news about Jenna, and waiting for answers was excruciating. The wave of hope I'd felt when the photograph of Jenna had appeared on my phone hadn't left me, but the initial excitement had given way to an unbearable tension as we waited to find out what the next step was going to be.

I'd hoped the police would have found Jenna by now, and we would be attempting some sort of reconnection. Even if everything worked out, and Jenna came home, it wouldn't be easy for Jenna to readjust. Would she even remember us?

Could I remember anything from when I was three years old? Not really. Some dim and distant images hovered at the edge of my memory— playing with a red tricycle in the garden, watching Kate climb the apple tree. Those memories were probably from when I was a year or so older than Jenna had been when she went missing.

If we got her back, it would be a difficult adjustment period for everyone. I couldn't even imagine how we would cope if this all turned out to be an elaborate hoax. I pushed away the negative thoughts, not wanting to consider the possibility Jenna wouldn't be coming home.

Neither of us was very hungry, and Mum only picked at her dinner, which only added to my concern. I was determined to take better care of her now that I was back home and make amends for my actions two years ago.

She was trying to be positive, but despite her best efforts, she couldn't hide her loss of appetite. It probably didn't help that we sat at the kitchen table, so close to the telephone, which kept reminding us there was still no news. Detective Sergeant Leanne Parker had said she would get back to us tomorrow, but that didn't stop me hoping they would, by some miracle, find Jenna before then.

"Have you spoken to Daniel this evening?" I asked.

Mum put down her glass of wine and shook her head. "No, I thought he could do with some space. He was really upset by the photograph."

I stabbed a spiral of pasta and moved it around the plate, coating it with some of the tomato sauce. "I thought I'd go into Oxford tomorrow and get a new phone," I said. "I ordered a sim card online, and it's going to be delivered tomorrow. Will you be home?"

"Yes, we were supposed to be having a coffee morning in aid of the church, but I don't feel up to it. Besides, I want to be here in case the police call."

"They have your mobile number, though, don't they?"

"Yes, but it's not the type of call I want to take in public."

I could understand that.

She rubbed her eyes and smothered a yawn. "I think I'll watch some mindless television and have an early night tonight, Beth. You don't mind, do you?"

"Of course not. It's been a stressful day."

The emotion of the day had left me drained, but I couldn't help feeling guilty. Waiting for answers was hard, but I should be feeling positive. I pushed my plate away and raised an eyebrow at Mum. "Finished?"

She nodded and lifted her plate, preparing to carry it to the sink.

"Leave it. I'll do that. You go and relax."

She smiled and patted my shoulder before heading off to the small sitting room. It had always been her refuge. When my father was alive, it had been their private sitting room — a room free from children and the associated mess and chaos. In the years after my father died, it had been her personal space, somewhere to retreat and get away from Kate, Daniel and Jenna when she needed some time alone.

I spent more time than necessary clearing up after dinner. There were only two pans, a saucepan I had used to boil the pasta, and a frying pan I'd used to fry up some garlic and onion before adding the tomatoes for the sauce. I scrubbed them carefully before washing our plates.

There was a dishwasher, but I washed and dried everything by hand before wiping down the kitchen counters. No doubt, I would find it difficult to sleep tonight and was in no rush to go to bed and be alone with my thoughts. Somehow, keeping busy with boring domestic tasks helped.

After I had said goodnight to Mum, I did everything possible to prepare for a good night's sleep, making myself a hot chocolate after soaking in a warm lavender-scented bath. Despite my best efforts, I lay awake beneath the cool, white sheets, staring up at the familiar swirls and patterns on the ceiling of my childhood bedroom. The memories were so numerous and strong here, it was impossible to banish them.

It had been easier in Dubai. Everything was fresh and new there, and nobody knew who I was. Here, everyone knew Jenna was missing and how Kate had taken her own life.

After miserably lying awake for an hour, I slipped out of bed and grabbed my handbag from the dressing table. In one of the sections of my purse, was a photograph I'd had printed after Kate had taken her own life. No one seemed to bother to print photographs anymore to make physical albums. Photographs were shared on Facebook or kept on phones. As my fingers closed around the glossy print, I smiled. There was something nice about a good old-fashioned photograph.

I sat back down, perching on the edge of the bed, and stared down at the photograph. It had been taken only a few months before Jenna disappeared. Jenna sat on Kate's lap, and they were both smiling. It was really only when Jenna smiled that you could see the similarity between her and Kate. Kate had dark hair whereas Jenna was very fair-haired and fair-skinned. But there was no doubt that Jenna had inherited Kate's smile. That broad, dazzling grin lit up their whole face. I would give anything to see them smile again.

I wondered how Kate would feel if she was still with us. Would she have handled things differently? Had I really tried hard enough to trace the number on my own before going to the police? I shuddered at the thought that whoever had taken Jenna may have unsuccessfully tried to contact me again. I couldn't get any more messages because the police had my phone.

But it was thoughts similar to these that had got me into trouble before. The police had the resources to track Jenna. They could do a better job than I ever could, and my own fumbling investigations would probably hinder rather than help the search for Jenna. I should have learnt that by now.

I put the photograph on the nightstand and then slid back under the sheets. It was silly, but with Kate's photograph beside me, I thought I might find it easier to sleep.

It didn't work. I was awake for hours and only just drifted off shortly before dawn. I'd never been good with a lack of sleep and woke up the next morning feeling wrung out and grouchy. I had a dull ache at the base of my skull, which was promising to turn into a killer headache. Pressing a hand to my forehead, I blinked. I wasn't wearing a watch and had no idea what the time was. I could tell by the way the sun was blaring in through the thin, cotton curtains that I'd slept later than usual. That didn't make any sense. I should have woken up early. After all, my body clock was still on Dubai time.

I shoved back the sheets and swung my legs out of bed, rubbing my bleary eyes. I padded towards the door and opened it. The delicious smell of coffee drifted towards me.

"Morning," I said to Mum and tried to smile as I walked into the kitchen.

She was standing beside the sink and looked at me over her shoulder. "You look like you got about as much sleep as I did."

"I probably only got a couple of hours."

I glanced at the antique clock on the kitchen wall and saw that it was just after nine AM. I really had slept in.

"Were you too warm? Or was the bed uncomfortable? It's getting on a bit now. We've had it for years, haven't we?"

Mum put a large mug of coffee on the table for me, and I quickly picked it up and breathed in the delicious scent. "It wasn't the bed's fault. It's comfortable enough. I just couldn't stop my mind turning things over, you know?"

Mum sighed and nodded. "I hope today will bring us some good news. I'm going to call Daniel in a little while and see how he is bearing up."

I blew over the top of my coffee, and then not wanting to wait for my shot of caffeine, I took a quick sip of the hot liquid, burning my tongue.

"Are you still going to Oxford today?" Mum asked.

I nodded. "Yes, unless we get any news from the police before then. I feel lost without my phone. Is there anything you need me to pick up for you?"

"Not really. Although, we're getting a little low on milk. You might want to pick some up on your way home."

I nodded and took another sip of the still too hot coffee. Mum was already impeccably dressed. Her short grey hair was carefully styled, and she'd applied her usual light layer of makeup. Despite that, she still looked pale and drawn.

"What time did you say that phone thingy was coming?" she asked.

"The sim card? I'm not sure. They said it would be delivered today but didn't give me a time."

Mum was moving about the kitchen as she spoke, as though she didn't want to pause for a moment and give herself time to think. "That's fine," she said. "I hadn't planned to do anything today anyway."

I smiled. "Thanks. I suppose I'd better get in the shower and get dressed." I pushed up from the table and picked up my half-full mug of coffee.

Mum picked up a towel to dry her hands and then she turned to face me. "How long will you be in Oxford?"

"I'll get the bus in, but I'll be as quick as possible because no one will be able to get in touch with me if there are any developments until I get a new phone and SIM card."

Mum moved closer to me and pushed my hair back from

my forehead. "I'm very glad you've come back home, Beth. Whatever happens, you can talk to me."

I hesitated before nodding. She meant she wanted me to talk to her before I went off the deep end again.

"You don't have to worry," I said. "When Jenna went missing and then Kate... I know I lost it a little. But I won't do it again."

Her shrewd hazel eyes fixed on mine, and I wondered if she believed me.

I left the kitchen to go to the shower room, which was on the ground floor. There was a further en suite bathroom upstairs, which had been recently fitted out with a large bath and a walk-in shower. The shower room downstairs had seen better days and needed updating. It hadn't changed since Kate and I shared it in our teens.

The shower was in a small glass cubicle, and I had forgotten just how small it was. My elbows knocked against the glass as I reached up to shampoo my hair. I had just started to rinse out the suds when I heard the phone ring.

Was that the police? Did they have news on Jenna?

I wiped the soap out of my eyes and scrambled to turn off the shower. Flinging open the door of the cubicle, I grabbed a towel. Dripping wet, I shoved open the bathroom door and ran down the hallway with slippery, wet feet.

Mum had answered the phone, and I was convinced by the rigid way she stood that it had to be the police. She turned around and nodded when she heard me behind her but didn't say anything. She was focused on listening to the person on the other end of the phone.

I stood there shivering and waiting.

"So you're telling me there have been no developments?" Mum said, her tone sharp. "Despite the fact you have the message and the phone number, you haven't been able to trace whoever sent it?"

I couldn't hear what the officer said on the other end of the line, but from Mum's expression, I guessed it wasn't very encouraging.

Mum closed her eyes briefly and let out an exasperated sigh. "No, of course, I don't have any concerns about that," she snapped.

What concerns? Were they asking her if she was concerned about me? Did they think I'd doctored the photo because I was so desperate for them to keep looking for Jenna? Surely not. I was overreacting.

"Well, I'm not sure that is good enough. If you haven't made any progress then maybe we need to release this to the press and find out—"

Mum stopped talking, and I imagined the officer on the other end of the line was trying to talk her out of contacting any journalists.

I had no love for the press after our last experience, but if the police weren't getting results, maybe some articles and news items on television would get some leads from the public.

After another minute or so, Mum put down the phone and shook her head as she looked at me. "As you must have guessed, that was Detective Sergeant Leanne Parker. They're no closer to finding Jenna. They can't even trace the phone number. I don't understand it. In this day and age, surely that's something they should be able to do in seconds."

I didn't know what to say. I was just as disappointed and irritated at the lack of progress.

Mum sighed and turned round to pick up the phone again. "I better give Daniel a ring. The sergeant said she'd already spoken to him this morning, so I'll see if they've told him anything different."

I nodded and turned around, heading back to the bathroom. My eyes were stinging from the shampoo I hadn't washed out properly. I got back in the shower to rinse out the shampoo and then realised I hadn't brought any conditioner with me. I towel dried my hair and tried not to tangle it too much, but it still took me about five minutes to brush it through, thanks to the lack of conditioner.

I'd been in such a rush to leave Dubai, I hadn't even packed my hairdryer, so I nipped upstairs to Mum's room to use hers. It was warmer upstairs, and the sunlight streamed through the Velux windows. The hairdryer was on her dressing table, so rather than unplug it and take it downstairs, I sat at the dressing table and dried my hair looking into Mum's magnifying mirror.

I barely recognised myself. The stress had given my face a

pinched expression. I turned away quickly from the mirror and concentrated on drying my hair.

Once I was finished, I went downstairs and called out to Mum, telling her I was going to use the computer again. I wasn't expecting any new emails, but I did want to check the plant ID forum, just in case.

It didn't take me long to log in and realise that I'd been holding out false hope. One person had liked my post, but no one had replied. With a huff of impatience, I logged out and shut down the computer.

CHAPTER FIFTEEN

As soon as I stepped out of the front door, I regretted the decision to go to Oxford. I would be uncontactable if anything happened. Attempting to push my worries away, I walked down the garden path and out through the gate. When had phones become so vital to our day-to-day existence? I felt naked without mine.

I walked quickly to the bus stop outside the Marlborough Arms, and the bus rumbled into view seconds after I reached the bus stop. A man, wearing a tweed coat and shiny brown shoes, who'd been waiting for the bus looked at me disapprovingly. "You're lucky the bus is two minutes late. If it had been on time, you would have missed it."

I smiled politely instead of telling him to mind his own business, which was what I really wanted to do.

The bus was busy, and as I walked down the aisle towards an empty seat, I spotted Dawn Parsons. I quickly looked away, but I wasn't fast enough. She had seen me, and worse than that, she knew I had seen her, too.

I walked past Dawn, keeping my gaze on the floor.

Please, don't let her talk to me.

I sat down in a seat as far away from Dawn as possible beside a young girl with bleached blonde hair and white earbuds in her ears. The sound of the bus pulling away was loud, but I could still hear the tinny music blaring out of the girl's headphones.

Despite my best intentions, I couldn't ignore Dawn. My gaze seemed to be magnetically drawn to the back of her head. She was even bigger than she used to be — definitely wider.

Despite the fact it was late May, and the weather was fine today, Dawn wore a purple wool coat, which strained across her shoulders. She had to be a good six inches taller than the woman in the seat beside her.

Her dark hair had been pulled back off her face, and she wore no make-up to hide her blotchy complexion. In all the years I'd known her, I don't think I'd ever seen Dawn wear makeup.

I chewed on the edge of my fingernail nervously. I had told Mrs Parsons I would try and find time to talk to Dawn. Now I had the perfect opportunity. I didn't have anything else to do. I didn't even have my phone to fiddle with and pretend to be busy, so nothing was stopping me slipping into the spare seat behind her and striking up a conversation. Nothing except the fact she made my skin crawl.

Dawn turned her head, and I quickly looked down at the floor, my hands clasped in my lap. Would I really ignore her if she spoke to me? Should I apologise?

She probably did deserve an apology. After all, she hadn't done any of the things I'd accused her of doing. That didn't mean I had to like her, though. The police had determined she'd had nothing to do with Jenna's disappearance, but being near Dawn Parsons made me feel on edge. I didn't want to be anywhere near her.

I forced myself to look away and stare out of the bus window. It was bright and sunny outside, but the bus windows were coated with a layer of grime, which made it hard to enjoy the scenery. The bus passed through a number of small villages and then finally pulled onto the Peartree roundabout, where we were stuck in traffic for a good ten minutes.

By the time we got to Oxford, everyone was impatient and eager to disembark. The bus pulled into the bus station, and the girl beside me grabbed up her bag and twisted in her seat to make it quite clear she expected me to stand up and get off of the bus quickly. But I pretended to rummage in my handbag, buying time. I wanted Dawn to get off the bus ahead of me, so I could get off and go in the opposite direction.

The bleached blonde girl beside me huffed under her breath impatiently, but I refused to be rushed.

Finally, Dawn heaved herself to her feet and plodded along the aisle. When she was safely off the bus, I stood up.

"Finally," the blonde who'd been sitting next to me said with a scowl.

I took a step to the side and gestured for her to go ahead of me. "After you, if you're in that much of a rush."

She scowled again, no doubt picking up on my sarcasm. We shuffled forward, and when I stepped down onto the pavement, I was glad to see that Dawn was already way ahead of me, walking up to the High Street.

I walked in the same direction, figuring I wouldn't run into her again as long as I walked slowly and gave her plenty of time to get out of the way.

There were a number of mobile phone shops in the city, but I wanted to get a replacement iPhone. But as I walked along the High Street, I realised I had no idea where the Apple Store was in Oxford, or even if there was one.

I couldn't believe I hadn't looked it up on the Internet last night. How stupid! In fact, I couldn't recall there ever being an Apple Store in Oxford.

I stopped a young man in a suit to ask him if there was an Apple Store. He had an iPhone clutched in his hand, so I figured he'd know.

He barely glanced up at me. "Nah, I think the closest one is in Reading," he said before looking back down at his phone and continuing to walk on.

This wasn't a good start, but I didn't have to have an iPhone. In fact, now that I wasn't sure I'd be going back to Dubai and resuming my job over there, I should start being more careful with my money. A cheaper phone would serve just as well for now.

The first shop I entered had lots of phones on display. Most of them were linked to contracts, though. I looked around in dismay for a few minutes before walking up to the counter and asking the young man with heavily gelled hair and traces of acne on his cheeks whether they had any phones to purchase without a locked-in contract.

"Yeah," he replied looking bored and waving his hand in the direction of the display beside the door. "There's a few over there."

He turned away, so I guessed that was the extent of his customer service. I thought about kicking up a fuss but decided against it.

I walked across to the display by the door and examined the phones. None of them looked particularly impressive, and they didn't have the prices on them. I picked one with a large screen with a dark grey metallic finish. I wouldn't be familiar with the operating system but how hard could it be?

"I'll take one of these," I said loudly to the man behind the counter. I didn't bother walking back over to him.

He looked up, irritated that I was disturbing him again. I could see the blue Facebook screen reflected in his glasses. Here was someone who obviously took his job seriously.

"What's the model number?" he asked sulkily.

"Why don't you come over here and have a look for yourself?"

His whole body slumped as though producing one big, sulky sigh and then he finally got up from his stool and stalked across the store.

He peered at the phone I pointed at and then walked back to his computer.

"We haven't got one in stock," he announced. "We can get one by Wednesday."

I stared at him in disbelief. I had come into Oxford today purely so I could get a phone and take it home with me today, not so I could order it. If I wanted to do that, I would have just done it online.

"Perhaps you could tell me the phones you do have in stock, so I'll be able to pick one."

Again the heavy sigh. He didn't answer but began tapping away on his keyboard, and I hoped he was checking stock rather than replying to a Facebook message.

A few seconds later, he looked up, rolled his eyes, then looked back at the computer screen and continued to type. I sighed and looked out of the window.

There was another phone shop over the street. I was just about to leave and try that one instead when he got up from the counter and walked over to me.

"We've got this one and this one and these are in stock today." He pointed at two rather unattractive phones.

"And if I pick one of those, I can take it home with me today and use my own SIM card with it, right?"

He nodded. "Yeah, they're not locked into a contract."

One of the phones he'd pointed out was narrow and thin, but I was used to a phone with a large screen and thought that would be annoying.

"Which is the cheapest of those two?" I asked.

He pointed to the dark grey one and told me a price that made me cringe.

"Fine," I said. "I'll take the dark grey one."

It seemed to take forever to fill in the form and process the order, but fifteen minutes later, I finally had my new mobile phone.

I left the shop gripping the plastic bag tightly in my hand, relieved to get out of the store and away from the unhelpful shop assistant.

The shopping area was busier now, even though there was still an hour until the office workers would be leaving their offices for lunch. I had ten minutes to kill before the next bus to Woodstock. Remembering Mum had asked me to pick up milk on the way back, I decided to go to the small Sainsbury's near Debenhams and then cut through to the back of the bus station. I didn't want to waste any more time than necessary. If there had been any developments in the police investigation, I wouldn't hear about them until I got back to Mum's.

I'd only walked a few steps when I saw Daniel not far ahead of me. He was dressed in his usual work gear of a dark grey suit and a light coloured shirt, open at the collar. Daniel never wore a tie. It was a throwback to his artist roots. Maybe he figured it made him look young and trendy and less like a 9-to-5 office cubicle worker.

A similarly dressed man was walking next to him, and they both held large takeaway cups from a coffee chain. I made no move to wave or call out. Instead, I just watched him. Something about the way he was behaving seemed off. As they walked towards me, I could see he was smiling.

The police had a vital lead in his daughter's disappearance, and Daniel was back at work, joking around with a colleague. Was that normal?

Why shouldn't he be at work? If the police wanted to contact him, they could contact him at work just as well as they could if he was at home.

He was just smiling with a colleague, probably being polite, that was all. I needed to give him a break. I was too hard on him. It was wrong to fall back into our old antagonistic roles. He was Jenna's father, and he must have taken her disappearance just as hard as Kate.

Determined to be more understanding I took a deep breath and stepped out of the shop doorway I'd been sheltering in.

I gave him a tentative smile and called out. "Hi." I held up the plastic bag in my hand. "I've just been to get a new phone."

The amenable smile that had been on Daniel's face as he chatted to his colleague disappeared when he saw me. His facial expression hardened, and he turned to the man next to him and said, "I'll see you back at the office."

His colleague nodded and looked at me curiously before walking on.

Daniel didn't say anything to me. I clutched the mobile phone bag to my chest. "I needed a new phone because the police took mine."

"I remember."

"Yes, well, I didn't like the idea of not being contactable at the moment. It set me back a bit, though."

Daniel didn't respond.

"Have you heard anything else from the police this morning?"

Daniel shook his head. "Nothing yet."

"You're back at work then?"

My gaze slid down, taking in his dark, sombre suit. It seemed odd to see him dressed for work, holding a cup of coffee as though it was just a normal day.

"Yes, I'm back at work. Do you have a problem with that?"

I frowned. "Of course not. I didn't think you would feel up to being back at work. I wasn't trying to criticise."

Daniel regarded me in a way that told me he thought that was exactly what I intended to do. "It's easier to be at work. The time passes faster. If I stay at home, I just sit there thinking, and it's driving me crazy."

I nodded. "Hopefully we will hear something soon," I said. "I'll let you get back to work."

Daniel said goodbye and then walked off without looking back.

Daniel and I had never hit it off, but before Jenna's disappearance, it hadn't really been a problem. Kate was so easygoing, and she always smoothed over any minor disagreements. Daniel irritated me, but all the things about him that wound me up now seemed trivial. I disliked his bragging, boastful behaviour, but when it came down to it, I'd never thought Daniel was a terrible person. I wasn't sure quite how we got to this point. He looked at me with intense dislike. It was no more than I deserved, I suppose, after putting him and Mum through the ringer after Kate died. He hadn't forgiven me for that.

I walked on, lost in thought, heading towards Sainsbury's. I ducked inside, grabbing two pints of milk before queueing up at the automatic checkout counter.

I was halfway along the road back to the bus station when a familiar figure caught my eye on the other side of the road.

I turned abruptly, causing the person behind to nearly crash into the back of me.

They muttered a few rude words under their breath.

"I'm sorry," I said, not even bothering to look at them. I was too focused on the person on the other side of the road.

It was Luke's brother, Philip Bowman.

I hadn't seen him since the day Jenna went missing. He'd had his own fair share of tragedy, and it was still apparent in the way his shoulders slumped in a way they never used to.

I held up my hand to wave and called to him across the street. He heard me and turned, and although he was some distance away, I could have sworn he paled when he saw me.

I called his name again, thinking perhaps he hadn't recognised me.

Looking left and right I waited for a gap in the traffic so I could cross the road and talk to him. But before I could, he quickly turned on his heel and stalked the other way.

I frowned. Didn't he recognise me? Still waiting for a gap in the traffic, I called out again, convinced he hadn't realised it was me. I'd spent so much time at his and Luke's house when we were teenagers. We'd been close, and I couldn't believe he would ignore me deliberately. I waited for a white van to pass in front of me and then darted across the road, but by the time I did so, Phil was already out of sight.

I walked on, looking in the shop windows as I went past, glancing down each alleyway, but there was no sign of him. Recalling the expression on his face when he'd seen it was me made me feel uncomfortable. Why was he trying to avoid me?

I walked on towards the bus stop, feeling strangely out of sorts. It had been nice seeing Luke yesterday, a reminder of how things had been before my world had turned upside down. After Daniel's coldness, I'd selfishly wanted to talk to Phil and brighten my mood. It hurt to be ignored.

It was probably just because Phil didn't want to talk about the past, maybe it was too painful for him. I could understand him wanting to build a new life and surround himself with people who didn't know how he'd lost his wife and young daughter.

The bus was already waiting in its designated bay at the station when I got there. I climbed aboard and showed my ticket to the driver. There were a number of other passengers already sitting in the downstairs seats, but I was relieved to see that Dawn wasn't one of them. I felt a wave of relief tinged with guilt, after all, I promised her mother I would try to find time to talk to her.

I sat back in my seat and thought about Phil Bowman's strange reaction. Did he purposely avoid me because he didn't want to talk to anyone who might mention his wife and daughter, or was there another, more sinister reason?

CHAPTER SIXTEEN

During the bus journey home, I tried to come up with a feasible explanation for why Luke's brother had completely ignored me. Had I imagined the look of panic on his face? Maybe he had simply been in a rush. But something about his reaction worried me. It wasn't nice to think that he had gone out of his way to avoid me, but the feeling of unease I couldn't shake wasn't just because my feelings had been hurt. I couldn't get rid of the knot of fear in the pit of my stomach.

When I got home, I found Mum sitting on the sofa, flicking through an old photograph album. Her eyes were red, and she'd been crying, but she smiled up at me as I walked in.

"Your SIM card was delivered," she said. "I left it on the kitchen table for you."

"Great." I held up the plastic bag I was carrying. "I got the milk and a new phone. It isn't the one I wanted, but it will do. I'll see if I can get it set up now."

I headed to the kitchen and grabbed the small envelope from the table. I unboxed the phone and looked at the manual that had come with it. It took me awhile to get to grips with the new phone because I wasn't used to the operating system, but as long as I knew how to use messages and I could use the phone to ring people, I was happy.

I'd be able to learn how to use the other apps and web browser later. The only app I downloaded was Facebook because I had formulated a plan as I travelled back on the bus.

The thing that worried me most about the police keeping my phone was that the person who sent the photograph of Jenna might try to get in touch with me again. Would the police tell us if there had been more messages sent to my old phone? I'd have liked to think they would, but after Daniel had suggested I could have altered the photograph of Jenna, I wasn't sure they trusted me.

I logged onto Facebook and posted a message, telling everybody my new phone number. Usually, I was quite careful about privacy settings, but I set the post to public. If the person who sent the photograph of Jenna wanted to reach me, I was determined to make it easy for them.

After I had posted the message, I set up my email account on the phone. Before I knew it, an hour had passed.

I called out to Mum and asked if she wanted a cup of tea as I moved across the kitchen to put the kettle on. I made the tea and carried it through to the sitting room, setting a cup on the coffee table in front of Mum. She'd moved on to flicking through another photo album now. I thought about sitting down and joining her on her trip down memory lane, but first, I wanted to check on the plant ID forum again. I was still holding out hope that somebody might be able to tell me something about the plant in the photograph and give me a clue as to where Jenna may have been when the photograph was taken.

I asked Mum if I could use her computer and then went to the iMac in the hall. I logged onto the plant forum and saw immediately from the red alert at the top of the screen that I had a message.

I held my breath as I clicked on the link and waited for the page to load. Below my original message, where I had attached the photograph of the hedge, someone had replied.

I muttered a curse as I read what they had written.

This is common ivy.

I shook my head. That was clearly rubbish. I was no gardener, but even I knew what Ivy looked like. Mum and Dad had always pulled it out of the garden, declaring it a weed. Why would somebody waste my time by posting this? Did people really have nothing better to do?

I opened up a new browser window and typed in common English ivy and then clicked on the images link. As I suspected, the hedge plant I posted didn't look anything like ivy. The leaves were a completely different shape, and in my photograph, the plant had small flowers on it.

I scrolled down the page a bit further and saw a plant that looked exactly like the one in the picture. I clicked on it to enlarge the image. I was certain it was the same plant, yet the label beneath the picture said it was ivy. Maybe there were different types?

I got up from the computer table and walked back to where Mum was sitting on the sofa. "Can you have a look at something for me?"

Mum looked up at me, surprised. She set the album to one side. "Of course."

She followed me back to the computer, and I pointed at the screen. "Did you know this was a type of ivy?"

She peered over her glasses and then nodded. "Yes, that's the mature form."

"But it looks nothing like ivy. We had ivy growing up the fence at the back of the house. I remember you and dad pulling it all out, and it didn't look anything like this."

Mum nodded. "Yes, it looks quite different when it's mature. It's the immature plant that climbs up things and sticks to them with those tiny suckers. When it's mature, it's quite an attractive plant and has flowers. Lots of gardeners have started to allow the plant to grow nowadays. It's very good for birds and bees apparently. It even produces berries in the winter."

"So, it's just about the most common plant in England, I suppose," I murmured with disappointment. "Typical."

Mum frowned. "Why are you so interested? I didn't think you were into plants."

I shook my head. "I'm not. I just didn't realise ivy could look like that."

I considered telling her about my stupid idea to identify the plants in the background of Jenna's photograph but then decided against it. Even to me, the idea sounded a little desperate and crazy, and I didn't want to cause Mum to worry about me again.

Mum walked back to the sitting room to pick up her mug of tea, but as she leant towards it, the doorbell rang.

I stepped towards the front door, but she held up a hand. "I'll get it."

I logged out of the forum and shut down the browser. I wasn't getting any closer to finding Jenna. It had been a stupid idea.

I heard voices behind me as Mum opened the front door and I recognised the visitor immediately. It was Pippa Clarkson. She carried a huge bunch of flowers, roses mixed with carnations, and held them out to my mother. Mum looked surprised as she took the flowers.

Pippa smiled brightly, her teeth dazzlingly white against her pink lipstick. Her hair was carefully styled as usual, and I wondered if she had just been to the hairdressers. I ran my hand through my own hair, which no doubt looked as though it hadn't seen the attention of a hairdresser for months.

"Hello, I hope you don't mind me popping in like this. I bought the flowers to welcome Beth back to Woodstock," she said brightly.

Mum seemed stunned into silence.

I stepped forward, smiling at Pippa. "That's very kind of you."

Mum finally regained her voice. "I'll put these in some water." Her tone was cold, and she didn't invite Pippa in, which was odd. Mum was usually polite to a fault.

But Pippa wasn't easily deterred. She hovered on the doorstep like a vampire who couldn't come in until you invited her.

"Do you have time for a cup of tea?" I asked.

Her smile broadened. "I'd love one. It will give us a chance to catch up. I can't wait to hear all your news."

She followed me into the kitchen, where Mum was shoving the flowers into a vase haphazardly. More odd behaviour. Mum loved flowers, and it wasn't unheard of for her to take over half an hour just to arrange them, but today, she selected an old chipped vase from under the sink.

Within thirty seconds, she had shoved all of the stems into the vase and placed the vase on the windowsill, brushing her hands together as though to say good riddance.

Pippa's eyes darted from Mum to me and back again. I could tell something was going on here, undercurrents of something that had happened in the past. I made a mental note to ask Mum about it later as I filled the kettle.

Pippa hovered beside the kitchen counter, clasping her hands together and looking around nervously.

I nodded at the table. "Why don't you sit down? Is normal tea okay for you?"

Pippa sank down into a chair at the table and nodded thankfully. "Normal tea will be great."

"Milk? Sugar?" I asked as I rummaged in the cupboard for another mug.

"Just a splash of milk, thanks."

Mum hesitated by the doorway, and for a moment, I thought she was going to walk away and leave me alone to deal with Pippa. That certainly meant something serious had gone on between them, but in the end, Mum pulled out a chair at the end of the table —as far away from Pippa as she could get— and sat down.

"So, tell me about Dubai," Pippa said. "I can't wait to hear all about it."

I poured the boiling water in the teapot and then turned around to face Pippa.

"It's been going well. I've got a nice job, and the sun shines most of the time."

"It must be nice not to pay tax!" Pippa said.

"Yes, it certainly makes a difference to my take-home pay."

"Did you go to the church meeting this morning?" Pippa asked turning to Mum.

Mum shook her head. "No, I had other things to do this morning."

"Oh, that is unusual for you. You never usually miss your church meetings."

Mum didn't reply, and an awkward silence followed.

"That was my fault," I said bringing the teapot over to the table. "Mum had to stay in and wait for a SIM card to be delivered for me as I went to Oxford to pick up a new phone."

"Oh, what happened to your old one?"

Mum and I exchanged a look. I didn't want to tell Pippa anything about Jenna, and I was absolutely certain that Mum didn't want to share the news by the way she was reacting.

"My old phone stopped working, and I decided a UK based SIM card would be cheaper to use while I was back."

Pippa nodded. "That makes sense. There's no point in paying more for your phone calls than you have to. So, do you have any idea how long you'll be staying? The weather is not too bad today, but it's been cold over the last few weeks. I bet you are already missing that Dubai sunshine."

"I'm not sure how long I'll be staying yet," I said and pushed a little jug of milk towards Pippa so she could add her own.

Pippa reached for the milk. "How strange. Didn't you have to book your holiday before you came home?"

"My employer is very flexible," I said, hoping that would shut Pippa down. It really wasn't any of her business.

I took a sip of my tea and tried to work out what was going

on with Mum. She was staring stonily down at the table and looked about as furious as I had ever seen her.

"It must be nice to have such an understanding boss," Pippa said.

"My boss can be a slave driver." She grinned at her own joke. Pippa ran her own business making scented candles. She had done very well for herself after she launched the candles on the Internet. In fact, when Jenna was a year old, Kate had started to work for Pippa part-time.

Pippa took a sip of her tea and then said, "I just wanted to say that if you need anything, you only have to ask." She turned to look at Mum, who was avoiding eye contact. "Day or night, you know where to find me."

My hands tightened around my mug of tea. Did she know about Jenna's photograph? Was that why she was offering support now? And if she did know about the photograph, who had told her? As far as I knew, only Mum, Daniel, the police and I knew about it.

I glanced over at Mum, wanting to know what was going on, but Mum was staring at her tea as though it were the most fascinating thing in the world.

I wasn't about to make a scene in front of Pippa, so I said, "That's very kind of you, thanks."

Pippa spent the next ten minutes telling us about the latest launch of her lavender candles. I tried to smile and ask questions in the right places and made encouraging noises as she chattered on.

"Well, I'd better not keep you all afternoon." She peered

towards the kitchen window. "Those grey clouds are looking menacing. I hung my washing out earlier. I'd better get back before it gets drenched."

I walked with her to the front door.

"Is your mother okay?" Pippa asked in a whisper as we got to the front door.

I nodded stiffly. "Yes."

She reached out to touch my arm. "Don't hesitate to ask if you need help."

Again, I nodded. Pippa had been a very close friend of Kate's, and it was kind of her to look out for me.

"Thank you. I appreciate it."

I closed the door behind Pippa and paused with my hand on the wood panelling. That had certainly been an interesting visit. I had no idea what was going on between Mum and Pippa, but I was certain something was causing the tension in the air during Pippa's visit. I turned away from the door and headed back to the kitchen, my mind full of questions to ask my mother.

CHAPTER SEVENTEEN

When I walked back into the kitchen, I asked, "So, are you going to tell me what that was all about?" I picked up our empty mugs and carried them over to the dishwasher.

"What do you mean?" Mum looked the picture of innocence.

"You know what I mean. I want to know what's going on between you and Pippa. The tension between the two of you was so thick I could have cut it with a knife."

Mum shook her head and looked irritable. "Are you going to load the dishwasher or shall I do it?"

I threw the remnants of the tea into the sink and pulled open the dishwasher.

"I'm doing it, but you're not going to get out of giving me an explanation by changing the subject. Tell me why you were so upset with her."

"I'm not upset," Mum said. "I just don't particularly like her."

She took the mugs out of my hand, pulled out the top drawer of the dishwasher and placed them at the back before shutting the door firmly.

"But you like everyone! And even if you don't, you're still polite to them anyway. I mean, you're always polite to Mrs Blythe who lives on the other end of Rectory Lane and nobody likes her. She is the most awful gossip."

Mum sighed. "I suppose it's just because I'm stressed today, and I'm not very good at being polite under these circumstances."

Her words made me feel bad. I reached out and put a hand on her shoulder. "Sorry, I shouldn't have pressed you. I just want you to know you can share things with me. I know I wasn't much help to you right after... it all happened, but you can rely on me now. I'm not going to fall apart."

"I know," she said with a smile. "I'm very glad you're home."

I avoided talking about Pippa after that. I was still certain something had gone on between them, but it was equally clear that Mum didn't want to talk about it.

I did suggest calling the police, though, to find out if they had any fresh information. But Mum said we should give them time to get on with the job. She did agree that if they didn't telephone us by four thirty, we would call Detective Sergeant Leanne Parker for an update.

After we'd eaten lunch, and cleaned the kitchen, I had

nothing to do and was going stir crazy. There were plenty of books in the house, but my mind couldn't focus on reading. Despite the forecast predicting rain, when I stepped outside and looked up, I could only see a few puffy white clouds in an otherwise bright blue sky.

I headed along Rectory Lane, in the opposite direction to the Parsons's house. I really didn't want to run into Dawn again today. I was keen to avoid her mother, too, because I didn't need a guilt trip right now. I wished I hadn't said I'd try to speak to Dawn. It was the last thing I wanted to do.

I didn't see anyone I knew as I walked the familiar streets. The town was strangely quiet today, almost empty of tourists, which was very unusual for this time of year. I paused beside the Woodstock Gallery and gazed in the window. The shop was empty. I'd always loved the small, eclectic shops in Woodstock. It was thanks to the tourists and their custom that we had the shops at all.

Heading away from the High Street, I walked towards the steps that led down to the main road when I noticed a group of people hanging around and blocking the pathway.

The stone staircase, which was surrounded by greenery, was normally a picturesque and peaceful spot in the town, but today, it was anything but peaceful.

People were jostling each other for position on the steps. Angry voices murmured in discontent, and I heard hoarsely whispered accusations. I had no idea who they were talking about.

I found and took a few steps closer to the group. That was

when I noticed they were standing outside the tall stone walls surrounding Robin Vaughan's residence.

"What's going on?" I asked a short, round woman with curly hair.

She turned around and faced me with a scowl. With a jerking movement, she pushed her hair back out of her eyes. "It's that dirty bastard. It's been in the papers."

"What has?"

The woman either hadn't heard my question or was ignoring me. She turned around to talk to the man beside her. I jumped in surprise when a tall man hammered against the large wooden gate nestled in the stone wall. "You can't hide in there forever!"

I tried again, asking somebody else this time. "What is it? What has Robin Vaughan done?"

A man with grey hair turned around and looked at me. His upper lip curled in a sneer as he leant heavily on his walking stick. "He's a pervert. He was arrested last week, but it's only just come out in the newspaper this morning. He's hiding in there now." He pointed at the wooden gate with his walking stick.

I felt a jolt of adrenaline as the man who had been banging on the gate now kicked it with his boot.

"Don't do any damage," somebody called out. "He'll call the police."

"Fat lot of good the police are," the man said kicking the gate again to show his contempt. "The bastard has been living under our noses for God knows how long. He should never have been allowed to live here in the first place."

The woman with the curly hair I'd spoken to first said, "I thought it was suspicious when he wanted to put up this wall. Just think of all the things he could have been doing to children while hiding behind this wall all this time."

My throat constricted and I put a hand against my chest. "Children..." My voice sounded raspy. "What children... Who?"

Somebody shoved a copy of the local paper into my hands, and I saw Robin Vaughan's picture splashed on the front cover. Before I could read any more than the headline, the elderly man with the walking stick turned to look at me.

"You look familiar... Don't I know you?"

Before he could ask me any more questions, I turned around and walked away, clutching the paper. I couldn't stay there. Blood was roaring in my ears and my chest was so tight I couldn't breathe properly. I had to get home and read the article. From skimming the first few lines, it was clear Robin Vaughan had been arrested for the possession of indecent images of children.

He was there that day at the fête. I could picture him clearly, remembering him holding court, surrounded by teenagers and wearing that horrible lairy shirt.

Had he taken Jenna? Had she been that close to us all this time? I tried to swallow away the urge to vomit. What had he done to her? And why had the police not told us about this?

When I reached the corner of Rectory Lane, I leant against the wall and threw up in the gutter. Bitter bile burned the back of my throat.

When I got my breath back, I wiped my mouth on the back of my hand and took off at a run. I needed to get home. I didn't want anybody else to tell Mum about this. It was going to crucify her.

I pushed open the front door and staggered into the house, Mum immediately knew something was wrong.

Her hands flew up to her mouth and her eyes widened. "What is it? What has happened?"

I showed her the newspaper. "Robin Vaughan has been arrested on child pornography charges."

I didn't say any more. I didn't have to. I knew Mum would think exactly the same as me. Had Robin Vaughan had something to do with Jenna's disappearance?

Mum pulled the newspaper from my hand and began to read. I walked into the kitchen and picked up the telephone.

Mum looked over her shoulder. "Who are you calling?"

"The police. I want to know why they didn't tell us we had a child sex offender living down the road."

Mum covered her mouth with her hand and smothered a sob as she looked back down at the article.

Infuriatingly, I couldn't get through to Detective Sergeant Leanne Parker or Detective Inspector Sharp. I left a message demanding they call me back as soon as they were free and then hung up.

I was so angry. How could they have not told us about this? How long had they known or suspected Robin Vaughan?

I felt the urge to vomit again and pressed a hand to my stomach. I clutched the side of the kitchen counter as black spots danced in front of my eyes. After a few deep breaths, I managed to stagger over to a kitchen chair and sat down resting my head in my hands.

"I'm going to phone Daniel," Mum said in a shaky voice. "He's going to need to know about this development. I don't want him to hear about it from anyone else."

Despite the tremor in her voice, she sounded strangely calm. I had a lump in my throat the size of a golf ball and couldn't respond, so I just nodded.

Mum took the cordless telephone out into the sitting room while I stayed in the kitchen and pulled the newspaper towards me. I poured over the article, looking for any little details or clues that might tell me whether Jenna was one of his victims. I held the newspaper so tightly that my fingers scrunched the edges. The sick bastard. I wanted to tear him limb from limb.

I could hear the murmur of Mum's voice as she talked to Daniel, and I could only imagine his reaction. It would crucify him, and he'd be finding out about it while he was at work. It was unimaginable.

Mum returned to the kitchen, clutching the telephone in front of her. I looked up and met her gaze.

"It can't have been easy to make that phone call. Did you

tell him I tried to call the police? He might have better luck."

"He already knew," Mum said.

All her poise from just moments ago disappeared. She put the phone down on the table and then sank into the seat opposite me. She shook her head. "The police had already told him before the article was published."

I frowned. "Then why didn't he tell you? Why did he let you find out this way?"

Mum blinked away tears. "I don't know."

I'd recovered from my dizzy spell and now I felt flooded with angry energy. I got to my feet, clutching my fists at my sides. "The thoughtless bastard."

"Don't, Beth. It doesn't help."

I shook my head. "I'm sorry but I'm done feeling sorry for him. He knew about this, and he didn't even bother to tell you. He let you find out from a newspaper article. What sort of person could do something like that?"

Mum closed her eyes and shook her head slightly.

I continued, "I thought I was being unreasonable and holding a grudge against him just because I don't like him, but I was right. He is horrible."

Mum didn't contradict me.

"After everything you did for him and Kate. Taking them in when he couldn't support his own family!"

"You know I was happy for them to live here, Beth. That doesn't have anything to do with it."

"It has everything to do with it. He was more than happy to let you look after Jenna for hours each day when Kate went back to work. You spent much more time with Jenna than he ever did. He probably only saw her for a maximum of thirty minutes during the week. You were the one who spent all that time with her. He knew how much you loved her, and he didn't even bother to let you know that Robin Vaughan had been arrested for possessing child pornography!"

Mum's shoulders shook in a silent sob, and I felt like the most evil person in the world. "I'm sorry. I'm sorry. I didn't mean to upset you even more. It just makes me so furious that he could do that."

I walked forward and put my arms around Mum, crouching by her side. "I'm sorry. I shouldn't have flown off the handle like that."

"It's upsetting he didn't tell us," Mum said with a sniff. "But we can't focus on that now. Maybe Daniel just forgot. He's got a lot on his mind. Maybe he thought the police would have told us…"

I remembered seeing Daniel that morning with his colleague, smiling and drinking coffee and a thought struck me. "When did Daniel find out?"

"He said the police telephoned him first thing this morning to let him know about the article. They don't believe Robin Vaughan was involved in Jenna's disappearance, but they are still investigating. So far the only evidence against Robin Vaughan has been the images on his computer."

I stayed crouching beside Mum, even though I could feel pins and needles tingling in my foot from my awkward position. He'd known. Daniel had known about Robin Vaughan when I'd seen him that morning.

The fury that flooded my system scared me. I could feel it bubbling away in my chest, itching beneath my skin. Anger was a destructive emotion. I stood up slowly and stiffly.

I didn't mention it to Mum because I thought there was no point in upsetting her further. Plus, she was right about one thing. We couldn't focus on Daniel's callous, selfish behaviour. That wouldn't help us track down Jenna, and flying off the handle wasn't going to help anyone.

But things had shifted. For one thing, we now had a solid suspect. A dirty pervert who lived only a few minutes away, and he had been there the day Jenna disappeared.

I'd also learned that I could never trust Daniel again. I was done feeling sorry for him.

CHAPTER EIGHTEEN

We sat in the kitchen waiting for the police to call us back and tell us what the hell Robin Vaughan had been getting up to right under our noses. Had he stopped at collecting obscene images of children or did he do more than that? We needed answers, and we needed them soon. My mind rebelling at the very idea Jenna had been taken away by somebody like Robin Vaughan, it was impossible to subdue the panic and keep calm.

I'd overreacted when I'd found out Daniel already knew about Robin Vaughan and upset Mum further. When would I learn to hold back? Maybe for once, I should put her feelings before my own. Furious with myself and sick with the thought that Robin Vaughan might have taken Jenna, I sat at the kitchen table in silence with my legs bouncing beneath the table with nervous energy.

Mum hadn't moved from the kitchen table either, and she looked worn down by the events of today. Her shoulders were slumped, and her light application of mascara was now smudged beneath her eyes. She hadn't bothered to reapply her lipstick as she usually did throughout the day.

Mum finally looked up at me and hesitated for a moment before saying, "There's something else we should talk about, Beth."

"What?"

The sharp ring of the telephone made us both jump.

Mum grabbed the phone, and from the look on her face, I could tell it was the police.

I waited anxiously, chewing my nails, as she spoke on the phone. She told them we didn't want a family liaison officer in our home, but we wanted to be informed of all relevant developments over the telephone.

When Jenna went missing, we hadn't appreciated having the family liaison officer. I had nothing against them and realised it couldn't be an easy job, but there was something horrible about going through the worst experience of your life and having an outsider hovering around all the time, watching you and making endless cups of tea.

I listened as Mum made it clear that we wanted to be informed separately from Daniel. Daniel was Jenna's next of kin, so it made sense that they'd told him about Robin Vaughan. I suspected the police thought Daniel would tell us himself.

Mum asked them specifically about Robin Vaughan and whether they thought he was involved in Jenna's disappearance. I held my breath as we waited for the answer, and then Mum let out a long breath and relief sagged through her body. It was clear the officer on the other end of the phone had told her they didn't think he was involved.

That didn't mean we could definitely rule him out, though. It was a huge coincidence to have someone like that living just round the corner when Jenna disappeared. I tried to remember if he'd looked at her strangely when we'd been at the fête. I hadn't noticed anything, but then I hadn't been looking out for a depraved pervert. I thought we were safe.

I was so lost in thought, trying to remember every moment I'd seen Robin Vaughan at the fête, I didn't notice Mum had put down the phone until she stepped in front of me.

"What did they say?" I asked.

"They apologised for not letting us know and promised that they'd update both us and Daniel with all future developments. They don't think Robin Vaughan had anything to do with Jenna's disappearance. There is no evidence to suggest he ever had any contact with Jenna, but of course, they can't rule anything out at this stage."

I rubbed my hands over my face. Could this day get any worse? "Did they say anything about the photograph of Jenna? Have they tracked down where it came from yet?"

Mum shook her head as she slumped down into the chair beside mine. "No, they still haven't found out who sent it."

The trail was growing colder and colder as each hour passed. I wished whoever sent the photograph would contact me again.

I glanced back at Mum, remembering she'd been about to

say something before the phone rang. Before I could ask her about it, the phone rang again, and Mum quickly snatched it up before handing it to me. "It's Luke."

I took the phone and then paused for a moment to try and collect myself. My mouth felt dry, and I didn't really want to talk to him or anyone else at the moment, but as Mum had already told him I was here, I tried to sound as normal as possible as I said, "Hi, Luke, how are you?"

"Good. I was just calling to see if you wanted to meet up for a drink tonight at The Black Prince. I'm getting off work early today."

"Oh, I'm not sure about tonight... Mum and I have got plans. Sorry."

Mum was frantically flapping her hand at me.

"Hang on a minute, Luke. Mum's trying to get my attention."

I pressed the mute button on the handset and then looked at Mum. "What's wrong?"

"Nothing is wrong. I think you should go. It will do you good."

I shook my head. "I don't want to. I'm definitely not in the mood to go out for a drink tonight."

Mum's eyes closed briefly, and her nostrils flared as she exhaled. "Please, Beth. I think it's for the best. Daniel said he was going to pop round after work, and I can't handle a scene."

In other words, she didn't want me around because I might upset precious Daniel.

Of course, that put my back up, and it was with great effort that I managed not to snap when I replied.

"Why do you want to see him?"

"It's complicated, but now is not the time for us to fall out. We just have to put our differences aside and focus on getting Jenna back. I'm not putting the blame solely at your door, Beth. I'm asking you to go out to avoid any arguments."

I thought it over for a second and then nodded, released the mute button on the handset and apologised to Luke for keeping him waiting.

"Not a problem," Luke said, as easy-going as ever. "I should be in The Black Prince for about five o'clock. Do you want to meet me there?"

"Sure. See you soon."

I hung up and then looked reproachfully at Mum. I couldn't help feeling hurt, but it was unfair of me. She wasn't picking Daniel's side over mine. She was trying to do what was best for all of us and would give us the best chance of working together to get Jenna back.

Mum could read me like a book. "Don't sulk, Beth. I'm only doing what's best. You know you won't be able to control your tongue with Daniel around. You'll end up saying things we will all regret."

I raised an eyebrow. "There's certainly some things I'd say. I wouldn't regret them, though."

Mum gave an exasperated sigh that took me right back to my teenage years. "Please, Beth."

I put my hands up. "It's fine. I won't be here. I said I'd meet Luke at the pub. I'd better go and get ready."

I headed to my bedroom to drag a brush through my hair and apply a little powder and lip gloss in an effort to look half-way human. I glanced in the mirror on the dressing table and cringed. My face looked white and pinched.

A short while later, I grabbed a warm jacket and headed out. The Black Prince was at the other end of town, set back on the main road, next to the river. It was a picturesque, old pub and had even featured in Colin Dexter's Inspector Morse series, the first book in fact.

Inside it had kept many of its old-fashioned, charming features, even though it had been refurbished since I'd gone to Dubai. The ceilings were low, and the windows were small, but the decor was a little brighter than the typical English pub.

Luke hadn't arrived when I got there, and there were just a couple of locals propped up at the bar.

I ordered a gin and tonic from a young barman I didn't recognise and then added a pint of Doom Bar to my order so Luke's drink would be ready when he got here. I carried the glasses over to a small table by the window and sat down, pulling out my new mobile phone.

I tapped on the screen and found I had enough signal to

download my emails. There was one email from Sylvia, telling me that she hoped I was sorting out my family problems and she was looking forward to seeing me soon. She also mentioned that my boss was running around like a headless chicken and was lost without me.

I'd had no messages or missed calls. I wondered how many people had seen my Facebook post with my new number. Had the person that sent the photograph of Jenna seen my new number? I hoped so and wished they would get back in contact.

I settled back in the cushioned chair as the warm May sunshine streaming through the window made me feel sleepy. I'd only taken a couple of sips of my gin and tonic when a shadow fell across the table, and I looked up to see Luke grinning at me.

"Thanks for getting the drinks in," he said, sitting down before lifting his pint and taking a long sip.

"You're welcome. So how was work? I didn't realise you worked part time these days," I said, smiling to show I was only teasing.

"The clinic usually shuts up shop at half-past five, but my last appointment cancelled. So it was your lucky day." He winked at me.

I rolled my eyes. " How fortunate."

"So, how have you been settling back into Woodstock? Is it like you'd never been away?"

Luke's friendly, open face and his warm smile made me want to confide in him and tell him about Jenna, but I couldn't do that yet. Instead, I told him about Robin Vaughan.

He nodded, his face serious. "I heard about that. Sickening, isn't it? Has he been charged?"

I nodded. "Yes, he was taken in for questioning last week, and then charged a few days later."

Luke put his pint carefully down on the table, avoiding eye contact, and I sensed he was building up to ask a question... "Have you spoken to the police about it... I mean, could he have..."

Luke struggled over his words, and I took pity on him. "You mean, could he have had anything to do with Jenna's disappearance?"

Luke winced and then nodded. "Yes, sorry. That wasn't a very tactful question."

"It was the first thing I wondered when I heard, too. But Mum has spoken to the police, and they don't think he was involved." I shrugged. "But we don't know anything for sure."

"God, how awful," Luke said and reached over to put his hand over mine and squeezed gently. "How is your Mum bearing up?"

"Considering everything that's going on, she is coping very well, but of course, she's upset."

Luke nodded and removed his hand from mine, picking up his drink again. "Poor Daniel. This news must have knocked him for six."

At the mention of Daniel's name, I tensed.

Anybody else would have missed my reaction, but not Luke. He picked up on it straight away.

"What is it? Are you and Daniel not getting on?"

I tried to make out the light of it. "Did we ever?"

Luke returned my smile. "No, not really. But you have to feel for the poor guy, though."

I wished he'd drop it. I didn't want to talk about Daniel. So, I changed the subject and mentioned I had seen his brother in Oxford.

"Yeah, Phil said he would be in Oxford. I think he stayed overnight at his old college. I usually try and meet up with him when he is here, but he said he was leaving early today."

"The weird thing is, your brother completely blanked me."

Luke frowned. "Really? Well, don't take it personally. You know what he can be like. Totally lost in his own thoughts. A typical academic."

I shook my head slowly. "No, it wasn't like that. I called out to him, he saw me, and then he just turned and walked away really fast, as though I was the last person he wanted to see."

Luke looked at me for a moment without saying anything. "That is odd."

"I can't think why he would have reacted like that. We

always got on quite well, didn't we? I mean, I always liked him. Maybe the feeling wasn't mutual."

Luke sighed. "It's not you, Beth. I think I mentioned yesterday that he's not quite back to his old self yet. He's never been very sociable, and well, after everything that happened, he retreated back inside his shell even more."

"So, he reacts that way to everyone, does he?"

Luke shrugged. I'd meant that as a joke, but he didn't smile. "He hasn't kept in touch with any of his old friends. He sees and interacts with colleagues at work, but he's lost a part of himself. My guess is that he avoided you because you're part of his past. You know what happened to his wife and daughter. He still can't talk about it."

I wanted to say I wouldn't have dreamed of being so insensitive as to mention his wife and daughter, but knowing me, I probably would have brought it up. I'd already talked about it to Luke yesterday, even though I knew it was a painful subject. After everything my family had been through with Jenna, I should have been more understanding.

"It's not a big deal. I just hope he is all right. When you see him, tell him I said hello."

Luke drained his pint. "Will do. Another?"

CHAPTER NINETEEN

I stayed in the pub with Luke for another hour and had two further drinks. Although I had gone to the pub to avoid seeing Daniel, once I was there, I started to relax and enjoy Luke's company. Of course, it was impossible to completely switch off, and I kept my phone on the table beside me just in case.

Luke told me stories about his veterinary clinic, and we reminisced about the past. I told him about Pippa's visit and Mum's strange reaction.

"Pippa was incredibly friendly, but Mum was cold with her. I don't think I've ever seen her react like that to anyone. I tried to find out why, but she didn't want to talk about it."

"Maybe it's hard for your Mum to see Pippa because it's a reminder that Kate isn't around anymore."

"You're probably right. Every memory I have of Pippa involves Kate. I don't know what is wrong with me. I keep thinking everyone has these ulterior motives and secrets they're keeping from me." I blurted out the words before I realised what I was saying. The alcohol had loosened my tongue.

"It's understandable," Luke said. "My brother is the same. Once you've been hurt, you put up your guard, and even when someone does something nice, it's hard to trust them. With Phil, it's almost as though he doesn't think he deserves anyone to be nice to him."

I stared down at the table and reached for my drink. That was a depressing thought.

After we had said our goodbyes, I walked back home slowly. It wasn't even dark yet, but I hoped I had given Mum and Daniel enough time to talk in private. On the way, I decided to take a detour and call in at the Parsons's house. I wasn't sure whether it was the Dutch courage from the alcohol or the fact I was feeling guilty for not talking to Dawn, despite telling her mother I would.

Dawn Parsons was a victim of circumstance. She'd been bullied and had turned into a bully herself, but her life hadn't turned out well. Surely I could show her a little compassion, for her mother's sake, if nothing else.

I took a left at the end of the High Street so I could take the long way around, which would take me past the Parsons's house on the way back home.

The sun was low in the sky, and swifts swooped above me in their crazy dance to catch insects on the wing. Despite the late hour, the birds hadn't yet stopped chirping. A blackbird appeared in front of me, darting across the road.

Some vehicles were parked up along Rectory Lane, but there was hardly any traffic at this time of night. As I approached the cluster of thatched cottages, I shivered. It was a warm evening but a chill prickled over my skin. As I got closer to the Parsons's cottage, I started to doubt myself. Was this really a good idea? I didn't want to interrupt them in the middle of eating dinner.

When I got closer to the cottage, I could see there was a flickering light coming from one of the downstairs rooms. It wasn't a warm light generated from a normal bulb, but a colder hue that made me think it could be from a television or computer screen. There was no sign of Mrs Parsons's car in the driveway. I didn't really want to see Dawn on her own, but I had come this far and decided I may as well get it over with.

Taking a deep breath, I walked forward, opening the small gate and heading up the garden path towards the front door. I glanced in one of the downstairs windows, the source of the flickering light. There was a bulky figure sitting in front of a computer screen. Dawn Parsons. For a moment, I just stood there on the garden path, staring in at her. The bluish glow from the computer screen picked out highlights in her dark hair and created a blue-tinged aura around her.

For some strange reason, I had the urge to turn around and run. But then Dawn shifted in front of the computer. It was too late now. She knew I was there. I couldn't back out.

I took a step forward, ready to knock on the door, when Dawn turned around. Her coarse features were illuminated by the light from the computer display. She scrambled out of her chair, a look of surprise mingled with panic on her face.

I had no idea why she would react that way. She retreated, disappearing from view, and I expected her to come straight to the front door, so I didn't knock or ring the doorbell.

A few seconds later, when the door didn't open, I grew restless, shuffling from foot to foot and wondering why I was wasting my time.

"For goodness sake," I muttered under my breath.

I pressed the doorbell and heard the cheerful chimes coming from inside the house. I waited for a good two minutes, but no one came to answer the door. I glanced back at the window in confusion. What was her problem? She clearly didn't want to see me and had decided to hide and pretend she wasn't home. It was ridiculous. She'd seen me watching her.

My mind started to work overtime, coming up with theories and possibilities as to why Dawn didn't want to see me. Maybe she knew something about Jenna. Maybe she was scared that if she talked to me, she would blurt out the truth.

I stepped back from the front door, tilted my head back and looked at the windows upstairs. There were no lights on and no sign that anyone was moving about inside.

Occam's razor. The simplest explanation was often the right one. Perhaps Dawn was still upset with me. I accused her of being involved somehow in Jenna's disappearance and insisted the police look into her, so it would certainly be understandable if she didn't want to talk to me. But if that was the case, why did Mrs Parsons ask me to come and talk to her daughter? If Dawn still held a grudge over my behaviour from two years ago, surely her mother wouldn't have suggested I talk to her.

Feeling irritated, and frustrated, I stepped off the garden path and onto the lawn before tiptoeing carefully around the flowerbed in front of the bay window so I could peer into the room that Dawn had recently vacated. The faint blue light from the computer screen gave the room an eerie feel, but I couldn't see anyone inside. From outside, I couldn't even make out what she'd been looking at on the computer – I saw a blue header and some text and photographs and guessed it was Facebook.

I was just about to step back when a sudden movement directly behind the window made me jerk backwards. A strangled cry left my throat as I staggered backwards, trampling the geraniums in the flowerbed.

My heart was still pounding when I realised it was just the Parsons's tabby cat. He'd leapt up onto the windowsill to take a look at the nosy person peering in. Wiping my sweaty palms on the legs of my jeans, I exhaled a deep breath and shook my head. I was jumpy tonight.

I took one last look at the upstairs windows and shrugged. Fine. If she didn't want to talk to me, I was okay with that. I'd done my best to talk to Dawn as Mrs Parsons had requested so I wouldn't feel guilty anymore. But when I began to walk away from the house, I felt a prickling sensation on my skin, just like last time, and I was convinced

Dawn was peering out from one of the windows, watching me.

By the time I was halfway down the lane, I'd managed to calm down. I was paranoid. Dawn's strange behaviour probably had nothing to do with Jenna's disappearance. It was far more likely that Dawn didn't want to talk to me because she held a grudge, which was understandable really. We'd never been friends in the past, so why did I expect her to want to see me now? She was never going to welcome me back to Woodstock with open arms.

I rolled my shoulders, trying to ease some of the tension that had built up steadily during the day. Meeting Luke for a drink had helped. I relaxed enough to smile briefly when I remembered how I'd reacted when the tabby cat startled me. I'd almost jumped out of my skin.

When I reached the gate to Mum's house, I saw the tall metal gate was already open. That was unusual. Mum only left them open when she was expecting somebody to visit or she had a visitor with her at that time. I had my keys with me so she wouldn't have left the gate open for me. Was Daniel still there?

I pulled out my mobile phone and checked the time. It was just after eight o'clock.

After I had passed through the gate, I saw a car I didn't recognise parked in the driveway. It wasn't Daniel's car. I increased my walking speed, marching up the driveway, wondering who the visitor could be. I was halfway up the driveway when a man, dressed in a tight navy blue suit, exited the front door. He had closely cropped fair hair and glanced at me dismissively as he reached out with his key fob to unlock the car.

I broke into a jog, trying to reach him before he slipped into the driver seat.

Was he a police officer?

"Hey!" I called out. "Just a minute. I want to talk to you."

Why hadn't mum told me the police were calling round? I'd had my phone with me all evening. I hated the idea of the police coming to deliver bad news when I wasn't there.

The young man in the tight blue suit turned around and looked me up and down. "And you are?"

"Beth Farrow. Mrs Farrow's daughter."

"Oh, I see." He pulled out his wallet from the inside pocket of his jacket, plucked out a card and handed it to me. "If there are viewings scheduled, it would be a good idea to make yourself scarce."

"I don't understand." I read the card he'd handed me. Blyton & Morrison Estate Agents. Underneath the name of the company was the word valuations.

"Valuations? Why are you valuing Mum's house?"

The man gave a little huff and then waved his hands to indicate I should get out of the way so he could open the car door. "I think you should ask your mother about that... Client confidentiality and all that."

"Client confidentiality? You're an estate agent."

"Nothing gets past you, does it?" And with that, he slipped into the driver's seat and slammed the door.

Cheeky sod. I clenched my fists, scrunching up his card in the process. Then I walked briskly up to the front door and let myself in.

"Mum?"

Mum appeared in the kitchen doorway. "Oh, Beth, you're back early. I was just about to make a cup of tea. Do you want one? I have a couple of lamb leg steaks to put under the grill if you haven't eaten yet. I thought they would be nice with some new potatoes."

I shook my head. "I've just seen an estate agent outside. He said he has valued the house."

"Oh, I see."

"Why is the house being valued? Are you going to sell? Why didn't you mention it?" I followed Mum into the kitchen. "Did you think I'd be upset?" We had a lot of memories tied to this house, memories of Dad, Kate and Jenna, but that didn't mean I expected Mum to live there forever. In fact, the more I thought about it, the more sense it made for her to downsize if that was what she wanted. Although I couldn't imagine how she would cope without her garden.

"I was going to tell you," Mum said.

"It was a surprise. I didn't realise you were thinking of moving."

Mum sat down at the kitchen table, pinched the bridge of

her nose between her thumb and forefinger and closed her eyes. "I don't want to move, Beth. If I had my way, I would stay here until the day I die, but needs must."

"Is it money?" I was surprised. After dad had died during surgery, his life insurance policy had paid out and left Mum comfortably off. "Is there anything I can do to help? I've got a bit put by, about ten grand, if that would help?"

Mum made a noise that was halfway between a sob and a chuckle. "Oh, Beth. Thank you, love. But I'm not going to take your money."

"I don't understand. I thought the mortgage was paid off, and you got the insurance money after Dad died."

Mum took a deep breath and nodded. "Yes, well, it's a long story."

"I'm listening," I said.

She took a deep breath, folded her arms and leant her elbows on the table. "Fine. I'll tell you, but I don't want you to do anything rash."

I didn't like the sound of this.

"You remember when Kate and Daniel moved in with me because they were having financial problems?"

I nodded. "Yes, they moved in here with you and paid you a small amount of rent each month."

"That's right. But things were worse than you thought. They were in quite a lot of debt. They were in negative equity with the house they'd bought, and Kate told me, they'd run up a great deal of credit card debt, spread over a few different cards."

My eyes widened. That was news to me. Kate had always been so careful with money.

My mother nodded. "Kate came to me for help, and I did what I could with the savings I had, but it wasn't enough. I had the council tax to pay every month, and the heating bills for an old house like this cost a fortune. The savings wouldn't cover their debt, but I did still have the equity in the house."

I didn't need Mum to continue. I could guess what happened. "So you remortgaged?"

She nodded. "It seemed the best thing to do at the time. I remortgaged to get a lump sum to pay off their debts, and the idea was that Kate and Daniel would move in with me and slowly pay me back. So, in essence, they were giving me the money, and I was paying it back into the mortgage."

I nodded. "Right. But if you're looking to sell, I guess something went wrong with that plan."

She nodded again. "For a while, it worked well, but after Jenna was born, there were a lot of missed payments. I paid the mortgage from my savings. What could I do? You know Jenna needed new clothes and new shoes. And Kate was working as hard as she could. She went out and got a full-time job to make sure there weren't any more missed payments."

"I thought Daniel had a good job? Where did his money go?"

177

She shook her head. "I don't know. It wasn't every month that he missed the payment. But it was enough that I had to cash in my ISAs to cover the difference."

I felt sick.

I wrapped my arms around my middle and leant forward. "Has he kept up the payments after Kate died?"

Mum wouldn't look at me as she shook her head. "No, after he moved out of here, he said he couldn't afford his own rent and to pay me back. He said I gave money to Kate, and he had nothing to do with it."

Mum shifted her gaze to look at me tentatively, and I knew she was waiting for me to explode in anger. But rather than red-hot fury, a cold rage trickled through me. "I could kill him."

"Beth, this is exactly why I didn't tell you. It's just money."

"How can you say that? He's cheated you out of thousands. You could lose your home. We both know Kate was good with money. She was never in debt. She was always the one that would have pocket money left at the end of the week, not me."

"I know. But nobody could have foreseen this happening, and to be honest with you, if it happened all over again, I'd do the same thing. Not for Daniel, but for Kate."

I clenched my fist on the rough surface of the scrubbed pine table. I hated Daniel.

"Right, well, we will get this sorted out. But I think right now we need to buy ourselves some time so we can focus on Jenna. So I'm going to transfer some money to your account, and you can keep paying the mortgage for as long as that money lasts, okay?"

Mum shook her head.

"No arguments, Mum. I am not letting him screw you over."

"I won't be able to pay back, love."

"I don't expect you to."

I was already thinking about what I could do in the future. It would take years to pay off the mortgage. But we'd cross that bridge when we came to it. After we'd found Jenna, we would sit down and work out a repayment plan we could afford.

"And after this is all over and we've found Jenna, then we can report him to the police because Daniel owes you that money." I jabbed a finger on the table to emphasise my point.

Mum looked tired as she shook her head. "No, Beth. I'm not going to do that. It's his word against mine."

"It's not. There will be financial records," I insisted. "The police will see you transferred money to them."

"Beth, please stop. This is why I didn't want to tell you. I can't deal with all this now on top of everything else."

Tears pricked at the corner of my eyes, and my throat felt raw. I'd never hated someone quite as much as I hated Daniel Creswell at that moment.

CHAPTER TWENTY

Mum was proud and didn't want to accept my money, but I insisted. We could worry about how we would make future payments later, but the ten thousand pounds should give us a nice period of breathing space. I felt thoroughly wrung out and was sure Mum felt the same.

"We can talk about all this later," I said as I walked out of the kitchen. "Can I borrow your MacBook? I'll transfer the money now."

"It's on the table," Mum said following me through to the sitting room and nodding at the coffee table.

I sat down and pulled the MacBook towards me. Opening the lid, I noticed a mobile phone I didn't recognise beside the computer. I picked it up and turned back to Mum holding the phone up so she could see it.

"Whose is this?"

Mum's shoulders slumped. "It's Daniel's. He must have left it here earlier."

I tensed but tried to control my reaction. "He'll probably come back for it then."

"Probably," Mum said. "I'm going to make a hot drink. Do you want anything?"

"No thanks," I said and turned my attention back to the computer and logged onto my bank's online banking website.

It took less than a minute to transfer the money.

"It's all done," I said to Mum as she walked into the sitting room cradling a cup of tea. "You should probably check it's gone into your account."

Mum set her cup of tea down on the coffee table, sat next to me on the sofa, and I handed her the MacBook. Before she had a chance to type in her details, I heard the front door open.

"He's got a cheek," I said. I couldn't believe Daniel still let himself into Mum's house as though he lived here.

"Beth." The warning tone was clear in my mother's voice.

I stood up as Mum put the laptop back on the coffee table. She picked up Daniel's mobile phone. When Daniel entered the house, he looked tense and irritable. His eyes narrowed slightly as he saw me standing beside Mum.

"We were talking about you earlier, Daniel."

Mum shot me a warning look, but I wasn't going to

mention the money just yet. "When I saw you in the city centre this morning, you must have known about the article with Robin Vaughan. So why didn't you bother to tell us? Mum had to find out from the newspaper article."

Daniel narrowed his eyes. "We've already discussed it. And I'm not going to get into it with you."

I opened my mouth to say something else, but Mum quickly cut me off. "Beth, please, just give Daniel and I a moment to talk alone."

A flush of red stained my cheeks. I felt like a child being sent away while the adults had an important conversation.

"Fine," I said stiffly and turned away from them before walking down the hallway towards my bedroom.

I opened the door, flung my jacket on the bed and shut the door behind me. This was ridiculous. It reminded me of the times my Mum and Dad would send me to my room for misbehaving.

The house, even this newer extended section, had solid walls, which provided good soundproofing. Right now, I would have preferred a modern plasterboard wall so I could hear their conversation. Their voices were muffled, and I had no idea what they were saying.

Mum was probably right to send me away. After I'd learnt how badly Daniel had treated her when she had remortgaged her house for him, I wasn't sure I would be able to control my temper.

Daniel was a lowdown sponger, but Mum was right, at this precise moment, the only thing that mattered was finding out where Jenna was and who was keeping her from us. Everything else was a distraction.

I sighed and walked away from the door, sitting on the edge of the bed and wondering how long their conversation was going to take. A headache was building behind my eyes, and I longed for a coffee.

We were due for another update from the police at nine AM. I wanted to encourage them to put all the resources they could into this investigation. Sometimes I was convinced they were trying everything they could to get Jenna back, but I had moments of doubt where I wondered if they believed I had made the whole thing up and somehow forged the photograph.

I kicked off my shoes and yawned as I picked up my mobile phone and tapped on the Facebook app. Then I heard raised voices.

I froze. I couldn't hear them clearly, but I was sure I heard my mother mention Pippa's name. Her voice was shrill, and she sounded upset.

Screw it. I wasn't going to just sit around while Daniel upset her. Yes, Jenna was our priority, but I wasn't going to let Daniel treat my mother badly any longer. I yanked open my bedroom door and stormed down the hallway.

I could only see Daniel's face in profile as he loomed over Mum. His face was flushed, and spittle gathered at the edge of his mouth as he growled, "It's none of your business, Rhonda."

He hadn't seen me.

"I think you should leave. Right now," I said coldly.

"Oh, it's Beth. She's come to moralise," Daniel said mockingly as he turned to face me.

I'd heard far worse insults in my time and wasn't going to let him get to me.

I stood my ground and folded my arms over my chest. "Didn't you hear me? It's time for you to go home."

"This is none of your business, Beth."

None of my business? It was my mother he was shouting at.

"Well, if you're going to stick around perhaps you can answer some questions. Firstly, when are you going to pay Mum back?"

Daniel flushed, his cheeks darkening even further. Like many bullies, he only thrived when people kept his bad deeds secret. He hated the fact I knew what he'd done.

"I'm not," he said through gritted teeth. "It was your precious sister who squandered the money. Not me."

"Bollocks."

"How would you know, Beth? When did you ever pay any attention to anyone except yourself?"

"What are you talking about?"

"You're a drama queen, Beth. You think the world revolves around you. Well, here's a newsflash for you: it doesn't."

"I should have guessed you'd try to spin it round and turn it back on me."

But Daniel knew he'd pushed a sensitive spot and continued, "Your mother was a wreck after Kate died. I had to support her emotionally and financially. Then I had to sort out that job in Dubai for you because you were practically a nutcase. Do you know we could have had you sectioned?"

Blood rushed in my ears, but I was determined not to be hotheaded. It wasn't true. I was never that bad. He was only saying that to hurt me.

"I'm not rising to the bait, Daniel," I said, struggling to keep calm. "I would just like to know when you're going to pay Mum back. After all, none of us believes Kate got into debt. The very idea is ridiculous."

"This is typical of you. My daughter is missing, and you bring this up now when we might have a chance of finding her again. You're always trying to find a way to twist things, Beth, to give yourself a starring role in the drama."

Daniel had raised his voice to a shout, and I took a step back. How could Kate have fallen for a man like this? He was deranged.

"Of course, getting Jenna back is our priority. But that doesn't mean I'm going to let you cheat my mother out of her money. You do realise she's going to have to sell the house because she can't afford to pay back the debt you owe her?"

"How is that my problem? I can't afford to pay rent on two places, and there is no way I'm moving back here. It was claustrophobic enough when Kate was alive. I couldn't bear it now. When I'm here, all I can think about is Kate and Jenna…"

His voice cracked at the end of the sentence, and he turned away fiercely as his eyes filled with tears.

"I thought it was typically women who turned on the waterworks to get what they wanted," I said coldly, surprising even myself with my callousness.

"Beth," my mother admonished. "I think you better go, Daniel. We'll see you tomorrow morning when the police come to give us an update."

Daniel nodded and then walked away from us, heading out of the sitting room to let himself out. When the front door had closed behind Daniel, I braced myself for my mother's angry words. I deserved them, too. I shouldn't have lashed out like that. Especially not now.

But rather than telling me off, she sighed and said, "My tea has gone cold. I'll make another pot."

CHAPTER TWENTY-ONE

I went to bed early but lay awake worrying that our chance to find Jenna was slipping away. By fighting amongst ourselves, we weren't helping our chances.

Staring up at the ceiling, I tried to figure out where I'd gone wrong. Things had quickly spiralled out of control. Kate would have wanted me to be more understanding. Daniel had been through hell after losing his wife and daughter, and some of what he said made sense. Everything here reminded him of the wife and child he'd lost. Why could I not be more sympathetic?

It was impossible to believe the story he was spinning about Kate building up mountains of debt. That just wasn't like her. Kate was the one who would save some of her pocket money so she would have money for sweets at the end of the week, whereas I would spend mine in the first two days. She'd always been good with money.

Maybe Daniel was right. I was self-centred, not stopping to think why Kate had to go back to work so quickly after Jenna was born. Now, I understood why she had been so keen to start working for Pippa. They'd needed the money desperately.

Before I said goodnight to Mum, I'd asked her why she'd mentioned Pippa's name when she was arguing with Daniel, but she hadn't given me a straight answer, and I hadn't wanted to push it. We'd had enough stress tonight. I guessed it had to have something to do with the money, though. Perhaps she was reminding Daniel that Kate had to go back to work for Pippa because he couldn't manage his finances.

Getting the money from Daniel wasn't going to be easy. We would need to get a lawyer and take him to court. Bank records would show the money trail from Mum's bank account to Daniel's, which would prove he'd received the money, but what if he said the money was only for Kate – after all, they'd had a joint account. How would that argument stand up in court? I'd transferred enough money to pay the mortgage the next few months, and after that, we would need to make a plan for the future.

It was just after ten o'clock when my mobile phone beeped. I sat up in bed and grabbed it, eager to open the message in case it contained information about Jenna, but it was a message from my boss in Dubai. He wanted to know where I'd filed a particular spreadsheet on his computer.

I rolled my eyes. The spreadsheet was in the same place it always was. I replied to his message and felt a twinge of guilt when I realised it was two AM in Dubai. He was working late. I'd enjoyed my job and took on duties above my pay grade, including tasks designated for him, but he'd been happy enough for me to take on more responsibility. Now, though, it meant I'd really left him in the lurch.

I bunched up my pillow, trying to get comfortable. Was there anything I didn't feel guilty about at the moment? Staring up at the ceiling until my eyelids grew heavy, I replayed the events of the day Jenna went missing, always hoping for a newly remembered detail. Fragments of the day went round and round in my mind until finally, exhausted, I fell asleep.

When I woke up, my mouth felt dry, and my head felt like it was full of cotton wool. I swung my legs out of bed and then staggered down the hallway to make a strong cup of coffee. I needed it.

Mum was already in the kitchen in her dressing gown. She poured me a mug of filter coffee. "How did you sleep?"

"Not well," I admitted. "You?"

"I managed to get a few hours, but I had to take a pill."

I frowned. "I didn't know you were still taking sleeping tablets?"

"I haven't taken one for a while, but I needed one last night. Perhaps you could make an appointment to see a doctor today and get a prescription. You might find they help."

I set my mug down on the table and pulled a face. "I don't need to take anything."

Mum sighed heavily and shook her head as though she'd

expected that answer. She sipped her coffee and then said, "It would make me feel better if you saw the GP, Beth. It's not a bad thing to get some support."

"I know that, and if I need help, I'll make an appointment."

"By the time you admit you need help, you'll be in a bad way. It's better to head it off in advance. I can't cope if it happens again, Beth."

That was emotional blackmail. And it was very effective.

The last thing I wanted was a repeat of the hell I put my mother through two years ago. I picked up my coffee mug again and nodded reluctantly. "Okay, fine. I'll call them."

"You don't have to take any medication," she said encouragingly, reached over for the telephone handset and phonebook and passed them to me. "Just talk to the GP. That's all I'm asking."

Mum headed off to take a shower, and I dialled the GP's number.

Dr Fitzgerald was my old GP. He'd looked after me and Kate since we'd been at primary school.

The call connected, and I was immediately put in a waiting queue. The silence was punctuated every thirty seconds by an automated female voice announcing my number in the queue. I yawned and took sips of my coffee as I waited.

When I finally got through to the efficient, brusque receptionist, she informed me I was supposed to telephone on a Monday morning to get a pre-bookable appointment.

"So, you're telling me I can't have an appointment?" I asked, confused, but not necessarily very upset about it.

"I can't give out any pre-bookable appointments during the week. They have to be booked on a Monday."

"Are you telling me to hang up and phone back next Monday, then?"

"I'm not telling you to do anything. I'm simply saying I can't make any pre-bookable appointments until Monday."

I pulled a face. "So, I won't be able to see the doctor until next week at the earliest?"

"That's right. Unless it's an urgent issue?"

"No, it's not urgent. Thank you."

I hung up, feeling quite relieved. Surely, Mum would be satisfied with the fact I'd tried.

I was just filling my mug with a second cup of coffee when Mum came into the kitchen to do the same. Her short, curly, grey hair was wet from the shower, and her skin was shiny from freshly-applied moisturiser.

"Well? Did you get an appointment?"

"I have to phone next Monday. That's when they give out pre-bookable appointments," I informed her and raised the coffee jug to refresh her mug.

Mum frowned and tutted. "Nonsense, I'll phone them."

I went off to get in the shower. When I was drying my hair, Mum poked her head around the bedroom door and told me Dr Fitzgerald would see me at two PM that afternoon.

I wondered how Mum had managed to get past the officious receptionist. She obviously knew some tricks I didn't. But it was pointless to argue. If it made Mum feel better, I would go and see Dr Fitzgerald this afternoon.

At just before nine, Mum and I were both back in the kitchen, watching the clock. The police were coming to update us, and Daniel would be arriving any moment. After last night, I wasn't sure how this morning's visit would go.

Mum fished around in the cupboard under the sink, wincing a little as if crouching hurt her knees. She turned around triumphantly, brandishing a viciously sharp looking pair of secateurs.

I raised an eyebrow. I'd never been a great gardener.

"I thought we could do some gardening after the police visit this morning and take our mind off things."

I was about to object and say we had much more important things than a few overgrown shrubs to worry about, but from the earnest look on Mum's face, I knew this was her way of trying to keep me busy. Her concern had motivated her to persuade me to visit the GP.

I took the secateurs from her, which were surprisingly heavy, and nodded. "Okay, but you'd better keep a close eye on me. I can't be held accountable for any scalped roses."

"If you think I'm going to let you near the roses, you've got another think coming," Mum said, trying to hide a smile.

When Daniel arrived at five to nine, we put our differences

aside to concentrate on Jenna. It wasn't easy, and the atmosphere was tense. If Inspector Sharp and Detective Sergeant Parker picked up on the undercurrent of tension between us when they arrived a few minutes later, they didn't mention it.

Mum made tea, and we all sat down at the kitchen table. I had still been holding the secateurs when the police arrived and put them on the table to the left of my cup. Of course, we had a tonne of questions for the officers, but unfortunately, they didn't have many answers. Inspector Sharp was, at least, able to tell us that rather than being sent from a mobile phone, the photograph of Jenna had been sent from a computer using an Internet messaging service.

Detective Sergeant Parker's cheeks were tinged with red as her boss spoke. She'd already hinted at that information when I'd spoken to her on the phone. I got the distinct impression she hadn't intended to share the information quite so early.

The message had been sent from a computer in a chat room, in Oxford, but unfortunately, there were no security cameras or CCTV in the immediate area, but they were still checking CCTV from premises along the same road.

Mum asked them whether they thought Robin Vaughan sent the message, but he had an alibi for the time the message was sent.

It felt like all our leads were terminating in dead ends.

"Are you absolutely sure about the location the message was sent from?" Daniel asked. "I mean, could somebody have tried to make it look like it came from an Oxford chat room?"

Inspector Sharp and Sergeant Parker turned to look at Daniel, and there was a long pause before Sergeant Parker responded. "We have no evidence to suggest the IP address was masked. Why do you ask?"

Daniel glanced at me and then looked away again quickly. "Would you be able to tell if it came from somewhere abroad, like Dubai?"

There was an awkward silence. No one wanted to acknowledge the insinuation behind Daniel's words. My hands curled into fists, but I forced myself to remain calm. How could he believe I would do something like that?

A few seconds passed, and I realised everyone was looking at me.

Sergeant Parker's gaze lowered, focusing on my clasped fingers wrapped around the sharp secateurs. My knuckles were white.

I uncurled my fingers and let go of the secateurs.

"We have no reason to believe that the message was sent from abroad, Daniel," Inspector Sharp said finally, breaking the silence.

I glared at Daniel. Maybe I should be flattered that he thought I was some kind of cyber-genius. I'd like to tell him exactly what he could do with his ridiculous theories, but this was all a distraction, and it wasn't getting us any closer to finding Jenna.

"Have any more messages come through on my phone?" I asked.

Sergeant Parker shook her head. "No, I'm afraid not."

"And what about Robin Vaughan... I mean, he was there that day, at the fête, I mean. He could have been involved, couldn't he? Maybe he had an accomplice snatch Jenna and take her back to his place? Have you searched his house?"

Inspector Sharp's eyebrows knitted together in a frown. "I know you want answers, Beth. But the Robin Vaughan investigation is separate to Jenna's case. If we find anything linking the two investigations, we will let you know, but right now, we don't believe Robin Vaughan was involved in Jenna's disappearance."

"But have you searched his house? Surely, you can tell us that much," Daniel's voice was clipped. He was furious and frustrated.

Sergeant Parker exchanged a look with her boss and then nodded. "We have. As part of our ongoing investigation into Robin Vaughan, we have searched his property. But again, I have to reiterate that at this stage, we don't believe he is involved in Jenna's disappearance."

"So who do you think is involved? It's been two years. Somebody sent that photograph, which means she is still alive. She is out there somewhere, so why haven't you found her?" Mum asked, her voice strained as she blinked back tears.

"I can't even imagine how frustrating this is for all of you, Mrs Farrow. But I want you to know we have a whole team dedicated to tracking down who sent that photograph. Please believe we are doing everything we can to find her. We have the best resources and officers looking for Jenna. "

I sighed and leant back in my chair. That was all very well, but it didn't look like their best was good enough.

CHAPTER TWENTY-TWO

I arrived at the GP surgery five minutes early for my appointment. The waiting room was chock-a-block.

There was already a queue at the counter, so I joined the end, waiting behind an old lady in a grubby-looking rain-coat. The queue moved slowly, and everyone kept a respectful distance from the reception desk, so they didn't overhear the medical complaints of the person in front.

A young man in a shiny suit and rimless glasses joined the queue behind me, and he smiled before a hacking cough engulfed him. I tried not to make it too obvious when I took a step forward, away from his germs.

I'd never liked coming to the doctors. The idea behind waiting in an overheated room, filled with sick people, was fundamentally flawed. It was the perfect place for germs to spread like wildfire. And I couldn't help wondering how many people came to the doctor's surgery for something like a bad back and left with the flu.

When I finally reached the front of the queue and told the receptionist I was there for my two o'clock appointment, she gave an impatient little huff.

At first, I thought she must have realised that I was the person who was supposed to phone back on Monday. Maybe she disapproved of me not following the correct procedure. I couldn't really blame her, but I preferred to deal with an angry receptionist rather than an angry mother.

The receptionist pointed towards a touchscreen monitor set up in the corner of the room. I hadn't noticed it earlier. The UK had obviously moved with the times since I'd been away. "You're supposed to check in over there. With your date of birth and the first letter of your last name."

"Oh, I see. Sorry."

"Don't bother, love," a voice said behind me. It was the old lady, wearing the grubby raincoat, who had been standing in front of me in the queue. She hobbled away from the touchscreen back to the reception desk. "It's on the blink. Screen won't respond."

The receptionist turned her attention to the old lady. "Are you sure you're pressing the correct buttons?"

The old lady looked at her scornfully. "I've been in here enough times to know how to work that infernal thing, and I'm telling you, it's not working."

The receptionist sighed and tapped the keys on the keyboard in front of her. "Name?" she asked.

"Patricia Morrison," the old woman said.

"Dr Ingram is on time today. He'll call you in when he's ready. Name?"

After a short delay, I realised she was talking to me now. "Beth Farrow. I've got a two PM appointment with Dr Fitzgerald."

"Fine, take a seat. He is running about twenty minutes late."

As it turned out, I didn't have to wait that long to see Dr Fitzgerald. Ten minutes later, his gruff voice called my name over the intercom system.

I got up, and as directed, walked to room three.

Dr Fitzgerald had to be close to retirement age. His fair hair was streaked with white, and his face had more wrinkles than I remembered. He had kindly, soft, blue eyes, and he looked up at me with a smile as I walked in.

"Take a seat," he said. "I won't keep you a moment."

I guessed he was looking at my records. He scrolled through some text on his computer with a serious expression on his face.

A few seconds later, he turned to face me, rested his forearms on the desk and interlinked his fingers. "How can I help you, today, Beth?"

"Well, I'm not ill," I said, thinking I'd get that in straightaway. "I'm sure you remember when my niece went missing two years ago?"

"Of course."

"I've been having trouble sleeping recently, and it's been worse since I flew back to the UK. I'm sure it's stress, exacerbated by the jet-lag. It will probably sort itself out, but my mother suggested I come and see you today."

"And your mother is a very wise woman," Dr Fitzgerald said with a gentle smile. "Now, tell me how the insomnia is affecting you."

"I struggle to fall asleep, and then when I do, it's only for an hour or so at a time," I admitted. "The following day, I'm tired and irritable and find it hard to focus."

Dr Fitzgerald nodded. "A lack of sleep can have a cumulative effect, Beth. I'd be happy to prescribe you something on a short-term basis."

I shook my head rapidly. "I don't want to take anything that's going to knock me out."

"Long-term, sleeping pills aren't a good idea, but we've come a long way from the old-fashioned tablets. Sometimes, people just need a little help getting back into a routine. Coming back home has been a shock to your system. You've been reminded of a traumatic event, and on top of that, you are suffering from a little jet lag, too, I suspect."

I wondered how much Mum had told him over the phone about our situation. The idea of an unbroken night's sleep was very appealing, but what if we had news of Jenna in the middle of the night?

"What if I needed to wake up urgently?"

He didn't ask me why I might need to wake up urgently. I suspected Mum may have dropped a hint about the development in Jenna's case.

"You'll feel a little groggy, Beth, but you will be able to function."

I nodded, considering his words.

As though he sensed me coming round to his point of view, he added, "But you'll feel far more groggy if you're trying to function on hardly any sleep."

That was a good point. I was already feeling the effects, and it had only been really bad for a couple of days. What would I be like after a week of this? A month? I had no idea how long our search for Jenna would take. Would our lives be in limbo for weeks or months? Or would this whole thing come to nothing, and somehow, we'd have to get back into the daily routine of our lives without Jenna?

"Okay, I said. "I'll take the tablets."

Dr Fitzgerald smiled. "Good. I'm going to give you a prescription for fourteen days, and if you have any unusual reactions to the tablets, or if there is anything else you want to talk about, make another appointment to see me."

"I will. Thank you."

"Before you go, Beth, I'd like to suggest referring you to a therapist. I do try to keep up with the latest developments in medicine. Therapy can be very helpful, especially after the tough time you and your family have been through."

I nodded. "I did see a therapist for a while, a year or so ago."

Dr Fitzgerald referred back to his computer screen and then nodded. "I can get you a referral to the same therapist if you would like?"

I didn't really, but I couldn't think of a good excuse to put him off. "Thank you."

I left the doctor's surgery and walked straight to the chemist on the High Street. It was an independent shop crammed with toiletries. A rack of sunglasses was by the door, next to a featured display of "touch of silver" shampoo.

There were two other customers already in the shop when I entered, both women in their mid-fifties. They were having a conversation about the Woodstock Museum. I wasn't close enough, or interested enough, to overhear every word.

I handed my prescription to the pharmacist, answered her questions, and then turned to browse the shelves stacked with perfumed soaps while I waited for the prescription to be filled.

I'd just picked up a small lemon-fragranced soap when I overheard part of the conversation between the two other customers in the shop. I'd heard them say a name I recognised – Robin Vaughan. Pausing with the soap gripped in my hand, I stayed perfectly still, straining to hear what they were saying.

"He wants stringing up," the first woman declared, and I turned around slowly so I could see them.

Noticing them properly for the first time, I realised that they were perhaps a little older than I'd first thought. Both were well dressed in expensive, casual clothes. The woman on the left wore tight-fitting jeans, which suited her slim figure, a pale blue, cotton shirt was tucked into her jeans and topped with a large, navy-blue, padded gilet. The other woman was taller and wore a cashmere twinset and a pair of chinos.

The cashmere-wearing woman tucked a lock of hair behind her ear and nodded in agreement with her friend. "And what about that little girl who went missing. It makes you wonder if he was involved, doesn't it?"

"Yes," her friend agreed. "You don't expect something like that to happen in Woodstock."

I couldn't listen anymore. I shoved the soap back on the shelf and walked past the two women before yanking open the shop door and stepping out onto the street.

I'd needed to get out of there before the place suffocated me. The shop was too warm, and the smell of the soap and other toiletries was cloying. The women were only saying what everybody was thinking. As the saying went, there was no smoke without fire.

The police told us they had no reason to believe that Robin Vaughan was involved in Jenna's disappearance, but did I really believe that? He'd been there, at the fête, the day Jenna went missing, and his recent arrest was incriminating. … How could they be certain he wasn't involved?

The bell above the shop door tinkled as the two women left the chemist. I waited until they were some distance away, heading down the High Street, and then went back into the chemist. Luckily, my prescription was ready, and I didn't have to wait for long in the hot, stuffy shop.

When I got home, I suffered through the third degree from Mum over the sleeping tablets. She wanted to know every detail about my visit with Dr Fitzgerald, and I humoured her because she was desperately worried about me. If only I could think of a way to reassure her, prove she could rely on me and convince her that this time, I was in control.

When she'd finished her quick-fire questions, Mum went back into the garden to attend to her roses. She mentioned something about greenfly and showed me a new spray she'd bought last week to obliterate the bugs. I promised I'd help out in the garden later but needed to go to the bank first.

The bank was only an excuse. I really wanted to go and see if Pippa Clarkson was at home. The argument between Mum and Daniel last night had worried me. Pippa's name had been mentioned, but I couldn't find out why. Mum didn't want to talk about it, and I was damned if I was going to ask Daniel. That only left me with one other person to ask— Pippa.

CHAPTER TWENTY-THREE

Pippa lived in a narrow, three-storey terraced townhouse opposite the bank. It was at the end of a row of similar houses, all old and expensive. Three stone steps led up to the bright red door, which contrasted with the sandy-coloured Cotswold stone.

I felt guilty for sneaking around behind Mum's back like this, but she didn't want to discuss her argument with Daniel, and I didn't want to upset her. The only way to find out was to ask Pippa.

I rang the doorbell and waited. It took so long for Pippa to come to the door I began to think she wasn't at home. Then I recalled she had a small wooden lodge in her garden where she and Kate had prepared the candles. She'd had the doorbell connected to the lodge so she could hear it while she and Kate were working, but maybe it wasn't working.

The last time I visited this house, I dropped off Kate's mobile phone and collected Jenna so Kate could work in peace. I pictured Kate walking towards me with a smile, her hand outstretched for the phone, and Jenna flinging herself at me and wrapping her arms around my legs in greeting.

I took a deep breath, turned and walked away from the door, but the door opened behind me.

Pippa looked immaculate as usual. She hesitated before smiling widely, her perfectly pink-glossed lips stretching over bright, whitened teeth. "Beth, what a surprise. Come in."

I walked back up the steps and crossed the threshold into Pippa's house. I'd visited the house a few times, usually because I needed to speak to Kate rather than because I wanted to visit Pippa. The house looked very different. It had always been well cared for, but now there was a sleek, modern feel to the house that didn't quite match the exterior.

The floor of the hallway was dark wood, and in front of me, I saw the old carpeted stairs had been replaced by a new minimalist staircase painted white. French-grey paint coated the walls and contrasted with the white woodwork.

"Have you decorated? It looks different."

Pippa waved a hand. "Oh, I did this about a year or two ago. I've had quite a bit of work done actually. Knocked down a wall or two and combined the kitchen and dining room into one room. The back has been extended, too. Come through and see."

She gave me a guided tour of the downstairs rooms, and I was impressed. The refurbishment must have cost a packet.

"I'll have to show you upstairs another time. It's a bit messy. To be honest, it looks like a bomb hit it. I keep promising myself I'll hire a cleaner but never get around to it."

She led the way through a small sitting room, decorated in various shades of beige and cream, into a large kitchen diner. It was light and airy, with double-width French doors that led out onto the garden. Sunlight flooded through the glass and made the room warm. A huge table, in the centre of the room, was covered with various glass jars, ribbons and labels. There was a strong floral scent that was quite overpowering as we moved closer to the stove.

"I was just about to take a break," Pippa said. "Join me for a coffee?"

"That would be lovely, thanks."

I walked towards the large French doors and looked out onto the small garden. The large extension had taken up quite a bit of the original outside space. The old wooden lodge was still there, but the curtains were drawn.

"Do you not use the lodge for work anymore?" I asked.

Pippa shrugged as she busied herself with a sleek chrome and black coffee machine. "Sometimes, I usually prefer working in here, though." She sighed. "Truthfully, I find it hard to work out there on my own. I miss Kate. It's not the same as when we worked side-by-side."

I was gazing outside, looking at the lodge, when the noise

from the coffee machine juddering into action made me jump. I turned back to Pippa and walked across to the granite-topped island in the middle of the kitchen.

Pippa pulled a plastic container of milk out of the large American-style fridge.

"Milk?" she asked, setting the container down in the centre of the island.

"Yes, thanks."

"Just like Kate," Pippa commented cheerfully, and then her facial expression froze. "Sorry."

I shook my head. "You can talk about her. It's fine. I don't take quite as much milk as Kate, though."

Pippa looked relieved and grinned. "Yes, Kate did like her drinks on the milky side. I used to tease her about that. We spent so much time together when she was working with me. I still find it hard to believe she is gone. She was a good person. I only wish I'd been a better friend."

"What do you mean?"

Pippa retrieved one cup full of coffee from the machine and slid another beneath the nozzle and pressed the button. The machine juddered to life for the second time.

She added a dash of milk to the coffee then pushed the cup across the island to me. "I just wished she'd felt she could come and talk to me. I hate to think she was in a desperate place and didn't have anyone to turn to."

I nodded stiffly as irritation twisted inside me. Why would

Kate have confided in Pippa when she could have spoken to my mother or me? Pippa wasn't really insinuating that Kate's family hadn't been there for her when she needed them, but it felt like a dig all the same.

"I don't think you should look at it that way, Pippa," I said, picking up the cup of coffee. "Kate was in pain. She didn't know how to cope with it, and there wasn't anything anyone could have said or done to make her feel better."

I swallowed hard and turned away so she couldn't see the expression on my face. No matter what I might say to Pippa, I couldn't help wishing Kate had held on so she could be here now when we had the chance to get Jenna back. Then again, there was nothing to say that we really would get Jenna back. The police seemed to be getting nowhere, and Daniel seemed to be convinced that the photograph had been manipulated somehow and wasn't really his daughter. I tried to push away those thoughts. Thoughts like that made it impossible to stay positive and focused.

When the machine had finished, Pippa retrieved the second cup of coffee and added milk.

"Shall we sit at the table?" she said, nodding at the table, which was covered with items from her candle-making business. We walked over to the table, and she said, "I'm sorry. Give me a sec, and I'll clear some space."

She shuffled some things around and then put a couple of coasters on the table. I took a seat with my back to the wall, and Pippa sat down opposite me.

"So, what brings you here today?" Pippa asked.

"Sorry," I said. "I should have called first and arranged something. It's just you said the other day to pop in for a chat anytime."

Pippa nodded enthusiastically. "Absolutely, and I meant it. You're always welcome. I just wondered if there was a particular reason behind your visit."

I hesitated for a moment and wondered whether I should just tell Pippa the truth. I was tired of games. I wished more people were direct and to the point. Secrets didn't do anyone any good. They festered beneath the surface until they grew so large and ugly they caused far-reaching, unpredictable problems.

I wrapped my fingers around the hot cup of coffee and nodded. "There is something I wanted to ask you. I overheard my mother and Daniel talking about you."

I didn't mention that they were arguing at the time, and my mother had practically screeched Pippa's name at Daniel, but I didn't need to. Pippa's reaction was enough.

She paled and blinked before looking down at the table.

"Oh, really?" she asked, aiming for nonchalance but not quite carrying it off.

"Yes, I wondered if there was something going on."

Pippa's gaze lifted and she fixed me with her light blue eyes. "Why didn't you ask your mother or Daniel about it?"

I had touched a nerve. She sounded defensive. I shrugged and planned to delay my reply, taking a sip of coffee first.

Pippa sighed and sat back in her chair. "Well, I can guess what it was about. I'm surprised they haven't told you yet. I told Daniel I'd tell you, but no, he thought he knew best and wanted to do it himself."

My grip on my cup tightened. "Tell me what?"

Pippa bit down on her lower lip. "I don't want to upset you, Beth."

"Just tell me."

"I've been seeing Daniel. I suppose the fact he is moving on must be difficult for your Mum. After Kate, I mean. You're not upset, are you?"

Pippa's explanation made things fall into place for me, but I wasn't upset. Pippa and Daniel were an odd pairing. Pippa didn't seem quite as soft and as accepting as Kate had been. I could see her and Daniel having some serious rows when their personalities clashed. But that was none of my business.

"I don't think Kate would have expected Daniel to remain single forever," I said carefully.

Pippa beamed and reached out to grab my hand. I had to stop myself pulling away as her hot fingers clutched mine.

"Oh, I am pleased to hear that. Daniel wouldn't admit it, but I think he was quite concerned about how you might react."

I bristled. "React?"

A warm blush spread over Pippa's cheeks. "Oh, I just meant he didn't want to upset you."

I knew exactly what he meant. He thought the news might send his crazy sister-in-law over the edge again.

I took a breath and shook my head. "It's fine. I'm not upset."

I'd intended to stay for a while and talk to Pippa about Kate. That was one of the main things I'd missed when I was in Dubai. Although it was easier to cope because nobody knew what I'd been through or quite how far down the rabbit hole I'd fallen afterwards, there was nobody there I could talk to about Kate. Nobody knew her. Nobody knew the way her hair curled stubbornly over her forehead, and no matter how hard she tried, she couldn't style it any other way. Nobody knew that when she got angry, her voice got softer. Nobody knew that when she was nine, she'd broken her Easter egg in half and shared it with me because I fell and scraped my knee.

Immediately after Kate died, I'd spent hours every day trying to remember details of the life we had shared from tiny tots to grown women. I was terrified I'd forget something important. Memories helped to ease the pain.

I folded my arms over my chest as though I were clutching those memories and didn't want to let them go. Now I was here, though, I didn't want to share my memories with Pippa. I wanted to leave and take my memories of Kate with me.

I made myself stay and finish my coffee and asked Pippa inane questions about her scented candles and her new range of reed diffusers.

"You've done really well for yourself, Pippa, and you

deserve it after all the hard work you put into building up the business," I said before draining the last of my coffee.

"I suppose I needed something to put my energy into after Mark left. I've always been like that. I like to have a project to keep me busy. I've had the building work on the house to supervise as well as the business, and it's kept me really busy."

"Do you keep in touch with Mark?"

Pippa's ex-husband, Mark Clarkson, had left her shortly after Jenna's disappearance. Although the fact they'd been going through a difficult patch had hardly been a secret. Their full-on shouting matches were legendary.

"Not really," Pippa said. "We've both moved on."

"He moved to Warwickshire, didn't he?"

Pippa nodded. "Yes, that's right. Another?" She held up her empty cup, but I shook my head.

"No, thanks. I'd better be going. I've held you up enough."

I got to my feet, and Pippa walked me to the door. "I enjoyed catching up, Beth. We should do it again sometime."

I nodded as I reached for the door handle. "Yes, that would be nice."

I meant it, too. I'd been dreading seeing Pippa again but had found talking to someone who had known Kate so well was comforting rather than upsetting.

"We could go out for a meal, and maybe I could persuade Daniel to come along."

I had to force myself to smile. "Maybe."

CHAPTER TWENTY-FOUR

After I had left Pippa's, I went straight home, and as promised, helped Mum in the garden. We left the back door open so we could hear the telephone if the police called. But yet again, the day ended with no new information, and we were no closer to finding Jenna.

After dinner, I could barely keep my eyes open. The lack of sleep was catching up with me, and I decided to have an early night. After saying goodnight to Mum, I cleaned my teeth, stripped off my clothes and changed into a long T-shirt and pyjama bottoms.

I sat on the edge of the bed clutching the bottle of sleeping tablets, feeling bone weary. Did I really need them? It was awful to be so tired yet unable to get more than a few hours sleep each night. My eyelids were drooping, so smothering a yawn, I left the bottle on my nightstand and slipped between the sheets. After thirty minutes of lying awake, tossing and turning, I finally gave in, grabbed the bottle of tablets and swallowed one of the small, blue tablets.

At first, I thought the tablet wasn't working. Ten minutes after taking it, I was still staring up at the ceiling, then finally, I closed my eyes and drifted off. For the first time in a while, I had a vivid dream.

I was alone, walking through Christchurch Meadow towards the River Isis in Oxford. There was a heavy fog descending, and long grass wound around my legs as I steadily made my way forward to the misty riverbank. When I got closer to the river, I could hear the sound of a child singing, and my heart rate increased. It sounded so much like Jenna.

Twinkle twinkle little star… How I wonder what you are…

I tried to walk faster, ignoring the grass and wildflowers wrapping their way around my ankles. But when I got to the riverbank it was deserted. I was too late.

Nothing grew by the river. The sandy earth was barren, but there was a faint footprint. I'd bent down to take a closer look when a movement caught my attention.

A little girl was playing close to the edge of the river. She had her back to me and was reaching for something she'd dropped in the water.

"Be careful!" I called out and began to run towards her.

I couldn't see her face, but from her blonde hair, I knew it was Jenna. I couldn't let her get away from me again. But before I reached her, a man stepped out in front of me. He seemed to appear from nowhere and held out his hands, grabbing my wrists.

He laughed. "What's the rush, Beth?"

When he spoke, I realised I knew him. It was Philip Bowman, Luke's brother. But he looked different. Happy. Gone was the gaunt, haunted man I'd seen just the other day.

He wore the same teasing, slightly bored expression I remembered from when Luke and I were just kids. I tried to pull away, but he wouldn't let me.

"She shouldn't be playing by the river, Phil. It's not safe."

Philip Bowman turned to look at the little girl and said, "You're quite right."

He released his grip on my wrists but kept a firm hold on my right hand, forcing me to walk at the same pace as him as he ambled along as though we had all the time in the world. It was maddening. I wanted to rush to Jenna, but he kept pulling me back.

"Isabel," he called in a singsong voice. "You shouldn't be playing by the river. It's very dangerous."

My head whipped around to face him. "It's not Isabel," I insisted.

I turned back to look at the little girl. She was still singing to herself, and now I could see it was quite clearly Jenna, but she didn't look any older than the day she'd disappeared.

"Jenna! Come here."

But she ignored me. Could she not hear me?

"Of course, it's Isabel," Phil said. "Don't you think I would know my own daughter?"

I shook my head. No. Isabel had been blonde with blue eyes, like Jenna, but they didn't look that similar.

"Don't be ridiculous. It's Jenna. We've found her."

Phil's grip tightened painfully around my fingers, and he turned to face me, his face filled with fury as he roared, "No. It's Isabel, my daughter."

The pain in my hand shot up through my arm and made me cry out and fall to my knees.

Jenna cried out in alarm, and I looked up just in time to see her fall backwards into the water. Finally, Phil let go of my hand, and I was able to scramble forwards on my hands and knees. But when I reached the water's edge she had disappeared beneath the surface.

"No!" I waded into the water, but Phil held me back.

He was shaking my shoulders. I couldn't fight him off...

"Beth! Beth! Wake up!"

My eyelids flew open, and I saw Mum's concerned, pale face staring down at me. Her hands were on my shoulders, trying to restrain me.

I blinked, slowly waking up. "Sorry...I must have had a bad dream."

I sat up when Mum released her grip on my shoulders. The

sheets were twisted around my legs, and my T-shirt was damp with sweat and sticking to my skin.

Mum looked frightened. I reached out to squeeze her hand reassuringly.

"It was just a dream," I repeated, as much for my benefit as hers. "I'm sorry. It must have scared you."

Mum pressed a hand against her chest and then sat on the edge of my bed. "I heard you screaming. I didn't know what to think."

The walls were thick in the old part of the house. I must have been quite loud for Mum to hear me.

"It was about Jenna," I said and pushed my hair back from my face.

"Yes, you called out her name. I'll get you a glass of water," Mum said, shooting me an anxious look before she left the bedroom.

I climbed out of bed and went to the bathroom to splash cold water on my face. It was just a dream. It didn't mean anything. It was simply my subconscious working over-time. The tablets probably hadn't helped.

The bathroom mirror caused me to cringe. My hair stuck up at all angles, and my face was deathly white. It had only been a dream, but it had felt so real. A niggling worry wormed its way into my brain. Could Phil Bowman have been involved in Jenna's disappearance? Was that why I'd had this dream? Could there be some forgotten detail buried deep in my mind? I shook my head. The idea was ridiculous. I'd known Phil Bowman for years.

~

The following morning, I woke up feeling pretty good. After the nightmare, I'd slept straight through and felt better for it. A sense of foreboding still lingered from the dream, but I pushed the paranoia to one side.

As soon as Mum walked into the kitchen, I could see she hadn't slept well at all. Her eyes were puffy and red, and despite the fact she'd applied her usual makeup, her face looked pale. We picked at our toast and drank cup after cup of coffee as we waited for the minutes to tick down to nine o'clock when we planned to call the police and see if there was any fresh information.

Unfortunately, we were disappointed. There had been no new developments overnight.

"No news is good news, I suppose," Mum said glumly as she hung up the phone after speaking to DI Sharp.

I groaned. "I can't believe they haven't made any progress at all. I was so sure that we were going to find her."

"And we will," Mum said firmly. "Just not as quickly as we'd like."

"Do you think it's possible the photograph was faked?"

Mum looked up with a startled expression on her face. Her hand froze in midair as she'd been just about to pick up her coffee mug.

I hurriedly tried to explain. "I don't mean I modified it. Of course, I wouldn't do that, despite what Daniel may think. I just wondered if there could be some sicko out there who thought it would be a funny thing to do... Maybe someone with a grudge."

Mum looked uneasy, but she shook her head. "No, why on earth would anyone want to do something like that?"

I shrugged. "I certainly ruffled a few feathers after Jenna's disappearance. I made some crazy accusations. Maybe somebody wants to get back at me."

Mum thought it over for a moment. "I really don't think so, Beth." She held out her hand for my empty coffee mug and took it over to the coffee machine.

The waiting around was killing me. I couldn't focus on anything. Every time I tried to pick up a book, I put it straight back down again. The babbling shows on television were inane and pointless. Every time I tried to concentrate on something else, my mind would drift back to puzzling over who could be behind the photograph.

For some reason, I hadn't told Mum that Phil Bowman had been in my dream last night. For one thing, I didn't want to worry her, and it would make me sound a little paranoid. On the one hand, the Phil I knew wouldn't ever abduct a child, but his daughter had looked so like Jenna. Grief could do strange things to people. I knew that better than anyone. Could the loss of his daughter have tipped him over the edge?

"Are you okay, Beth? You're looking anxious," Mum said as she set my freshly-filled coffee mug down on a coaster.

"Last night's nightmare unnerved me a little, but I'm fine. I might phone Luke and see if he's free for lunch today."

It would do me good to get out of the house, and I could do a little digging. From what Luke had already told me, it was clear Phil was still suffering from the loss of his wife and daughter. Of course, a person couldn't just rebound from something like that, but I'd like to know more about how he was coping now. He'd certainly reacted very strangely when I'd spotted him in Oxford. I wasn't planning to make any crazy accusations at this stage, but asking Luke a few questions couldn't hurt.

Mum smiled. "That's a good idea. Hopefully, it will take your mind off things for a little while. I always liked Luke."

Everyone liked Luke. Polite, friendly, compassionate and kind to animals. He was perfect. There was nothing not to like.

"You could do much worse you know," Mum added. "He's a nice boy."

I gave an over-the-top groan and then grinned. "One, Luke and I are just friends, and two, he's not a boy anymore."

Mum raised her eyebrows and took a sip of her coffee. "Well, he'll always be a boy to me. Do you remember when he grazed his knees and put holes in his trousers, trying to coax the injured fox out from under Mr Patterson's car?"

I smiled at the memory. "I'd forgotten about that."

Luke liked to save animals and could never bear to see one in pain. He'd had to come back to our house so Mum could clean him up, put a bit of antiseptic cream on his knees and try to mend his trousers. His own mother would have killed him if she'd seen the state of him.

I sent Luke a text, inviting him for lunch, my treat.

Ten minutes later, he sent a reply:

Great. Lunch at 12:30 suits me, but come to the clinic first. Someone just brought in an abandoned kitten, and he's adorable.

I smiled. Typical Luke.

CHAPTER TWENTY-FIVE

I arrived at Woodrow and Bowman Veterinary Surgery at just after noon.

The receptionist greeted me with a friendly smile. "Can I help you?"

"I'm here to meet Luke."

She gave me a speculative look. "Oh, I see."

She was weighing me up, no doubt, wondering who I was and what sort of relationship I had with Luke. To be honest, I didn't mind her curiosity. For once, it was nice not to be recognised as the woman who'd lost her niece. I took a seat in the corner, and waited, picking up a magazine to flick through.

A couple of minutes later, Luke walked into the waiting area and spotted me sitting in the corner. He grinned and started to make his way over to me, but the receptionist cut him off as she quickly strode around the reception desk and stopped directly in front of him.

"Oh, Luke, there's someone waiting for you."

From the way her gaze shifted from Luke to me, I guessed she was waiting to be introduced. But Luke appeared oblivious. He simply smiled and thanked her before making his way over to me.

"Do you want to see Spike?"

"You've called the kitten Spike?" I smiled, put the magazine back on the pile and stood up to follow Luke into the treatment area.

"Wait until you see him," Luke said. "Then you'll see why we've given him that name."

A veterinary assistant was already in the room, trying to feed the tiny kitten using a syringe. The kitten seemed to be getting the milk formula everywhere but in its mouth. Immediately, I saw why the little tabby cat had earned his name. The hair between its ears stood up on end, giving it the look of a miniature mohawk.

"Hey," I said looking down at the tiny little thing as I walked up to the bench.

The veterinary assistant smiled at me. "I'm Claire, and this cute little chap is Spike."

"I'm Beth," I said and melted as I looked at the tiny kitten again. "Nice to meet you, Spike." I stroked the kitten's soft fur and felt some of my tension ease almost immediately. "Where did you find him?"

"Someone brought him in this morning." The smile left Claire's face. "They found him in a plastic bag dumped behind the Co-op."

I pulled a face. "Poor little thing. Any brothers or sisters found with him?"

Luke moved to stand beside me. "No sign of his litter mates. I'm hoping they fared better than Spike."

"How could anyone abandon a kitten?"

"People can be very strange," Claire said.

"And cruel," I added.

Luke moved over to the sink to wash his hands. "I'm heading out for an hour for lunch, Claire. I'll be back before one thirty to take over from Michael."

"Right-oh," Claire said before turning her attention back to the kitten and making another attempt to get a syringe full of formula into the kitten's mouth.

As we left the veterinary surgery, the receptionist shot us yet another curious look.

"I think you've a fan there," I said teasingly to Luke after we'd walked out of the front door and through the car park. "She is desperate to know who I am."

He pulled a face. "That's Martha. She makes it her business to know everything that goes on in Woodstock. She terrifies me."

I tried not to laugh.

"She is extremely efficient, but also slightly scary. She'll interrogate me when I get back from lunch."

I grinned. "Well, you can tell her we ate at The Feathers. I made a reservation."

"You made a reservation? Now, I'm worried."

"Worried?"

"You know me, I'm happy with pub grub. The Feathers is expensive, so you're making me nervous. I'm starting to think you must want something from me."

Luke was only teasing, but he was so close to the mark, I flushed. "Don't be daft. I just fancied trying something different."

As we got closer to The Feathers Hotel, Luke nudged me. "Do you remember how we use to laugh at the people coming out of this restaurant?"

I'd forgotten. The Feathers Hotel used to have a supper club, and Luke and I used to watch the comings and goings of all the old, wealthy clientele. We'd found it hysterical to go around, with our noses in the air, mimicking the old fogeys, as we'd called them, and announcing airily we were off to the supper club.

Childish, but it had amused us at the time.

"Well, now I'm one of the old fogeys, I suppose."

Luke grinned. "I'm not complaining, especially if it's your treat."

After we'd been shown to our table by a waitress, we both ordered water. Luke because he was working after lunch, and me because I needed to keep a clear head. The restaurant was expensive. There were even linen tablecloths, Luke pointed out, teasing me again.

We drew the attention of the regular lunchtime crowd. A couple of corpulent businessmen, dining out on an expense account, sat at the table to my left. The other tables were filled with ladies who lunched, all looking alike in the way they dressed and styled their hair.

Luke didn't seem to notice anyone else in the restaurant. He'd always had a way of making me feel like I was the most interesting person in the room.

He fixed me with an open, friendly gaze and asked me what I'd been up to. I was already having second thoughts. What had I been thinking? He'd see through me as soon as I started to ask him questions about his brother, Phil. This had been a terrible idea. I wanted to confide in him, not use him to get details about his brother. I played for time, telling him briefly about my chat with Pippa.

Now that I was in Luke's company, my crazy theory went out the window. The idea of his brother being involved in Jenna's disappearance seemed ridiculous.

The waitress bought over my prawn and avocado salad and Luke's pan-fried chicken and sweet potato mash.

After the waitress left us, Luke asked, "When are you going to tell me what this lunch is really about?" His eyes were kind, but he wasn't teasing anymore.

I shrugged and tried to inject humour in my tone when I

said, "It's just lunch. You should be thankful I'm feeling generous and enjoy it."

He gave me a mock salute and began to eat his chicken.

"I don't suppose you've spoken to Phil since I saw him the other day?" I tried to sound nonchalant but failed miserably. I grabbed my glass of sparkling water and took a gulp to hide my nerves.

Luke shook his head. "No, not yet. It's not the kind of thing I wanted to ask him about over the phone. I thought I would see him at the weekend."

I nodded. "Good idea."

I put down my glass of water and then smoothed my napkin over my lap again nervously.

"After what happened with his wife and daughter, he must have been pushed very close to the edge."

Luke watched me carefully, but I refused to raise my gaze and meet his. Instead, I stabbed a piece of avocado with my fork, focusing on my salad as though it was the most fascinating thing in the world.

"He was devastated," Luke said simply, and I could hear the pain in his voice over the loss of his sister-in-law and niece as well as for his distraught brother.

Why did Luke have to be so nice? He was making digging for information really difficult.

"After I saw him in Oxford the other day and he reacted so strangely it made me wonder…"

Luke stopped eating, put his knife and fork down and waited for me to continue.

Surely there was a better way to phrase this. There had to be some way I could ask him questions about Phil without sounding like I suspected his brother of one of the worst crimes imaginable.

"Well, it got me thinking. I mean, Jenna and Isabel looked very like, didn't they?"

"I don't think I like where this is going, Beth. Tell me what you mean."

My insides were in knots as I met Luke's gaze. "Maybe he took Jenna because she reminded him so much of Isabel."

"What the hell? What planet are you on, Beth? Phil would never do anything like that."

I bid a hasty retreat, nodding frantically. "I know, I know. But his strange reaction to me made me think and..." I wasn't making any sense and was digging an even deeper hole.

"You know Phil. You must know he could never do anything like that."

How well do we ever really know anyone? The Philip Bowman I knew from years ago was very different from the man he was today. I leant forward across the table.

"I don't know him. I used to know him, but I don't know him that well anymore. I can't say what he would or wouldn't do."

The look of hurt on Luke's face made my throat tighten. I

reached for my water and took another gulp, but it didn't ease the dryness in my mouth.

"People don't change that much, Beth. No matter what you might think, he is the same person underneath. There is no way my brother would have taken Jenna. He knew more than anyone what it was like to lose a daughter. He would never put anyone else through that."

Sure, what Luke said made sense, but Phil was his brother so he was bound to take his side. I had to admit Phil was unlikely to be involved in Jenna's disappearance but my suspicions wouldn't go away.

"But he moved away shortly afterwards. And he's got a place in London where nobody knows him… I mean, have you even seen his new place?"

"Yes," Luke replied loudly, and the people at the next table turned to look at us in surprise. He lowered his voice. "You are being ridiculous, Beth. What's got into you?"

He pushed his chair away from the table, and for a moment, I thought he was going to storm off, but he said, "I am going to the gents'. When I come back, you are going to tell me what has put this crazy idea into your head."

I swallowed hard and put my head in my hands as he walked past me.

The last thing I wanted to do was upset Luke, but ignoring my suspicions was impossible. They were like an itch that demanded to be scratched. If I didn't find out more about Phil, I would never know if there was something more I could have done to find Jenna if only I'd addressed the right questions to the right people.

I reached for the bottle of sparkling mineral water to top up my glass and that's when I noticed Luke had left his mobile phone on the table.

I didn't know where Philip lived, but Luke probably had his address in the contacts list in his phone. I stared at the phone. What harm would it do? I could get Phil's address, just to scope it out. I'd soon see if he had a child living with him and no one needed to get hurt. No one would find out. It was the easiest way to end my suspicions.

Before I could talk myself out of it, I reached forward and snatched up the phone. With my pulse quickening, I pressed the central button, hoping I'd be quick enough to get the address before Luke returned.

I mumbled a curse under my breath when I realised the phone was locked, and I didn't know the pass code.

I put the phone back on the table and felt thoroughly miserable. What was I doing? This was Luke. One of the people I trusted most in the world. And I was trying to... God knows what I was trying to do.

What sort of person was I?

When Luke returned, I couldn't look at him. I felt cruel, evil and a thoroughly nasty person for even entertaining those thoughts about his brother. I didn't want Luke to think badly of me and needed him to understand. Although I'd told nobody about the photograph of Jenna outside my Mum, Daniel and the police, I knew I had to confide in

Luke. It was the only thing that would stop him thinking I was a nutcase.

After I had finished explaining, the angry expression on his face melted away, and he unclenched his jaw.

"Oh, Beth, you should have told me."

"The police told us that the less people who know, the better. They don't want the information getting out and interfering with the investigation. You know, people phoning up and saying they know things when they don't, giving them loads of false leads to sift through like last time."

"So that's why Phil acting oddly made you put two and two together and come up with five."

I opened my mouth to dispute that but then thought better of it. I wasn't going to persuade Luke that his own brother had been involved, and I didn't want to create a rift between us by arguing my point.

He reached across the table and put his hand over mine. "You do know that Phil would never have done anything to hurt Jenna."

I shook my head wearily. "I never thought he'd hurt her, but it would be understandable if he'd reached his breaking point and because they looked so similar...."

Luke shook his head. "No, absolutely not. He wouldn't. And you have to know that if for one second I suspected he had, I wouldn't protect him."

I nodded. "I know. Look, don't mention the photograph to

anyone, especially not Phil. I don't want him to know I thought..."

"Of course, I won't mention it to anyone," Luke promised.

We finished our lunch. I only picked at my salad, but Luke cleared his plate. He asked me a couple more questions about the investigation, mostly concerning Robin Vaughan, and he was disappointed to hear the police didn't have much on him at all.

"It's a bit of a coincidence that he was there at the fête on the day it happened," Luke said, echoing what Mum and I had already mentioned to the police.

"I know. We just have to be patient and see what they can dig up, but waiting is not easy."

That was the understatement of the century, I thought, as I turned to signal the waitress and ask for the bill.

After the bill was settled, we left the restaurant, and outside, I said goodbye to Luke. I'd only taken a couple of steps when I spotted someone standing motionless on the other side of the road.

Dawn Parsons.

I shivered. She was staring at me, a blank expression on her round face. For a moment, on the edge of the pavement, I hesitated. Why was she just staring at me like that? Was she trying to intimidate me?

I'd had enough of her creepy spying. I took a step off the pavement only to reel back at the blast of a car horn. A car had pulled out of a parking space and accelerated far too fast, almost plowing into me. Shaken, I stared after the blue Astra as a young girl with red streaks in her hair asked me if I was okay.

"I'm fine, thanks. The car seemed to come out of nowhere."

She scrunched up her nose and made a rude signal at the driver, who'd already reached the junction with the main road. "They were driving far too fast."

I nodded. "Yes, I'm lucky the car didn't hit me," I said, although I was shaking and didn't feel particularly lucky.

"My heart was in my mouth when I saw you step out. It's a miracle the car didn't hit you."

I managed to smile and nod in agreement as the young woman said goodbye and went on her way. I scanned the other side of the street for Dawn, but there was no sign of her.

She had disappeared.

CHAPTER TWENTY-SIX

It's just for my own peace of mind, I muttered to myself as the Paddington train clattered over the tracks, heading towards London.

Fortunately, it had been easy to track down Phil Bowman. At first, I had been furious with myself for not remembering where Phil worked because I was sure Luke had told me during one of our conversations. Luke mentioned something about a university, but I couldn't recall which one. In the end, it didn't matter. A quick Google search soon told me he was working at Imperial College, even helpfully listing the department and building number.

My plan, if I could even call it that, was to wait for him to finish work today and see what he did and where he went. Of course, just seeing Phil again wouldn't be enough to rule out the possibility that he'd played a role in Jenna's abduction, but following him home, should give me the opportunity to see if he was living alone. A big confrontation with Luke's brother was the last thing I wanted.

Speaking to him directly would be a bad idea. I really didn't want this getting back to Luke. It was better for everybody if Luke believed I'd dropped the matter completely.

In all honesty, I really did want to believe Luke. The thought that somebody I knew had taken Jenna was sickening, but on the other hand, if Phil had taken her, it was very unlikely she'd be hurt.

Much of what Luke had said over lunch made perfect sense. If anyone had asked me a few years ago whether Phil Bowman could have abducted a child, I would have insisted he couldn't.

But things were different now. I knew better than anyone how grief could twist your mind and play havoc with your thought process.

I leant back in my seat and gazed out of the large window as the train sped past open fields. It was nice to get away from Woodstock for a few hours.

Catching Dawn Parsons watching me earlier had set me on edge. Almost getting knocked over by a car had stopped me confronting her there and then, but I had half a mind to head over to her house when I'd finished in London. Mum would definitely not approve of that, though, and she would be horrified if she found out what I was up to this afternoon. In fact, I didn't want anyone to find out what I was doing because they'd assume I'd gone crazy.

Maybe I was crazy. My actions were ridiculous, but I

couldn't rule Phil Bowman out without making sure, and following him home was one way to ease my worries without everybody thinking I was losing my marbles.

It didn't take me long to get from Paddington to the science building where Phil worked, and although the University had been helpful enough to list his lectures online, I didn't know what time he would be finishing today. His scheduled lectures ended at four PM, but he could have other meetings or work that kept him later. My only option was to wait.

There was a bus stop nearby, and I stood beside it, trying to blend in, keeping a close eye on the glass double doors at the entrance. I hoped there wasn't another way out. If there was, I could miss him, and my crazy plan would be over before it started.

I'd made it to London by three thirty and thought I had a good chance to catch him as he left work.

Bus after bus departed as I waited. The minutes ticked past, giving me time to think and realise how foolish my plan was. What if Phil recognised me? Would I really be able to follow him all the way home without him noticing? If he took a bus, there was no chance I'd be able to follow without him spotting me. If he'd driven to work, I didn't stand a chance.

I let out a frustrated sigh. Why hadn't I considered that? But parking spaces were at a premium in central London, and surely, university staff weren't that well-paid. There were only a few parking spaces outside the front of the building. My gaze shifted from the entrance to the side of the building, trying to see if there were another, larger car park. But there was nothing except more buildings.

My heart sank as I looked further to my left. A bicycle rack jammed full of a variety of bikes, old and new, racing bikes with drop handles along with more practical road bikes. Great, Philip had cycled everywhere when he lived in Woodstock and Oxford. If he'd cycled here today, I might as well leave now. There was no way I would be able to keep up with him. This was a waste of time.

A large bin lorry rumbled past, followed by a black cab, with an irate driver. I took a step back as they pulled closer to the kerb. Cycling in central London carried certain risks. The heavy traffic would deter all but the most dedicated cyclists, and surely Phil wouldn't enjoy cycling here. My spirits lifted a little, and I leant back against the bus shelter as yet another red double-decker bus pulled to a stop in front of me and the passengers filed off.

A man with messy hair, a patchy beard and a grubby-looking jacket shuffled up to me. He'd been waiting at the other end of the shelter and had been here longer than I had. I guessed he wasn't here to wait for a bus either.

"Whatcha doing?"

I shook my head and avoided eye contact, not wanting to get into a conversation. "I'm waiting for someone."

The man hitched up his baggy trousers and nodded thoughtfully. "Me too. But they don't come. They never come."

I didn't know how to respond so said nothing. Looking

back over my shoulder, I saw a group of students exit the building, but there was still no sign of Phil Bowman.

"Spare a quid for a cup of tea, love?"

I turned back to the man and guessed he must have fallen on hard times. Shoving my hands in the pockets of my jeans, I pulled out some coins. My purse was safely tucked away in my handbag, but I never carried much cash with me anyway. I'd had the foresight to purchase an Oyster card just in case Phil used public transport to get home. Handing over a handful of change that probably only amounted to about two pounds earned me a toothy grin.

"Cheers, love. I hope he turns up soon, whoever he is."

"Thanks," I said and turned back to watch the glass front doors.

By the time six p.m. came around, I was starting to lose hope. I tapped out a text message to Mum, telling her I'd be late home as I had to pop into London for something. The message I sent was vague, but I would have to come up with a better explanation on my way home.

I was just tucking my phone back into my handbag when I saw him.

Phil Bowman. He wore light brown trousers and a heavy tweed jacket, not really suitable for the warm May weather we were experiencing at the moment. His floppy, fair hair fell forward over his forehead, and he wore his usual rimless glasses.

He was heading straight for me.

I froze, shrinking back behind the shelter, wishing it wasn't made from see-through Perspex. Luckily for me, he walked right past without a second glance. I let out a shaky breath and set off in pursuit.

If he turned around, I planned to act surprised and pretend I just happened to be in the area. Okay, so that was stretching belief a little bit, but he wouldn't be able to prove otherwise, and as long as Luke didn't find out, I would be in the clear. To start with, I kept my distance, but I was terrified of losing him. As we walked away from the University, the number of people jostling on the pavement increased, and I had to get closer or risk losing him.

I bit down on my lower lip, concentrating on the top of Phil's fair head, as I weaved through the crowds of people and tried to keep sight of him. He took a sudden right, heading down into an underground station. I followed him, rummaging through my handbag for my Oyster card, not daring to take my eyes off Phil.

How on earth would I follow him onto the same platform and then get on the same train without him noticing me? I should have at least worn a hat or something. Luckily, the platform was busy, and I managed to wedge myself amongst a large group of colourfully-dressed, foreign tourists. I could keep an eye on Phil from my place in the crowd without him spotting me.

The train rolled up to the platform less than thirty seconds later, but I didn't dare get on the same carriage as him. Instead, I picked the next one along and slumped down into a seat. Through the grimy window, I watched him look around the carriage.

He remained standing, swaying a little as the underground train jerked along the track towards the dark tunnel, but he didn't bother to hold on to the metal pole or the handhold loops that dropped down from the ceiling. He was a seasoned underground traveller.

I shifted to the side as somebody sat down in the seat beside me, but I didn't pay them any attention. Clutching my handbag to my chest, I bit down on my thumbnail and watched Phil in the next carriage.

He stared straight ahead, not really looking at anything, but seemingly lost in thought. Unlike the other people in his carriage, he didn't pull out his phone and study the screen. I wondered whether any of them got a signal down here. As the train rumbled into the next station, I held my breath and leant forward, ready to get off the train quickly if Phil disembarked. But he didn't.

My phone buzzed in my handbag. I guessed it was Mum replying to my text message, but I didn't look at it. I had Phil Bowman in my sights, and I wasn't going to lose him.

The journey on the underground seemed to take forever. I lost count of how many stops the train made and didn't dare take my eyes off of Phil to glance at the map of the underground displayed on a sign above my seat. The only thing I cared about was keeping my gaze fixed on Phil.

When the train stopped again, and he walked towards the doors, I jumped up, making my way to the exit. To my irritation, a short lady with a ginormous suitcase was also getting off at this stop. She pulled the suitcase across my foot and then left it in front of me, blocking my path.

Christ, I was going to lose him.

Murmuring apologies, I pushed around the lady with the suitcase, who grunted something not very polite in return.

I didn't care. The only thing I was concerned with was following Phil.

I followed him along the winding corridors, terrified he was going to spot me, but he didn't once look back over his shoulder. Then again, how often did any of us do that? We were all lost in our own little worlds, focused on our own lives, giving little thought to the people around us.

The day Jenna went missing, I had no premonition, no alarm bells sounding, no sixth sense warning me to keep a closer eye on Jenna. I hadn't picked up on anything that indicated someone lurked close by, someone who was about to snatch the most precious thing in my sister's life away.

I tried to follow Phil through the gate at the exit of the underground station, but the gate refused to open. In my panic, I slammed the Oyster card hard on the top of the sensor. My actions caught the attention of one of the underground staff, who started making his way towards me. Thankfully, on the third attempt, the sensor read the card and the gates opened, allowing me to dart forward and race up the stairs after Phil.

I was too disorientated even to pay any attention to the name of the station. The only thing I focused on was Phil.

When I burst out of the underground station into the

daylight and fresh air, I was terrified I'd lost him. I looked in every direction, but there was no sign of him.

People were pouring out of the station behind me, making disapproving tutting noises because I had dared to stop rather than go along with the tide of commuters.

But I couldn't move until I knew which direction Phil had taken. Had he turned left or right out of the station? I was just beginning to think I would have to take a gamble when a bus pulled away on the other side of the road, and I saw Phil.

There was a crossing a few yards away, and I ran up to it, jabbing the button. The road was far too busy to run across safely without waiting for the pedestrian crossing, and I'd already had one near miss with a car today. I didn't really want to repeat the experience.

But as Phil walked further and further away, I grew desperate. A red single-decker bus was coming towards me, slow and steady, and on the other side of the road, there was a white van, travelling at a sedate pace.

I went for the gap, racing forward. I heard a collective gasp from the people who'd been waiting at the crossing beside me. I passed in front of the bus with plenty of room to spare, but the white van was a close call. A horn sounded.

I held up a hand in apology and jogged to the other side of the pavement before ducking into a shop doorway. The blast from the van's horn had drawn the attention of people nearby, and the last thing I wanted, was for Phil to turn around and see me.

After a few seconds, I dared to move forward again. Had he seen me?

But Phil was walking at a steady pace, and there was nothing to make me think he'd spotted me. I fell into step behind him, walking quickly to close some of the distance between us.

I followed him for at least ten minutes. We left the busy streets, full of shops and people, and I pulled back a little. Phil's pace slowed a little as we approached a school. A primary school.

My heart beat faster. Was he here to pick up a child? Jenna should have started school by now. By the time we were level with the school, my heart was hammering in my chest.

Then I noticed he'd only slowed to pull his phone out of his pocket and he carried on walking past the school without looking back.

How stupid. It was almost seven o'clock at night. He wouldn't be picking up a child from school at this time.

Phil took the next left, and I followed him into a much quieter, residential road. Then he took the second turning on the left into Brierley Crescent.

He stopped at the third house along, a narrow, terraced house, and jostled in his pockets for his keys. I waited on the other side of the road, half hidden behind a small birch tree and a parked car.

When Phil disappeared inside, I stood there wondering what to do next. How could I tell whether he had a child in there with him?

A light came on downstairs, but it was still light enough not to need them everywhere. Upstairs, I could see two windows. One looked like a bathroom window, with a blind pulled halfway down.

There was a Velux window in the roof, so I guessed the attic had been converted. The house wasn't huge, but there would certainly be enough room for a man and a small child to live there.

Yellow curtains hung in the bedroom window. Was that an unusual colour choice for a man living alone? Not necessarily, but they could be the colour curtains someone might pick out for a child's bedroom.

I ran my fingers through my hair, debating what to do next. I had come so far to get answers and had managed to get absolutely nothing.

I tapped my hand against the side of my leg, trying to think what to do. I *should* turn around and go home. I *should* admit my fears to someone else and talk it through. And I definitely *should* see that therapist. By anyone's standards, including my own, I was going too far.

But what would I say to the police? They were hardly going to investigate a man because I'd had a bad dream. They would laugh me out of the station, and who could blame them?

I doubted myself, so why would anybody else take me seriously?

Did I really think Phil could harm Jenna? No. He couldn't

have. At least, I was ninety-nine percent sure he couldn't have.

As I stood there, trying to talk myself out of this craziness, I came to realise it was pointless. I'd come this far and wasn't about to give up now. I looked over my shoulder to check for traffic and then crossed the road.

Luke was going to be furious, and if my Mum found out... Well, it would only add to her stress levels, but I couldn't leave here without knowing for sure.

I reached up and pressed the gold-coloured doorbell and stared at the green door until it opened.

When he opened the door and recognised me, Phil Bowman stood perfectly still, and his face paled dramatically.

CHAPTER TWENTY-SEVEN

Phil stared down at me for so long I thought he was going to shut the door in my face, but after a moment, his pained expression faded, and he let out a heavy sigh.

"Beth, what are you doing here?"

I hesitated. Should I tell him the truth? No. If I told him the reason I was here, he would tell me to leave, and I needed to get inside to prove to myself that he didn't have Jenna.

"I was just passing," I said and waited to see if he pointed out my obvious lie.

Phil frowned. "How did you know where I live?"

I could tell him that his brother had given me the address, but I didn't want to drag Luke into it.

"I'd been to visit a friend, and as I was walking back to the underground station, I saw you and thought I'd say hello."

"Right," Phil said, making it clear with that single word he didn't believe me.

"Are you going to invite me in?" I plastered a smile on my face, trying to look like this was a normal social call.

He hesitated for a moment, keeping his hand on the front door, and then finally took a step back, allowing me to enter.

The hallway walls were painted magnolia, and the floor was covered with light-coloured wood. I wasn't sure if it was real wood or veneer, but if it was veneer, it was pretty good quality.

He led me down the hall and into an open plan living area. There were no pictures or mirrors on the walls. The kitchen was at one end, all chrome and black appliances and black tiles on the floor. A small, round dining table was wedged in behind a cream leather sofa. The living area looked a little bit bigger than it had from outside, but that was because it was sparsely furnished.

There were no photographs anywhere. It didn't look like a home.

"So, what can I do for you, Beth?" Phil asked.

"I'll be honest with you, Phil," I said, intending to be anything but. "I saw you the other day in Oxford and tried to say hello. I'm pretty sure you saw me, but you looked a bit anxious. I wanted to make sure you're okay."

I hated myself for the false note of concern in my voice because I did care about Phil. Even so, my worry for Jenna trumped any concern I had for Phil.

"Right." Phil pushed his glasses back on the bridge of his nose and blinked a couple of times. "Sorry about that. I wasn't expecting to see you, and to be honest, I don't choose to spend time with people from Woodstock these days. I can't stand people looking at me with pity and asking how I'm getting on all the time."

That I could understand. The concern of people who were practically strangers could be suffocating. It felt like they were delving into your life when you didn't want or need their interest.

But I wasn't a stranger. I'd spent a lot of time with Phil and Luke when we were younger and thought he would consider me a friend.

It was laughable that I was feeling hurt because he didn't consider me a friend when I was wondering whether he was a child abductor.

"I don't want to pry. I just want to know if you are okay."

Phil stood rigidly beside the kitchen counter. He was determined not to make me feel welcome or offer me a drink. I could tell he was only barely holding himself back from telling me to leave.

And that made me feel uneasy. The man who lived in this house was not the same Phil Bowman I'd known years ago. The cold, detached man in front of me was nothing like Luke's nerdy, teasing, older brother.

"How long have you lived here?"

Phil blinked a couple of times as though surprised by my question. "Just over a year."

"It's nice. I mean, it looks like the perfect place for a man on his own, a great bachelor pad," I said and could have kicked myself as soon as the words left my mouth.

Phil nodded stiffly.

"I meant the design, you know, the black and chrome, not that..." I trailed off. "Do you live here alone?"

Phil frowned, and a muscle twitched at the corner of his mouth. He was losing patience with me rapidly.

"Of course, who else would live here?"

He practically spat the words at me, and feeling nervous, I took a step back. I'd been so concerned about people thinking I was crazy that I hadn't told anyone where I was going. If something happened to me, no one would connect that to Phil.

"I told Mum I was popping in to see you," I lied. "She asked me to say hello."

Phil nodded, and despite the atmosphere between us, he managed a small smile. "Give her my regards. I always liked your mum and dad."

Both Luke and Phil had spent time with my parents. They'd shared family events with us-going out for meals, sharing birthday celebrations, barbecues in the garden. The type of family gatherings that Luke and Phil's mum never had time for. I suppose it was because, for most of their childhood, she'd been a single mum, struggling to bring up two boys. She didn't have much time or money to spend on those sorts of things.

Because Phil was older than us, he'd spent less time at our house than Luke, but he'd still come along to the occasional barbecue and meals to celebrate our birthdays. My mum and dad had taken Luke out for his seventeenth birthday when they learned his mother was going to be on a business trip. Phil had tagged along, playing it cool, but when we got home, I overheard him thanking my mum and dad sincerely.

As memory after memory hit me in quick succession, I felt my doubts about Phil lessen. The Phil I'd known would never have taken Jenna. I felt lightheaded and clutched the side of the kitchen counter.

"Are you all right, Beth?" Phil asked as he grabbed my elbow.

I closed my eyes. "Yes, sorry, I just skipped lunch today."

"Come and sit down." He waited for me to sit down at the small dining room table before going back into the kitchen and grabbing me a glass of water. He set it down in front of me.

"Drink that and try to relax. I haven't got much food in the house, but I could stretch to a bowl of cereal if that would help."

I shook my head. "Thanks, but I'll be fine. I'll get some dinner on the way home."

I rested my forehead in my hands for a moment and then took a sip of the water as I considered my options.

If I had any sense, I'd say goodbye to Phil and go straight

home. There was no sign of a child living in this house, no teddy bears, no toys. Nothing.

The back of my throat ached, and to my horror, my eyes filled with tears. I was losing it again. Just like last time.

Phil pulled out another chair at the dining table and sat down beside me. "Oh, Christ, Beth. Don't cry."

"I'm sorry," I said, wiping my eyes and sniffing back tears. "I don't know what's wrong with me." I watched him carefully. "Out of everybody, you should understand."

Phil's expression grew guarded. "Understand what?"

"I keep thinking about the day Jenna went missing, trying to work things out in my head, and I can't. It's driving me crazy."

Phil was quiet for a moment and then said, "You feel guilty."

Only three simple words but they packed so much emotional punch I felt like he'd thrown a bucket of cold water over me. I managed to nod.

"I feel guilty, too. That's why I can't talk to people about them. I was driving, and by rights, it should have been me who died that day. It was my mistake. I should have been the one to pay, not my wife and daughter. How can anyone function normally after something like that?"

I nodded again. "Exactly. Anyone else would be furious with me, or hurt, but I thought you'd understand."

Phil's forehead crinkled in confusion, and he reached up to shove his glasses back on the bridge of his nose again.

"I'm really sorry, Phil. I don't really believe it…" I struggled with the words. "I had to come and see you to put my mind at rest. Deep down, I always knew you could never have done it."

"You're not making any sense, Beth."

How could I expect Phil to make sense of what I was saying when I didn't understand the way my own mind was working?

"I remembered how alike Jenna and Isabel were, and I got it into my head…." I paused to wipe away a tear and take a breath. "For some stupid reason, I fixated on the idea you might have taken her because she reminded you of Isabel and –"

"Jesus Christ."

I broke off and looked up at Phil. He was never going to forgive me for thinking these things. I shouldn't have told him. I shook my head, unable to explain further.

"And that's why you're here today? To see if you can find Jenna? You think I'm hiding her here?"

"I don't know where else to look."

My voice shook as I spoke, and Phil looked away from me as he shook his head in disgust.

After a moment, he placed his hands flat on the table and narrowed his eyes. "So, what are you waiting for? Go and have a look around. Knock yourself out."

I hesitated. He was being sarcastic. I knew that much, but a chance to look around was what I wanted and why I'd come here in the first place.

"You don't mind if I have a quick look around?"

His face paled. "Jesus, you really do think I had something to do with it, don't you?"

"No... Not really, but this way I get to make sure and stop thinking about it."

He flicked a hand. "Go ahead. I'll wait here."

I got up from the table, pushing the chair back so it rasped against the floor tiles. Trying to ignore Phil's eyes boring into my back, I walked out of the open plan area and back into the hallway. There was a small door under the stairs. When I opened it I saw it had been converted into a small downstairs toilet.

I shut the door behind me and went upstairs. Although the stairs were laid with a thick new carpet, the stairs still creaked beneath my feet.

Upstairs, there were two bedrooms and one bathroom. The one with the yellow curtains was at the front of the house, and I checked that first. It had white walls, and the bed was made up with white linen, with a bright yellow cushion as an accent piece resting on the pillows.

A guest room. No surprises there.

The main bedroom, I guessed was Phil's room. It was decorated in various shades of grey, and there were no toys, puzzles or books to be seen. I walked forward and opened the wardrobe. No children's clothes hung from the rails.

I made my way back to the top of the stairs, and my gaze drifted up to the hatch in the ceiling. I'd seen the window in the roof from outside. Was there another room up there? Was it for storage?

I was about to ask Phil if he had a ladder so I could look in the loft room because, well, why not? I'd already made a complete fool of myself. I might as well go for broke.

The doorbell rang.

I froze at the top of the stairs, feeling awkward, and decided to wait upstairs until Phil had dealt with his visitor.

The front door wasn't visible from my spot on the upstairs landing, and when Phil opened the door, I couldn't see him.

I waited silently.

"I wasn't expecting you," Phil said.

"Nice to see you, too," came the reply.

I recognised that voice. My stomach flipped over. I closed my eyes and covered my face with my hands. *Luke.* Jesus. He was never going to forgive me for this.

"It's good timing really," Phil said as I heard the door shut. "Beth just turned up."

"Beth?"

"Yes. Beth. Beth Farrow."

"What's she doing here?"

"Looking for Jenna. You should go upstairs and talk to her. Apparently, she thinks I could be hiding Jenna because she

256

looked like Isabel. She's checking the bedrooms as we speak."

I heard Luke curse swiftly followed by the sound of his footsteps as he began to climb the stairs.

I froze. There was no way out. I'd been caught red-handed.

CHAPTER TWENTY-EIGHT

I winced at the expression on Luke's face. The mixture of fury and disappointment made me feel even worse.

"I'm sorry. I just had to make sure."

"Don't you think he's been through enough," Luke said in a low, dangerous voice, barely above a whisper. "How could you, Beth?"

I didn't have an answer for that question. Luke was right. My actions today had been completely selfish. Even though I was aware my turning up on Phil's doorstep would upset him, I hadn't been able to stop myself. A compulsion drove me to follow every clue that could lead me to Jenna no matter who I hurt along the way.

"Did you know I'd be here?" I wondered if I'd been that obvious. Maybe my motives were more transparent than I'd thought.

Luke shot me a scornful look. "After you expressed such concern for Phil, I thought I'd better check on him and try to persuade him to come out for a beer and a chat tonight. I had no idea you were here."

I followed Luke down the stairs, and Phil met us at the bottom.

"Did you drive?" Phil asked.

Luke nodded.

"Good, maybe you should take Beth home." Phil turned to look at me. "I take it you're satisfied with your search?"

"Well, I didn't look in the loft. Have you had it converted?"

"Jesus Christ, Beth!"

Luke practically growled behind me. He took hold of my forearm, opened the front door and pulled me out of the house. "That's enough. Get a grip."

I stood on the cracked pavement and watched miserably as Luke said goodbye to his brother. My gaze drifted up towards the Velux window in the roof. There was probably quite a good size room up there.

Phil noticed me staring. "It's just storage space. I don't even have a ladder indoors."

"I'm sorry," I started to say, but Phil turned around and shut the door on me .

"Come on," Luke said as he strode ahead. "I'll take you home."

I had to walk quickly to catch up with him. He'd parked his car, a grey Volvo estate, around the corner.

Luke's hands gripped the steering wheel tightly as he drove out of London. The traffic was still busy. I said nothing for the first fifteen minutes of the journey, wanting to give Luke time to calm down. He had every right to be angry, and I knew him well enough to know he needed time to think before he would consider my point of view. Even so, it took a lot of effort to keep my mouth shut and not beg for his forgiveness.

After fifteen minutes, he reached over and turned the radio on. He kept the music low, but it was better than enduring the weight of silence that had been hanging over us.

"Why didn't you tell me you were thinking of going to visit Phil?" he asked once we were on the motorway.

"Because you would have tried to stop me," I said honestly.

He huffed under his breath. "Yes, I would because it was a crazy thing to do."

"You won't mention this to Mum, will you?" I felt like a teenager asking someone not to tell tales to my mother.

But it wasn't because I wanted to stay out of trouble. I wasn't worried about my own skin this time, not like ten years ago when I'd had to persuade Luke to cover for me because I'd been given an after-school detention due to smoking behind the sports hall.

"I'm not sure," Luke said.

I straightened and turned towards him. What did he mean?

I'd never seriously considered the possibility of Luke ratting on me.

"She worries about me," I snapped. "She doesn't need more on her plate at the moment, Luke."

"Then you should have thought about that before you did something so stupid." His gaze shifted to meet mine briefly before he focused back on the road and slowed the car to a crawl behind a red Fiesta.

"You can't do things like this, Beth," he said quietly, staring straight ahead. "This is how it happened last time."

I swallowed hard, not trusting myself to answer. It hurt to hear those words, mostly because I knew they were true. It was reckless and stupid to rush off to London based on a far-fetched theory, but I couldn't seem to stop myself. The *what if* question played at the back of my mind, taunting and tempting me until I couldn't resist and had to take a chance just in case.

Luke was wrong, though. This wasn't how it had happened last time. I'd learned from the past and knew no one would listen to me without solid proof. This time, I hadn't confided in anyone. The police wouldn't want to know if I didn't have feasible evidence.

I felt thoroughly miserable and must have looked it, too, because Luke reached over and squeezed my shoulder.

"It's not the end of the world," he said. "But I'm going to need you to promise me if you even consider doing something like this again you will talk it over with me or your mum first."

"Because I can't trust my own judgement, you mean?"

"Well, I wasn't going to put it exactly like that, but yes. Seriously, Beth, I'm worried about you."

I leant back in the seat and turned to look out of the passenger window as we crawled through the traffic. "I'm sorry. I didn't mean to upset Phil. That was the last thing I wanted to do, but it's like I have a compulsion. Once the crazy idea he might have had something to do with Jenna's disappearance was in my head, it niggled away at me until I couldn't think about anything else. I just wanted to rule him out."

"Right, the next time you feel like that, tell me. We'll talk about it."

"You'll try to talk me out of it, you mean."

"Only for your own good."

Luke hadn't forgiven me completely, but he was coming around to the idea. It was more than I deserved. By the time we drove into Woodstock, the atmosphere between us had thawed considerably.

As he turned onto the High Street we passed the local Co-op, and I said, "Could you drop me here? I want to get something from the shop."

I still felt a little light-headed but hadn't wanted to tell Luke I hadn't eaten because he'd insist on us stopping for food, and I wanted some time alone.

Guilt was weighing heavily on my shoulders. I'd screwed

up and needed to mull things over without feeling judged or seeing the disappointment in Luke's eyes.

Luke pulled over to the side of the road. "Do you want me to wait?"

I shook my head as I unclipped the seatbelt. "No, don't be silly. The house is only around the corner, and I'm not planning to buy that much from the shop." I reached for the door handle. "I really am sorry. Thanks for the lift home."

"You're welcome."

Luke waited until I was just about to step into the Co-op before driving off. Even though I'd wanted to be alone, I felt hollow seeing him leave.

I took a deep breath and stepped inside the little supermarket, grabbed a basket and headed for the convenience food aisle. I wanted something easy to cook. I was regretting texting Mum earlier and telling her not to save me anything. I looked down at the ready meals despondently.

Scooping up a chilled chicken tikka masala with rice, I studied the front of the packet. The picture of curry on the front looked good, but when I pulled back the cardboard and looked at the food beneath the polythene, it didn't look so appetising.

"Hi, Beth."

I turned around and saw Pippa standing behind me, clutching a bottle of wine.

"Everything all right?" She looked down at the microwave meal for one in my hand.

I shrugged. "Fine, it's just been a long day."

"For me, too." She raised the bottle of wine and then tilted her head to the side. "I don't suppose you fancy joining me, do you? I was thinking about getting an Indian takeaway." She nodded at the packet in my hand. "I'm pretty sure it will taste better than that."

Tired, and bone weary after my disastrous evening, I was going to refuse, but Pippa's warm smile made me reconsider.

I placed the ready meal back on the shelf and nodded. "An Indian takeaway sounds perfect."

After queuing at the checkout to pay for the wine, we headed over to the local Indian restaurant. We sat in the small reception area, crunching our way through a mound of poppadoms, and I listened to Pippa tell me how she'd spent her day dealing with shoddy suppliers.

I let her words wash over me and tried to relax. Pippa's problems were minor in the grand scheme of things, but I tried to nod at the right moments and sound supportive. Perhaps Daniel was right. Maybe I was too self-involved.

We carried the takeaway back to Pippa's house and ate it at her kitchen table. The chicken biryani was as good as I'd remembered, and we shared the chicken tikka masala, using nan bread to mop up the sauce as we sipped Pinot Grigio.

"Ugh," Pippa said as she took another sip of her wine and screwed up her nose. "It's not cold enough for me. I know it's sacrilege to dilute good wine, but I'm going to put an ice cube in mine. Do you want one?"

I shook my head. My mouth was too full of chicken biryani to respond.

"You're right," I said when Pippa sat back down and placed her wine glass on the table. "This is a million times better than a microwave meal."

"I think that has something to do with the half a pound of ghee they put into each curry. It's fattening but delicious." She grinned and cheerfully took another bite.

Pippa had fairy lights set up around the French doors that led to the garden. They weren't very bright but gave out a subtle glow, lighting up the plants on the patio.

"You've made your house look lovely," I said and meant it.

It was hard not to compare it to Phil Bowman's house. Pippa's house was a real home, comfortable and warm, and a direct contrast to Phil's austere house.

"Thanks," Pippa said, raising her glass to chink it against mine. "Have you decided if you're going to go back to Dubai?"

I took a sip of my wine before replying. "Not yet, but the way I'm feeling at the moment has made me want to stick around."

I wondered whether Pippa knew about Daniel's debts and thought about mentioning it. It was bitchy of me to consider going behind his back, but I was still furious with him. But telling Pippa wouldn't do much good. It wouldn't make me feel better or get Mum's money back, and it would upset Pippa. She had done very well for herself and had worked hard for her success. I hoped Daniel wasn't viewing Pippa as an easy target for money.

I needed to push Daniel's debts out of my head until after we found out what had happened to Jenna.

One way or another, things would work out. I could go back to work in Dubai and send money home so Mum could pay the mortgage, or I could get a job here and live at home while I paid off the loan. We would get through it somehow. Everyday problems I could deal with. They seemed small in comparison to the mystery surrounding Jenna's disappearance.

"How are things going with you and Daniel?" I asked.

I wanted to ask whether Daniel had told her about the photograph of Jenna, but by asking the question I would give the game away.

Pippa smiled happily and leant forward. "Between you and me, things are going very well." She waggled her eyebrows suggestively. "In fact, I think he might be on the verge of asking me to marry him."

I nearly choked on a mouthful of chicken tikka. "Really? Wow."

The smile left Pippa's face. "You think it's too soon, don't you?"

"No, not at all. I think it's great news." I raised my wine-glass. "Congratulations."

"Well, he hasn't actually asked me yet, but I'm sure it's only a matter of time."

"So, are you and Mark divorced now?" I knew they'd separated when Mark moved to Warwickshire, but I didn't know whether they'd gone through the formalities of a divorce.

"Oh, yes, that's all done and dusted now. Between you and me, it feels like a lifetime ago."

After we'd finished the bottle of wine, Pippa made us coffee. I turned down the whiskey she generously added to her own cup. I wanted to take my prescription tablets tonight, and I'd already had wine. Mixing them with alcohol was probably unwise.

We cleared the table before rinsing off the plates and then stacking the dishwasher.

"Thanks for tonight," I said as I drained the last of my coffee.

"No problem. I enjoyed it. If you're sticking around, we should make it a regular thing."

"I'd like that." I said, realising to my surprise that I meant it.

I needed to start living a normal life and that meant interacting with people, making friends and keeping them. Once we'd found Jenna, I wanted to believe everything would be back to normal.

Pippa walked me to the door, and as she switched on the

light in the hallway, I saw a children's puzzle resting on the telephone table. I hadn't spotted it as we came in.

The sight of it produced a bittersweet memory as I remembered how Jenna had loved puzzles. Her favourite one had been a puzzle of a pig splashing in muddy puddles, and she couldn't get enough of it. She'd been good at them, too, and Kate had been very proud of her ability to fit together the pieces of a puzzle meant for older children.

Pippa followed my gaze. "It's a present for my cousin's little girl. I've not seen her for ages. I know presents are no substitute for visiting, but it eases my conscience a little bit."

"I'm sure she'll appreciate it."

I said goodnight to Pippa and walked down the steps to the pavement. The air was fresh and cool now, and the sun had long since set. The combination of wine and a large dinner made me feel sleepy, and I was glad I only had a short walk home.

My route took me past the Parsons's thatched cottage, reminding me of Dawn's odd behaviour earlier. I turned away refusing to look at the creepy cottage with its dark, glinting windows. I had more than enough to worry about now without adding Dawn Parsons to my list.

CHAPTER TWENTY-NINE

Mum was still awake when I let myself in. It was after ten o'clock, and she was in the kitchen making hot chocolate.

She looked up as I entered the kitchen. "Did you have a nice evening?"

I knew she was trying to contain her curiosity, even though she wanted to give me the third degree about where I'd been.

"Sorry I'm late. I bumped into Pippa on the way back and joined her for an Indian."

"Want one?" Mum held up her mug.

She'd been mixing the cocoa powder and milk into paste. It was her special technique to make old-fashioned hot chocolate. She made it that way to avoid lumps because, according to Mum, there was nothing worse than lumpy hot chocolate. The shops stocked a dozen different instant varieties these days, which could be made with hot water, but Mum insisted they just didn't taste the same as proper old-fashioned cocoa.

I nodded. "Thanks."

My stomach churned in protest. After stuffing myself with Indian food, a sugary chocolate drink was not what I needed. But I wanted the comforting smell and taste of my favourite childhood drink.

"Did you hear anything from the police?"

Mum shook her head. "No, I would have called you if there'd been any news.

"I suppose they're still looking into Robin Vaughan, but as far as I know, they haven't found any links with Jenna's case."

I sat down at the kitchen table as Mum watched the milk heating on top of the stove.

I put my elbows on the table, leaning forward, suddenly feeling so, so tired. Mum wasn't going to ask me what I'd been up to today. It wasn't her style. Even when Kate and I were young, she would wait to for us to come to her with problems, thinking we were more likely to confide in her if she didn't badger us. Though I could tell it took an effort for her to avoid the questions she must want to ask.

I didn't think Luke would spill my secret, but things had a way of getting out, and I didn't want Mum to find out what I'd been doing this afternoon from someone else. It was my mistake, and I needed to own up to it. If I told her about it now, calmly and rationally, hopefully she wouldn't panic and think I was losing it again.

"I went to see Philip Bowman today."

Mum turned around, keeping one hand on the handle of the saucepan. "Philip Bowman? Why did you need to see him?"

I took a deep breath. "It was because of that weird dream I had. It's been bothering me."

"The nightmare?"

I nodded. "It was disturbing. Of course, it was just a dream, but I had to go and check."

Mum left the saucepan unattended and walked over to the table. "What do you mean? What did you have to check?"

"The dream I had was about Phil, and he had Jenna with him. He insisted Jenna was his daughter, Isabel." I shrugged. "I can't explain it. I know it sounds ridiculous, but the dream set me on edge."

Mum put a hand to her mouth. "Beth, what have you done?"

"Nothing. It's nothing to worry about. I just wanted to be honest with you. I went to see him today, talked to him and looked around his house, and there was absolutely no evidence he had anything to do with Jenna's disappearance."

Mum looked shocked. "Did you tell him you suspected he had something to do with it?"

"Not in so many words. I suppose that was implied, though."

"That poor man. He lost his wife and daughter just before Jenna went missing."

"Exactly. That's why I went to see him. I thought it might have tipped him over the edge."

Mum looked at me doubtfully. "I wish you would have told me what you were planning before you went to see him."

"That's what Luke said," I muttered.

"I always knew that boy had a good head on his shoulders," Mum said approvingly.

I shot up from my chair. "The milk!"

The pan had started to bubble over. Mum swore under her breath and quickly removed the milk from the heat.

When we'd cleared up the mess on the stove, we sat down opposite each other each with mugs of hot chocolate, and Mum asked, "You will let me know if you have any more of these…theories, won't you, Beth?"

I nodded, wishing I hadn't mentioned it. "I will. But it's not a big deal, honestly. I'm sure Phil understood."

I didn't actually believe any such thing. I thought Philip was hurt and furious, and quite rightly, too.

Mum blew over the top of her mug to cool the chocolate and shook her head. "Was there anything else that made you think he was involved in Jenna's disappearance?"

I shook my head, feeling foolish. A normal person wouldn't act on the basis of a dream. Then again, I'd known for quite some time that I wasn't normal by most people's standards.

CHAPTER THIRTY

The following morning, we had our coffee in the kitchen as usual. We had settled into a routine, drinking two pots between us every morning.

"Maybe you should make an appointment with Doctor Fitzgerald and ask for some of the same sleeping tablets he prescribed me. They have been helping. I slept okay last night," I said to Mum, noticing she looked even more tired this morning.

She nodded absently. "Yes, I might do that."

She poured fresh coffee into our mugs and set them on the table before turning back to the kitchen counter.

"Any plans for today?" Mum asked as she unwrapped a loaf of bread and stuck two slices into the bright red toaster.

She glanced at the clock, and I guessed she was counting down the minutes to 9 o'clock when the police were due to ring with an update. I tried to prepare myself for disappointment. There would probably be no news as usual, but I couldn't help hoping there would be some fresh developments in Jenna's case.

How could we have reached a dead-end? In this technologically advanced time, surely there was some way to trace the person who had sent the photograph of Jenna.

"I haven't made any plans," I said. "Maybe I could help you in the garden?"

"That would be nice. It's the Woodstock Women's Group's annual luncheon today. Would you like to come?"

I could think of better ways to spend my time. I shrugged. "It doesn't really sound like my sort of thing."

Mum peered closely at the toaster, and when she was satisfied the toast wasn't yet ready, she sat down opposite me at the table. "I would like you to come with me, Beth. It will do us good to keep busy. It won't be as bad as you think, and it's being held at the Bear Hotel this year, so the food will be decent."

"Will there be space for me? They must have catered for a set number of people."

Mum smiled and had a glint in her eye, which I was pretty sure meant: *you're not getting out of it that easily.* "It won't be a problem. Betty Booth-Ingleton had to cancel because she sprained her wrist, so there's a spare place."

How convenient. I was pretty sure Mum wanted me to go to lunch so she could keep an eye on me, and after my behaviour yesterday, it was probably no more than I deserved.

"Okay, I'll go."

"Good," Mum said.

She got up from the table as the slices of toast popped out of the toaster. I got up to and went to the fridge to get the butter. At the back of the top shelf, something caught my eye. It was a jar of home-made blackcurrant jam.

I smiled. Kate and I used to love that jam. I remember the first batch my mother made. She gave it to us on thickly-sliced wholemeal bread with a generous helping of butter. Kate and I had eaten it until we felt quite sick, our mouths and fingers sticky from the sugary jam.

I reached out and pulled the glass jar from the fridge. "I didn't know you kept jam in the fridge these days."

Mum glanced over to see what I was holding and then nodded. "Well, I'm sure it would be fine in the cupboard considering the amount of sugar that is in it, but the health and safety police advise everything to be stored in the fridge these days. Everyone has cut down on preservatives, but of course, that means everything goes out of date quickly."

"But this is home-made. You know exactly what goes into it, and there are no preservatives."

Mum began to butter the toast. "Yes, but it's only me here now, and I don't get through a jar very quickly, so I tend to keep it in the fridge to stop it going off. It was different when Jenna was here. It was her favourite, and she would have some everyday if she was allowed…" She trailed off, and I saw the effort it took for her to swallow back her tears.

I filled the sad silence by saying, "Yes, she loved it, and so did Kate and I when we were kids."

Mum nodded, still too choked up to reply.

I added a little dollop of blackcurrant jam to my toast for old times' sake, and it tasted so good, I managed to eat two slices, but Mum only nibbled at her single slice of toast.

"I hope you eat more at lunch," I said gently.

She pushed her plate away. "I've got a lump in my throat, I can't seem to swallow properly."

I knew exactly how she felt.

Detective Inspector Sharp called at nine AM, and as I had expected, he didn't have anything new for us. He did tell us they were following a new development in the Robin Vaughan case, but he couldn't elaborate because it didn't directly relate to Jenna. Of course, that didn't stop my mind working overtime, wondering if this new development would bring us closer to the truth.

I'd managed to push the idea of Phil Bowman being involved in Jenna's disappearance to the back of my mind. I'd embarrassed myself yesterday and hurt Luke in the process. I wouldn't make the same mistake again, even if the roof window at Phil's place niggled away at me. So, there was one room I hadn't explored. There was nothing sinister about it. He had been out at work all day. Did I really think he would leave a five-year-old child alone in an attic all day while he was at work?

No, I needed to focus my attention elsewhere.

After breakfast, I sent a text message to Luke, apologising once again and asking if he wanted to meet up tomorrow. When he didn't reply immediately, I assumed he was still very angry.

I turned my phone over and over in my hands, thinking about how to convince Luke my apology was sincere. As I restlessly paced the kitchen, I realised how ridiculously I was behaving. I'd apologised to Luke yesterday, and he had accepted my apology. Just because he hadn't replied to my message immediately, didn't mean he was ignoring me. He was at work and probably very busy.

Daniel had been right. I was selfishly acting as though I were the centre of the universe, and that wasn't a very attractive trait.

CHAPTER THIRTY-ONE

The Bear Hotel in Woodstock used to be a thirteenth century coaching inn. It was said that Elizabeth Taylor and Richard Burton had stayed there on numerous occasions in the seventies. The decor had been sympathetically updated and hadn't lost any of its character. The dark wood beams were still in place and some of the rooms were unusual shapes with low ceilings.

The Woodstock Women's luncheon was to be held in one of the small private dining rooms.

Many of the women were already milling about and chatting when Mum and I arrived. For some reason, nerves hit me as I stepped into the room. A dozen pair of eyes turned to look at us, and I froze.

Within a few seconds, the conversation level was back to normal. I had to remind myself that nobody else knew about the photograph. From the way some of the women turned to look curiously at me, it made me wonder if any of them knew more than they were letting on.

Most of the women had gathered at the end of the room beside the large window. A table had been set up in front of the window and was laden with glasses of wine and fruit juice. When Mum went over to talk to her friends, I took a moment to study the main dining table and find out who I would be sitting next to at lunch.

I tried to hide a grimace when I saw I was going to be wedged between Mrs Parsons, Dawn's mother, and Elizabeth, Pippa's mother.

Mrs Parsons wasn't really a problem, but she might give me a hard time because I hadn't given Dawn the pep talk she wanted me to. Well, I'd tried, and it hadn't gone well. Not only had her daughter ignored me, she had also bolted out of the room and hidden upstairs when I knocked on the door. I took that as a definite sign she didn't want to talk to me. I would have to find some way to let Mrs Parsons down gently.

Pippa's mother, Elizabeth, was worse than Marjorie Parsons. She was well known in Woodstock for being a snob. Still, I supposed I could put up with it for an hour or two. It wasn't as though I had anything better to do.

I walked over to the table beside the window and picked up a glass of white wine. I took a long sip. It wasn't as cold as I would have liked, but it tasted pretty good.

As soon as I'd swallowed my first mouthful of wine, Marjorie Parsons made a beeline for me. "Beth, how lovely to see you. I didn't know you were coming today otherwise I would have persuaded Dawn to come along, too."

I made a sound that was a cross between a disbelieving snort and a laugh before feeling guilty over how rudely I was behaving.

"I'm not sure Dawn really wants to speak to me, Mrs Parsons."

Mrs Parsons's brow furrowed in a frown. "Oh, I'm sure she does. She always looked up to you and Kate."

I couldn't make up my mind. Should I tell her how Dawn had reacted when I called around? If I didn't, she would think I couldn't be bothered.

I took a deep breath and blurted out the truth. "I did call on Dawn. She saw me from the downstairs window, but she didn't answer when I rang the doorbell."

The smile slipped from Marjorie Parsons's face. "Oh, I find that very hard to believe."

I bristled at the insinuation. Did she realise she was implying I was lying?

"Well, I rang the doorbell then I knocked on the door, but she still didn't open it." I shrugged and then took a large gulp of my white wine.

"Maybe she had some music on or perhaps she didn't hear you over the television."

I resisted the urge to roll my eyes. Dawn had seen me all right. She had looked straight at me and then scurried out of the room, but I didn't want to press the point with

Marjorie. She was only concerned about her daughter and that was natural. It wasn't her fault that her daughter was so odd.

A short lady I didn't recognise tapped the edge of her glass with a spoon and informed us it was time to sit down. I followed Marjorie to the table.

"Oh, we're sitting together," she said, smiling. "How lovely. You can tell me all about Dubai!"

I plastered on a smile as I slid into my seat. I kept the smile stretched over my lips as Pippa's mother sat down on my left hand side.

"Hello, Beth," she said in a bored tone. "How are you?"

But she didn't wait for me to reply before turning her back on me and talking to the person on her left.

I wasn't really surprised. I had no social connections and as such I wasn't worth Pippa's mother's time. It was surprising Pippa had turned out as well as she had with a mother like Elizabeth.

She didn't bother to turn around again until we were halfway through the main course. She looked at me through narrowed eyes and said, "I hear the Far East has done you a world of good. I'm glad to hear you have put all that break-down business behind you now."

My cheeks flushed, and it wasn't only because I was on my third glass of wine. "Actually, I've been in the Middle East, not the Far East."

I hadn't had a breakdown, not really. I had found coping

after Kate's death incredibly hard, which was understandable. I hated being gossiped about, and I knew anything I said to Elizabeth now would soon be spread amongst her little network.

"Well, I knew you'd gone abroad somewhere to recover," she said, waving her hand dismissively. "This chicken is rather tough." She poked it with a fork. "Your mother said you're practically back to normal now. That *is* good news."

I gave her a tight smile hoping she would change the subject. Unfortunately, Elizabeth didn't take the hint.

"It was such a tragedy, and I think your Mum took it very hard. Not only did she lose her granddaughter and daughter, she also had your problems to deal with. I hope you realise how lucky you are to have a mother like that."

I stared at the woman in disbelief. I was getting very close to telling her exactly what I thought about her comments. I especially resented the fact she was talking to me as though I didn't realise how difficult my mother had found the last couple of years, and implying that was my fault. I mean, I knew I had to take some of the blame. But it wasn't as though I'd intended to make things worse for her.

People like Pippa's mother thought they could say anything they damn well pleased from their perch of superiority.

I gestured for the waitress to top up my wine glass.

"Don't you think you've had enough. It's only lunchtime," she said mildly. "It's a bad habit to get into. In a year or two, you'll soon find wine at lunchtime puts a few pounds on the waistline."

"I don't drink like this every day," I snapped.

"I should hope not."

Marjorie Parsons, who had more sensitivity than Elizabeth, could see I was feeling stressed and put a hand on my arm. "It *is* ever such a nice wine," she said. "Fruity and not too dry."

Pippa's mother barely glanced at her. "It's not dry enough for me."

Childishly, just to make my point, after the waitress had topped up my glass, I gulped down half of it in one go.

That earned me a disapproving look from Pippa's mother.

"Dear me, Beth. That really isn't very ladylike."

I snapped and I resorted to the one thing I knew that would put Elizabeth in her place. It was wrong of me, but I was furious with the stuck up cow.

"I'm not interested in being ladylike. I'm all about equality now. Society has moved on." I turned to her and gave her my coldest smile. "Oh, I meant to say congratulations."

Elizabeth blinked at me. "What for?"

"Daniel and Pippa getting married, of course." I gave her a very unladylike wink and then downed the rest of my wine.

Of course, I regretted it almost immediately. The momentary satisfaction of seeing Elizabeth's face pale and her hurried attempts to pretend she knew all about it was satisfying, but only briefly.

Pippa had told me she expected Daniel to propose, and I'd

betrayed her confidence just to get one up on her horrible mother. What was the matter with me? I didn't even know myself any more. The old me would never have dreamt of betraying a confidence like that.

When the lunch was over, Mum scurried over to my side and asked me, "What was that all about? It looked as though there was some disagreement between you and Pippa's mother."

I didn't want to get into it so I just said, "You know what Elizabeth is like. She just made a few cutting comments. Nothing to worry about, though."

Mum watched me carefully for a moment, weighing up whether to believe me or not, but in the end, she smiled.

"Shall we head home?" She adjusted the strap of her handbag.

"Actually, I need to pop into the bank, and then I thought I might have a bit of a stroll around town."

"Oh, okay. I'll see you at home then."

I smiled brightly. "Yes, I won't be long."

I went to the ladies' room, reapplied some lipstick and waited for the other women to leave. I didn't really need to go to the bank. I did need another drink, though, and didn't want to put up with any disapproving comments or glances. Wasn't that the first sign you had a problem?

Hiding your drinking? Or was it drinking alone? I was intending to do both.

I washed my hands with the rose scented soap and took my time drying them. When I finally left the ladies' room and went back into the main part of the hotel, the Woodstock Women's group had left.

With a sigh of relief, I walked into the main bar and ordered a gin and tonic.

I took my glass over to a table by the window. There were a couple of people in the main bar, tourists I guessed from the look of them, but I didn't pay them any attention.

I gazed out of the multi-panelled window down towards the small green hollow that lead to the steps. I couldn't see Robin Vaughan's house from my seat, but I could picture it in my mind, those tall sandstone walls with the grey slate roof peeking out just above. The roof was the only thing you could see as you walked past those walls. I shivered, realising those walls had hidden his dirty secrets in the middle of town. I'd always considered Woodstock a safe haven before Jenna had been taken.

I gulped down my gin and tonic, barely tasting it. What had the police learned about Robin Vaughan so far? Had he ever done more than look at vile images online?

There had been talk around town of him employing a fancy lawyer to help him get off the charges. It made me feel sick.

I went to take another sip of my gin and tonic, and to my surprise, I realised my glass was empty.

I went back up to the bar, ordered another double and then

returned to sit moodily at my table. I fished my mobile phone out of my bag and saw that Luke still hadn't replied to my text message. He had his own life to live, and his own family problems to deal with. Who could blame him for not wanting to get dragged into mine?

I stared angrily towards the stone steps. They were like a siren's call. I needed to go down there. If I looked him in the eye, would I be able to tell whether he knew anything about Jenna's disappearance? Would he let me in if I rang the bell?

An elderly couple shuffled past my table. He had a newspaper tucked under his arm, and had loosened the collar of his shirt.

"Warm out there today," he muttered to no one in particular.

I didn't turn around. I wasn't the mood for conversation.

They sat down at a table behind mine.

"Look at that, it's disgusting." The man chucked his newspaper down on their table.

Despite my original intention to ignore them, curiosity made me turn. I couldn't make out the smaller text on the front page but I could see the lurid headline – Robin Vaughan fights to clear his name.

My fingers tightened around my glass.

"Nasty man," the woman commented and pulled a compact mirror out of her old-fashioned handbag.

"Well, that's the problem with society these days. He can afford a fancy lawyer, so he'll get off scot free, won't he?"

"Probably," his wife murmured in agreement as she peered into the mirror to check her make up.

"Shame he won't go to prison," the man grumbled. "I've heard what they do to the likes of him if he goes inside. Dirty scumbag."

"Terry!" his wife exclaimed, leaning forward. "Mind your language," she said, chastising him.

I tried to tune out the rest of their conversation, but it was too late. A seed had been planted in my mind.

I didn't know who Terry was, but he had a point. With a well-paid lawyer, Robin Vaughan did have a good chance of getting away with whatever he'd done. And if he got off these charges, did that mean the police would think twice about investigating him in relation to Jenna's disappearance?

I leant forward, resting my head in my hands. I couldn't face that. I couldn't bear the thought of him getting away with whatever he'd done.

I stood up and left the table without leaving a tip. I strode out of the bar and headed straight for Robin Vaughan's house.

CHAPTER THIRTY-TWO

It wasn't my wisest decision, and I probably should have known better after how things had gone yesterday with Phil. Although I'd had too much to drink, I couldn't blame the alcohol completely. The obsessive thoughts had taken over my mind, and I couldn't let things go.

Less than two minutes later, I was standing outside the walls surrounding Robin Vaughan's residence. There was nobody around, absolutely no sign of the angry mob who'd surrounded his fortress. People moved on fast. Fury and outrage had ebbed away as the residents of Woodstock went back to their everyday lives. In time, his crime would be a distant memory. Would he get away with it?

I moved closer to the gate and placed my finger on the intercom button, hesitating for only a moment before pushing it hard. There was a small camera lens at the top of the intercom, so he'd be able to see me if he was home. The thought of him watching me turned my stomach.

There was no answer. Was he out or just ignoring me? I tried again. But still, there was no answer. I gave the gate a shove, but it didn't budge. It was made of heavy, solid wood.

I swore and thumped the gate with the side of my fist in frustration. He was there. He just didn't want to speak to me. The coward.

I only wanted to talk to him. I had to find out whether he'd had anything to do with Jenna's disappearance.

I placed my hands on the sandstone wall and felt the rough surface scratch my fingers. I looked more carefully at the stone. It was crumbly in spots, but it was a relatively new wall, and having been made in the traditional way, there were many crevices and cracks. The walls were about seven foot high. Close up, it looked imposing but not quite the impenetrable fortress I'd thought. I nodded as I walked along the base of the wall, looking for the most suitable crevices I could use as a handhold or foothold.

Pausing at a good spot, I looked up. Could I really scale the wall? Did I dare?

I looked around, making sure I really was alone. There was a large, old house opposite, but I couldn't see any signs of life.

I pivoted back to the wall. Could I really climb over it without breaking my neck? And even if I got over the wall, would I be able to get inside the house?

Maybe not. But I could look in the windows, and if Robin

Vaughan was at home, it might pressure him into opening the front door to talk to me.

I reached up for the first crevice, stuck my foot in a hole at the bottom of the wall and tried to pull myself up. My first attempt wasn't successful. I slipped back down, and the rough stone scraped my hands.

I tried again. This time I made it to a second handhold and hung there perilously for a moment before dropping back to the floor.

It wasn't as easy as it looked.

Again, I reached up, this time trying to move faster, my feet scrabbling against the wall. I kept moving, even as my feet slipped and my grazed fingers began to bleed.

When I made it, puffing and panting, to the top of the wall, I hung there for a moment trying to get my breath back. I hadn't expected it to be quite so hard.

I didn't stay draped over Robin Vaughan's wall for long. If I was discovered, it wouldn't be easy to explain.

Motivated by the fact I didn't want anyone to see me perched on the wall, I flung one leg over and straddled the dusty top of the wall.

Then slowly, I slid down the other side, trying to slow my descent with my hands and feet and failing miserably. I plummeted down and landed with a bump at the bottom of the wall.

I felt a little woozy and when I tried to stand, a pain shot up my ankle. I was sober enough to realise that was going to hurt even more later.

Brushing my hands together, I looked around to get my bearings. I'd come down in a lawned area, surrounded by a few well-maintained shrubs. There were no flowers in the garden. The house was straight ahead of me, but I couldn't see anyone from where I stood.

The security cameras were in full view, but it was too late to worry about that now.

I marched up to the front door, my original plan to sneak around and look in the windows long forgotten. I needed to look Robin Vaughan in the eye and ask him whether he knew what had happened to Jenna.

I pressed my thumb on the doorbell and kept it pushed down. I could hear the cheerful chime inside.

"Open up, you bastard. I know you're in there," I muttered.

There was no movement from inside, but I wasn't going to give up easily. I must've stood there for a full minute with my thumb firmly on the doorbell. When the front door finally opened, I blinked in surprise.

The man facing me looked nothing like the flash, cocky Robin Vaughan I'd seen at the fête. The media-friendly, loud, colourful clothes were absent and he looked at least ten years older.

The pathetic man standing in front of me was barely recognisable. He had on a dark red dressing gown that hung open to reveal he wore a grubby white T-shirt and boxer shorts underneath. His mid-length hair stuck up at all angles as though he'd only just woken up. He clutched a bottle of whiskey in one hand as his bleary eyes watched me fearfully.

His lower lip trembled before he spoke. "What do you want?"

His fear gave me courage. I pushed open the door further, barging in and forcing him to stagger back.

"Who are you?" he demanded but there was no power in his voice, and I ignored him and walking further inside the house.

The place was ostentatiously decorated — black and grey flock wallpaper, gilt mirrors and red velvet curtains, which due to the size of the windows must have been custom-made.

I took the first doorway on my left and walked through a large sitting room. This room was decorated in the same shade of purple as a Cadbury's chocolate bar. A large archway led into another room — a modern kitchen.

"I don't understand what's going on." Robin Vaughan said as he trotted after me.

He didn't try to stop me. He just stood there shivering, looking like the pathetic figure he was.

"I'm going to look upstairs," I told him and turned, heading for the staircase.

He scurried after me. "What for? Are you with the police?"

I ignored his question. If he wanted to think I was with the police that was fine by me. He might be a little more forthcoming.

I went from bedroom to bedroom and even checked all the bathrooms, but there was no sign that a child had been here.

After I checked the last room upstairs, I leant back against the wall and let out a shaky breath. Even if Jenna had been brought here after she'd been taken, there was no reason to believe she would still be here now.

Two years. A lot could happen in two years.

Besides, the police had searched his home. If there was anything to be found, they would have found it. It was stupid of me to think I might pick up on something they'd missed. Did I think I possessed some sort of sixth sense? That I would somehow know if Jenna had been here?

I turned to look at Robin Vaughan who'd been following me from room to room. "What have you done?"

He shook his head. "Nothing, I haven't hurt anyone."

I looked at him scornfully.

"You're not with the police are you?" he asked. "Well, you better leave because the police are on their way."

I narrowed my eyes. "No, they're not. You didn't have a chance to ring them."

"I pressed my panic button before I opened the door."

I scrutinised his face, trying to guess whether he was lying to me. If the police were on their way, I was going to be in a hell of a lot of trouble.

"I haven't done anything wrong," I said, even though I knew climbing over someone's wall and trespassing was wrong. "You let me in."

He didn't have an answer to that, and his eyes darted backwards and forwards as he lifted the bottle of whiskey to his lips.

"Have you brought any children here?" I asked him.

He shook his head "No! Honestly, the police got the wrong end of the stick. They found something on my computer, but it wasn't mine. I dunno how it got there."

I looked scornfully at the pathetic, lying worm. "You're sick."

He held the bottle of whiskey to his chest, dribbling onto his white T-shirt.

Then his gaze lifted and he blinked a couple of times. "It was your niece that went missing, wasn't it?"

I clenched my fists at my sides and stepped closer to him. "What do you know about Jenna?"

He shook his head frantically, swaying as I took another step forward. "Nothing! I had nothing to do with that. I'm not a monster."

I shoved him in the middle of his chest. "Yes, you are. That's exactly what you are!"

He opened his mouth to defend himself but the doorbell

rang. A voice travelled up to us through the front door Robin Vaughan had left wide open when he chased after me. They called out, identifying themselves as police.

So, he hadn't been lying about that panic button, after all.

I thought about making a run for it then decided that would be an even worse decision than the other bad choices I'd made today. I headed for the stairs, determined to get my side of the story heard before Robin Vaughan.

I was met at the bottom of the stairs by two uniformed PCs.

"Who are you?" A stern-faced female PC asked. Her hair was streaked with grey, and her mouth was set in a thin, firm line as she waited for me to answer.

"I'm a neighbour. I just came to see if Mr Vaughan was all right. He wasn't answering the intercom."

Robin Vaughan was making his way slowly down the stairs, clutching the banister with one hand and his bottle of whiskey with the other.

"Is everything all right here, Mr Vaughan?" the female PC asked.

He nodded. "Yeah, she's leaving now."

"Why did you press the panic button?"

"Because she broke in," he pointed at me with his whiskey bottle.

"I did not. You let me in."

"Perhaps we should talk about this outside, please. What's your name?" the young male PC asked, looking at me suspiciously. He was tall and looked much younger than his female colleague. His sandy hair flopped forward over his forehead.

"She's the woman whose niece went missing a couple of years ago. She came here to accuse me. It's not fair. I'm being persecuted."

"We'll deal with this, Mr Vaughan. Is the rest of your house secure?" The female PC asked in a cold voice. I could tell she didn't want to stay here any longer than she had to. I didn't envy her this part of her job, protecting someone like Robin Vaughan.

I didn't hear any more of their conversation as the young, sandy-haired officer escorted me outside.

"Name?" he asked.

"Beth Farrow." There was no point in lying. It would only come back to haunt me.

He nodded. "Mr Vaughan mentioned your niece—"

"My niece is Jenna Creswell. She went missing from Wood-stock two years ago."

I deliberately used the word *is*.

His eyes softened a little. "So, this wasn't just a neighbourly visit then?"

I shook my head. "I didn't do anything wrong. I didn't hurt him, and he let me in."

He looked at my bloody fingers and then shifted his gaze to the wall. "I'm going to guess you scaled that wall."

I stared at the ground.

"Look, you probably don't want to hear it, but here's my advice. You stink like a brewery. Go home, sober up and come to the station tomorrow to make a statement."

I pulled a face. "Why do I need to make a statement? Nothing happened. There was no crime."

He raised an eyebrow. "You're lucky I'm not taking you in now. Go home, sober up, sleep on it, and I'll see you tomorrow. My name is PC Dawson." He handed me a card with his name on it and the address of the Thames Valley police station.

I sighed. I suppose it could have been worse, I might be able to get out of this without Mum finding out, or Daniel for that matter. I wondered whether the police departments would talk to each other and whether Detective Inspector Sharp or Sergeant Parker would find out. If they did, they were bound to mention it in front of Mum and Daniel.

What a waste of time. I still had no evidence Robin Vaughan had anything to do with Jenna's disappearance. What had I expected to happen? Did I really think he would admit everything to me just because I confronted him?

I blinked away angry tears and ran a hand through my hair in frustration.

"It's not so bad," the PC said. "I'm sure you'll just get a ticking off. But it's above my pay grade to ignore something like this. Come on, where do you live? We'll give you a lift home."

So with my cheeks burning with mortification, adding to

the rosy glow I'd already had from the alcohol, I was taken home in a marked police car.

Mum came rushing out, and I knew she assumed the police were here with news of Jenna, which of course, made me feel like even more of a failure.

I felt like I'd reached rock bottom, but I was wrong. There was worse to come.

CHAPTER THIRTY-THREE

By early evening, my pleasant alcohol buzz had worn off and morphed into the hangover from hell. My head was pounding, which hadn't been helped by Mum's sudden urge to vacuum every room in the house.

It would have been better if she'd yelled at me, or at least discussed what I had done. But she completely ignored it, acting as though it hadn't happened. The hurt and disappointed look on her face said it all, though.

She shot me worried looks when she thought I wasn't looking, and I knew she didn't want to talk about it in case she pulled the loose thread that would finally cause me to unravel completely.

Luke finally sent me a text message, saying he was sorry he'd had a busy day but tomorrow would be fine to meet up.

After swallowing two paracetamol, I tried to make myself

useful by unloading the dishwasher and watering Mum's bedding plants.

I was filling the watering can from the garden tap to water some geraniums when someone frantically hammered on the side gate.

By this time, Mum had finished vacuuming and was now wiping down the windowsills in the sun room in a desperate attempt to keep busy. She paused and looked at me before quickly walking to the side gate to open it.

The gate was on the left side of the house and led directly from the driveway into the back garden.

After Mum had opened the gate, I recognised the woman standing there. Patricia Morrison, who'd been our neighbour for over twenty years and lived three doors away.

"What is it, Patricia? What's wrong?" Mum asked.

"You'd better come quickly. I knew you wouldn't want to miss this. The police are carting off Dawn Parsons, and they're searching the house."

"Dawn? Why?" I asked, brushing my hands together and walking quickly through the side gate, determined to find out what was going on.

Mum and I charged around the side of the house and out onto the road and Patricia followed us.

"I don't know," she admitted. "But everyone is saying it's got something to do with your granddaughter, Rhonda,"

Patricia looked at Mum nervously as she spoke.

Mum pressed a hand against her chest and took in a deep breath as we saw police cars parked outside the Parsons's house. We walked quickly towards the thatched cottage. A number of residents had already gathered outside.

A policeman in a bright yellow jacket was attempting to persuade the crowd to step back out of the way, but people kept nipping forward to get a better view.

I didn't know what to do. I was repelled and didn't want to get any closer, but at the same time, I had to know what was going on.

Mum clutched my forearm. "It can't be anything to do with Jenna, Beth."

I don't know who Mum was trying to convince. Me or her. I linked my arm through hers as we walked towards the melee. As we drew level with the house, a female officer emerged with Dawn Parsons just behind her.

Dawn looked down at the floor as she lumbered towards the waiting police car.

From where I stood, I had a view into the living room — the room with the computer Dawn had been using when she wouldn't answer the door. A man in a white suit leaning over the computer.

"If this had something to do with Jenna, the police would have told us, wouldn't they?" Mum asked.

I couldn't respond. I didn't know what to say.

We stood beside the police car, and Dawn got closer and closer to us.

One of the neighbours called out, "What's this all about, Dawn? What's happened?"

"If you could move back please, ladies and gents," the beleaguered police constable in the yellow jacket said, holding out his arms and ushering them back.

Dawn had almost reached the police car. If I didn't say anything now, I might not get a chance to speak to her for a while. A thousand questions whirled in my mind, but I couldn't form a coherent sentence. I kept thinking back to the day Jenna went missing and remembering Dawn's thick fingers covered with the greasy face paint.

"Dawn!" I yelled.

She looked up sharply, her gaze meeting mine for a split second. She looked at me defiantly before ducking her head and disappearing into the back of the police car.

The police car left almost immediately, but some other vehicles stayed parked outside the Parsons's residence.

"They're doing something with her computer," I said, nodding at the living room window.

A forensics officer was putting the computer in a box.

"I need to talk to Marjorie," Mum said, stepping away from me and marching up the Parsons's driveway.

The officer maintaining the perimeter caught sight of her before she reached the house.

"Hey! You can't go in there."

Mum turned around and gave him a cold stare. "I am visiting my friend."

"It's not a good time right now, madam. As I'm sure you can see."

"I'm concerned about my friend's welfare," Mum said sharply. "Perhaps we could ask Marjorie whether she wants to see me or not?"

A look of relief passed over the young officer's face when DI Sharp stepped out of the house and onto the garden path.

"I don't think that's a very good idea, Mrs Farrow. Not right now."

"Has this got anything to do with Jenna?" I asked him.

"Let's go to your house so I can give you an update."

He smiled kindly at Mum and then me, but it was the kind of smile that made me nervous. He was trying too hard to be reassuring. It meant he had bad news to deliver.

I reached out to grasp Mum's hand.

"I would have appreciated an update earlier before we came upon a scene like this," Mum said.

"I'm sorry we couldn't let you know earlier. But we had to keep this quiet. We didn't want anyone tipping off Dawn."

"We wouldn't have tipped anyone off." Mum folded her arms over her chest.

"Quite so," Inspector Sharp said, refusing to get drawn into a debate. "My colleague, Sergeant Parker has gone to update Daniel Creswell. She is going to bring him here, and you can ask us questions."

"Have you found Jenna?" I asked in a quiet voice.

My throat was dry. After all this time, were we about to get the most devastating news?

Inspector Sharp shook his head as we walked along the lane towards our house. "No, not yet. But we are getting closer. We believe the photograph of Jenna was sent by Dawn."

"Dawn sent me a picture of Jenna?"

"We believe so," Inspector Sharp said as we reached the gate we'd left ajar.

Mum pushed open the metal gate, and we followed her along the garden path to the front door.

Inspector Sharp hadn't got very far with his explanation when Daniel and Sergeant Parker arrived.

"Have you heard?" Daniel asked as he burst into the kitchen.

Mum and I nodded, and Daniel sat down at the kitchen table. Sergeant Parker joined him, murmuring a polite greeting as she sat down.

"I'm so confused. None of this is making any sense," Mum said.

"I'll do my best to explain. Dawn sent the photograph of Jenna from an Oxford Internet Café. We have CCTV evidence of her entering the cafe. She used a public computer to access a website that can send text messages to mobile phones."

"But why would Dawn do that?" Daniel asked, and immediately before DI Sharp could reply, added, "Did she modify the photograph to make Jenna look older?" Daniel's gaze flickered to me. "Did you know about this?"

I shook my head and clenched my fists so tightly that my nails dug into my palms.

"Of course she didn't," Mum said.

"We have no reason to believe that the image was tampered with," DI Sharp said. "We will, of course, be questioning Dawn to ascertain how she got the photograph of Jenna."

"Do you think she was involved in Jenna's abduction?" Daniel asked.

"Does this mean Jenna is still alive?" Mum asked.

Inspector Sharp held up his hands to fend off questions. "I don't have all the answers for you yet. We will be questioning Dawn for the next few hours, and I will update you as soon as we get any fresh information. Sergeant Parker and I need to get back to the station so we can begin interviewing Dawn as soon as she's processed. Detective Sergeant Parker will be your point of contact, and she will phone you later this evening with an update."

After answering a few more questions, Detective Inspector Sharp and Detective Sergeant Parker left us alone with Daniel. We were all dazed and confused. None of this made any sense.

"Well, it looks like you were right about at least one of your stabs in the dark," Daniel said coldly. "Dawn Parsons was one of many people on your list of suspects."

I sat forward, leaning on the kitchen table and rested my forehead in my hand. He was expecting a reply, but I was too wrung out to argue.

We were so on edge that we all jumped when the doorbell rang.

Mum began to stand, but I put a hand out to stop her. "I'll get it."

I opened the door and was surprised to see Pippa standing there with a look of concern on her face.

"Oh, my God, Beth. I'm so sorry. I just heard that Dawn Parsons was taken away by the police! I was so worried, and I knew Daniel would be here so…"

I took a step back, opening the front door wide. "He is here, come in."

Pippa stepped inside and shot me an apologetic look. "I really am sorry to intrude at such a time, but I was so worried."

She walked quickly through to the kitchen.

Daniel stood up. A frown creased his forehead as she rushed up to him.

She grasped his hands. "Oh, I'm so sorry. Did you find out anything? Was it Dawn who sent the photograph?"

Daniel nodded. "It looks that way."

I couldn't help noticing how he softened his voice when he talked to her. He certainly didn't use that tone with me.

"Can I make anyone a drink?" I offered. My head was still pounding, and I couldn't think straight. I needed strong black coffee.

Daniel shook his head. "No, thanks. I should get going."

"Tell us if you hear anything, Daniel," Mum said.

He nodded. "I will."

The atmosphere was subdued as we said goodbye. I'd expected us to feel full of nervous energy now we were closer to finding Jenna, but it was like an unspoken cloud of fear hung over us. All of us were terrified of facing what could have happened to that sweet little girl.

If only I hadn't let go of her hand. If only I'd kept my eyes on her all the time. If only...

CHAPTER THIRTY-FOUR

After Daniel had left with Pippa, Mum and I sat at the kitchen table and discussed the situation, but neither of us could understand how Dawn was involved.

"Maybe, someone blackmailed her into taking part..." Mum suggested.

I kept glancing at the antique clock, wishing the phone would ring with fresh news. "I didn't think it would take so long. Why doesn't she just tell the police what she knows?"

"Do you think the police got it wrong?" Mum asked, stirring her tea. "Maybe Dawn just happened to be in that Internet cafe. Maybe they identified the wrong person?"

I folded my arms across my chest and shook my head. "I doubt it. I saw her face when she got into the police car. She looked guilty."

I knew guilt. The amount of guilt I'd experienced over the

last two years had made me an expert on it, and I could recognise it in another person.

"I want to speak to Marjorie," Mum said. "But I don't want to leave the house in case the police ring to update us."

"They have our mobile numbers."

"I know, but I don't want to take the call at Marjorie's."

I felt the same, and I had a feeling that Marjorie wouldn't have any answers anyway. She was blinkered and thought Dawn was a perpetual victim. People often saw what they wanted to, especially where family was concerned.

After an agonising, interminable wait, Detective Sergeant Leanne Parker telephoned at nine pm. Mum snatched up the phone and put it on speaker so I could hear both sides of the conversation.

"I'm calling because we promised you an update, but I'm afraid we haven't got very far with Dawn's interview. We are taking a break for the evening and will be getting straight back into the questioning tomorrow."

"Taking a break?" Mum asked with disbelief in her voice. "Surely you can't take a break until after you've found out what she knows about Jenna."

There was a pause on the other end of the line before Sergeant Parker responded. "I'm sorry, Mrs Farrow. I know you're desperate for news, and I wish I had more for you, but legally, there's only a certain amount of time we can question Dawn. Anyone in police custody is entitled to meal breaks and time to rest."

"Then why didn't you pick her up earlier?" I asked, leaning close to the phone.

"It took time to arrange the warrant," Sergeant Parker replied calmly. "We have been trying to get her to open up, but she is only giving yes or no answers to our questions. I'm hopeful we'll get more out of her tomorrow."

Mum looked at me, horrified. How would we get through the night when the truth about Jenna was almost within our grasp?

"But it's your job to get her to talk," I said. "She must have said something. Are you sure it was Dawn who sent the message? Has she admitted that much?"

"No, as I said, she's not been forthcoming. But she's under stress at the moment. When we start again tomorrow morning, the interview should be more productive."

I took a step back from the telephone. Unbelievable. Jenna had been taken by God knows who, and the police were pussy-footing around Dawn, who'd decided she didn't want to talk about it.

"Do you think Dawn took her? She was there. She could have." I was talking to Sergeant Parker, but I was looking at Mum.

Her skin had turned a strange shade of grey, and I reached out to grab her arm and steady her before she fell. I dragged over a chair and told her to sit down.

"Is everything all right?" Sergeant Parker asked.

"Mum's just feeling a bit dizzy." I put a hand on Mum's

shoulder, and she rested her head against my arm. "So what's the next step?"

"We'll come at Dawn again fresh tomorrow and offer her some inducements to talk."

At that point, I didn't care what they offered Dawn. I just wanted her to talk and tell us what she knew about Jenna.

"Is there any proof Dawn took the photograph?" I asked.

"Beth, we found the photograph on Dawn's phone. We think she must have emailed it to herself to access it from the computer in the chat room and then sent it to your phone from there. We know the message didn't come from Dawn's phone, so she was trying to cover her tracks. The fact the photograph was found on her phone leads me to suspect Dawn took the photograph. But we don't know that for sure. There are things we can look into, such as the time-stamp on the image to find out when the photograph was taken, and possibly find out where the photo was taken. We are looking into that now and will update you as soon as we have more information."

I nodded, forgetting that she couldn't see me. "Right, so you're not doing anything else tonight?"

"The work on Dawn's phone will continue as a priority, but we won't be questioning Dawn until tomorrow morning. We'll commence the interviews at eight thirty. I will contact you as soon as we take a break to give you an update."

"Okay. Thank you."

I hung up, wondering what on earth I was thanking her for. She was only doing her job, but it was frustrating beyond belief to think we were so close to finding out what had happened to Jenna, but there was nothing we could do but wait.

I turned my attention to Mum. "Are you feeling any better now?"

She nodded. "Yes, but I don't know how much more of this I can take. I just want to know one way or the other."

I squeezed her shoulder. "I'll make us a cup of tea."

I walked towards the kettle, but Mum stood up and shook her head.

"No. We haven't got time for that. The police don't have any answers for us, so I'm going to talk to Marjorie. Are you coming?"

I wasn't going to let Mum go alone, so I nodded and followed her out of the kitchen. I grabbed my jacket from the coat stand and then handed Mum hers.

It had been a warm day but the night air was chilly, and I wasn't one hundred percent convinced Mum was recovered after her dizzy spell. I didn't want her catching a chill.

As we approached the Parsons's thatched cottage, we saw Marjorie was still up because the lights were on downstairs. There was no sign of any police vehicles now, so I guessed they'd completed the search.

"Are you sure you're up to this?" I asked Mum as we walked up the Parsons's driveway.

"Yes," Mum said firmly as we reached the front door and she pressed the doorbell.

That pretty chocolate box cottage looked sinister at night. The thatched roof cast long shadows in the moonlight, and I suppressed a shudder as I looked up.

Marjorie's face appeared in the living room window. She looked at us sadly for a moment and then came to the front door. When she opened the door, it was immediately apparent she'd been crying.

She shook her head and opened her mouth, but no words came out.

"I'm sorry this has happened to you, Mrs Parsons," I said and meant it.

She may have been taken in by Dawn and didn't want to think badly of her, but Mrs Parsons had always been kind to us, and she didn't deserve this.

She stood back and opened the door wide so we could come inside. As we entered the sitting room, the Parsons's tomcat jumped up onto the windowsill, knocking over a pale lilac, pillar candle.

"Oh, Thomas, you naughty kitty," Mrs Parsons said, flapping her hands and shooing the cat away. She bent down to pick up the candle and put it back on the windowsill.

There was something familiar about that candle. When Mrs Parsons moved away from the windowsill, I picked it up. It smelt of lavender, and a purple ribbon was tied around the middle.

"This is lovely," I said. "Did you buy it?"

Mum looked at me as though I'd lost my mind. Asking

questions about a candle at a time like this must have seemed odd.

Mrs Parsons blinked at me in confusion.

"It's Dawn's. She was going to throw it away, but I told her I'd keep it if she didn't want it. I don't understand why she bought it if she didn't like it." She shook her head. "But it seems as though there are a lot of things I don't understand about my daughter."

Before we could reply, Mrs Parsons continued, "I was just about to make a cup of tea. Would you like one?"

Mum huffed with impatience.

But I said, "That would be nice, Marjorie, thanks."

Mum frowned but didn't contradict me.

As Marjorie left us and headed to the kitchen, I turned to face Mum. "It isn't her fault. We have to tread gently if we want to get anything out of her. Dawn's her daughter, and she won't want to believe she could have been involved in Jenna's disappearance."

Me being the one to tell Mum to calm down was a total role reversal.

"I know that. I don't know what you thought I was going to do, Beth. I'm perfectly calm."

She went to perch on the edge of the sofa, and I sat down beside her. As we waited, I tried to prepare what I was going to say to Marjorie.

Naturally, she would be defensive, but we needed her to

confide in us. I wanted us to be on the same side.

When Marjorie came back, carrying a large tray laden with a teapot, a jug of milk and three cups, I smiled and stood up to take the tray from her. I put it down on the coffee table.

"I just don't understand what's happening," Marjorie said as she stooped down to pour the tea.

"What did the police tell you?" Mum asked, edging forward on her seat.

"Not very much," Marjorie said as she handed Mum a cup of tea. "The police turned up on the doorstep, and when I answered the door, they asked if Dawn was home. We'd been watching television together, just like any other night, and when I led the police into the living room, Dawn turned white. She looked terrified. I've never seen her look so scared."

Marjorie passed me my cup of tea, and I thanked her. "Did Dawn tell you why the police are interested in her?"

"She didn't tell me anything. I got upset and demanded to know what's going on, but then they cautioned Dawn and said anything she said could be taken in evidence or something like that... Well, she took them at their word because she didn't speak again. She didn't even say goodbye."

"We think this had something to do with Jenna's disappearance," Mum said.

Marjorie nodded sadly. "The police must have made a mistake. There was some talk about a photograph, and they wanted to take Dawn's computer away. But I don't see how Dawn could be involved in Jenna's disappearance. She wouldn't do anything like that. She couldn't. She doesn't have it in her."

Marjorie picked up her own cup of tea with a shaking hand and turned to me. "You know her, Beth. Dawn could never have done something like that."

I was getting sick of her assumption I knew Dawn and that we'd been friends at some point. We hadn't. I'd once felt sorry for her, tried to reach out and it hadn't worked out well. That was all.

"Actually, Mrs Parsons, I really don't know Dawn very well, at all. We were at school together, but we weren't friends. She was a bully."

Mrs Parsons's face paled, and her eyes widened. "A bully? No, you've got that wrong. Dawn was never a bully. She was the one who got bullied. She would cry herself to sleep because of what they did to her at school."

"I'm not saying Dawn didn't get bullied. She did, but she was no angel. I stopped to speak to her on the way back from school once. I was only eleven and about half the size of Dawn, and do you know what she did when I tried to be friendly?"

Marjorie shook her head.

"She shoved me into the brook. And then she left me there. That's what I know about Dawn, Mrs Parsons."

With a smothered sob, Marjorie sunk down into an armchair and then put a hand over her eyes, as though she wanted to block out the truth. Maybe I'd gone too far. But if we convinced Marjorie her daughter wasn't a sweet, hard done by victim, she might be willing to help us.

"You never told me that," Mum said, turning to face me.

"It was a long time ago. Look," I said, trying to keep my voice even and calm, "Dawn wasn't perfect, but none of us are. Maybe she made a mistake. We need to know how she was involved in Jenna's disappearance. Was she helping someone? Did she just happen to stumble across someone snatching Jenna and..." I trailed off, not really sure where I was going with this. Had Dawn known who had taken Jenna all this time? Had she snatched Jenna herself?

"Dawn isn't perfect, but I know she would never have harmed so much as a hair on Jenna's head. Dawn is a kind-hearted girl. I'm sorry she did that to you when you were just children. But that isn't her typical behaviour. She's a good girl. She visits old Mrs Taverne two days a week and helps with her cleaning and ironing. She even does her shopping, and she doesn't get paid. She does it because she wants to help."

I looked down at my untouched tea. Where did we go from here? Marjorie wasn't prepared to accept Dawn's involvement, and any moment now she could ask us to leave.

"Tell me about Dawn," I said. "Which friends has she kept in contact with? Did her behaviour suddenly change two years ago?"

Mrs Parsons thought for a moment and then shook her head. "She's been getting more isolated over the past few years, but I didn't notice any change in her that I could pinpoint to the time Jenna went missing. She has a hard time making friends, and she lost her last job just after Jenna went missing, I think."

"Any boyfriends? Did you ever suspect she was sneaking off to see anyone?"

Mrs Parsons shook her head. "No, she preferred to stay at home. We watch the soaps together in the evenings. Occasionally, she'd go out on one of her walks."

"Where did she go on these walks?"

"Oh, I'm not sure exactly. She stayed local, though. She got one of those little gadgets that measure how many steps you do in a day. She used it to monitor her progress on the computer. In fact, her route will probably be on there. She showed me once and..." Mrs Parsons's voice trailed off as she turned her head to look for the computer and saw the empty space on the desk in the corner of the room.

I nodded slowly thinking things over. What if Dawn had discovered something on one of these walks? Could she have seen Jenna here in Woodstock?

"Maybe Dawn was trying to help. Her sending the photograph of Jenna to Beth could have been her attempt to help," Mum suggested.

Marjorie nodded frantically. "Yes, that must be it. She must have stumbled across something and didn't know what to do. She wouldn't have been a part of taking Jenna. I'm sure of that."

No matter how convinced Marjorie was, I was going to reserve judgement. Could Dawn have seen Jenna near

Robin Vaughan's house? But why would no one else have seen her?

"Did Dawn ever make any trips to London?" I hated myself for asking the question. Deep down, I didn't want to believe Luke's brother was involved, but I had to ask.

Marjorie shook her head. "No, why do you ask that?"

Mum watched me quizzically.

I picked up my cup of tea, even though I had a lump in my throat which made it hard to swallow. I took a sip and listened while Mum asked Marjorie Parsons more questions. But we went round and round in circles before we finally had to admit defeat.

Marjorie Parsons didn't hold any answers. At least, not the ones we needed.

CHAPTER THIRTY-FIVE

Mum went to bed, but I knew there would be no point in me trying to do the same. I couldn't sleep with all this hanging over me. I curled up on the sofa with the television on, the sound turned down low, and stared at the screen, not paying any attention to the film flickering over the screen.

At two AM, I heard a creak on the stairs and sat up. I was cold, and from where I'd been curled up on the sofa, my neck and back felt stiff.

Mum shuffled into the front room and gave a little start when she saw me.

"You couldn't sleep either?" I asked.

"It seems to be getting quite a habit," Mum said. "I needed a glass of water. Do you want one?"

I shook my head but stood up and stretched and then

followed her into the kitchen. "What do we do if Dawn doesn't talk?"

"She has to. Eventually. I just hope it won't be too late."

Mum didn't say too late for what. She didn't need to. In the pit of my stomach, I had a horrible, sinking feeling that had grown in intensity over the past few hours. Maybe we were already too late.

Whatever role Dawn had played in Jenna's disappearance, I found it hard to believe she was the mastermind.

Mum turned on the tap and filled her glass. "Did you tell anyone about the photograph of Jenna?"

I frowned, not quite following the change in conversation. My mind was fuzzy from lack of sleep. "No, of course not."

Mum took a sip of water and then set the glass down on the draining board. "I think Daniel must have told Pippa. He promised he wouldn't tell anyone."

"Well, that's not surprising. We know Daniel doesn't have a very good moral compass." My words were vindictive, covering a layer of guilt. I ran a hand through my hair. "Actually, I did tell someone about the photograph. Sorry. I should have mentioned it sooner."

Mum's eyes widened as she looked at me. "Why, Beth? Who did you tell?"

"It was only Luke. I'm sure he won't tell anybody. It was after I'd made that scene with his brother. I felt I owed him an explanation and... Well, I told him about the photograph so he would understand."

Mum sighed. "The problem is we can't be certain he hasn't told anybody else."

I couldn't argue with that. My gut reaction told me that Luke would keep my secret, especially one so important, but as far as Mum was concerned, I'd gone against my word.

"You're right. I shouldn't have told him. I was shaken up by the whole situation with Phil. I just wanted him to understand."

"I know, love."

We hadn't bothered to switch on the light in the kitchen. The full moon illuminated the kitchen without any need for artificial light.

"What do we do if Dawn doesn't talk?" Mum asked.

"She will," I replied with more conviction than I felt.

Mum refilled her glass with water, said goodnight and went back to bed. The sofa wasn't comfortable enough for me to spend all night on it, so I went to bed, too, fully expecting to lie awake for hours.

I lay on my back, interlaced my fingers and rested them my stomach. I closed my eyes and tried to recall every moment of the day Jenna went missing, focusing especially on where Dawn had been. I'd seen her at the face-painting station, but when Jenna went missing, Dawn had disappeared, too. Where had she gone? She told the police she went to get something from the car... But had she? Or had she been part of a plan to snatch Jenna?

I tried to concentrate and remember every little detail, but for some reason, my mind kept returning to the exchange between Daniel and Kate just before I had taken Jenna to the bouncy castle.

There had been tension between them, and I'd meant to ask Kate about it later when I got to speak to her alone, but after Jenna had gone missing, we had no time for anything else.

Had Kate suspected something was going on between Daniel and Pippa? Had Daniel and Pippa started their affair before Kate's death? Or even before Jenna went missing?

Whatever it was, something had been bothering Kate, and I puzzled over what could have been worrying her. Fragments of that day floated through my mind in no discernible order, and after a while, frustrated, I reached over for my mobile phone and illuminated the screen to check the time.

It was then I saw I'd missed a text message.

I sat bolt upright in bed and opened the message. It was from Marjorie Parsons.

She'd sent it earlier in the evening. Why hadn't I checked my phone earlier?

She'd sent it at eleven thirty. Hours ago.

I quickly read the message:

I thought of something else to tell you about Dawn. It's nothing urgent. Give me a call or come over tomorrow and I'll explain. Marjorie.

I considered phoning her straightaway, but it was now three AM.

I got out of bed and walked down the hallway towards the stairs. The window on the landing was the only one that looked out onto the lane. From there, I could see the front of Marjorie Parsons's cottage.

I opened the window to get a better view, and the cold night air, fragranced with Wisteria blossoms, made me shiver. As I'd expected there were no lights on in the Parsons's cottage. Of course, Marjorie had probably been tucked up in bed for hours.

I was going to have to wait until tomorrow to talk to her. In any event, she probably just wanted to tell me something inconsequential in an attempt to persuade me that Dawn was a good person. I couldn't blame her for that. In fact, I admired her loyalty to Dawn.

If the police couldn't get anything from Dawn during their questioning tomorrow, then perhaps we could rely on Marjorie to persuade Dawn to tell us whatever she knew.

I was about to shut the window when I saw a movement along the lane. A figure was standing outside Marjorie Parsons's house.

I froze, staring. Although the moon was bright tonight, I couldn't make out who it was from this distance. It looked like a male figure, but I couldn't say for sure.

The pubs and restaurants were all long shut. This was a quiet, residential lane and only led to more houses.

I was immediately suspicious. Were they simply out for a

walk? Perhaps they were suffering from insomnia, like me. But why had they stopped walking and lingered beside the Parsons's cottage?

After a moment or two, the figure started walking again, away from the cottage and towards our house.

I took in a sharp breath and pulled the window shut, trying to be quiet. The glint of moonlight must have reflected on the glass and made the figure look up. Although I couldn't see their face, I was sure they were looking directly at me.

I stayed motionless. Logically, that was the sensible thing to do. But I hadn't stayed still because I was sensible. I was frozen with fear. There was something about the shadowy figure that felt very wrong.

I finally started to breathe normally again when the figure carried on walking. I didn't dare move, though. It seemed to take ages for the figure to walk past the beech trees, and when he did, I gasped.

The branches no longer obscured his face, and the moon-light clearly illuminated his features. It was Daniel. Daniel Creswell.

I hugged my arms around my body and waited for him to carry on walking. I half-expected him to walk up to our gate, but he passed by without stopping.

I stood there for a moment, my heart thudding in my chest as I tried to think of a feasible explanation for why he would be walking along the lane at this time of night. He didn't even live in Woodstock anymore. He lived in Oxford.

Had he been visiting Pippa? If so, why had he been walking

down Rectory Lane? Pippa's house was on the High Street. I would have liked to think it was because he was frantic with worry over his daughter. Had he been drawn to the Parsons's house, looking for answers?

My legs felt shaky as I walked downstairs to my bedroom. Unable to rid myself of the unsettled feeling, I climbed back into bed. I knew Daniel was awake. I could call him and ask why he was wandering about at this time of night.

Maybe there was a logical explanation. The situation was getting more and more complicated, and I had no idea who to trust.

I'd never liked Daniel, and I liked him even less after I found out he had cheated my mother financially. But I'd never once doubted his love for Jenna, and I'd never seriously considered the possibility he had something to do with her disappearance.

Various memories flashed through my mind as I remembered Daniel being short tempered with Jenna on a few occasions. It was never anything physical, but what if he'd lost his temper, just once, and hurt her?

I put my hands over my face and groaned. That couldn't have happened. Jenna was in a public place when she went missing. There were too many confusing threads to this mystery, and I felt like I was going around and around in circles.

I closed my eyes. I didn't want to take a sleeping tablet tonight because I wanted to be awake early tomorrow morning. A groggy head was the last thing I wanted if

Dawn decided to make a full confession. Yes, that was unlikely, but I couldn't help hoping.

I would have to wait until tomorrow morning to find out what Marjorie wanted to tell me about Dawn. I turned over in bed and stared up at the ceiling, willing the time to pass quickly.

All I could do was pray tomorrow would deliver the answers we'd been waiting two years for.

CHAPTER THIRTY-SIX

I woke at seven AM the next morning, feeling terrible, and headed straight for the bathroom to take a shower. After I had dressed, I walked into the kitchen, with my hair still wet, yawning.

Mum was already there, sitting at the table. "Coffee?"

I nodded. "I'll get it."

I picked up her cup and got a mug out of the cupboard for myself. Lifting the filter coffee jug, I poured us both a generous serving.

"I'm going to see Marjorie Parsons this morning," I said, glancing at Mum over my shoulder. "She sent me a text message last night, but I didn't see it until the early hours. She said she wanted to tell me something about Dawn."

"Really? I'll come with you."

I shook my head after I took a sip of my hot coffee, burning my tongue. "It's better if you stay here, in case the police call with news. I'm sure Marjorie just wants to tell me about another one of Dawn's good deeds and try to persuade me her daughter is a good person deep down."

Mum's shoulders slumped in disappointment. "It can't be easy for Marjorie, but surely she must accept Dawn knows something. Otherwise, she would never have had the photograph."

I nodded. "We should try to keep Marjorie on side. If the police don't have any luck with Dawn, her mother might be able to persuade her to tell us what she knows."

"If anyone could do it, I suppose Marjorie could, but right now, she doesn't believe Dawn could be involved."

I shrugged, took another sip of my coffee and then set it down on the counter. "Marjorie always gets up early, doesn't she?"

"Yes, she's an early riser. She told me she hasn't slept later than six AM in years. She always volunteers for the early shift if we need to do something for the Woodstock Women's group."

"Right," I said, leaning over to give Mum a quick squeeze. "I'll go now. I won't be long, and I'll probably be back before the police telephone to give us an update on Dawn's interview."

I left Mum in the kitchen and headed for Marjorie's house. As I approached the thatched cottage, I shivered, remembering Daniel lingering there last night. I decided to ask him about it later.

There were no lights on in the cottage, but it was a bright, sunny morning so that wasn't unusual. I rang the doorbell, stepped back and waited.

No response.

Marjorie's car was in the driveway, so she hadn't gone out. I tried again, keeping my finger pressed against the bell a little longer this time.

When I still didn't get an answer, I took a couple of steps back so I could see the upstairs windows. One set of curtains were closed. Was that Marjorie's bedroom?

She was supposed to be an early riser. Typical. Today of all days, Marjorie had chosen to sleep in.

I had her telephone number from the text message, so I pulled out my mobile phone and dialled. It rang and rang and then cut through to an answering service.

Frustrated, I hung up and then peered through the letterbox.

"Marjorie! Are you there? It's me, Beth. I hope I'm not too early."

I straightened up and waited, but still got no response.

A few moments later, I peered through the letterbox again and saw Thomas the tabby cat strolling towards me.

"Where's your owner?"

I got a meow in response.

I tried the bell again. Just when I was about to give up, I heard a car behind me.

I turned to see a marked police vehicle parking at the side of the lane. They hadn't parked in Marjorie's driveway but had parked outside her house.

Two uniformed officers exited the vehicle. Both male, one about a foot taller than the other.

The taller of the two officers spoke first. "Can I help you, Madam?"

"I've come to visit Marjorie Parsons. She sent me a text message saying she had something to tell me." I didn't mention the fact that she'd sent it last night.

"I see."

"There's no answer. I think she's still asleep."

Yesterday had been stressful. It wouldn't have been a surprise if Marjorie overslept this morning, but something about this situation made me nervous. I kept thinking about Daniel's shadowy figure lurking outside the cottage last night.

The officer looked up at the closed curtains upstairs. "You might have to come back later. Mrs Parsons is coming into the station to answer some questions this morning."

"Oh," I said. "I didn't realise. Have you spoken to her this morning?"

The tall officer narrowed his eyes. He had either picked up on my concern, or he thought my behaviour was suspicious. "The interview was arranged yesterday. When did you get the text message from Mrs Parsons?"

The shorter officer stepped around me and pressed the doorbell himself, obviously not taking me at my word.

"It was last night," I admitted. "But I didn't get it until it was too late to visit her, so I decided to come first thing this morning."

The shorter man took his thumb off the doorbell and walked around me again, this time heading across driveway to the side of the house and then disappearing around the back.

I turned back to the taller PC. "Is there any news on Dawn Parsons? Has she said anything yet?"

The officer's expression tightened. "I'm afraid I can't talk about an ongoing investigation. Perhaps you should go home now, and call on Mrs Parsons another time."

From his cold tone, I guessed he'd assumed I was a nosy neighbour.

"My name is Beth Farrow. Dawn Parsons has been arrested in connection with the disappearance of my niece, Jenna Creswell."

His face softened a little. "Oh, sorry. I thought…" He gave me an apologetic smile. "I'm afraid I couldn't tell you anything about Dawn's interview, even if I knew something, which I don't. I'm sure your liaison officer will be in touch, as soon as there is some news."

"Right. Thanks." I turned to walk back home when I heard a shout.

The officer who'd gone around the side of the house had

rushed back to the driveway. "Signs of a break-in," he said to his colleague. "A glass panel on the back door has been smashed."

Both officers sprung into action, seemingly forgetting about me. They radioed in, and then both of them went around the back of the house.

I stood there not knowing what to do. Someone had broken in?... Christ, I hoped Marjorie was okay. Was this some odd coincidence? Daniel Creswell had been outside last night. Could he have broken in and demanded answers from Marjorie? Had there been an altercation? My mind was running wild with theories of what could have happened when I heard more shouting from upstairs. The police officers had obviously gone inside.

The lane remained strangely empty despite the commotion. It wasn't until I heard the peal of sirens that the neighbours began twitching curtains and poking their heads out of their doors.

I watched the commotion as I stood on the edge of the driveway, trying to keep out of the way of the paramedics and the police who had taken over the scene.

I knew something bad had happened, but when I saw Marjorie carried out of the house on a stretcher, her face grey and her eyes closed, I feared the worst.

I rushed to her side. "Marjorie! Can you hear me?" I turned to one of the paramedics. "Is she going to be okay? What happened to her?"

There was no sign of blood or any trauma to Marjorie's face, which was the only part of her I could see.

"Are you family?"

"I'm a friend. I live just over there." I pointed to Mum's house.

"She'll be taken to the John Radcliffe. The best thing you can do is get in touch with her family and contact the hospital for information."

I nodded. The only family member of Marjorie's I knew was Dawn, and she wasn't going to be able to get to the hospital in a hurry.

With a shaking hand, I clutched my mobile ready to dial Mum's number. I needed to tell her about Marjorie before she came outside to find out what was happening herself.

Before I connected the call, the tall officer I'd been speaking to earlier walked past me, and I reached out to grab his arm.

"Can you tell me what's happened?"

At first, I thought he was going to tell me he could only discuss the situation with family, but then he seemed to relent. "It looks like Mrs Parsons took an overdose. I imagine she was devastated after learning her daughter might be involved in something criminal."

"But Marjorie would never do that. She goes to church."

The officer raised a fair eyebrow. "Does that make a difference?"

"Yes," I said firmly. "Marjorie would never try to take her own life. She considered it a sin."

"Well, forensics will be here soon, and I'm sure they'll tell us if it was a suicide attempt or anything else more nefarious."

"I thought there was a break-in?"

"There was a broken window pane in the back door. Could be unrelated, but we'll look into it." He turned and began to walk away.

"Wait! There's something else."

He turned back to me. "Yes?"

"Daniel Creswell was outside this house at two AM this morning. I looked out of my window and saw him."

The officer's confident expression wavered, and then he said, "Are you sure about this?"

I nodded. "Absolutely positive."

Daniel may be Jenna's father, but as far as I was concerned, I owed him no loyalty, at all.

CHAPTER THIRTY-SEVEN

When I got home, Mum had lots of questions for me, but there wasn't much I could tell her. She was understandably concerned about Marjorie and looked shocked when I told her Daniel had been lurking outside last night.

Before she could ask me any questions about Daniel, the telephone rang. Mum rushed over to the phone, almost tripping in her haste. From the way she gripped the handset, I guessed it was the police on the other end of the line.

After listening for a moment, she looked over at me and shook her head. I took that to mean that Dawn still wasn't talking.

After a moment, Mum held out the phone to me. "Sergeant Parker wants to have a word with you."

I took the phone, wondering whether this had something to do with Marjorie, or whether Sergeant Parker wanted to tell me off for trespassing on Robin Vaughan's property yesterday.

"Hello."

"Beth, this is Leanne Parker. We've told Dawn the news about her mother, and she is very upset."

"I suppose that's going to delay your interview?"

"I'm afraid it's inevitable. She will be visiting her mother in the hospital, but I think this shock might force her to open up to us."

I stared at the floor and didn't respond. Why wasn't Dawn talking? Was she frightened? Had somebody threatened her? Or was she just scared of getting in trouble?

"Would you be able to come into the station this morning, Beth? It's nothing serious. I've just got a few questions to ask you to help me with some forms I need to fill in."

"Yes, I can do that. What time?"

"As soon as you can make it. I'll send a car to pick you up. Could you come in now?"

I hesitated. Sergeant Parker had said this wasn't urgent, but for some reason she wanted me to get to the station quickly. I was about to ask more questions when I realised I was being paranoid. No doubt, she just wanted to get the paper-work off her desk.

"Yes, I can come in now."

"Great. I'll see you soon."

After I had hung up, I explained to Mum I needed to go to

the station to answer some questions. It wasn't a hardship. I'd been planning to go to the station anyway to deal with the fallout from yesterday.

I opened the gate and got myself organised, grabbing my jacket and making sure I had everything I needed in my handbag, and then I walked into the living room to wait beside the window and look out for the police car that was coming to collect me.

But before the police car arrived, I saw we had another visitor. Daniel Creswell had walked through the open gate and was striding up the driveway. I flung open the front door and stepped out onto the path, closing the door behind me.

"What are you doing here?"

He looked furious. His face was flushed, and his eyes were wild as he stood in front of me and thrust a finger in my direction. "It was you, wasn't it?"

I swallowed nervously. "What are you talking about?"

"Don't deny it. Somebody told the police they'd seen me outside the Parsons's cottage last night. It had to be you."

I took a step back and put my hands out in front of me to try and ward him off. I'd seen Daniel riled up plenty of times, but never like this.

He loomed over me. "You selfish cow. You didn't stop to think how it would affect me, did you? Or maybe you wanted the police to be banging on Pippa's door. Is this some sort of game to you?"

"Hang on. You're not the victim here. I saw you outside

Marjorie's house. Don't try to deny it. I haven't done anything wrong. I only told the truth."

"Why couldn't you have asked me for my side of the story before you went to the police? You owe me that much at least."

"I don't owe you anything."

He clenched his jaw and looked down, spotting the fact I was clutching my jacket and my handbag. "Where are you going?"

"The police station. I have an appointment with Sergeant Parker. I don't want you talking to Mum when I'm not here."

"That's nothing to do with you."

"Yes, it is. I'd be concerned for Mum's safety if you visited her when I wasn't there."

Daniel looked as though I'd slapped him. "Is that really what you think of me?"

Right now, I didn't trust him at all. "All I know is that something happened to Marjorie last night, and I saw you hanging around outside her house. I also know that you've taken a loan from my mother and refused to pay it back, putting her at risk of losing her home. So I don't think very highly of you, Daniel. Surely that can't come as a surprise to you?"

His anger seemed to leave him like evaporating steam. He bent forward at his waist, as though staggering under the weight of grief. His face crumpled.

"I couldn't sleep. I was staying at Pippa's, but I needed to get out and think. After the news we had about Dawn, I was drawn to the house. I didn't do anything though. For God's sake, Beth. You have to believe that."

"It doesn't matter what I believe," I said, walking past him as I spotted a police car coming down the lane. "I'm going to the police station now, and I'm going to tell the officer in that car you're bothering us if you don't leave now."

Daniel's shoulders slumped, and he scowled at me as he shook his head. Then he turned and stalked off up the lane without another word.

I took a deep breath and walked towards the police car. Just before I reached the car, a man in his fifties, walking a Jack Russell, passed me. He looked at me and beamed.

I tried to remember whether I'd spoken to him before. He looked vaguely familiar, but I didn't know his name.

"Good for you, love. I hope you put the frighteners on that dirty sod." He walked past me, grinning.

I stared after him, and it dawned on me that word must have spread around Woodstock. People had heard about me confronting Robin Vaughan yesterday. Great. First, I was known around the town as the woman with the missing niece, and now, I was known as some kind of vigilante, crusading agent against paedophiles.

I didn't reply and instead turned to face the police officer who'd just climbed out of the vehicle.

"Beth Farrow?"

I nodded. "That's me."

"I've got instructions to take you to Thames Valley head-quarters."

"That's right. I've been expecting you."

I slid into the back of the police car and buckled up, closing my eyes briefly. As the car pulled away, I tried to forget about Daniel.

Was Sergeant Parker right when she suggested Marjorie's misfortune might help to persuade Dawn to open up? I hoped so because if she didn't talk soon, it could be too late.

Maybe Dawn would talk to me. After all, she sent the photograph to me. She must have wanted to help and to let me know Jenna was still alive. So why hadn't she sent the photograph to Daniel? As Jenna's father, he was the logical choice.

I could confront her at the hospital. Under normal circum-stances, I wouldn't dream of using Majorie's misfortune to my advantage, but all bets were off now. All I cared about was finding Jenna, and if I had to apply pressure to Dawn when she was emotionally fragile, I would do it without hesitation.

I rested my head against the cool glass of the window as the police car pulled out onto the A44. The Oxfordshire coun-tryside flashed past as I began to formulate a plan.

CHAPTER THIRTY-EIGHT

My plan fell apart the moment I stepped inside the police station. I was shown inside by the officer who'd driven me there.

Just as we passed a line of blue visitors' chairs, a door opened on my left, and Dawn Parsons appeared. I stopped walking abruptly, causing the officer to stumble into me and mutter an apology I barely heard. All my careful planning on the car journey had been for nothing. I'd planned to confront Dawn at the hospital later, but now she was standing in front of me, I was too shocked to say anything.

My surprise was reflected on Dawn's face. Her eyes widened as she stared at me. She wasn't alone, but at first, I didn't notice the police officers escorting her. When I came to my senses, I walked quickly towards her, before anybody could stop me.

I thought the police would have some reason for keeping us

apart while she was being questioned, but I had questions of my own, and I couldn't wait any longer.

Before I even asked my first question, Dawn was shaking her head and stepping back away from me, as though I was the monster and the person to fear.

"What did you do, Dawn? Where is Jenna?"

Dawn's mouth hung open, making her look gormless and stupid. Was it all an act? Was there an evil, scheming mind going on beneath that slow, lumbering exterior?

"Dawn! You have to talk to me. Tell me what you know."

I'd planned to talk to Dawn calmly. She might confide in me if she thought I was her friend. I was still holding out hope that she really did want to help me find Jenna and that was why she had sent the photograph. But I couldn't keep the anger out of my voice. If she knew where Jenna was, why didn't she just tell me?

My plan to confront her at the hospital might have worked. I thought Dawn would be emotionally fragile after visiting her mother and when I showed up, under the guise of visiting Marjorie, Dawn would be overcome with gratitude and confess everything to me.

But everything was spiralling out of control. Dawn was looking at me as though she were terrified, and the officer who'd been escorting me had now reached my side and put a cautioning hand on my elbow. At any moment, I expected him to pull me away.

"You sent me the photograph," I said and gripped the

sleeve of Dawn's blouse. "I know you are trying to help. Please, tell me. Help me find her."

Dawn's eyes were stormy and conflicted as she stared at me, opening and shutting her mouth like a goldfish. She looked behind her, and that was when I saw Detective Sergeant Leanne Parker watching the two of us. I hadn't even realised she was there.

I tugged on Dawn's sleeve to get her attention. "Please. Your mother wants you to help me."

I was clutching at straws, but it was all I had.

"You should...g...go and see Mrs Taverne," Dawn stuttered.

"Mrs Taverne?" I stared at Dawn not understanding what on earth Mrs Taverne had to do with any of this.

Dawn nodded and then Sergeant Parker stepped forward. "This way, Dawn." She looked at me. "I'll be with you in just a minute, Beth. Dawn is going to visit her mother now."

I stared after them in confusion as Sergeant Parker led Dawn outside. Had Dawn just fed me a load of nonsense to shut me up? Or did Mrs Taverne really know something about Jenna's disappearance? The old woman was legally blind and almost deaf. She was also in her eighties, and the idea of her being involved in a child's abduction was absurd.

She was a sweet, kindly woman who had been involved with the local church and had played the piano for our recitals when I'd attended Woodstock Infants' School.

"You can wait here," the officer by my side said. "She won't keep you waiting long."

I sat on one of the blue chairs he pointed to and waited. From where I sat, I could see through the large glass windows and watched as Dawn got into a marked police car to be taken to the hospital. Sergeant Parker didn't come back inside immediately. Instead, she paused to talk to two uniformed officers. I tried to guess what she was saying by reading her lips, but I was hopeless at it. The only word I thought I recognised was Mrs Taverne.

Sergeant Parker walked back into the police station and greeted me with a smile. "Sorry for keeping you waiting. Follow me. It won't take long. Can I get you a cup of coffee?"

"No, thanks," I said as I got to my feet. I was still feeling off kilter from my run-in with Dawn, but I knew I had to keep my wits about me. Sergeant Parker said she wanted to ask me some routine questions so she could finish off some paperwork, but I wasn't about to let my guard down.

I followed her through a door locked with a security number pad, and we walked along a narrow corridor, bright with artificial lights.

"Do you know what Dawn was talking about? Have you any idea why she mentioned Mrs Taverne?" I asked.

Sergeant Parker turned to face me and cocked her head to one side. "Do you?"

I shook my head. Typical police officer. Answering my question with one of her own.

"No. Did you ask those officers you spoke to outside to go and talk to Mrs Taverne."

"We are following up all leads, Beth. I don't know what Mrs Taverne has got to do with this case, but we will look into it."

Sergeant Parker greeted a colleague who walked past us and paused outside an interview room. She pulled keys from her pocket, unlocked the door and opened it, allowing me to enter ahead of her. I was starting to feel I'd been brought here under false pretences.

There was a selection of papers in piles on the desk, which stood in the centre of the small room. An old-fashioned tape recorder sat at one end of the desk. There was only one window in the room — a narrow, long strip, close to the ceiling, showing a glimpse of the blue sky outside.

Sergeant Parker sat down and nodded for me to do the same. She smiled at me.

"This shouldn't take long, Beth." She shuffled some of the paperwork and selected a form.

I waited, trying to focus on Sergeant Parker, but my mind kept wandering. Had those officers gone directly to speak to Mrs Taverne? What did an old lady who'd lived in Woodstock all her life have to do with Jenna's disappearance?

Sergeant Parker brought me back to the present by tapping her pen against the desk. "Before we start, I need to tell you I'm aware of the incident yesterday at Robin Vaughan's residence."

"Ah, right. I thought you might have heard about that."

"It was a reckless thing to do, Beth. I've spoken to the officers who attended the incident, and they're happy to hand things over to me. Robin Vaughan isn't going to press charges."

"I should think not!"

"You did trespass onto his property and trick your way into his house, Beth. You're lucky this isn't going to go any further."

I didn't feel particularly lucky at the moment. I wanted to get to the hospital and talk to Dawn again, but instead, I was listening to Sergeant Parker give me a ticking off.

Arguing my case wasn't going to get me anywhere, and since it looked as though I was going to get off with a warning, I nodded and tried to look repentant. "I won't do it again."

"Okay, well, we'll leave it at that. I wanted you to come in today to ask you some questions about your relationship with Dawn prior to when Jenna went missing."

"My relationship with Dawn?"

Sergeant Parker nodded, rested her elbows on the table and looked at me intently. "Yes."

"I didn't have any kind of relationship with Dawn. We weren't friends if that's what you mean. We went to the same school and travelled on the same school bus when we were in secondary school. That's all we had in common."

"We haven't been able to get Dawn to open up about Jenna,

but she has told us about some bullying incidents in the past."

I rolled my eyes. "Seriously. A five-year-old child is missing. Is Dawn seriously trying to make herself out to be the victim?"

"So, you don't know anything about this bullying?"

I shook my head, unable to believe we were wasting time on this. "She was bullied at school. Lots of kids are. I didn't bully her, and neither did Kate if that's what you're getting at."

"I'm just trying to gather information. I'm not 'getting at' anything."

I said nothing. I'd warmed to Sergeant Leanne Parker when we'd met her for the first time. At least, as much as I could under the circumstances. Now, I was starting to change my mind.

I glanced at the clock on the wall, wondering whether the officers would be at Mrs Taverne's house yet. Dawn had to be at the hospital by now.

"Who was involved in the bullying, Beth?"

"I can't remember. It was a long time ago, and Dawn wasn't in the same year as me. Can you tell me what happened to Marjorie?"

"It looks like she took too many sleeping tablets. Luckily, she was found in time."

"So she's going to be okay?"

"The doctors are optimistic."

"The first officers on the scene said there were signs of a break-in."

Sergeant Parker nodded slowly. "Yes. We are looking at that. Nothing was taken, but when Marjorie came around in the hospital, she was adamant she had never taken sleeping pills in her life."

I frowned. "Do you think someone tried to poison Marjorie?"

"It's too early for me to comment on that yet. Let's finish up here. I think I have all I need to complete the paperwork."

I raised an eyebrow as I reached for my handbag. "If I were a cynical person, I might think you'd engineered me running into Dawn like that earlier."

Sergeant Parker's cheeks coloured, telling me I was right, and I thought that was an unfortunate tendency for a police officer who tried to play her cards close to her chest.

"A coincidence," she said, and her cheeks were reddened further.

"Timed perfectly."

Sergeant Parker opened the door, and I followed her out into the corridor.

"Do you think Dawn was involved in taking Jenna?" I asked.

"I can't say for sure—"

"I'm not asking about the facts. I'm asking you what you

believe. Do you think Dawn was involved in a plot to abduct Jenna?"

Sergeant Parker took a deep breath before replying. "I don't know whether she was involved in a plot or conspired with others."

The disappointment must have been clear on my face. For once, I wanted one of the police officers involved in this case to tell me their personal opinion, their gut reaction.

"There is one thing I know for sure, though," she said, locking the door behind us. "I'm convinced Dawn knows what happened that day."

CHAPTER THIRTY-NINE

I took a taxi back to Woodstock. Detective Sergeant Parker offered to arrange transport for me, but I turned her down. I intended to go straight to Mrs Taverne's house but didn't want the police to know that.

Unfortunately, when the taxi approached the end of the High Street and pulled up outside Mrs Taverne's three-bedroom terrace, which was next to Pippa Clarkson's house, I saw that the marked police car was still there and muttered a curse under my breath. The officers must be still questioning Mrs Taverne.

I thanked the taxi driver and paid him and then stood on the edge of the pavement wondering what to do next. After crossing to the other side of the road, I waited beside the old Barclays Bank. I wanted to know as soon as the officers left so I could talk to Mrs Taverne as soon as possible.

What could she know about Jenna's disappearance? I

couldn't help thinking Dawn had sent me on a wild goose chase. Perhaps this was her way of avoiding confrontation.

The sun was hot, and I was thankful for the shade from the trees in front of the bank. I leant back against the wall, wondering whether I should wait somewhere less conspicuous. I was considering my options when my mobile phone beeped.

I pulled out my phone, thinking it was probably Mum wondering where I was, but the message was from an unrecognised number. My heart skipped a beat, and I held my breath as I opened the message. Could it be another message from Dawn about Jenna? But wouldn't the police be watching her closely while she was visiting Marjorie in the hospital?

I soon saw it wasn't from Dawn.

We need to talk. Meet me by the Churchill statue at Blenheim asap.

Robin Vaughan.

I stared at the message. My gut reaction was to ignore it. Robin Vaughan was the last person I wanted to meet right now. How could I delete the message, though? What if he wanted to confess his involvement in Jenna's disappearance?

I gritted my teeth. It was no good. I couldn't ignore it. I would have to meet him.

I typed out a text message, telling him I'd be there soon, and with a last, lingering glance at Mrs Taverne's house, I turned off the High Street and headed down the steps that would take me out onto the main road.

I passed Robin Vaughan's house on the way. It would have been much easier to meet him there without all this cloak and dagger stuff. Who knew a music producer would be so dramatic?

When I got to the main road, I pulled out my phone again to call Mum. Although I didn't want to worry her, there was no way I was going off to meet Robin Vaughan without telling anyone. I'd seen enough episodes of Crimewatch to know that was a terrible idea.

Of course, Mum thought meeting Robin Vaughan was a ridiculous thing to do. At first, she tried to persuade me not to go and to tell the police about the message, and then when she realised I was going to go and meet him anyway, she wanted to come along. It took me a few minutes to convince her that wasn't a possibility.

"I don't think he's a threat," I said. "I'm going to meet him in public, so I'm sure it will be fine."

"I really don't think it's a good idea, Beth."

"You're probably right, but I have to talk to him just in case he wants to tell me something about Jenna."

I changed the subject then, telling Mum about Marjorie's suspicious overdose and relaying what Dawn had told me about Mrs Taverne.

Opposite the Black Prince pub was a blue wooden gate, which looked like it led to a private residence, but actually led to the public right of way to Blenheim. I wasn't planning to visit as a tourist, and so I pushed open the gate with one hand and kept my mobile clamped to my ear with the other.

I turned right when I got to the walkway. Rabbits, disturbed from their foraging, darted to safety as I approached.

"I can't understand how Mrs Taverne would be involved," Mum said. "I think Dawn fed you a line. I'd like to get my hands on that girl and shake the truth out of her."

I knew how she felt. "Well, I'll try to find out what, if anything, Mrs Taverne knows after I've finished with Robin Vaughan."

"Beth, call me as soon as you finish with this meeting and let me know you're safe. If I don't hear from you within twenty minutes, I'm going to call the police."

"I will. I promise."

After I had hung up, I walked faster, squinting at the tall column in the distance. I could just make out the statue of John Churchill perched on top of the column, but I was still too far away to see if Robin Vaughan was there already.

As I rounded the corner by the lake, I surprised a flock of geese, which in turn flapped their wings and made an awful racket. I carefully skirted around the group. Geese could be vicious, and an altercation was the last thing I needed today.

I marched on, and when I reached the hill, I was already out of breath. There was a figure beside the column, and I guessed it was Robin Vaughan. It was just my luck that there was nobody else around at the moment. I had a hollow feeling in my stomach, and I started to suspect agreeing to meet him here had been the wrong decision. I kept climbing steadily until I reached the top.

He turned to face me, and I could tell he'd been drinking. He wasn't clutching a whisky bottle now but was unsteady on his feet, and his bloodshot eyes were wide and staring as I walked up to him.

"What's all this about?" I asked, trying to sound more confident than I felt.

He licked his lips and moved closer to me, making my skin crawl.

"I told the police I didn't see your niece that day, but I did."

A thin smile stretched over his lips, and I felt sick. I imagined myself punching him in the face. Violence was never the answer, so they said, but if I'd been holding a knife right now…

"What did you do?" My voice was barely a whisper.

His smile disappeared and was replaced with a frown. "I told you I didn't *do* anything. But I saw her."

I shook my head and began to turn away. "Is that all you've got to tell me? You saw her. So did a hundred other people at the fête. How exactly does that help me?"

"Because I saw her with a woman. It wasn't you or your sister. I don't know her name, but—"

I cut him off. "Was it Dawn Parsons?"

"Who?"

"Dark hair, taller than me, about five foot ten, and a large build?"

He shook his head. "I'm not sure, maybe."

He smiled as though he was enjoying this, and I realised he was wasting my time.

"You've made this up, haven't you?"

He scowled at me and pushed his reddened face close to mine. "I'm trying to help."

"Of course you are. You're quite the moral citizen, aren't you?"

He pulled back as though hurt. "Why are you so nasty?"

I looked at him in disbelief. "Because you're wasting my time. Even if you didn't have anything to do with Jenna's disappearance, you are still an evil, sick man."

He took a step back away from me and stumbled as he stepped into a rabbit hole. I imagined shoving him and sending him hurtling down the hill. But I just stood there with my arms at my sides.

"I thought you'd want to know about the woman."

"Some nameless woman, whom you've probably invented to take the heat off of yourself. Are you expecting me to go to the police with this? Do you think it will clear your name?"

He shrugged. "It might. I didn't do it. I never touched her. The police are wasting their time."

"And you're wasting mine. What else can you tell me about

this woman? Was she taking Jenna off somewhere? Did Jenna look upset?"

"No, she looked happy enough."

"And the woman? What did she look like?"

"Quite average really. I wasn't paying much attention. At the time, I didn't know it was going to be important."

"So that's it?"

"What?"

"That's all you have to tell me?"

He hesitated as though he thought it might be a trick question and then he nodded.

I turned and walked away. He didn't bother to follow me or call out. I had been an idiot to believe Robin Vaughan was going to tell me anything useful.

When I reached the bottom of the hill, I pulled out my mobile and gave Mum a ring to reassure her I was safe.

"Oh, thank God. Did he tell you anything?"

"Nothing useful. It was a waste of time. He said he saw Jenna at the fête with a woman, but he couldn't describe her. To be honest, I think he made it up."

"Nasty man."

"I'm going to head to Mrs Taverne's house now and see if she can shed any light on why Dawn told me to speak to her."

"I'd offer to come with you, but I just had a call from DI

Sharp. They are resuming their questioning of Dawn soon, but he got called away when he was on the phone. I don't want to get your hopes up, but it sounded like there had been a development."

My fingers tightened around the phone. "Really? What did he say?"

"Nothing concrete. But I could hear a voice in the background. They said something about Dawn's financial records. Then DI Sharp said he had to go, but he'd call me back soon."

I sighed and raised my head, looking up at the clear blue sky as the swallows and swifts swooped overhead. Had the police finally made a breakthrough?

"Do you think I should come straight home?" I asked.

"Well, I'm not sure how long it will be before DI Sharp gets back to us. You may as well go and see Mrs Taverne, and I'll give you a ring if anything happens."

I agreed and said goodbye to Mum before hanging up. After two years of pain and inertia, feeling like we were never going to get to the bottom of Jenna's disappearance, it finally seemed things were starting to go our way.

CHAPTER FORTY

It didn't take me long to get to Mrs Taverne's house. She lived next door to Pippa Clarkson, and architecturally her house was similar although not as well maintained.

Old net curtains hung in the windows on the ground floor to stop passers-by peering in. I climbed the stone steps to her red front door and used the brass knocker.

It seemed as though I waited for ages for Mrs Taverne to open the door. I bit my lip and shuffled from foot to foot. She was in her eighties now, and she'd been hard of hearing twenty years ago, so I wondered whether she even heard me knock. I was contemplating trying again when I saw a shadow move beyond the glass panel in the door.

She finally opened the door but kept the chain on and peered over the top of it, the skin around her eyes wrinkling as she squinted at me.

"Yes?"

"Mrs Taverne, I don't know if you remember me. I'm Beth Farrow, you used to play the piano when I was at school."

Mrs Taverne stopped frowning, but she didn't smile. Her eyes looked sad. "Beth, I was so sorry to hear about the troubles your family has endured over the past couple of years."

Her words gave me pause. She'd known both Kate and me as children, and of course, would have heard what happened after Jenna went missing.

"Thank you. I wondered if I could come in and ask you a few questions."

Mrs Taverne blinked in surprise and then she pushed the front door shut. I was stunned. What had I said to upset her?

It wasn't long before I realised she was just closing the door so she could remove the security chain. She pulled the door open again and stepped back.

"Of course, dear. Come in."

I followed her inside. The hallway was dark, with no windows. The dim light wasn't helped by the dark red striped wallpaper. The carpet was thick beneath my feet, but the swirled pattern was old-fashioned, and it was worn in the centre from years of foot traffic.

I wondered when the house had last been decorated. Decades ago, I assumed. But painters and decorators were expensive, and when you got to Mrs Taverne's age, with her infirmities, it wasn't possible to do the job yourself.

I felt a pang of guilt as I followed her into the small sitting room. It wouldn't have hurt me to visit Mrs Taverne now and again and ask if she needed help.

"Can I get you a cup of tea, dear?" Mrs Taverne said. She clasped her hands in front of her chest and looked at me through blue, cloudy eyes.

"That would be lovely. Shall I give you a hand?"

"There's no need. Please, sit down and make yourself comfortable. I won't be long."

She turned away from me and left the room, following a practised path. I wondered just how bad her eyesight was now. Her hearing didn't seem too bad, but she wore hearing aids in both ears.

I sat down on the floral print sofa, which was surprisingly soft and comfortable, and waited. I needed to ask my questions sensitively. The last thing I wanted was to accuse Mrs Taverne of being involved in some kind of plot. But I was intrigued by her relationship with Dawn. Marjorie Parsons had said her daughter came here because she was kind and goodhearted, but that didn't tally with the Dawn I knew.

My mobile beeped, and I pulled it out of my pocket. I had a message from Mum.

The police have found out Daniel sent Dawn money. I think it is hush money. DI Sharp is going to call me back in twenty minutes and explain.

My breath caught in my throat. Why had Daniel sent Dawn money? Was it payment for something? Blackmail?

Payment to make sure she kept her mouth shut when the police asked her questions?

I'd never suspected Daniel had anything to do with Dawn? I wasn't aware he'd ever said more than a couple of words to her. Did Dawn know what had happened to Jenna and Daniel paid her to keep quiet? But that didn't make any sense. If Jenna was still alive, why would Daniel want to keep that quiet?

Maybe it had nothing to do with Jenna. Maybe Dawn had some dirt on Daniel. His relationship with Pippa was out in the open now, but what if it had started earlier... What if it started before Kate died, or even before Jenna went missing? I thought back to the day of the fête and the tension between my sister and Daniel. Was that the reason Daniel had given money to Dawn?

How must he feel now that he'd realised he'd given money to silence somebody who knew what had happened to Jenna? Was the blackmail the reason Dawn had chosen to send me the photograph of Jenna and not Daniel?

I put the phone down on the seat cushion beside me and rested my head in my hands. Every new discovery resulted in fresh questions. I felt like we were never going to get to the bottom of it. So many secrets. So many lies.

Daniel would never talk to me about this, and I couldn't talk to Dawn as she was still in police custody. I wondered if Pippa knew about Daniel's payment to Dawn? Had it been a one-off thing or were the payments still ongoing?

One thing that supported my theory that Pippa and Daniel's relationship started earlier than I'd originally thought was the fact that Pippa's husband, Mark, had left Woodstock suddenly. Maybe he would know when their affair started.

I picked up my phone again, and this time, opened the Facebook app. I was friends with Mark Clarkson, although I hadn't seen a post from him in some time. I scrolled through my friend list until I found Mark's name and then clicked onto his profile page.

I frowned when I saw he hadn't updated Facebook recently. His last post had been two years ago this month. I ran a hand through my hair as I stared at my mobile screen. It didn't mean anything. Maybe he just got bored of Facebook, or he wanted a fresh start after his split from Pippa.

I typed out a pm asking him outright if he knew when Daniel and Pippa began their relationship. It was direct, but there wasn't any point agonising over word choice. Whichever way I asked the question, it wouldn't avoid hurt feelings.

The only things on Mark's wall were posts from other people wishing him happy birthday last November, and he hadn't responded to any of them. Not even to his sister.

I clicked on his sister's profile. I didn't know her well, but she'd visited Woodstock from time to time and often drank at the Woodstock Arms. Her profile page was full of cat memes, and at the top, was a GIF of a dancing baby.

I sent her a pm, too, asking after Mark.

The rattle of a tea tray made me get to my feet. I took the tray from Mrs Taverne and carried it into the sitting room.

"This looks lovely," I said, feeling guilty over the trouble she'd gone to.

She'd arranged three types of biscuits on a gold-rimmed, pretty plate. Ginger nuts, bourbons and custard creams.

"I'm afraid it's all I had in. I don't get many visitors these days, so I just keep a selection of my favourites."

I felt another twinge of guilt. "I love bourbons."

After we poured the tea and sat opposite one another, Mrs Taverne on a high-backed chair and me on the sofa, I started asking questions.

"I've just spoken to Dawn, did you hear what's happened to her?"

Mrs Taverne's teacup rattled against her saucer. "Dawn? No. Is she all right?"

This was going to be harder than I'd thought. "Dawn is being questioned by the police. They think she knows something about Jenna's disappearance."

I paused to let my words sink in and watch Mrs Taverne's reaction.

"Jenna? The little girl who went missing?"

"Yes, my niece. Kate's daughter. We never found out what happened to her after she went missing."

"And the police think Dawn knows something about it?" Mrs Taverne shook her head and stared down at her teacup.

She was either a tremendous actress, or she knew nothing

about Jenna's disappearance. "Yes, in fact, they are very confident Dawn knows what happened that day."

"I can't believe it. She is such a kind girl. She offered to help me with my cleaning, and she often gets my shopping."

On the spur of the moment, I decided to tell her about the photograph. I needed her to believe that Dawn had kept secrets so she would confide in me and tell me anything she knew.

"I received a photograph of Jenna. She looked older than she did when she disappeared. So we believe it's a recent photograph. I didn't know who sent it, but the police found the photograph on Dawn's phone."

"Oh, my goodness. Have they found the child? Do they know what happened?"

I shook my head. "No, and that's why I am here."

Mrs Taverne looked even more confused. She leant forward, and with a shaky hand, put her tea cup on the coffee table. "Why?"

"Because when I asked Dawn about it this morning at the police station, she told me to come here and speak to you."

"She did? I don't understand."

Disappointment surged through me. It had been stupid to get my hopes up. Dawn hadn't wanted to help. She'd told me to see Mrs Taverne to get me out of her hair.

"Dawn has been difficult," I said. "I'm not sure why she told me to come here. She might just be wasting my time, but can you think of any reason she would send me here?"

Mrs Taverne shook her head.

"Did Dawn ever bring anybody here to meet you? Or did she mention a friend, anyone I might be able to talk to?"

"No, Dawn came across as a very lonely girl. I appreciated her coming here, and she's been a great help to me over the last two years, but I've told her plenty of times she should be mixing with people her own age."

"What sort of things did Dawn help you with?"

"Dusting. I can't see the cobwebs and dust with my poor eyesight. She goes shopping for me once a week, and she does some ironing, too. She always does it in the third-floor box room. I told her she should do it downstairs where there is more room, but she says the light's better up there."

I nodded slowly. "Do you think I could take a look at the box room?"

Mrs Taverne nodded. "Of course, there's not much up there. The room is so small the ironing board only just fits inside."

I put my tea on the coffee table and stood up. "Thank you. I won't be a minute."

"Take as long as you need. It's the first room on the left. You won't mind if I don't escort you up there, will you? Living in a three-storey house at my age isn't ideal. I do find the stairs difficult."

I left Mrs Taverne in the sitting room and made my way to the staircase. I looked up the dark stairs and shivered. The stairs creaked as I put my foot on the first step.

What could be in the tiny room at the top of the stairs?

Could the small room hold the truth behind Jenna's disappearance? Did Dawn have some kind of evidence hidden up there? Or were there more photographs?

There was only one way to find out. I gripped the bannister and continued to climb.

CHAPTER FORTY-ONE

Upstairs, it was darker still. I paused on the landing and looked around. There were four doors, all dark wood and unpainted, and they were all shut. I walked towards the door on my left as Mrs Taverne had instructed.

The handles were old-fashioned, brass knobs and felt cold to the touch. The door opened smoothly, and I was surprised when I looked into a bright, tidy room. I'd been expecting something dim, and dark up here. But the large sash window let in plenty of light. The room was wallpapered with a cream coloured paper printed with tiny pink roses. There was a small patterned rug in the centre of the room, but otherwise the floorboards were bare and unpolished.

A large, antique wardrobe stood in the corner of the room. It was huge, far too big for a room this size.

I looked around and saw an ironing board propped up against the wall behind me. There was nothing here to indicate why Dawn had asked me to come and see Mrs Taverne.

I sighed. What had I expected? A shoebox full of secret correspondence or some hidden evidence underneath a loose floorboard? What a gullible idiot. There was nothing here.

Crossing the room in two steps, I took a closer look at the large wardrobe. I pulled one of the doors, and it creaked open stiffly. Inside, old blankets and patchwork quilts were neatly arranged on the shelves. On the other side, three heavy, full-length woollen coats in drab colours hung from the rail. Glancing down, I saw two pairs of old-fashioned sandals and a scuffed pair of winter boots.

Frustrated, I closed the doors with a shove. Dawn gave me the creeps, but I had never thought she could be this vindictive. It was bad enough she wouldn't tell me what she knew about Jenna's disappearance, but to waste my time like this was cruel.

I turned to the window and looked down at the small garden. Metal garden furniture was arranged on the patio. The garden itself had been paved, presumably to save on the physical work of mowing a lawn. There were two raised flower beds on either side, and both of them were overgrown with weeds.

Next door, Pippa's garden was startling contrast. Her garden was bigger, as she had the house at the end of the terrace. The grass was green, and there was no sign of dandelions or daisies. Of course, that was probably because she'd had it re-turfed after the building work and the new patio had been laid.

I was about to turn away when for the first time I noticed the hedge at the back of Pippa's garden looked remarkably similar to the hedge behind Jenna in the photograph. I gripped the side of the windowsill and leant forward to get a better look.

I was so close to the window, my breath steamed up the glass. It was just Ivy. One of the most common plants in England. So what if Pippa had some Ivy in her hedge? Did I really think Jenna had been playing in that garden without anyone noticing?

But someone did notice, a little voice in my head whispered. Dawn noticed.

I folded my arms over my chest and shook my head. That idea was ridiculous even for me. Why would Pippa hide Jenna? And if she'd been here for two years, why hadn't anyone but Dawn noticed? Pippa welcomed visitors. She'd never tried to dissuade me from coming to her house. And she was in a relationship with Daniel. He stayed over. Were Daniel and Pippa in on it together?

"Is everything all right up there?" Mrs Taverne's reedy voice carried upstairs.

"Yes, thank you. I won't be much longer."

I turned back to the window. None of this made any sense. Neither Daniel nor Pippa had any reason to take Jenna.

Besides, where would they have kept her for two years without arousing suspicion?

My gaze fixed on the cedar lodge in Pippa's garden. It had been installed as a studio when Pippa started her candle-making business. She'd worked there with Kate. Why didn't she work out there anymore? She worked at the kitchen table now. Wasn't that odd?

There were large windows in the lodge, but the curtains were closed. I swallowed hard. Was that to keep out the sun, or to hide what was inside?

I pushed away from the windowsill and turned my back on the window. This was another crazy idea. I couldn't trust my instincts. I put my hand in my pocket, and my fingers tightened around my mobile. Luke had asked me to speak to him before I acted on any more crazy ideas.

I left the room, shutting the door behind me and walking down the dark staircase.

Plastering a smile on my face, I said, "Thank you very much, Mrs Taverne."

"Did you find anything useful?"

I shook my head. "I'm afraid not. I think Dawn just wanted me to go away and stop bothering her."

Mrs Taverne's face fell. "Oh, I am sorry."

"Let me help you. I'll wash up our cups," I said, walking over to pick up the tray.

"There's really no need. I can do that. It's the one thing I can still do," she said firmly as she took the tray from me.

I followed her to the kitchen. "I'm not sure when Dawn will be able to come and help you again, so I'll leave you my number in case you need any help."

"That is very kind of you. But I'm sure I'll manage."

I left Mrs Taverne's house and fought against the urge to go next door to Pippa's. I crossed to the other side of the road but hesitated on the pavement. The sensible thing to do now was go home and talk it over with Mum. She'd probably tell me I was ridiculous, and with some distance and time to think it through, I'd probably agree with her.

But I didn't do the sensible thing. My feet felt rooted to the pavement. I could just take a quick look. What harm could it do? I could come up with some excuse to visit Pippa and go out into the garden...

I turned around and marched across the road before I could change my mind. When I drew level with the front door, I paused and looked at the side gate, which was painted a pretty duck-egg blue. If that was open, I could sneak around into the garden and look into the lodge without needing to come up with an excuse.

I glanced at the windows. I couldn't see anyone inside, so I decided to take a chance and quickly walked to the side gate. To my surprise, it wasn't locked.

I smiled. See, I knew it. If Pippa had something to hide, she would keep this gate locked at all times. I would just take a quick look to put my mind at rest.

I closed the gate quietly behind me and walked softly along the narrow strip of land between the house and the fence, squeezing past the rubbish bin. Emerging in the garden, I paused and listened. If Pippa had the French doors open, she might hear me. But if I kept to the outside of the garden, she wouldn't be able to see me from the downstairs windows.

I paused behind a blooming fuchsia, considering what would happen if Pippa found me here now. How would I be able to explain why I was creeping around her garden?

I pushed those thoughts aside and made my way slowly to the large cedar lodge.

When I was almost there, I glanced up at the house next door, looking at the window in the small box room in Mrs Taverne's house and wondering how many times Dawn had stood up there looking down at Pippa's garden.

Could I imagine Jenna playing here with Dawn watching over her? I shuddered.

Taking a quick look back over my shoulder at Pippa's house to make sure she wasn't watching me, I snuck around the side of the lodge, ready to peer into the windows. But it was no good. The blue curtains were thick and heavy, and I couldn't see anything.

Did the lodge used to have curtains when Kate worked here? I couldn't remember.

What a waste of time. I moved to the next window, but it was just the same. Finally, as a last resort, I tried the handle on the door of the lodge, and to my surprise, it opened.

Holding my breath, I pushed the door open slowly.

The lodge was empty.

It looked almost the same as the last time I'd seen it. The air smelled a little musty, and the floor was covered with a layer of dust. Pippa had installed the lodge, sparing no expense. There was a small sink on the far side, and she had a custom-made heating stove to melt the wax.

Cupboards, which used to contain all the essential oils and fragrances for the candles, lined one of the walls. The large table in the centre of the lodge that Pippa and Kate had worked at side-by-side was empty apart from a few glass jars and scattered wrappings and ribbons. The only thing different in the lodge was a large chest freezer in the corner. I didn't remember that being there before.

The silence was eerie.

A movement inside made me jump, but then I realised it was just the breeze moving the curtains.

A hysterical bubble of laughter threatened to overwhelm me. I was losing it. What would Daniel do if he found out I was creeping around out here? He'd never let me live it down.

I took one last look at the scattered items on the table and then left the lodge and shut the door. If I could just get out of there without anyone noticing, I could pretend it never happened.

My cheeks were flushed as I made my way across the lawn and then sneaked down the side of the house, through the side gate and out onto the street. I'd been lucky no one spotted me. Luke was right. I needed to stop acting on these crazy suspicions when I had no evidence.

I walked away from Pippa's house and pulled out my mobile, dialling Luke's number. At that point, I wasn't sure whether I wanted to confess what I'd just done, or whether I wanted to hear his voice to make me feel better. But he didn't answer straight away, and my phone beeped to tell me I had a call waiting.

It was Mum. I immediately ended the call to Luke and answered Mum.

"Beth? Any luck?" She sounded a little breathless.

"No, it was a waste of time. Are you okay?"

"I think you should probably come home now. I heard back from DI Sharp. They have an arrest warrant for Daniel. They've been to his flat in Oxford, but he's not there."

I stopped walking and put my hand against the trunk of a tree, leaning on it heavily. "They're going to arrest Daniel? Why?"

I could never be accused of being an admirer of Daniel Creswell, but deep down, I'd never believed he could hurt Jenna. After learning about the payments he'd made to Dawn, I'd thought they were to cover up some kind of an affair, but if the police were arresting him... Surely, that meant it was more serious.

"Yes, DI Sharp told me if he turns up, I should call the police straight away and not let him in. The detective said he could be dangerous."

Dangerous? I remembered how Daniel had loomed over me menacingly, furious I'd reported him to the police for lurking outside Marjorie Parsons's house.

"What's the arrest warrant for?" I asked. "They don't think Daniel abducted Jenna that day, do they?"

I shook my head. He couldn't have. He was there in the immediate aftermath.

"I'll tell you all about it when you get home."

"I'm on my way. I'll be there in a couple of minutes."

After I had hung up, I shoved my mobile in my pocket, and that was when I saw Daniel's car. I froze. He was here, parked just outside the bank, opposite Pippa's house. I was sure his car hadn't been there earlier.

I turned back to look at the house. Was he in there now? The police said he was dangerous. Would he harm Pippa?

Frowning, I walked back towards the house. One of the windows downstairs had the blinds drawn, very unusual for this time of day. I pressed a hand against my churning stomach as I reached again for my mobile to call the police.

Before I could do so, my phone rang again. It was Luke.

"Beth, sorry I missed your call. I was—"

"Luke, I need your help. The police have issued an arrest warrant for Daniel and say he could be dangerous. He's at Pippa's house, I think. At least, his car is parked outside. Can you call the police? DI Sharp is in charge of the case. And let Mum know, too."

"Hang on a minute, Beth. Where are you?"

"I'm just outside Pippa's house."

"Okay. I'm calling the police now, but whatever you do, keep your distance. Don't go inside."

"Thanks," I said, ignoring his advice as I headed for Pippa's front door.

CHAPTER FORTY-TWO

I wasn't planning to go straight inside. My judgement wasn't great at the moment, but I wasn't that stupid. Plus, there was a good chance my presence might alert Daniel to the fact the police were on their way, and I didn't want to take that risk.

Standing on the top step, beside the front door, I paused, listening. I couldn't hear anything at all, which was a good thing. If Daniel was in a violent temper and Pippa's life was in danger, I would have heard something. Unless, of course, he'd already taken his anger out on Pippa, and I was too late.

Usually, from this spot, I would be able to see into both of the downstairs windows. I could see into the room on the right — the formal dining room – but that was empty. The blinds were drawn on the window to my left. I stared at them for a moment wondering what to do.

Had Daniel closed the blinds? I'd never known the blinds to be closed during the day in all the time that Pippa had lived there. That made me very nervous.

I already knew that the side gate was open so it would be easy to slip around the back and look in the windows. I was very concerned for Pippa's safety. The look in Daniel's eyes when he'd found out I'd reported him to the police revealed the anger and hate he usually kept hidden.

I left the front steps and felt my mobile phone vibrate in my pocket. I pulled it out and saw I had a Facebook notification. At first, I thought it might be from Mark Clarkson, but then I saw it was a reply from his sister.

Hi, Beth, lovely to hear from you. I'm afraid the family had a falling out with Mark a couple of years ago, and we haven't been in touch. It's sad really. If he does get in contact with you, please tell him I'd love to hear from him. xx

It didn't look like I would get any answers from her, so I had to hope Mark would get in touch. I set my mobile to silent, and then walked around to the side gate. Following my earlier path, I made my way to the back of the house. This time, instead of circling the perimeter of the garden, I made my way along the external wall of the house. I ducked beneath the open kitchen window as I heard voices coming from inside. Pippa's voice.

I froze beneath the window, trying to listen to what she was saying.

"You've been a disappointment, Daniel. I'm sick of it. I've given you so many chances."

I waited for Daniel's reply, but none came. Pippa didn't sound scared. She sounded angry.

I waited there, crouched on the floor, but they'd either walked away from the window or stopped talking. After a moment, I moved on, heading for the French doors. I took time to build up the courage to peer inside, expecting Daniel to pull the door open and drag me inside at any moment.

But when I finally peered around the edge of the door frame and looked into the large kitchen diner, I was so shocked that for a moment, I forgot I needed to hide.

Pippa stood in the dining area of the kitchen with her hands on her hips. Daniel sat on one of the chairs that had been pulled out from the dining table. But there was something about him that didn't look quite right.

His hair was dishevelled, and his shirt was untucked. He lolled forward in his chair as though he were drunk. Maybe he had been drinking, and that was the reason he wasn't arguing back.

Pippa paced back and forth in front of Daniel, and I wished the French doors were open so I could hear what she was saying.

Daniel shifted in his seat, and his head rolled back until he was facing me. For one horrifying moment, I thought he'd seen me. I pushed back, moving away from the window and pressing my back against the wall. I waited for the shouts and for one of them to yank open the door, but they didn't.

He couldn't have seen me. Or maybe he was too drunk to process the fact he'd spotted me.

I should have gone back to the front of the house and waited until the police arrived. It didn't look like Daniel would be going anywhere in the state he was in, and Pippa seemed unharmed. I forced myself to move, heading back past the kitchen window and keeping my head ducked down low.

But then I heard Daniel's voice through the open window.

"Where is she? Can I see her?"

"She's upstairs in her room. As she always is. Waiting for you to come to your senses. You have no idea how hard it's been for me. Every time I thought you may have earned the right to know the truth, you would do something stupid like tell me another sob story about Kate. Do you really think that's what I wanted to hear? Bloody Kate. She wasn't the perfect wife you thought she was. She told me Jenna drove her crazy. She wished she wasn't tied down. She hated her life with you."

If I'd paused to think about them, Pippa's words might have stung. But as it was I couldn't get past her first sentence. *She's upstairs in her room.*

She couldn't be. They couldn't have kept Jenna here, not with the police crawling about after she was taken. Somebody would have noticed something. It wasn't possible to keep a young child hidden away.

I twisted around and made my way back. This time, I held my breath as I darted past the French doors. Pippa had her back to me, Daniel was staring ahead, glassy-eyed. I carried on moving until I was outside the small room Pippa used as a study. The window was ajar, and I straightened up, grabbing hold of the PVC frame, and prising the window open further.

The window wasn't huge, but it was big enough for me to squeeze inside. The window ledge was large, which helped. I pulled myself up and through the window, quietly. The small key wedged in the window's handle scraped my arm, but other than that, I made it through the window quickly and practically silently.

I slid down, barely avoiding the desk, and when my feet hit the soft carpet, I paused, listening. Had they heard anything? After a few agonising seconds, I crossed the room to the door.

Pippa was still berating Daniel. "It's too late, Daniel. I've given you enough chances. Taking care of your daughter has been a thankless task. But I did it for you."

Daniel's reply was too slurred for me to make it out.

None of this made any sense. If Pippa and Daniel had colluded together to take Jenna and keep her from Kate and the rest of our family… How had nobody noticed? They couldn't have kept her here all the time. I'd been in this very house and heard nothing. I would have sensed something if Jenna was in there, wouldn't I? It would be impossible to keep a five-year-old child so quiet that a visitor wouldn't hear them.

And Mark was still living here when Jenna went missing. He definitely would have noticed.

I slowly pushed open the study door and looked out into the hallway. They were still in the kitchen, so I stepped out into the hall and crept along to the staircase.

I wanted to run up the stairs but forced myself to move slowly so I wouldn't attract their attention. My shoes were muddy from the garden and left smudges on the cream carpet, but that was the least of my concerns now. At the top of the stairs, I was greeted by four white doors.

All of them were closed, but only one had a key in the lock.

I stared at it. They'd locked her away up here. No wonder Pippa hadn't wanted to show me the upstairs of the house when she gave me that guided tour. My heart was thundering in my chest when I reached out and unlocked the door. The key turned with a click, and I grabbed the handle and shoved the door open.

Inside, was a girl's bedroom, decorated with pink cushions and My Little Pony posters, and the cream carpet was strewn with toys. There was no window, and the walls were coated with strange, spongy material that I guessed had to be some kind of soundproofing.

A single bed covered with teddy bears, was in the corner of the room, up against the wall, and crouched down beside it, clutching a doll to her chest, was Jenna.

CHAPTER FORTY-THREE

I stared at the little girl, who cringed as I walked into the room, and hesitated, not wanting to scare her.

She looked different. Her chubby cheeks that used to dimple every time she saw me had slimmed down. Her hair was a shade or two darker, and those pretty blue eyes watched me distrustfully. But she was definitely Jenna. There was no doubt in my mind.

I crouched down, thinking that meeting her at eye level was better and less threatening than looming over her, but she still looked terrified. Jenna had no obvious injuries, but being kept up here for so long must have had an effect on her mental state.

"It's okay, Jenna. Everything is going to be all right. Do you remember me? I'm Auntie Beth."

I watched Jenna closely for some flicker of recognition, but her expression didn't change.

Pippa's voice was still droning on downstairs. The police would be here soon, so I had two options. One, I could remain in this room with Jenna, lock the door and take shelter from Daniel and Pippa, or two, I could try to persuade Jenna to escape with me now.

I knelt down and extended a hand, but Jenna scooted back further from me. There was no way I was going to get her out of here without Pippa and Daniel noticing, but I didn't want to stay in this room.

Jenna's prison had been carefully disguised as a little girl's ideal bedroom, but underneath all the furnishings and toys, it was still a prison. On the surface, the room was every little girl's dream. But there were no windows, and the bright pink walls seemed to close in on me, making me feel claustrophobic, even though it was a large room.

I tried again. "Jenna, I need you to come with me now and be as quiet as you can." I smiled. "We're going to play a game."

She shook her head firmly, and I jumped when I heard something smashing downstairs.

The noise jolted me into action, and before I could think better of it, I reached out to grasp Jenna's arm.

She screamed.

It wasn't just a little yelp, either. It was a full on red-faced, gut-wrenching scream.

I panicked. "Shhhh, Jenna. Be quiet."

I rushed over to the door and tried to grab the key from the lock on the other side. I pushed the door closed, but I wasn't fast enough. It burst open, hitting me hard on the side of the head.

Dazed, I took a step back. Pippa stood on the threshold glaring at me. She held out a hand to Jenna, and to my shock, Jenna darted out of her hiding place and clung to Pippa's arm.

Pippa's face was a mask of concern. "Don't be scared, Jenna. This is your Auntie Beth. Don't you remember her?"

Jenna looked up at me doubtfully as Pippa stroked her hair.

"Thank God you're here, Beth. We need to get help. Daniel's crazy. He took Jenna, but I only just found out. He is forcing me to go along with it."

I stared at her. Daniel was a mess downstairs, but Pippa was perfectly controlled as always. Her lipstick and hair were immaculate. She didn't look like a woman being made to go along with anything.

I touched the side of my head and winced. Warm, sticky blood coated my fingertips. My stomach rolled, and bile rose in my throat.

"We should call the police," I said, not wanting to tip her off to the fact the police were already on the way. "But first, I should take Jenna somewhere safe."

I reached out to Jenna and tried to smile reassuringly. This time, she didn't cringe away from me, but I must have looked a fright with blood trickling down the side of my face.

Pippa cocked her head to one side and narrowed her eyes. "You don't think she's safe here with me?"

I wanted to rip Jenna away from her clutches, but I tried to play along and pretend I believed her. "Of course, but she's not safe with Daniel here."

Pippa sighed. "You don't believe me, do you? That's disappointing. I've only ever been kind to you, Beth. I thought I'd be able to make this work."

"It doesn't matter what I think. We just need to get Jenna out of here."

"No," Pippa said coldly. "You don't get to barge into my home and start giving out orders."

Her distressed expression evaporated and was replaced by a hard, bitter glare.

"I don't understand," I said. "Did you take Jenna? Was Daniel involved?"

Pippa shook her head in disgust. "Daniel is pathetic. He couldn't even admit what he wanted. It was up to me to make him see what he really needed."

"And what did he need?"

"Me, of course. He always wanted me."

"He was married to Kate."

"He was mine first," Pippa said through clenched teeth. "Your sister stole him from me."

I glanced down at Jenna, who was watching us both and looking confused.

"But what about Mark? He was still in Woodstock when you took Jenna. He must have been involved."

"Mark? Don't make me laugh. He's even more spineless than Daniel. He couldn't see it through…" Pippa trailed off as she looked down at Jenna. "This isn't a subject to talk about in front of a child, Beth."

She was mad. Absolutely crazy.

"How could you?" I whispered. "Kate was your friend. You helped her, gave her a job."

Pippa pulled her arm away from Jenna's grip and tucked her hair behind her ears as she leant forward, closer to me. "Kate was a mess. She was always moaning about Daniel and her life, but she never did anything about it. She was pathetically grateful for the job, but she never worked hard. She expected everyone to help her. Daniel, your mum, me, we all had to pander to her and make sure she was all right."

"That's not true!"

"You just don't want to see it. Now she's gone, you act like she's some kind of martyr, but she was a terrible mother. She left Jenna with your mother all day."

"Only because she had to work. Plenty of women have to do that. It didn't mean she was a bad mother."

"When Kate couldn't get someone to watch her, she used to drag poor Jenna here. She had to sit in the corner and occupy herself while her mother worked."

I knew that had happened, but only on a couple of occasions when Kate couldn't organise childcare. Pieces of the puzzle began to fit into place. Jenna had spent plenty of time with Pippa and wouldn't have thought twice about going with her, without raising a fuss.

But how had Jenna been kept in this house the whole time without anyone noticing?

"You locked her up." I held up the key I'd extracted from the lock. "What if there had been a fire?"

"I work at home. I only ever leave her for a few minutes. She's better off with me than she was with Kate."

I wanted to smack the smile off Pippa's face but decided the better option was to keep her talking until the police arrived.

"How did you persuade Mark to go along with it?"

Pippa smiled as though she remembered a fond memory. "It was easy. I told him I'd booked him a fishing trip for the weekend and sent him off to Wiltshire. He was as pleased as punch, but he wasn't too happy when he got back and found out I'd taken Jenna."

"But you were there when we searched for Jenna?"

"It only took a couple of minutes to take her to my house. I gave her my iPad to keep her occupied and came back to join the search party." Pippa looked incredibly pleased with herself.

"The police talked to everybody. They visited every house in Woodstock. How did you keep her here without anyone noticing?"

"They did their house-to-house enquiries and asked questions, but they didn't search our house. I don't think anyone would ever have found out if it hadn't been for Dawn, the little bitch."

There was a groan from downstairs, and Pippa rolled her eyes. "I've wasted too much time on him already. I should have known Daniel would let me down. After everything I did for him…" She shrugged and then looked at me with a trace of a smile on her face. "It's so sad. Daniel couldn't live with what he's done, so he decided to commit suicide."

I moved towards the door, but Pippa blocked my path. "Why do you care? You've never liked him."

"We have to help him."

"Oh, no, we don't. Daniel has typed a full confession on his computer, including a nice section on how he bullied me into going along with his plans. The trouble is, what do I do with you, Beth? Now that you know, you've become a thorn in my side."

"You're going to blame it all on Daniel and pretend you're a victim?"

"I think it's only fair. After all, if he hadn't been—"

Jenna tugged on Pippa's shirt. "Mummy, can I watch My Little Pony now."

I stared down at my niece in horror. Mummy. She'd called Pippa *mummy*.

I lunged for Pippa, trying to push her out of the door, but missed.

Pippa laughed. "Now, now, Beth. Not in front of the child."

Jenna whimpered and clutched Pippa, which brought me to my senses. Even if Jenna had some distant memories of me from two years ago, the state of me now must be terrifying to her.

I used my shirt to try and dab away some of the blood, which was stinging my eyes.

"Everything is okay, Jenna. You don't have to be scared." My hands balled into fists at my sides as Pippa watched me with an amused expression.

She held out her hand. "Give me your phone."

I thought about refusing, but maybe I was better off playing along for now. The police were on their way, and Luke knew I was here. I yanked my phone out of my pocket and thrust it towards her.

She took it and glanced at her watch. "I'd better get a move on. It's time for Plan B."

Pippa disentangled herself from Jenna and walked out into the hallway, leaving Jenna hesitating at the door.

Pippa nodded. "It's okay. You can come downstairs now."

Jenna smiled and her face lit up, reminding me of the little girl whose mood used to change like lightning. She stepped out into the hallway, bouncing on the balls of her feet. Going downstairs was a treat for Jenna. It broke my heart. Leaving this room clearly wasn't something she was allowed to do often.

Jenna skipped after Pippa, and they descended the stairs. I felt dizzy and detached as I followed them. Black spots danced in front of my eyes, and I gripped the bannister with each shaky step.

What should I do now? Grab Jenna and run? I didn't want to traumatise her any more than necessary, but I needed to get her away from Pippa. The woman was unhinged, and I had no idea what she was planning to do next. Surely the police would be here soon. I only had to hold out for another few minutes.

We walked into the kitchen diner, where Daniel was still slumped in a chair. Now I could see him close up, it was clear he wasn't drunk. Pippa must have drugged him.

Seemingly unaware of her father, Jenna rushed past him and went to the large pine dresser set back against the wall behind the table. She opened a drawer and pulled out a colouring book and colouring pencils before sitting down at the table and starting to colour in a Disney Princess.

The situation was surreal. I realised I had my back to Pippa, which was not a good idea. I staggered a little as I turned around and watched Pippa as she shut the kitchen window and locked it before putting the key in her pocket.

She walked into the hallway and then returned carrying her laptop.

"What are you doing?"

"Getting ready to leave," Pippa said. "I just have a few loose ends to tie up."

I didn't like the way she looked at Jenna when she said loose ends.

She couldn't leave yet. I had to keep her here until the police arrived.

"What's your Plan B?" I asked.

Pippa looked up from her MacBook. "I'm hardly going to tell you that, Beth."

I tried another tactic to keep her talking. "How was Dawn involved? Did she see Jenna in your garden when she was cleaning Mrs Taverne's house?"

Pippa looked indignant. "Oh, she would like everyone to believe that, wouldn't she? But no, Beth. That isn't how Dawn found out. She knew from the very beginning."

"Dawn was involved in the abduction?"

"I didn't say that," Pippa said, frowning at something on her computer screen. "I said she knew."

That made no sense. My head was pounding now, and I really wanted to pull out a chair and sit down. Jenna was still colouring happily.

Daniel made a gurgling sound, and we all looked at him. Vomit splattered the front of his shirt, and his bloodshot eyes looked up into mine. "Help me," he slurred.

I wanted to tell him that help was on its way, but of course, I couldn't do that without tipping Pippa off.

"What have you done to him?" I asked Pippa.

"Just a few of my prescription drugs. I suffer from terrible migraines and insomnia. Unfortunately, Daniel's taken more than the recommended dose."

She was enjoying this. "You drugged Marjorie too, didn't you?"

"I had to make Dawn realise I was serious. She wouldn't listen. I tried to play nice. I bought her things, gave her little gifts."

"The candle? I saw that when I went to their house."

Pippa shrugged and then pressed a button on the computer, and the printer in the hallway hummed into life. "I gave her lots of things, but it was never enough. It was her own fault."

"So you poisoned Marjorie as a warning for Dawn to keep quiet."

Pippa rolled her eyes as she walked past me. "Ten out of ten."

In the hallway, she plucked a sheet of paper from the printer and smiled in satisfaction. I crossed the room and grabbed it from her. It was an itinerary. Car hire. Ferry passage...

Before I could read any further, Pippa grabbed it back from me. "That's very rude, Beth."

"The police will catch you before you get very far," I said. "Once we tell them what you've done—"

Pippa leant close to me, so close I could feel her breath on my cheek. "That's only if there is someone left to tell them what happened."

Her words chilled me, but I put my hands up to shove her away. "You really have lost it."

Pippa laughed but before she could respond there was a hammering on the front door.

CHAPTER FORTY-FOUR

Thank God. That had to be the police. At the same time as I rushed for the door, Pippa grabbed onto my shirt and clutched a handful of my hair with her other hand.

"No," she hissed.

"Pippa? Is Beth there? I need you to open the door." The voice carried through the solid front door. It wasn't the police. It was Luke.

A horrifying thought hit me. Did he think this was one of my wild imaginings? Had he come to check out the situation himself before calling the police?

I elbowed Pippa hard in the ribs, and when she released her grip, I ran towards the front door. I called out to Luke as I tried to pull down the handle only to find that the door was locked and the key was nowhere to be seen.

"The door is locked. I can't open it," I shouted to Luke.

"Pippa has drugged Daniel. Jenna is here, but I can't find the key to unlock the front door. Get the police."

Luke shouted back that the police were already on their way, and I breathed a sigh of relief. I shouldn't have doubted him.

I turned around to inform Pippa that she was going to get what she deserved when I noticed she was no longer standing in the hallway.

My stomach lurched. *Jenna*. Why had I let my attention be diverted?

I ran back into the kitchen diner and felt some of my anxiety melt away when I saw Jenna was still sitting at the table, colouring. Why was she just sitting there while all hell was breaking loose? That wasn't normal behaviour for a five-year-old, was it?

Pippa was nowhere to be seen, and Daniel had passed out.

"Jenna, where has Pippa... Mummy gone?" I asked as I walked to the kitchen and grabbed the washing-up bowl out of the sink.

"She's gone out," Jenna said. "I'm allowed to stay down here, though." She looked at me stubbornly as though she was expecting me to send her back to her bedroom.

I knelt down beside Daniel and put a hand beneath his chin. He was unresponsive. I then tried to wake him up by lightly slapping his face.

"Did she say where she has gone?"

Jenna shook her head.

"Do you know where the key to the front door is kept?"

Jenna shook her head again and then went back to her colouring.

Daniel wasn't fully awake, but he was groaning. I lifted the washing-up bowl and held it level with his chest. Then, feeling pretty sick myself, I pushed two fingers into his mouth, making him gag. It took three attempts before he vomited up the contents of his stomach.

Jenna pulled a face. "What's wrong with him? Is he poorly?"

I nodded. "Yes, he is very poorly. He's going to have to go to the hospital."

I went into the kitchen and leant heavily against the sink as I washed my hands. Pippa had left my phone on the kitchen counter, so I grabbed it and quickly typed out a text to Mum. I didn't want to worry her, so I didn't mention the fact we were locked in the house. I told her I'd found Jenna, though, and she was safe.

After I had pressed send, I tried to open the French doors, but they were locked, so I started to search for the front door keys. I checked the kitchen drawers first but had no luck. Luke banged on the front door again. I could hear him shouting but couldn't make out what he was saying.

I walked towards the front door. Now that Pippa was gone, I was starting to believe that this was all going to work out. The police would track her down before she got too far. And when the police got here, they would be able to break the lock on the front door. Daniel would soon be on his way to the hospital in an ambulance and Jenna would be safe.

Luke was hammering on the front door so loudly I couldn't hear what he was shouting. I waited until he'd finished banging before putting my palms flat against the door and calling out to him.

"Luke, Pippa has left. Did you see her leave?"

There was no response. Luke must have moved away from the door. I frowned and walked into the sitting room, intending to open the blinds and see what was going on outside.

As soon as I walked into the small sitting room, the smell hit me.

The smell of something burning. I raced back into the kitchen diner and saw a wisp of smoke. Where was it coming from? It wasn't the kitchen.

I followed the smell to where I'd entered the house, the small study. Dark grey smoke was billowing out of the room, and I could smell petrol mixed with the acrid scent of smoke.

I covered my mouth and nose with my shirt and reached out to grab the handle to pull the door shut and burned my hand in the process. I grabbed the rug from the hallway and pressed it tightly against the bottom of the door, trying to stop the smoke spreading.

Scrambling to my feet, I raced back into the kitchen and saw Luke outside the French doors, searching for a way to get in. As soon as he saw me, he mouthed the word *fire*. That was why he had been banging on the door so urgently. He must've made his way around the side and into the garden.

"Jenna, we need to find the keys," I said. "A key to a door or a window. It doesn't matter which one. Do you know where they are?"

Jenna slid down from the chair she'd been sitting in, shaking her head slowly and edging towards the door that led to the hallway.

"Where are you going?"

"Upstairs. I want to go back upstairs."

I knew I was scaring her, but I had no choice. I pulled her away from the door and shut it firmly. "No. You have to stay down here."

She shrunk away from me and looked terrified, but I couldn't help that now. I'd prefer her to be afraid of me than allowing her to go upstairs when a fire was burning through the house.

"It smells funny down here," Jenna said as I began to rummage through the pine dresser, desperately looking for a key. "Who's that man?"

She was referring to Luke who was now trying to prise the French doors open. He'd taken the bottom part of a parasol from Pippa's patio furniture and was slamming it into the lock.

"That's Luke. He's trying to help us get out because…" My

voice trailed away as Luke finally smashed the lock and slid the door open.

"Luke, thank God."

There was a gash on his hand, and his blood dripped onto the tiles, but he didn't seem to notice.

"Are you okay?" He addressed the question to me, but he was staring at Jenna. "I can't believe it."

"We need to get Daniel outside, too," I said.

Luke nodded and walked behind Daniel, grasping him under the arms, ready to drag him outside. "What's wrong with him?"

"Pippa drugged him. I don't know exactly what she gave him, but he has been sick."

As Luke pulled Daniel out through the French doors, I followed with Jenna. I took her hand, and although she tried to pull away, she didn't put up too much of a struggle.

"I know this is scary, Jenna. But we need to get out the house because there's a fire and it's dangerous."

"I'm not allowed to go outside."

I took a breath of fresh air and closed the French doors behind us.

"You are now," I said.

The next few minutes passed in a blur. Sirens were blaring as both the police, the fire service and paramedics turned up. I tried desperately to comfort Jenna as members of the fire service entered the property behind us, but she was rigid with fright. She wasn't used to being outside, and the sheer number of people and the amount of noise was overwhelming for her.

She'd forgotten her initial fear of me and buried her head against my hip. Her hands pressed against her ears, trying to block out the noise.

The paramedics had attended to Luke's cut hand at the scene, and Daniel was taken away in an ambulance. They wanted to examine Jenna and me, but she wasn't making it easy, screaming and slapping their hands away. I didn't know what to do. She didn't trust me, and it was horrible to see her so scared.

One of the paramedics, a young woman with short blond hair, spoke softly to Jenna and then looked up at me. "I think it's better if we get her somewhere quiet. Perhaps, we could put her in one of the vehicles?"

I nodded and tried to follow the paramedic with Jenna clamped to my side. Then a voice from the crowd made me stop.

"Beth!" It was Mum.

She rushed towards us, weaving past the people standing in her way. Her voice had caused Jenna to look up. I felt her small hands relax their grip as she looked at her grandmother.

I crouched down beside her. "That's Granny. Do you remember her?"

Jenna didn't answer my question with words, but with

action. She let go of me and raced towards Mum, who scooped her up in her arms.

As Jenna buried her face in Mum's soft woollen cardigan, I swallowed the lump in my throat and walked towards them, brushing away my tears.

CHAPTER FORTY-FIVE

The following twenty-four hours were happy but stressful. We'd got Jenna back, and of course, we were thrilled and thankful, but after two years of being hidden away, Jenna had some huge adjustments to make. We all did.

Daniel remained in the hospital under the watchful eyes of the medical staff overnight. He'd had his stomach pumped, but it looked like he was going to recover. Until he was discharged from the hospital, Jenna was staying at Mum's. She had turned into Mum's shadow, never wanting to let Granny out of her sight.

She'd asked for Pippa a couple of times, and Mum's face blanched when she called Pippa mummy. It was a difficult situation. We didn't know what to do for the best. Did we tell Jenna the truth and insist she stop referring to Pippa as Mummy, or would that upset her and cause more psychological damage?

The police had been great. They'd sent a child psychologist with a trained officer to Mum's house to talk to Jenna, but they didn't rush her or apply any pressure. Jenna could open up in her own time.

Pippa had been picked up by the police just outside of Oxford and would be subjected to the full weight of the law.

Luke had helped us so much in the first few hours. Neither Mum nor I felt up to going shopping for the things Jenna needed, and so Luke took on the task. As well as the essentials, he also picked up a few toys and colouring books.

Jenna didn't sleep well that first night, which was understandable. She ended up sleeping in Mum's bed, and the following morning Mum looked shattered.

"Are you sure you don't want me to stay here?" I asked. "I could look after Jenna while you catch up on some sleep?"

Mum shook her head as she topped up her mug of coffee. "No, I'm fine. You go and see Daniel. He must be desperate to find out how Jenna is getting on."

She blew over the top of her mug and watched Jenna, who was sitting on the floor, watching cartoons. "I can't believe we've got her back, Beth."

I smiled and reached out to hug Mum, and we both watched Jenna for a moment as she sat cross-legged on the floor in front of the television. The challenge ahead of us was daunting. We wanted Jenna to be a normal little girl again, but it wouldn't happen overnight.

After I had finished my coffee, I said goodbye to Jenna and

Mum and headed to the John Radcliffe hospital to visit Daniel.

Now that he was out of immediate danger, he was in a normal ward. When I walked towards his bed beside the window, he stirred, pushing himself into a sitting position.

As soon as I reached his bedside, he asked, "How is she?"

I nodded. "Pretty good, all things considered."

I sat down in the chair beside his bed. He looked a lot better than the last time I'd seen him. He had more colour in his cheeks, and his eyes didn't look so bloodshot. "How are you?"

"I'm fine. I should be getting out of here this afternoon. There's so much to do." His voice was hoarse. I guessed that was from whatever the doctors had used to pump his stomach. "I need to organise the flat and convert the spare room into something suitable for a little girl. I don't even have a spare bed yet. I can't believe that after all this time..." He grinned at me and then suddenly his face fell. "I keep thinking about Kate. I feel this unbelievable happiness to have Jenna back, but then I think about Kate."

He reached over to grip my hand. "I didn't know what Pippa had done. You have to believe me."

I nodded slowly. I did believe him. At one point, I'd thought him capable of abducting his own daughter, but I didn't mention that. As things had unravelled, it became clear to me that Daniel had no idea what Pippa had done. I still found it hard to believe she'd managed to get away with it, hiding Jenna beneath our noses for all that time. It was hard to comprehend.

"When did she tell you?"

Daniel rubbed his hands over his face. "I found out the same day as you. She told me she had a surprise for me... And I had no idea. She started talking about family and children, and I thought she was going to say she wanted us to get married and start a family, but I couldn't, not after Jenna. I tried to let her down gently, but she flipped and screamed at me. She said Jenna was upstairs. I didn't believe her at first. I've been inside that house so many times...and I never knew."

"The room was soundproofed," I said. "But didn't you think it was odd that room was locked."

He leant back against his pillows and shook his head. "No. Maybe I should have, but she said she used the room for storage. Could you pass me that glass of water."

He nodded to the glass on the nightstand. I passed him the water and waited for him to finish drinking and continue.

"She must have put tablets in my drink. I didn't realise she'd drugged me until it was too late. When she told me about Jenna, I tried to get upstairs, but I could barely move. I was sure she was going to kill me." He shook his head. "I never suspected her for a moment. She was always so sympathetic."

The question I wanted to ask Daniel was a difficult one, but I had to know.

"Pippa said Kate stole you from her."

Daniel looked incredulous. "Stole me?"

I nodded. "Were you seeing Pippa when Kate was still alive?"

I held my breath as I waited for him to reply, but I think deep down, I already knew the answer.

Daniel paled and blinked rapidly as he turned away. After a pause, he answered, "Yes, we had a fling. It didn't mean anything."

"It clearly meant something to Pippa," I said cuttingly and felt resentment burning in my stomach. If he'd managed to keep it in his pants, maybe none of this would have happened. Maybe Kate would still be alive.

I closed my eyes. Recriminations weren't going to help now.

"I know you're right," he said, his voice almost a whisper. "I'll regret it for as long as I live."

"What did she mean by saying Kate stole you from her, though? Were you seeing Pippa first?"

Daniel shook his head. "No, it was nothing like that. Pippa and I went on a few dates when we were in the sixth form at school, but it was nothing serious. I loved Kate. I was an idiot to have a fling with Pippa, but it only lasted a few weeks, and then I ended it because I thought Kate was getting suspicious. I told Pippa that day at the fête that she had to stopped calling me…"

His voice trailed away as I stared at him. "I guess we know why Pippa chose that day to take Jenna, then."

I'd intended to come here and build bridges with Daniel, but it was hard. I couldn't even bring myself to look at him.

"I know what you did, Beth."

I turned back to him. "What do you mean?"

"You could have left me there to rot. The doctor said if you hadn't made me sick, more of the drugs would have passed into my bloodstream, and I probably wouldn't be here now." His intense gaze met mine. "I'm sorry."

The ward was starting to feel stuffy, and I glanced at the large sash window, wondering whether I'd get told off for pushing it open. "One thing, I couldn't work out was why you transferred money to Dawn."

"I didn't."

"The police said they saw money transferred from your account to Dawn's. They checked your bank statements."

Daniel frowned and rubbed his forehead. "I have no idea how that is possible unless Pippa used my computer."

"But your online banking must be protected by a password."

Daniel looked sheepish. "The computer remembers my login ID, and the password is Jenna's name and the year she was born."

"You should probably change that," I said, shaking my head.

A nurse came over to check Daniel's vital signs. "One last

check, Mr Creswell," she said. "Then, you'll be able to go home this afternoon."

"I'll leave you to it," I said, standing up. "When do you want to pick up Jenna?"

"I think it might be better if she stays with you tonight, and I'll pick her up tomorrow. I'll come around to see her just as soon as they let me out of here, though."

I nodded. "I'll let Mum know."

I was deep in thought as I left the ward, still angry and hurt by Daniel's behaviour. Our wounds and past hurts weren't healed, but we were both trying. No matter what Daniel or I had done in the past, we had to ignore our personal grievances and get along for Jenna's sake.

My throat was dry, and my head ached. I decided to grab a coffee before I got a taxi home. When I entered the cafe area near the main entrance, I saw Dawn.

She was alone, with no police escorts. As far as I knew, she still had to be questioned in relation to Jenna's abduction. As I waited in the queue to pay for my cup of coffee, I could feel the weight of Dawn's gaze.

When I'd been served, I carried my coffee across the room and stood beside Dawn's table.

She raised her head slowly until her dark eyes met mine.

"I've just been visiting my mother," she said. "She had a relapse, and they had to bring her back in."

I put my coffee cup on the table and sat down opposite Dawn. "I'm sorry. Is she going to be all right?"

Dawn nodded. "They think so. They've put her on one of those IV drip things. She was dehydrated." She looked at me nervously and licked her lips. "What are you doing here?"

"I've just been to see Daniel."

"I heard what happened. Is he all right?"

"Not really, Dawn. He's just had his stomach pumped and looks like death warmed up, thanks to Pippa." I wanted to add thanks to you as well, but I managed to bite my tongue.

"She's evil," Dawn said. "Absolutely evil."

I took a deep breath and asked, "How did you find out Pippa had Jenna?" I had to know. The truth might be brutal, but I had to know if Pippa had been telling the truth and Dawn had known since the day Jenna went missing.

Dawn's face crumpled in distress. "I saw Jenna with Pippa at the fête. She was carrying her towards the car park, but I didn't think anything of it until after everyone was searching for her."

"Why didn't you tell the police what you'd seen?"

"I wasn't sure she'd actually taken her, and when I asked Pippa, she threatened me. She said horrible things to me. I was scared."

"Why didn't you tell me? You sent me the photograph of Jenna. Why not just tell me that Pippa had her?"

Dawn shook her head and played with the empty paper cup in front of her. "I didn't want people to find out it was me telling you. She said she was going to do something awful if I told anyone."

My phone buzzed in my pocket, and I pulled it out. It was just Mum asking me to pick up some groceries on the way home. I replied to her text message and put the phone back in my pocket.

I lifted the coffee cup to my lips and took a sip, hoping the caffeine would go some way to easing my headache. "I wish you had told me earlier," I said simply.

Dawn bowed her head as fat tear drops rolled down her cheeks and hit the table top. "So do I."

CHAPTER FORTY-SIX

A week passed. We struggled to get our lives back to normal, but I wasn't sure what normal was anymore.

Jenna was now living with Daniel, but they weren't far away, and Mum and I saw Jenna frequently. Daniel had organised some compassionate leave from work so he could help Jenna settle back into a routine. When he was due to go back to work, Mum had agreed to help out as she had before.

Jenna would be going to school in September, and Mum would pick her up after school and look after her until Daniel finished work.

Considering the fraught and emotional tension between us, I was getting along well with Daniel. I'd promised Mum I wouldn't raise the money issue again, and I planned on staying in Woodstock. Now that we had Jenna back, I couldn't imagine leaving.

Understandably, Jenna was still very confused. She didn't like groups of people and hated wide-open spaces. We were all worried about how she would react when she started school in September, but we would cross that bridge when we came to it.

Jenna had pointed to a photograph of Kate a couple of days ago and asked who it was. We probably didn't handle the situation well, telling Jenna it was her mother only confused her. Helping Jenna to adapt was a learning process, and we had a long way to go.

All of us, our whole dysfunctional family, had enrolled in therapy sessions. Jenna would still see the child psychologist on her own, but we would work through any issues as a family.

We had to judge carefully how much to tell Jenna. Was it better to get the whole truth out in the open now, or should we let her settle in and feel secure in our family unit before telling her what had happened? It was a balancing act, but we would muddle through together.

I planned to pop around to deliver some bread and milk to Mrs Taverne before Sergeant Parker was due to visit and give us an update on the case against Pippa.

When I left the house, I spotted Marjorie Parsons pottering about in her front garden.

It was good to see her up and about again. After her relapse, we were all concerned that she might not make it.

I waved at her as I passed and called out good morning, but I didn't pause to chat because I wanted to get Mrs Taverne's shopping and get back home before Sergeant Parker arrived.

I bought the bread and milk in the Co-op, glancing at the newspapers, which all had the same headline. Robin Vaughan had been charged. He'd had nothing to do with Jenna's abduction, but he'd been charged for his crimes. No doubt his trial would bring a media circus to our little town, but it would be worth it to see him punished.

After paying for the shopping, I walked along the High Street towards Mrs Taverne's house. I wondered if I would ever be able to look at Pippa's house again without shivering and feeling revulsion. I was still some distance away when I spotted the police cars.

My pace quickened. The police presence had already drawn a crowd.

"What's going on?" I asked to no one in particular when I reached a group of people waiting beside a police cordon.

"They're digging up the back garden," a young girl, who was leaning on the handles of the pushchair, replied.

"Why?"

She shrugged as the young child in the pushchair began to cry. "I don't know. Maybe they're looking for bodies."

I shuddered.

"She reached down to put a dummy in the toddler's mouth and then looked back up at me, narrowing her eyes. "I recognise you. Aren't you—?"

"Sorry, I have to go." I pushed my way through the crowd to get to Mrs Taverne's front door.

Thankfully it wasn't long before she opened it. She must have seen me from her sitting room window.

"Did the police tell you what this is about?" I gestured to the police cars parked on the road behind me and handed her the small bag of shopping.

She shook her head. "I've no idea. They turned up an hour ago. I can see them working in the garden from the upstairs window. Do you want to take a look?"

I hesitated, feeling sick. I wasn't sure whether I wanted to look. But after a moment, I nodded and followed Mrs Taverne inside.

She put the bag of shopping in the kitchen and then led the way to the box room. I climbed the stairs behind her, feeling more nervous with each step. I had a horrible feeling I knew why they were digging up the garden.

Mrs Taverne and I stood side-by-side in the small box room and looked out of the window. Neither of us spoke for a long time. The garden was swarming with forensics officers wearing white suits that covered every inch of their body. The patio slabs had been lifted, and the previously perfect lawn now looked like a muddy row of trenches.

Mrs Taverne put a hand on my arm. "It's hard to believe evil can be carried out so close to home."

I turned away from the window. "I'm sorry I can't stay long today. I'm expecting a visit from the police. They are going to give us an update."

Mrs Taverne nodded. "Of course, I understand."

"Will you be all right here with all this going on outside?"

Mrs Taverne gave me a smile. "If the noise bothers me, I can always turn down my hearing aids. It's one of the benefits of getting old."

I left Mrs Taverne's and walked home slowly. Pulling out my mobile phone, I opened the Facebook app and checked my messages. There were no new ones, but I clicked on the message from Mark's sister and felt tears prick the corner of my eyes.

We'd had a happy ending. Getting Jenna back was the best possible outcome for us, but for others, like Mark's sister, this story would have a tragic ending.

When I got back home, I told Mum what I'd seen, and so we were both prepared when Sergeant Parker came to talk to us an hour later.

Sergeant Leanne Parker's face was grave as she accepted Mum's offer of a cup of tea and sat down at the kitchen table.

"I know you're going to have lots of questions for me. I'll do my best to answer them all. But first, tell me, how is Jenna doing?"

Mum switched the kettle on to boil and then turned around to face Sergeant Parker. "She's doing very well under the circumstances. She's a resilient little thing. We are the ones walking around on eggshells. But Daniel says she slept right through for the past two nights. No nightmares."

Sergeant Parker ran a hand through her hair and smiled. "That's good news. We've had reports from the child psychologist about Jenna's progress. She seems to be adapting well, but these sorts of things can have long-term consequences."

Mum nodded. "We're prepared for that."

After Mum made the tea and set the teapot on the table, Sergeant Parker got down to business.

"Pippa has made a partial confession, which is good news. That's going to make it easier for us to charge her. It's not going to be smooth sailing, though. I have to warn you that she is going to probably say all sorts of things about Kate being a bad mother during her defence."

Mum put the milk jug down on the table a little harder than was necessary. "That's absolute rubbish."

Sergeant Parker nodded. "Absolutely. I doubt her trying to use that in her defence is going to sway anyone, but I think it's best that you're prepared."

As Mum began to pour the tea, I asked, "I visited Mrs Taverne earlier. She lives next door to Pippa."

"So you probably want to know why the police were there again earlier?"

"I saw you had a team digging up the garden."

Sergeant Parker took a deep breath and nodded. "Yes, I'm sorry to tell you we found a body buried beneath the patio."

Mum covered her mouth with her hands, and I looked down at the table.

"It's Mark, isn't it?" I asked. "He didn't move away. She killed him."

Sergeant Parker rested her forearms on the table and looked at Mum and me in turn. "We believe it is Mark's body, but we don't have the full story yet. At this stage, Pippa is refusing to talk about Mark."

"What made you dig up the garden then? I got a message from Mark's sister last week. She said they'd been estranged for a while. Did she contact you?"

Sergeant Parker shook her head. "We got the information from Dawn."

"Dawn?" Mum's forehead wrinkled in confusion.

"Yes, in fact, that's how Pippa blackmailed Dawn into keeping quiet about Jenna. We don't yet know the timeline, but we think Pippa poisoned Mark soon after Jenna was abducted. It's possible he objected strongly, and that's why Pippa took action. According to Dawn, she stored his body in a chest freezer."

I felt like I'd been punched in the stomach. *A chest freezer.* "The one Pippa had in her garden lodge? That was why she didn't want to work out there anymore."

Sergeant Parker nodded once. "We're going to run some forensic tests on the freezer, which will give us more answers we hope. Dawn said Pippa showed her Mark's frozen body and threatened that if she went to the police or uttered a word about Jenna's abduction, Pippa would tell everybody that Dawn was involved and had helped to abduct Jenna and poison Mark."

Sergeant Parker paused for a moment to let her words sink in, and I leant back in my chair, reeling.

Mum shook her head. "But that's ridiculous. It was an empty threat. Why didn't Dawn just come forward? No one would have believed she was involved."

"Pippa is a strong character. I have no doubt she manipulated Dawn and held some power over her. She gave Dawn gifts but also threatened her. She promised Dawn's mother would end up like Mark unless Dawn cooperated."

"How awful," Mum said and picked up her cup of tea to take a sip.

Maybe I should have felt sorry for Dawn. She was easily led, and despite everything, she'd taken a risk to send me the photograph of Jenna. But I couldn't help thinking, that if she had come clean sooner, all the tragic events that followed could have been avoided.

I wanted to forgive her and was grateful she had sent the photograph, but if she had spoken up when it happened, Kate might still be alive.

Sergeant Parker tucked her hair behind her ears and then clasped her hands in front of her on the table. She shifted nervously in her chair, and I suspected she had more to tell us. Whatever it was, we probably weren't going to like it.

"There's more, isn't there?" I asked.

She nodded slowly. "Yes, and this next part is going to be very hard to hear."

I sat forward and quickly glanced at Mum. She looked as pale and nervous as I felt.

"It's about how Kate died," Sergeant Parker said.

"We know how she died," I said. "She took an overdose in her car."

Sergeant Parker nodded. "Yes, but she wasn't alone. We don't have any traffic camera footage to prove it, but we believe Pippa was with Kate that day. Bear in mind, this is only what Pippa has told us."

"Please, just tell us, Sergeant," Mum said, and I held my breath waiting for her to continue.

"Pippa said she helped Kate purchase enough tablets. As you probably know, you can only buy a certain number of paracetamols at once in UK shops. She said she sat in the car with Kate as she took the tablets and stayed with her until the end. She told her it was the right thing to do."

"Do you believe her?" I asked. "Do you think she encouraged Kate to take her own life or is she just making this up now to hurt Daniel and us?"

Sergeant Parker shook her head. "It's hard to say, Beth. And it is equally hard to prove after two years. I'm sorry I had to be the one to tell you this, but if it comes up later in the case against Pippa, I wanted you to be prepared and know the whole story."

Devastated, I struggled to process what she had just told us.

My hands balled into fists, and my fingernails dug into the soft flesh of my palms.

Mum stood up abruptly, the legs of her chair grating against the tiles on the kitchen floor. She turned and walked out of the kitchen, leaving me sitting at the table with Sergeant Parker.

CHAPTER FORTY-SEVEN

Four weeks later, I sat beside Mum in the garden on a hot, sunny Sunday, watching Jenna organise a picnic for two of her dolls and a teddy bear. She'd had a few tears earlier because she'd had to get out of the paddling pool. Now, she was sitting happily on the grass, playing with Spike the kitten.

I had taken Mum to Luke's veterinary surgery a few days ago, and she hadn't been able to resist the tiny kitten with its cute mohawk. Jenna was enchanted by the tiny ball of fur and was incredibly gentle with the kitten as it climbed all over her.

We were expecting Daniel to arrive to pick her up at any moment. He'd had the past four weeks off work, and had used his compassionate leave to spend time with Jenna and decorate the spare room in his flat for her.

We had all kept a close eye on Jenna over the past few

LOST CHILD

weeks, but she seemed to be getting along well. I had managed to get a job in Oxford. It was only temporary work in an office, but the day-to-day tasks were interesting, and it allowed me to help out with the mortgage while Mum decided what to do with the house.

I leant back in the garden chair, enjoying the sensation of the warm sun on my skin as a couple of swifts swooped overhead and bees buzzed over the fuchsias in the flowerbed next to me. I smiled as I listened to Jenna's laughter. I would never get bored of that sound.

"How was Marjorie?" I asked Mum, who had been to visit her yesterday.

"She's much better. She is still taking it easy and very worried about Dawn, though," Mum said as she adjusted the cushion behind her back.

Dawn was still being investigated by the police, and no one really knew whether she would be charged. It all depended on whether the CPS believed they had enough evidence against her. Pippa wasn't exactly a reliable witness. On the other hand, the evidence against Pippa was overwhelming, and we had been assured by Inspector Sharp and Sergeant Parker that Pippa would be going to prison for a very long time.

At times like this, watching Jenna play happily in the garden, I couldn't help thinking about Kate. It was hard not to spend all my time wishing she was here with us. But life had to go on.

Mum had stopped locking the electric gate at the front

425

during the day. She was more relaxed now that she wasn't living on her own.

Not long after Daniel had collected Jenna, there was a knock on the side gate.

"Are you expecting anyone?" I asked Mum as I stood up.

She shook her head, and I walked across the garden to see who it was. When I opened the gate, I saw Luke and his brother Phil. Luke grinned at me, and Phil gave me a polite nod.

"Come on, Mrs F.," Luke called out to Mum. "We've come to take you to lunch."

Mum flushed with pleasure and got up to take Spike indoors. "Sounds lovely. Just give me a minute."

I went inside to grab my handbag but couldn't resist taking a backward glance at Phil. He seemed like a different person. He stood up straighter and looked less tense. Guilt was a terrible emotion. I should know. But today, I felt positive about the future. It seemed like guilt had lessened its grip on Phil, too.

Mum and I walked back out into the garden, and I locked the back door behind us. We joined Luke and Phil and walked out of the side gate, along the path, towards the lane.

"This is just like old times," Mum said smiling at Phil.

Almost, I thought, wishing Dad and Kate could be with us.

Luke must have caught the expression on my face because

he reached out to put an arm around my shoulders. "It's a new start, a chance to make new memories."

Mum and Phil walked slightly ahead of us down the lane, chatting happily, and I smiled up at Luke.

"I think you're right."

We couldn't go back, but there was a lot to look forward to. We had Jenna back, and for the first time in a while, I felt like I was ready to face the future.

A NOTE FROM D. S. BUTLER

Thank you for reading Lost Child! If you enjoyed this book, please give it a review on Amazon. Your kind words and encouragement help all authors, and reviews help other readers find books they'll enjoy.

This book is a departure for me. I usually write police procedurals and gritty East End stories. Lost Child is different. When I first conjured up the characters of Beth and Jenna, I knew this story would be unlike anything I'd written before. It's certainly a change in direction, but I hope you like the book.

Next up for me, is a Dani Oakley novel and then I'll be working on another D. S. Butler book.

If you would like to be one of the first to find out when my next book is available, you can sign up for my new release email:

www.dsbutlerbooks.com/newsletter

All the best,

Dani

www.dsbutlerbooks.com

ALSO BY D S BUTLER

Deadly Obsession

Deadly Motive

Deadly Revenge

Deadly Justice

Deadly Ritual

Deadly Payback

Deadly Game

If you would like to be informed when the next book is released,
sign up for the newsletter:

http://www.dsbutlerbooks.com/newsletter/

Written as Dani Oakley

East End Trouble

East End Diamond

East End Retribution

ACKNOWLEDGMENTS

I would like to thank my readers for their support and encouragement.

My thanks, too, to all the people who read the story and gave helpful suggestions and to Chris, who, as always, supported me.

To Nanci, my editor, thanks for always managing to squeeze me in when I finally finish my books!

And last but not least, my thanks to you for reading this book. I hope you enjoyed it.

Made in the USA
Middletown, DE
29 September 2017